CRITICAL ACCLAIM FOR JANE HADDAM'S
GREGOR DEMARKIAN NOVELS

"A delightful read for lovers of classic crime stories."
—*Romantic Times* on *Skeleton Key*

"[A] smoothly running mystery marked by lively characters, good descriptions, and enough misdirection to keep a reader's interest high." —*Publishers Weekly* on *Skeleton Key*

"A sophisticated style, excellent delivery, and riveting plot make this an excellent choice for all collections."
—*Library Journal* on *Skeleton Key*

"A real winner . . . Sure to grab readers from the first page . . . A fine entry in a fine series." —*Booklist* on *Skeleton Key*

"Bound to satisfy any reader who likes multiple murders mixed with miraculous apparitions and a perfectly damnable puzzle."
—*Chicago Tribune* on *A Great Day for the Deadly*

"A rattling good puzzle, a varied and appealing cast, and a detective whose work carries a rare stamp of authority . . . This one is a treat."
—*Kirkus Reviews* (starred review) on *Bleeding Hearts*

MORE . . .

TRUE
BELIEVERS

Jane Haddam

St. Martin's Paperbacks

This is a work of fiction. The characters, incidents, and dialogues are products of the author's imagination and are not to be construed as real. Any resemblance to actual events or persons, living or dead, is entirely conincidental.

TRUE BELIEVERS

Copyright © 2001 by Orania Papazoglou.
Excerpt from *Somebody Else's Music* © 2002 by Orania Papazoglou.

Library of Congress Catalog Card Number: 2001058899

ISBN: 0-312-98286-0
EAN: 80312-98286-7

Printed in the United States of America

St. Martin's Press hardcover edition / May 2001
St. Martin's Paperbacks edition / April 2002

St. Martin's Paperbacks are published by St. Martin's Press, 175 Fifth Avenue, New York, NY 10010.

10 9 8 7 6 5 4 3

To KARIN SLAUGHTER, *in honor of the fact that she managed to make me crazy every single day for three straight years*

ACKNOWLEDGMENTS

Anybody who has ever written a book knows that nobody can write a book — no one person, that is. If you try to do something like this alone, you end up looking like an idiot.

This time, I've received the help of many people who prefer not to be acknowledged publicly. They got me clippings on priest pedophilia cases from one end of the U.S. to the other, and local newspaper reports on anti-gay activism from Florida to Kansas. I thank them all.

A special thanks is due to all the people at St. Martin's Press, including my editor, Keith Kahla, and Teresa Theophano, the best editorial assistant in the history of the planet. Keith has been a welcome and knowledgeable ear — and voice — in my continuing struggles with this series. Teresa has suffered valiantly through my neuroses (I've got lots) and cheerfully dealt with the fact that the word "technoklutz" was invented for me.

Finally, I need to thank my sons, Matthew and Gregory DeAndrea. They keep me the opposite of sane . . . but who wants to be sane, anyway?

PROLOGUE
THE OUTWARD AND VISIBLE SIGN . . .

1

It was still full dark when Marty Kelly left home, so dark that
there were halos around all the streetlights, as if the lights had
metamorphosed into miniature blue moons. For a while, it
seemed odd to him that he should be standing out here in the
night like this. He'd done enough of this kind of thing in his
life, in spite of the fact that he was only twenty-six, but all
the other times he'd been anything but stone-cold sober.

"Alcoholics," Bernadette had told him, the first time he'd
brought her to this place. "Alcoholics and druggies. This place
is full of them."

At the moment, this place was full of nothing. Marty could
see with perfect clarity down the long alley between the trailers, and there wasn't so much as a light on in one of the living-
room windows. Even Marty's own mother seemed to be
asleep. Marty shifted from one leg to the other, put his hands
in his pockets, tried to think. If Bernadette found out that
Geena's trailer was dark, she'd want him to go down and
check. It was Friday night. Geena worked on Friday nights, if
she was able—and for some reason she still got work, almost
as much of it as she'd gotten when Marty was small and her
face had looked less like a piece of onionskin that had been
crumpled into a ball and thrown into a wastepaper basket. In
those days, the men had come in the afternoons as well as at
night, and when they did Geena would shove Marty into the
back bedroom and fix the door so he couldn't get out. If the
man was fast, it didn't matter. If he wasn't, Marty would find
himself sitting on the bedroom floor for hours, hungry, bored,
ready to explode. When he had to relieve himself, he would

get an empty beer bottle out from under the bed and go in that, praying like crazy that he didn't have to relieve himself in the other way. When the fights started, he would wedge himself into the small closet and shut the door, hoping like hell that nobody would find out he was there. Every once in a while, the fights got bad enough to make somebody notice. Something would crash through the living-room window. Something would spill out into the alley where other people could see. Then the police would come, and he would have to hide even more carefully. He would have to practically stop breathing. If the police found him, they would call the child-protection people, and that was the very worst thing of all.

"She might be sick," Bernadette would say, if she were standing out here next to him. "One of those men who visit her might have done something to her. You can't just leave her alone. You have to go see."

Marty turned back to look at the truck. Bernadette was sitting upright in the passenger seat, her seat belt already on, her eyes closed. Her sense of duty was one of the things he loved most about her, mostly because he'd never met anybody else who had it. Bernadette believed that wives cleaned house and got dinner for their husbands. Their trailer was always spotless, and if she had to work late and couldn't be there when he got back from the station, she left a covered dish in the refrigerator with instructions for him to heat it in the microwave. Bernadette believed that good people went to church on Sunday and that they did more for their church than sit at Mass looking holy. She volunteered for two different missions, and helped out at the Episcopalian church across the street when they had need of it. She hadn't even seemed to mind that most of the people at the church across the street were gay. Bernadette was holy, but she wasn't one of those people who had her nose stuck in the air.

Marty had learned to nurse a single beer all Saturday night so that he'd be in shape when the alarm went off at six on Sunday morning. Sometimes, he stopped cold in the middle of installing a carburetor or changing the oil on some car that hadn't had it changed in the last six years and felt a kind of shock. He was still living where he had always lived, but he might as well have been living on a different planet. He didn't know anybody else whose trailer looked like his or who had a savings account, either. It was incredible what happened when you kept your drinking to a six-pack a week and didn't do drugs at all. In the beginning, he had only gone along because he was in love, and because he couldn't believe that Bernadette loved him back. In the end, he had had to admit that she was right about everything.

"*Used* to have a savings account," he said now. He was looking at his mother's dark living-room window again. It was the first of February and very cold. In any other year, there would have been snow. He turned back to look at Bernadette. She hadn't moved.

"Listen," Bernadette had told him, when they were first going out. "It's not luck. It's not that you have to get lucky. It's that you have to have a plan. If you have a plan, you can do anything. Don't you see?"

One of the things Bernadette had done was to make him stop playing the lottery. She had made him take the money he would have spent on lottery tickets and put it in a jar behind the kitchen sink. At the end of a month, she had dumped it all out on the kitchen table and shown him how much there was—and there was nearly three hundred dollars, enough for the utilities two months running, enough for a payment on the truck. Marty thought he would remember it all the rest of his life, the way she had been that night, her red hair caught back in a barrette, her great blue eyes looking bluer than usual in her pale, freckled face. She had been so beautiful, she had made him hurt.

"You have to have a plan," she had told him again. "You have to think things through."

He'd never been too good at that: thinking things through. He wasn't good at it now. He had a sudden vision of the first time she had fallen down in front of him, bucking and shaking, her eyes rolling back in her head—but the vision went black in no time at all. He knew what he had done, the first time she had gotten sick and every time thereafter, but he couldn't remember himself doing it.

He forced himself to look at Geena's window, yet again. He forced himself to walk down the alley to Geena's front door. The inner door was open, in spite of the cold, but at least the storm windows were in the outer door. He'd put them in himself, in November, because Bernadette had reminded him to. The windows were all clean, too, because Bernadette had cleaned them, the way she went down to Geena's when Geena was sleeping off a drunk to do the dishes or vacuum the floors or get the laundry to the Laundromat so that Geena wouldn't smell.

"She's your mother," Bernadette had said, running her fingers along the edge of a sewing needle she had been trying to thread for the last half hour. "You have to honor your mother, even if she hasn't been a very good one."

Sometimes, Marty wondered what it was God thought he was doing. He was supposed to have some very important plan—and there had been times when Marty had claimed to understand it—but the truth was that everything seemed to be a mess. Nothing made sense. Nothing ever went right for more than a minute at a time.

Marty went into Geena's trailer and turned on the light. He could hear Geena snoring in the back. He could see the small plastic statue of the Virgin Bernadette had put up on the wall next to the front door, as if that alone would be enough to make Geena want to change. Bernadette had statues of the Virgin everywhere, and rosaries, too. She had a Miraculous Medal with a blue glass background that she wore around her neck, always, no matter what. Even in these last few months, when they had not been going to St. Anselm's at all, Bernadette had not stopped wearing that medal.

Sometimes, when Geena fell asleep drunk, she fell asleep naked. Marty didn't know how old she was, but he thought she might be going through the menopause. She got hot at night, and even hotter when she was plastered, and then she took off her clothes and left them on the floor. He held his own breath and listened to hers. It was even and untroubled. It didn't sound as if she were sucking in her own vomit. If she were lying naked, he should cover her—but he didn't want to see her that way. It made him sick to his stomach, and angry in a way he couldn't explain.

He listened for a moment more, and then went back outside, closing the inner door behind him, because that would at least let Geena's trailer warm up. The moon over his head was full and clear. The air around him was very sharp. His hands were cold enough to feel stiff. He walked back to the truck and got in behind the wheel, moving carefully so that he did not startle Bernadette. He found himself wishing that her eyes were open, so that he could look into them, so deeply that he could see the bottom of her soul.

Instead, he got the truck started and the heater turned on, then headed out down the dirt track toward the town road. It was going to be a long drive into Philadelphia, and there would be traffic even at four o'clock in the morning. If they got there too late, Mass would be starting, and they wouldn't be able to do what they needed to do. He should have listened to Bernadette in everything, without exception, even in those times when he had been so frightened he hadn't been able to listen at all.

He had just turned onto the two-lane blacktop when Bernadette shifted in her seat and seemed to shudder. He leaned over and put his right hand over hers, to comfort her in sleep.

It was only when he felt the marble coldness of her skin that he remembered, for the first time in an hour, that Bernadette was dead.

2

On any other day of his life, the Reverend Daniel Burdock would have been asleep at four o'clock in the morning. He would at least have been to sleep sometime before then. Even in college, when everybody else he knew was spending two days a week trying to figure out if they could stay up forty-eight hours straight, he had been able to leave the party and sack out at a halfway-reasonable hour. Now he had been awake and restless for almost a full day, and it didn't look like it was going to come to an end anytime soon. He had a terrible premonition that he was going to show up at the funeral this afternoon and keel right over—of exhaustion, or a heart attack, or simple frustration. Something was going to happen. He couldn't go on like this. He couldn't go on thinking like this. This was the way people like Timothy McVeigh thought, before they went out and did something stupid.

The truth of it, of course, was that he was in no danger of keeling over at the funeral, or anyplace else. He had never been so awake in his life. He had been drinking coffee for ten hours straight, and even if he hadn't been, he would have been

wired to the gills. Now he was pacing back and forth along
the long choir gallery that overlooked the body of the church,
his vision cut off at intervals by the thick granite columns that
framed the gallery's archways. It was a beautiful church, St.
Stephen's Episcopal. If he had been able to imagine the church
he wanted when he first entered the Yale Divinity School, this
would have been it. Catholic without being Catholic, Gothic
even though it was in the middle of Philadelphia, bells and
smells, chants and rituals, stained glass and tapestries—it
hadn't been this beautiful when he'd first come here, twenty
years ago. He could still remember himself sitting in the high-
ceilinged office of the then-bishop of Philadelphia, and being
told, without qualification, that it was a lost cause.

"The future of the Episcopalian Church is in the suburbs,"
the bishop had said, his fat little head bobbing back and forth
on a neck so thin it made him look like a Tootsie Pop. "That's
what we've got to accept. That Catholics have a lock on the
city of Philadelphia."

The Catholics were across the street, at St. Anselm's. Daniel couldn't see them from here, but he could from his office
upstairs. Sometimes, when Father Healy was in the middle of
doing something totally outrageous, Daniel would watch them
for hours, trying to figure out whether they were dangerous or
just annoying. He always came to the conclusion that they
were just annoying. Every once in a while, one of the papers
or one of the television stations came out to interview both
the priests in the "next-door-neighbor churches," as if merely
being next to each other ought to make them as loving and
squabbling as brothers. Then, too, the papers liked the contrast.
Dan was tall and spare. Robert Healy was small and wiry. It
was always Dan's figure that was easiest to see in the photographs that inevitably appeared in the *Inquirer* and the *Star,*
although the quotes always seemed to come from Robert
Healy. No reporter on earth ever wanted to talk to him long
enough to get any real news. No reporter on earth ever wanted
to get too clear on what was going on in St. Stephen's, either,
but Daniel was used to that. It was the unspoken agreement
among everybody who had anything to do with this church.
St. Stephen's would be left alone to be what it had become,
as long as St. Stephen's left them all alone as well—as long
as St. Stephen's did not force the issue.

Daniel stopped in the very last archway and looked down on the pews and the altar. Scott Boardman's casket was laid out in front of the Communion rail, draped with flowers. The first three rows of pews were dotted with the figures of men who had come to sit vigil. Under ordinary circumstances, of course, there would have been a wake instead of a vigil, and it would have been held in a funeral home. In Scott's case, they had all wanted to have the body here, and to stay with it, a little while longer than they would have been allowed to in a secular place. The one woman down there was Scott's mother. Scott's father had not come, and would not come, to see his son in death. Daniel rubbed his face and closed his eyes and wished suddenly that he had an answer to it all, to people, to what they were, to what they wanted and what they wanted to do without. He wished he had an answer to himself.

The door to the gallery stairway swung open, creaking. Daniel made a mental note to have the hinge oiled—and then felt stupid for having done it, as if a creaking hinge could rival in importance the fact that someone was dead. He wondered suddenly what it would be like to be someone like Chickie George, someone who could not hide who and what he was.

The gallery door creaked shut. Daniel put his head up and turned. Aaron Wardrop was standing at the back of the gallery, looking down on him for once, because of the graduated tiers of steps.

"Well?" he said.

"Well, what?" Daniel asked him.

They were whispering. They had to whisper. The church was a gigantic man-made cavern. Everything echoed off the granite of the arches and the columns.

Aaron came down the steps to sit beside him.

"You can't have had any sleep. Any at all. You're going to give yourself a heart attack. You're fifty-six."

"I was thinking about Chickie George," Daniel said.

"Chickie's behaving like a saint." Aaron leaned over the archway rail. Chickie was kneeling in the second pew from the front on the right of the center aisle, his hands folded on the back of the pew in front of him, his eyes closed, his body still. "We're all incredibly proud of Chickie at the moment. He's been here since midnight."

"Don't you ever wonder what it would be like, to be like

Chickie? We all get frustrated with him, I know. He's such a flaming stereotype in some ways—"

"Well," Aaron said, "flaming would be the word."

"Yes, exactly. But maybe that's better than what we are. You and me. Maybe it's more honest. Or maybe it just— precludes prevarication."

"I don't think it's a choice, Daniel. I don't think people decide to be flaming queens, not to put too fine a point on it. Any more than they decide to be gay."

"I don't think they decide, either." Daniel had put his coffee cup down on the floor next to his feet. Now he reached into the pocket of his trousers and brought out his open roll of soft mints. He offered them to Aaron and was refused. He took one himself. Somehow, at seven o'clock, he was supposed to go downstairs and lead a Matins sung prayer. At the moment, he didn't think he could remember the words.

Aaron sat down on the edge of the archway lip with his back against the rail. "So," he said. "What's all this about? Scott? It's odd about Scott, isn't it? You'd think it would be easier. He didn't die from AIDS. He didn't get beaten to a pulp in some back alley somewhere just because a couple of good old boys got liquored up and let loose."

"He fried his system on cocaine and died of a convulsion at the age of thirty-two."

"People do that, Daniel. People do it who aren't gay men."

"Scott did it because he could never accept who and what he was. And I'm at least partially responsible for that. St. Stephen's is at least partially responsible for that."

Aaron turned around to look over the rail. Scott's mother looked like she might have been asleep, she was that still. "He was molested at the age of eight by his own priest," he said. "You know that. We handle the settlements the archdiocese made, and not just for Scott. All the men who were victims over there are screwed up now. And on top of that, Scott's father was a son of a bitch. Is a son of a bitch. You know all this as well as I do."

"In two weeks," Daniel said, "it's Valentine's Day Sunday. And they'll be back. Roy Phipps and our friends from down the road."

"And?"

"And I'll go stand out there while they're having their demonstration. Wouldn't it be a good idea if I didn't go alone?"

"We'd go if we thought we could. It's not safe."

"Is it safe for me?"

"You've got the collar to protect you." Aaron stood up.
"Look, I don't understand what you're so upset about here.
It's not like we're all in the closet. It's not like St. Stephen's
is in the closet. Everybody knows—"

"Everybody knows, but they never say it out loud."

"Maybe that's the best we can do at the moment. Look,
what's going to happen to us if you decide to make an issue
of this and get kicked out of the clergy? Even Spong couldn't
make them budge on this, and he's got a lot more clout than
you do. What happens if St. Stephen's gets shut down? Or if
they put a conservative in here, or some asshole who thinks
his mission in life is to convert gay men to heterosexuality?
This is an incredible place, Daniel. This is the first place I've
ever found where I can hear God. I don't want to lose it."

Daniel got up. The adrenaline was back. Over the course
of this night, he had sometimes felt as if he had ingested methamphetamine in a time-release capsule. Every hour or so, it
surged back at him. He looked down at the altar, at the plain
gold cross that hung above it. Some of the men in the pews
were in pairs, pressed up close to each other or holding hands.
Others were solitary, like Chickie George, mostly because they
were always solitary. They were the ones who knew where all
the back-street bars were, and which of the leather shops
would run a private account.

"Do you believe in it?" Daniel asked Aaron. "What it is
we say we believe every Sunday. The virgin birth. The Resurrection. Do you believe in it?"

"I don't know what you're getting at."

"I'm getting at the fact that I do believe in it. I'm not John
Shelby Spong. I don't think it was all a myth. I don't think it
was all a metaphor. I think it really happened. The Annunci-
ation. The miracle of the loaves and the fishes. The walking
on water. But most of all, the Resurrection. And that's the
point."

"I think I'd feel a hell of a lot better if you'd start making
sense," Aaron said.

"I *am* making sense." Daniel leaned over the rail and
looked one more time at Chickie George, and then at Scott's

mother, a pale woman in a worn brown coat who looked exhausted beyond belief. He wondered what she made of it, what she made of them. He wondered if she realized that all the men in this church were gay, and not only the ones like Chickie.

"I'm going to go take a shower," Daniel said. "I feel like I'm covered in crud. Are we going to have picketers at this funeral?"

"I don't think so. It wasn't AIDS."

"And he wasn't famous. Thank heaven for small favors. I'll talk to you later."

"Right," Aaron said.

When Daniel went out the gallery door, it squeaked one more time, so he didn't bother to shut it behind him. The stairwell was steep and winding. Everything had been done that it was possible to do to make this church look as if it had been built by the same people who had built the Houses of Parliament. Back in the nineteenth century, when Philadelphia had been a rich city and the Episcopal Church had been the richest denomination in it, that had probably seemed like a perfectly sensible thing to do.

Daniel got to the bottom of the stairs and headed across the foyer to the side hall that led to the rectory at the back. The doors to the church had been propped open, but he didn't even bother to look inside. He felt light-headed beyond belief, and annoyed with himself for more reasons than he was able to enumerate, or even define. Maybe it was just the lack of sleep. Maybe it was just that he had always thought that Scott would make it through, when he was good and ready—and instead, all he had been ready to do was die. He knew all the good arguments against making decisions on the basis of emotion, but at the moment none of them seemed to apply. Hell, he thought. Sometimes, if you didn't make a decision on the basis of emotion, you didn't make a decision at all.

The back hall ended at an arched doorway. The doorway led into another hall. Daniel hurried through and came out in the rectory mudroom. There was a wooden bench against one of the walls. Under it, there were boots and shoes, the kinds of things Daniel wore when he was not wearing his collar. On another of the walls there was a rack with hooks. The hooks held snow parkas and barn jackets and a long yellow rubber slicker he'd bought once to keep out the rain, but never worn. Looking in this room, you could imagine yourself in the house of any upper-middle-class WASP in America: the sort of person who bought his suits from Brooks Brothers and his outdoor things from L. L. Bean; the sort of person who had been to a decent prep school before going on to Princeton; the sort of person who had tickets to the symphony every season. It was a very good description, Daniel thought, of the sort of person who belonged to the Episcopal Church.

He went through the mudroom into the kitchen and looked around. It didn't look like anyplace he had ever been before. It didn't even look like his coffeepot, sitting there at the edge of the stove.

He thought his head was about to explode into a million and one different pieces, and when it had finished doing that it was going to reconstruct itself—as something other than a head.

3

Sister Mary Scholastica had never met a parish coordinator before she came to St. Anselm's Roman Catholic Church, but now—two weeks into her tenure—she was sure that the title was nothing but a polite term for bitch.

Well, not "bitch" exactly. Scholastica's order, the Sisters of Divine Grace, wore recognizable habits. They weren't elaborate habits, like the ones Mother Angelica and her sisters wore on EWTN, but they were impossible to miss. A black dress that went to just below the calf line, black stockings, a black veil with a white brim that showed only the smallest amount of hair at the very front of the head: there was no way to mistake the fact that Scholastica was a nun, even before you saw the large metal crucifix that hung around her neck. Habits were more than a witness to the world. They were also a constraint. Considering what it was they constrained, Scholastica was willing to admit that that might not be a bad thing. If she was ever going to call Sister Harriet Garrity a bitch, she was going to have to wait to do it in her bathrobe—and that wouldn't work either, because she would never be in her bathrobe in any place where anybody outside her order would have a chance to see her. She went over and over the rules in her mind. It was barely past four in the morning. She was tired beyond belief, and she was not thinking well. All she came up with was a mishmash of emergency scenes: the convent was on fire and she was out in the parking lot in her bathrobe because of that; she was confined to a hospital bed for something like a broken leg or a bad case of sciatica; Sister Harriet burst in through the convent door in a mad attempt to free them all from patriarchal oppression. Patriarchal oppression made Sister Scholastica's head ache, but not nearly as much as Sister Harriet Garrity did. She should have taken a Tylenol when she'd still had a chance.

What she did instead was to put the big mug she'd brought from the motherhouse on the table, and to put a tea bag into it. Sister Harriet's note was sitting right there at the edge of the place mat, written in thick black letters that must have been made with a felt-tip pen. She caught the kitchen crucifix out of the corner of her eye and nodded to it, automatically, the way she'd been taught to nod to churches when she was young. The memory surprised her. When she was in grade school and all nuns wore habits even more obvious than her own, Catholic men used to tip their hats when they passed a Catholic church. They used to do it on the bus and on the sidewalks, all the time, so that even non-Catholics never thought anything of it. The kettle began to screech, and she took it off to pour water over her Red Rose. What a very odd thing to remember—and to pine for, which was really what she was doing. Men tipping their hats when they passed a church. Parishes with three priests in the rectory to see to all the parish business. Nuns who knew when to shut up. Sister Harriet Garrity. Scholastica put the kettle back on the stove.

Please inform the parents of the girls in the First Communion class, Sister Harriet's note said, *that it is no longer considered religiously appropriate for girls to dress like brides for their First Communion.*

Scholastica picked up the note, folded it in half, then unfolded it again. She put it down. She picked it up again. She put it down again. The kitchen door snicked open, then shut. Scholastica looked up to see Sister Peter Rose coming across the floor to her, dressed in one of those infamous bathrobes and with nothing at all on her head. Some of the older nuns wore their veils or their old white linen nightcaps just to get out of bed to go to the bathroom, but Peter Rose was barely twenty-six. She had a good head of hair, which now seemed to be held back by a rubber band.

Peter Rose stopped in front of Scholastica and bowed slightly, the way they'd all been taught to do in the novitiate.

Scholastica said, "Well, since I make the rules for this house, and I'm talking, I suppose we're not observing the grand silence this morning."

Peter Rose pulled out a chair and sat down. "You've been pacing for hours. Are you all right?"

Scholastica passed the note across the table. Peter Rose picked it up and read it.

"Ah," she said. "Harriet, up to her usual. I think she already suspects that you're not going to be as much of a pushover as Marie Bernadette."

"Was she a pushover?"

"She was sick, that was the problem," Peter Rose said. "Cancer makes you weak, and chemotherapy makes you weaker. She didn't have a lot of fight in her, at the end. She shouldn't have been kept on here so long."

"She wanted to stay. It seemed like the best thing to do, as long as she was able."

"I suppose. I'm glad you're here, though. Things have been insane around this place far too often lately. And the school needs—more energy than it's been getting."

Scholastica took the tea bag out of the mug and put it on a small square paper napkin. She dumped a heaping teaspoon of sugar into the mug and stirred. The clock on the wall seemed to be moving incredibly slowly, far more slowly than it ever had before. It was as if the world had decided to stay dark and asleep forever.

Scholastica put the teaspoon on the napkin. "Tell me something," she said. "Does Father Healy know about this?"

"I don't think so."

"Why not?

"Because he isn't having a fit about it."

"Exactly," Scholastica said. "He's going to have a fit about it. You know that, and I know it. It's just the kind of thing he can't stand. And after he's had a fit about it, the parents are going to have a fit about it, because they've probably already bought those First Communion dresses. White dresses. Little veils. Crown things for the tops of the heads."

"I had a really gorgeous one when I made my First Communion," Peter Rose said. "The crown had pearls all around it, and the veil had pearls in it. I kept it for years, just to look at."

"Well, I used to close the door of my room and put mine on and pretend I was getting married. My point, I think, is that this is going to be a very unpopular decision. It won't stand, because I don't think Father Healy will allow it to stand, but between the time it's made and the time it's countermanded, there's going to be a very big fuss. I resent this woman attempting to make that fuss center on me."

"But it won't center on you," Peter Rose said, startled. "You'll tell Father Healy it was Harriet's decision and—"

"And it will center on me, because I'll still be delivering the news. Which means I won't be delivering the news. I refuse to."

"You're just going to ignore the note?"

"I'm going to write her one back saying I can't possibly make such an announcement unless I've been told to make it by Father Healy, and that she should talk to Father Healy about it instead of me. And I'm not going to budge. Not at all. I think that's the only thing I can possibly do."

Peter Rose got up. "I think I'm going to make myself some tea. Or some coffee. Do we have coffee I don't have to use the percolator for?"

"We have those coffee-bag things, in the pantry cupboard."

"Oh, right. I wish you didn't sound so—I don't know. Angry, I suppose. But it's more than angry."

Scholastica drummed her fingers on the table. Then she picked up Harriet's note again and turned it over in her hand. "I hate these things," she said finally. "I hate the petty infighting, and the manipulations and the rhetoric that gets thrown around like garbage as soon as the situation heats up. Liberal Church. Conservative Church. Whatever happened to the Church speaking in one voice?"

"The birth-control encyclical."

"Marvelous. I entered the convent at the age of eighteen, and I still have to think about birth control."

Scholastica got up and wandered across the room, to the

big windows at the back that looked out over the courtyard toward the church. It was already lit up in there, but then it would be. Father Healy believed in keeping the church open twenty-four hours a day, in case somebody suddenly felt a need for conversion while walking down the street at two o'clock in the morning. What they really got, this time of year, was homeless people looking to get in out of the cold. Some of them genuflected when they first came in. Some of them just found an empty pew at the back and stretched out to sleep right away. Most of them were either so mentally ill or so alcoholic that they couldn't really follow a coherent line of thought. When seven o'clock Mass came around, some of them got up and tried to follow it, and some of them came to the front for Communion. When Mass was over, all of them came downstairs to the coffee hour that Father Healy adamantly refused to alter or cancel. There were six or seven different kinds of muffins, and coffee cake, and orange juice, and coffee and tea. None of the regular parishioners came, except for the three older women who set up the buffet. There were things Scholastica did not like about Father Robert Healy. He was young and stiff and far too rigid in his theology, and he tended to see things as issues that she thought ought to be decided on the basis of emotion. Still, in this one thing, she could not have imagined him any better than he was.

Over in the church, somebody seemed to be moving back and forth in front of the Stations of the Cross—not praying them, just moving back and forth in front of them. Scholastica went back to the kitchen table and sat down.

"Well," she said.

"It will be all right," Peter Rose said. "It's just Harriet. Everybody knows Harriet. Even the archbishop is fed up with Harriet."

"Maybe I just can't understand why a woman like that wants to be a nun. Oh, never mind. I think I'll go get some work done before we pray the Office. I still think of it as Matins, can you believe that? I still think of all the hours by their old names, but it doesn't work, because they got rid of one of them."

"I haven't the faintest idea what you're talking about," Peter Rose said.

Scholastica drained the last of her tea—she couldn't remember drinking it at all, but she must have—and brought her mug to the sink to rinse it out. When she was in the novitiate, her postulant mistress had been relentless in stressing the importance of doing "small work" for oneself whenever it was possible: washing out a cup instead of leaving it in the sink; wiping off the base of a statue when you noticed it was dusty; putting away your cloak as soon as you came in from outside.

"If everybody all over the world did that kind of thing all the time," Sister Carmelita had said, "the world would be a much better place, and hundreds of people who slave away at menial tasks would be free to get an education and better themselves."

Had she ever really been young enough for that to have made perfect sense?

"Sister?" Peter Rose said.

"Don't mind me," Scholastica said. "I'm just drifting off. Thinking of my postulant mistress. Who did you have for a postulant mistress?"

"Mary Alice."

"Oh, all right then. The soul of common sense. Oh, you're on the house phone today, aren't you?"

"That's right."

"Good. I'm expecting a phone call from a woman named Bennis Hannaford. If it comes in, could you hunt me down at school instead of just taking a message? I've been in Philadelphia for two weeks, and we haven't caught up with each other yet. I'm rather anxious to see her."

"All right. As long as you're all right yourself, right now. You're sure you're not still, I don't know, ready to breathe fire?"

"I'm fine."

She was, too. She put the mug and the spoon in the dish rack. She wiped her hands on the dish towel that was kept on a little rack next to the sink. Then she went back to the table and got Sister Harriet's note.

"Idiot," she said, folding it up and putting it into her pocket. She was suddenly very glad that they had these ready-made habits now, instead of the old ones. In the old ones, there had been a slit in the robe where the pocket was supposed to be, and then there had been a separate pocket that they'd had to pin on with straight pins. The pockets were always coming loose and falling down. The pins were always digging into the tops of everyone's legs.

I'm too tired to be let loose without a leash, Scholastica thought, then gave a little nod to Peter Rose and went out of the kitchen into the back hall. She had a lot of work to do today, Sister Harriet or no Sister Harriet. She had a school to run, and a CCD program to coordinate, and on top of everything else, it was Lent. She rubbed the palm of her hand against the fifteen-decade rosary that hung from her belt.

When she got to the vestibule, she could see out the windows by the side of the door, across the street to St. Stephen's. It was lit up, which it wasn't very often at night, and for a moment Scholastica felt confused. Then she remembered: there was going to be a funeral there today. That young man, Scott Boardman, whom she had seen a hundred times hanging around the wrought-iron gates, zoned out of his mind—Scott Boardman had finally taken a dose of cocaine strong enough to kill him. Scholastica made the sign of the cross and a quick prayer for the repose of a soul, then found herself hoping that those nuts from down the street wouldn't be here today with their signs.

"Idiots," she said, out loud. When she was in the novitiate, it would have been called "speaking without necessity during the grand silence," and she would have had to proclaim herself for it when it became her turn to speak in Chapter of Faults. There were some things Scholastica didn't miss from the old days at all.

She looked back at St. Stephen's, said another prayer for Scott Boardman, and hurried out across the convent's front parlor toward the side door that led to the side door of the school. If she really put her mind to it, she could get the entire seating plan for the First Confession breakfast worked out and down on paper before she had to come back to the convent at six and pray the Office.

4

The Cardinal Archbishop of Philadelphia had started his religious life in the Order of Discalced Carmelites, and now, fifty years later, he found he was a Carmelite still. It wasn't the asceticism that convinced him that he hadn't changed, much, from the days when he had walked the grounds of the monastery at Avery Point, with its low brownstone buildings and its chapel built as a perfect replica of the one St. Teresa had had for her nuns in Avila. The Cardinal Archbishop had always been something of an ascetic, even as a child. He liked order. He like quiet, too. It had seemed to him better to have a life that was cleared of inessentials, because in such a life it would be so much harder to be confused. Maybe the problem was that, as a small child, he had been confused too often. As far as he could tell, the only thing his father had done that he was supposed to do was to marry his mother. It hadn't lasted long. His mother had been highly religious and, he thought now, highly insane. She was one of those women who went to Mass daily, and whose life at home was a vortex of competing superstitions. They had had to kiss bread before they threw it out, to offer up the most minor bruises and cuts, to bless themselves from the fonts of holy water screwed into the frames of every door in the house, even the door in the bathroom. People called his mother a good Catholic woman, but the Cardinal Archbishop had known better, even at the age of five. He had known that there was something deeply evil about her, and that this evil was dangerous not only to him, but to the very idea of the Christian Church. By the time he was fourteen, he could see how most people brought up the way he was would turn against religion. It was almost wrong not to turn against something that crushed your life the way his mother's version of religion was crushing his, hemming in every move, stifling every thought, turning his nights into restless struggles with demons who refused to name themselves. He had known, then, that his only way out was to find a Catholic boarding school to take him. He had found one in the school connected to Avery Point. It had been a perfect match. There was nothing at all insane about the Carmelites. They lived with little and asked for less. Their schedules were as streamlined as monoliths. In the chapel in the mornings, chanting the Office in the cadenced Latin that had been in use everywhere then, with the light coming in through the east-wall windows in straight undecorated slants, the world had finally straightened itself out, and made itself right, and been clear. There were people who said of him that he had no emotions at all, and that his faith was a sham he put on to justify the power he had accrued to himself by the careful application of his ambition to the hierarchy of the Church. This was so far from true, he often found it funny. The only thing that bothered him was that so many people assumed he had no faith. Why was it that so many people were so very sure that only stupid people could believe? His faith had come in on the light from the east window in the chapel at Avery Point. That was God, pure and simple, offered up to anyone who would have Him. Maybe the truth was that he believed in God but not in the elaborate rituals of the Church, even though he went to great pains to ensure that those rituals were observed. Maybe it wasn't so odd that his mother had gone mad, when life outside a monastery was such a tangled heap of mess.

Right now, life in the Archdiocese of Philadelphia was mostly a struggle with money. It was—what? four o'clock in the morning? he'd been here so long, and he still lived without watches, so he couldn't tell—and he had yet to make sense of the figures laid out in this chart. The chart had been prepared by the firm of accountants he had hired, from New York, to audit the archdiocese's books. He couldn't hire a firm in Philadelphia because it seemed as if every single male human being between the ages of thirty and fifty was somehow part of The Scandal, even if they were Jewish, or had only immigrated to America in the last five years. He tried to think of what it was that had gone on here on his predecessor's watch, but it was like thinking of his mother. As far as he could tell, the old man had simply panicked. Decisions had been made that made no sense at all—to pay hush money that hadn't hushed anyone up; to make denials to the press that could not be maintained for an entire week; to claim ignorance where no ignorance had been possible. What had begun as just another priest-molests–altar-boy five-day wonder had exploded into the nastiest priest-pedophilia scandal in the history of the Church in America—and he had been sent here to clean it up. That was why he had been made an archbishop, and why he had been made a cardinal less than a year later, and why, sometimes, there were rumors that he was destined to become a Pope. The Cardinal Archbishop wanted to be Pope the way Sylvester Stallone wanted to be a girl. The more time he spent in the active life of the Church, the more certain he was that he wanted to end his time on earth at Avery Point, in the quiet, and the simplicity, and the lack of complication.

On the far side of the room, the door to the office opened, and Father Doheny stuck his head through, worried. He was young, but the Cardinal Archbishop was always struck by how very different he was than he himself had been at the same age. Father Doheny was the picture of the secular priest. He was destined for a parish. He exuded enthusiasm. Now he came in and shut the door behind him.

"Your Eminence, what are you doing? It's the middle of the night."

"What are *you* doing? It's the middle of the night for you, too."

"I saw your light on and got worried that you were awake. And working. You are awake and working."

"Not quite. Most of the time I'm just sitting here staring at these papers and thinking how ironic it is."

"How ironic what is?"

"Well," the Cardinal Archbishop said, "everybody outside the Church, everybody in Philadelphia, even CNN, thinks that the problem of the scandal has been solved, and that I've done it. As far as I can tell, I'm being forgiven my failures of personality because I came in here and cleaned up the mess left by my predecessor. Who, I may remind you, was not himself responsible for the scandal. He wasn't archbishop here when any of the incidents actually occurred."

"I don't think they really think you have any failures in personality," Father Doheny said.

The Cardinal Archbishop raised his right eyebrow into a perfectly straight, lethally sharp point. During his novitiate year at the monastery, he had been required to give up that habit for six straight months because his novice master had thought that his ability to do it was his greatest vanity. His novice master had been right.

"They think," he said carefully, "that I'm a son of a bitch."

Father Doheny looked pained.

"Never mind," the Cardinal Archbishop said. "They're right. The Church needs sons of bitches sometimes. Otherwise, we'd get Her into trouble, and we wouldn't be able to get Her out. That doesn't change the chief difficulty in this case, however, which is that the public humiliation of the scandal may be over, but the repercussions have only begun to be felt. Have you looked over these numbers?"

"Once or twice, Your Eminence, yes."

"And?"

Father Doheny hesitated. "We appear to be operating in the red."

The Cardinal Archbishop smiled. It was not, he knew, a friendly thing. "We are operating in the red. We most certainly are. To be a little more precise, we are hemorrhaging money, to the tune of twenty-five thousand dollars a week. Give or take the change. Twenty-five thousand dollars a week is one million, three hundred thousand dollars a year."

"Are we really going to lose that much this year?"

"We lost that much last year. We're living on loans, Father, and for the life of me I don't know what we're going to do about it. If we were somebody other than who we are, we could go back into court and ask that the restitution payment schedule be reworked so that we could actually pay it. Under the circumstances—"

"We'd get killed," Father Doheny said.

"Exactly. Which is what would happen to us if we declared bankruptcy, as well. Never mind the little problem that a court would be reluctant to grant us the relief, and with good reason not to do so. All the usual routes of financial recourse lead to the same place, and that's a resurgence of the nastiness The Scandal brought us to begin with. Which means we're just going to have to increase our revenue."

"Maybe we could make an appeal to the people," Father Doheny said. "Tell them the truth and ask them to help out."

"Would you expect them to?"

Father Doheny hesitated again. "No," he said finally.

"No," the Cardinal Archbishop agreed. "The people feel that this is something that has been visited on them as well as on the Church as an institution, and that it's our fault as well as our responsibility. And they do have a certain amount of justice on their side. It's one thing to ask the people in the pews to dig into their pockets a little more deeply to fund a new parish school or a new mission or even a new cathedral. It's quite another to ask them to do the same thing because one archbishop didn't have sense enough to realize that a man

who has molested children in his last three parishes is going
to molest new ones in his next six, or because another archbishop couldn't count and committed the Church to payments
in excess of the gross income of his archdiocese. Note I said
gross. If he'd only overshot the net, we might not be in so
much trouble."

"So what do we do?"

"I don't know, Father. I'm sure that if we pray on it, God
will tell us in time. For the moment, however, what we have
to do is nothing. No fuss. No muss. No bad press. There are
other numbers besides these." The Cardinal Archbishop waved
at the computer, as if he could make the other numbers appear.
"The decline in Mass attendance and parish membership that
followed the worst of the scandal has been halted and reversed.
We have some very successful parishes, now. St. Bonaventure.
St. John the Baptist. St. Anselm, of all places, considering how
closely it's connected to this mess. We have some very successful missions, too, homeless shelters, soup kitchens. If we
can continue the way we've been, maybe we can make an
appeal to the larger donors that sounds like something other
than a con game. I wish the old Archbishop had kept his
mouth shut on national television."

"Yes, Your Eminence."

"You ought to go off and get yourself some breakfast," the
Cardinal Archbishop said. "It's getting very close to the time
for the Sisters' Mass, and you're saying it this morning if I
remember rightly. There's no need to worry about me."

"You never sleep," Father Doheny said. "You never seem
to eat, either."

"I do as much of both as I need to." The Cardinal Archbishop stood up. It was something he tried not to do, unless
he was deliberately attempting to intimidate someone. The
combination of his extreme height and his extreme thinness
made him seem like a ghost of the Inquisition. "Go get some
breakfast," he said again.

"Yes, Your Eminence."

Father Doheny turned around. The Cardinal Archbishop
could almost hear the gears going around in his head. The
walls were so bare here now. In the days of the old Archbishop, they had been full of framed photographs: the Archbishop with the mayor; the Archbishop with two different

presidents; the Archbishop with the Pope. This Cardinal Archbishop kept only one crucifix on one wall, and that one made of plain wood and unpainted. Even the official publicity shot of the Pope, duly signed by the Pontiff himself, or with a stamp of the Pontiff's signature, and sent out to every parish and parish school, had been banished to Sister Marie Claire's reception desk outside.

"Well," Father Doheny said. "I'll see you later, then. At the seven o'clock."

"At the seven o'clock," the Cardinal Archbishop agreed.

Father Doheny went out, leaving the door open, so that the Cardinal Archbishop could hear his footsteps going down the corridor outside. If it had been another time of day, the Cardinal Archbishop would have taken pains to shut the door himself. Now he knew that no one would come in, except perhaps for Sister Marie Claire, who might, like Father Doheny, see the light on in his office and wonder.

He sat down behind his desk again and clicked the mouse a couple of times to get rid of the screen with the accountants' numbers on it. He could go over the figures as often as he wanted to, but the problem came down to simply this: right at this moment, they couldn't take a breath wrong without collapsing. And it would not be a pretty collapse. The waters were full of creatures that fed on blood, and that hunted the Church and all Her people. They preferred dead bodies to living ones. They waited just out of sight. If the archdiocese had to declare bankruptcy, or even if it only found itself unable to meet a payroll or two, it would all be over. The archdiocese would survive in name only, and maybe not even in that.

He got up again and went across the room to the filing cabinet. There was a small CD player sitting on top of it, his one personal indulgence. He opened the filing cabinet's top drawer and took out his CD of the John Eliot Gardiner production of Bach's *St. Matthew Passion*. It was the story of pain and destruction and despair, perfect for Lent, and perfect for the mood he had been in all week.

This was the part of active life he hated so completely: the desperateness of it; the feeling that everything mattered too much and even the smallest thing could destroy you. This was why he wanted to go back to Avery Point. At least there, silence was as absolute as the Fathers could make it, as anyone

could make it, because only when one was silent could one
hear the whispering voice of God.

5

It wasn't true that Edith Lawton had moved onto this street
just to be able to say that she was surrounded by churches,
which was what her enemies said about her—but it wasn't
true that she had been dragged here by her fundamentalist
Christian husband, either, which was what Edith said about
herself. Lately, Edith had a great deal of trouble sorting out
what was true about her life and what she had made up. There
seemed to be two people living in her head. There was the
Edith Lawton who had been Edith Hull back in high school,
the one who had never finished college and married at twenty.
That Edith Lawton was angry all the time, even in her sleep,
and embarrassed, too. How could she have known that it
would matter so much, in the long run, that she had never
finished her education? She had been so sure that being a
writer would be different. Being a writer was what she had
had in mind for herself from the beginning. What she had
imagined was that she would slave away for a few years in a
back bedroom, getting rejection slip after rejection slip, until
the day when her talent was discovered. Talent was something
she knew she had had all along. She could still remember the
stories she had read about writers when she was growing up:
Hemingway and all those people going to Paris to learn how
to really live; Somerset Maugham sailing to Asia on a tramp
steamer; Truman Capote coming to New York at the age of
eighteen and never looking back. Now, when she met real
writers, they were nothing like that. They had multiple de-
grees. They could swear in Latin. They felt comfortable talking about the medieval roots of deconstruction or the effect of
orchard farming on church history. Or some of them did.

That was because some of them were people like Bennis
Hannaford.

The other Edith Lawton, the one she had invented, was a
writer—of sorts. She didn't make any money at it, and she
didn't get her pieces in magazines whose names would be
recognized by the reader in the street, but she at least got

published, which was doing better than most of the people she met at the "freethought" conferences she attended two or three times a year. "Freethought" was the word "the secular community" preferred to call atheism. The word "atheism" itself was supposed to have been tarred and feathered by the antics of Madalyn Murray O'Hair, and that might actually be true. God only knows, Edith thought—and then mentally crossed out the "God," because she couldn't say that aloud to the people she knew, not even as a throwaway expression. She had to be very careful around the collective population of "the secular community." At the moment, they were her only claim to an identity. She was fifty years old, and she had the feeling that it had gone on too long. She had grown too old. She had made too many of the wrong decisions. She was never going to be the person she wanted to be. She was never going to be anything, really, except Edith Lawton, the class act of *Free Thinking* magazine and one of the distinctly more minor stars of The Secular Web. Even on The Secular Web, though, she wasn't able to compete with the heavyweights, with people like Jeffrey Jay Lowder and Farrell Till. Those people put up detailed analyses of biblical scholarship and Roman Catholic theology. She put up short essays about whatever came into her head in the week before her self-imposed deadline, and far too often she seemed to get things wrong. Mostly she was just a picture on a page or on the Internet, an apple-cheeked woman with too much hair and eyes far too small for her face, trying too hard to look literary.

Now it was five o'clock in the morning, and the alarm had gone off, and she did not want to get up. The world outside her windows was dark. In spite of the fact that she got up at this hour every morning, she had no idea what time it began to get light. She closed her eyes and let herself experience her body, just so that she could reassure herself that she wasn't getting fat. The last thing she wanted was to turn into one of those fat old atheist women who seemed to infest the movement like a plague of locusts. She sat up and swung her feet off the side of the bed onto the carpet. In the street below her, trucks rumbled endlessly and air brakes screeched. It was February. If she went to the window and opened it, she would be able to feel ice forming on her hand.

What she did instead was to get her robe and go to the

bathroom. She brushed her teeth. She took clean underwear and a clean nightshirt out of the linen cupboard and put them aside to put on after she had had her shower. Then she turned the water on as hot as she could stand it and stepped under it. This bathroom was the only completely apolitical place in the house. The bathroom downstairs had two bumper stickers on magnetic backs tacked to the side of the shower she never used. One said: GOD, PROTECT ME FROM YOUR FOLLOWERS. The other said: GOD IS JUST PRETEND. Soap got in her eyes, and she brushed it out. It was a terrible thing to say, but sometimes she thought the bumper stickers were the best thing about the freethought movement. At least they had something in the way of public support. Freethought itself seemed to be—invisible.

She turned off the water and stepped out of the shower. She toweled herself off, although not quite dry. She let her hair hang over her shoulder in wet clumps of permanent wave curls. Then she put on clean underwear and a clean nightgown and her robe and headed down the stairs to the kitchen. She got to the landing before her stomach started to knot up.

"Will?" she called, into the dark of the stairwell.

There was no answer, but that didn't mean he wasn't there. She could hear him there, moving around between the sink and the kitchen table. She thought about going back to her bedroom and brushing out her hair, but that was stupid. It was worse than stupid. After twenty-five years of marriage, it was more like crazy. Then she realized she had said it, in her head: *her* bedroom, not *theirs*. Will had only been sleeping down the hall for ten days, and already she was taking it as permanent.

She undid the belt of her robe and tied it again. She went very carefully down the last of the stairs, straining to hear whatever could be heard. The percolator was on. She could smell the thick scent of the French vanilla coffee Will liked to have for breakfast. He'd made toast, too. He'd even burned it.

She went across the living room and down the back hall. It took everything she had not to stop on the way to brush her hair. Her big pocketbook was sitting on the coffee table in front of the hearth. She could have gotten the brush out of that and used it. The hall was narrow and claustrophobic. It was always what she had liked least about this house. She couldn't remember now why they had bought it in the first place. Will had wanted to live out on the Main Line, or in Bucks County, or anywhere it was green. The thought of being stuck out in the suburbs had scared her to death.

She got to the kitchen door and stopped. Will was sitting in his usual place at the table, his legs stretched out awkwardly in an attempt to make himself more comfortable. He was so tall and thin, anybody who looked at him could tell that he'd played basketball in high school—in much the same way, Edith thought, that anybody could tell he had once been an Eagle Scout. She cleared her throat. He looked up, impassive, and then looked down again. He was reading the *Philadelphia Inquirer*. His face was open and smooth, as if he had nothing on his mind this morning but the sports scores and that odd knocking noise the car had started to make on the way home from work yesterday. He had the face of someone who had never had anything but a clean conscience at every split second of his life.

Edith came around to the other side of the table and got a coffee cup and saucer out of the cabinet. She put them down on the counter and reached for the coffeepot. The coffeepot was full, which made her feel suddenly and light-headedly relieved. At least he wasn't trying to starve her. At least he wasn't acting as if she didn't exist.

She put the coffee cup down in front of her usual place at the table, and then she saw it: the latest copy of *Vanity Fair*, open to that incredible two-page spread that was the start of the article on Bennis Hannaford. Edith brushed wet hair off her forehead. She had seen the piece before. Will had to know that. She had seen the piece and noted the obvious, which was that *Vanity Fair* had tried to make Hillary Clinton look glamourous and almost succeeded, but with Bennis Hannaford they hadn't even had to try.

She flipped the magazine shut and pushed it into the middle of the table. Then she sat down and said, "Well, that was nice of you."

Will looked up. Edith found herself wishing, uneasily, that he would let more emotion into his face. As it was, it was as if a rock were looking at her.

"I thought you'd be interested," Will said flatly. "She is a friend of yours. Or was. She was a friend of yours. Isn't that the way it works with you?"

Edith stirred the coffee in her cup, even though she hadn't put any sugar or milk in it. "I don't know what you're doing this for. I really don't. None of what happened here has anything to do with Bennis Hannaford."

"She went out of her way for you, do you remember that? She sent you books. She gave you advice. She suggested magazines that might be willing to take your work, real magazines, not that rag you have your face in once a month—"

"Thank you very much for supporting me in my professional aspirations."

"She told you how to put together a book proposal. And it worked. You sold the book."

"To a freethought publisher. Don't make it more than it was. To a freethought publisher, not to the mainstream."

"Well, Edith, she told you. You're not going to make it into the mainstream writing about how God doesn't exist."

"None of this is about Bennis Hannaford," Edith said.

"Right," Will said. "This is about the fact that I came home early from work last week and you were in our very own bed in our very own house with our very own lawyer, fucking like a rabbit."

"Oh, for God's sake," Edith said.

Will's coffee cup was empty. He got up and put it—and his saucer, and his spoon, and his crumb-filled breakfast dish—in the big stainless-steel sink. Edith didn't think she had ever heard Will use that word before. He didn't use words like that. He almost never said "hell" or "damn." He really was an Eagle Scout.

Will turned on the water and rinsed off his breakfast things. He put them in the dish rack on the counter and wiped his hands on the towel they kept threaded through the handle of the refrigerator.

"There's a funeral on at St. Stephen's today. Be careful when you go out. What's-his-name will probably be there with his pickets."

"Roy Phipps."

"Whatever. I think you're wrong, you know. I think this does have something to do with Bennis Hannaford. And with—who was it, before? When we had just started going out. That woman at the Foundation for Secular Studies, or whatever it was called. You've got this habit, do you know that, Edith? You always kill the ones you love."

"I don't know what you're talking about."

Will looked around—as if he might have something left to do, as if he'd forgotten that he'd done it all already. He wiped his hands one more time and put the dish towel back. Edith just wished that he'd get mad at her. He should be screaming, shouting, stomping around the house. He should have put his fist through a wall. She could still see him standing in the doorway to the bedroom last Wednesday afternoon, leaning against the doorjamb as if he were watching two cats play in the sun. They had been in the sun, too, she and the—the lawyer. She couldn't make herself say his name anymore: Ian Holden. They had been lying, stark naked, on top of the quilt instead of under it, because they'd both been too damned hot and in too damned much of a hurry. She'd been sitting straddled on top of him and yelling "heigh ho, Silver!" at the top of her lungs every time she'd let her body rise and fall back down into the saddle she'd made of him. She'd been acting more like fifteen than fifty—but she had certainly looked fifty. She'd seen it in the stripe of light that had fallen across them from the opened door. Her hands were pocked and lined. Her breasts sagged.

"Look," she said.

"I have to get to work," Will said. "I've got a project deadline I'm not sure I'm going to make. I've been a little distracted lately."

"I've said I'm sorry. I don't know what you want me to do except say I'm sorry."

"Annie Heston."

"What?"

"The woman from the Foundation for Secular Studies," Will said. "I remembered her name. I think it's interesting you didn't seem to."

"I don't see why we can't talk about what happened," Edith said. "I don't see why we have to go at this as if we were a couple of teenagers playing at how all love is such an agony we're never going to be the same again."

"Right," Will said.

He walked out of the kitchen and down the long hall to the

living room. Edith heard him open and close the front-hall closet. He would be getting the puffy down vest that was all he ever wore to work no matter how cold the winter. She got out of her chair and went after him, hurrying just a little. When she reached the living room, he was just opening the front door.

"You can't leave like this," she said. "You can't keep leaving like this. It's been going on for days."

"You used to tell me you hated it, being on top," Will said. "You used to say it made you feel too self-conscious to concentrate on the sex."

"Oh, for Christ's sake," Edith said.

Will went out the door and down the front steps. He did not close the door behind him. Edith went to it and stood in the draft it made to watch him get into his new Jeep Cherokee and get it started. He'd get out again any minute now to scrape ice off the windshield. Either that, or he'd waste a pile of gas letting the ice melt under the power of the defroster. Why was she thinking about the defroster? Why wasn't Will parking the Jeep in back, where it would be off the street and safe from car thieves?

Will did not get out of the car to scrape ice off his windshield. Edith found herself thinking of her first husband, the one she had married at twenty, the one who really had been a fundamentalist Christian of sorts. She looked up the street at St. Stephen's, but nothing seemed to be happening there. Something was happening at St. Anselm's, but then it always was. She looked into the St. Anselm's parking lot and saw a man trying to get something large and bulky out of the passenger side of the cab of a pickup truck. The illuminated clock on top of St. Stephen's said it was twenty after five.

Edith stepped back into the house and shut the door. She went back across the living room and down the hall and into the kitchen. Her "office" was a sunroom off the kitchen that had once been a porch. Will had enclosed it for her when she had decided that she needed a private space to work in and that the upstairs bedroom was too airless and too isolated to suit.

She turned on the computer and waited for it to get into gear. She looked at the wall where she tacked up the things that made her feel better, at the eight-and-a-half-by-eleven print of her author photo. Now that she'd seen the pictures of Bennis Hannaford in *Vanity Fair*, she knew it wasn't a real author photo. It wasn't what she would have if her book was being published by a real New York publisher, instead of by the Freethinker Press. She wondered what would happen to her, now, if Will walked out. She hadn't had a regular day job in years. She didn't make enough from what she wrote to pay the heating bill on the house, never mind to pay the taxes and keep it up. She couldn't go back to being a secretary in a world where secretaries had to know things about computers that she was only able to guess. Most of all, she wondered if the fact that Will had walked in on them was going to mean that she and Ian would have to give it up. Then her computer desktop was in front of her, and she found herself clicking her way onto the Internet and onto the Secular Web.

Sex was like a drug, that was the truth of it, but religion was an even bigger drug, and if it weren't for religion, she wouldn't be in the trouble she was in right now. She wasn't quite sure how that worked out, but she kept it firmly planted in her mind, because it was going to form the theme of her next column, the one that she should have put up a week ago, but that she hadn't because of Will.

If there had really been a God, she would not be stuck here, in this converted back porch, while Will refused to talk to her and Bennis Hannaford was on the pages of *Vanity Fair*.

6

There were a lot of people out there who thought Roy Phipps was failing, that he was some kind of fringe fanatic whose only real accomplishment was to make himself look stupid on the six o'clock evening news. Roy Phipps knew better. Roy was, in fact, an expert on the subject of success and failure—not only about what they meant, but about how they happened. Sometimes it struck him, as nothing else did, what a very different life he would have led if he had done what everybody else wanted of him. In this case, "everybody" meant his advisers at Princeton, the men who had seen him through his four years of academic isolation, the ones who had thought they had, in him, a case study of a local boy making good.

There had been times in those days when he had sat in one professor's office or another and silently imagined the tape playing inside the older man's head: poor boy, fine mind, great future. They were, Roy thought, right about all three things. Nobody could have been poorer than he had been when he had first come up to New Jersey from Millard's Corner, West Virginia. He had come up early, at the beginning of the summer, because he knew that if he didn't, he would never be able to save enough money to buy a set of clothes that didn't have holes in it. Even the Negroes in Millard's Corner had had more money than the Phippses, and most of them had had sense enough not to have eleven children in the bargain. Roy's childhood had been a sink-or-swim nightmare in a sea of perpetual failure: his father, always either too sick or too drunk to work; his mother, so tired she spent most of her time sitting on what was left of their sagging front porch, staring out at the hill in front of their house, doing nothing; his older brothers, always drunk or crazy or banged up so badly they had to spend a week in the hospital. They had had no electricity and no running water. When they had wanted water, they had to go out to the yard and pump it by hand. They had had no money, either, because whenever money came into the house it went out again: for food, for milk, for used clothing at the St. Vincent de Paul Shop in the next town. Sometimes there was no money for weeks, and then the older boys brought back kill from the woods in the back or even from out on the highway. They would skin it and give it to their oldest sister, Loretta, who had been named after Loretta Lynn. Loretta would gut it and cook it in a big cast-iron pot that had never been cleaned very well in all the time that Roy had known it. On those nights, Roy had gone out back and lain in the grass rather than eat, because he hadn't been able to stand it: the ersatz broth already crusting over with animal fat; the pieces of squirrel or racoon or muskrat floating to the surface. Sometimes the moon would rise up over him and fill him full of light. That was when he would know, for sure, that he was different than they were—better, and colder. He was so cold, he was a block of dry ice. Anybody who tried to touch him would get burned. When the day finally came to leave, he hitchhiked into Wheeling and got the bus at the Greyhound station without bothering to say good-bye. They wouldn't have known where he was going. He had forged his mother's signature on the papers that needed signing for Princeton. None of them knew he had ever applied to college. His mother didn't even know that he had managed to stay in high school.

Now he stood feeling the steam of coffee rising into his face from a very full cup and watched Will Lawton the atheist get into his truck and turn on the motor. Edith Lawton the atheist was standing in the doorway of her house, barefoot, as if she didn't have to care if her toes fell off from frostbite. He had been watching them all this week, and he was fairly sure that they were either not talking to each other at all, or only talking barely. He would have to pay attention. The members of this church were fascinated by the two atheists on their own block. Roy had had to warn them more than once not to go down there to gawk. That was all they needed, under the circumstances—a few members arrested for "harassing" the heathens, a big black-and-white picture in the *Philadelphia Inquirer* of a few Christians being led away in handcuffs for practicing "hate." It wasn't that Roy Phipps had anything against hate. In fact, he heartily approved of it. God hated the wicked, and he expected the righteous to hate them, too, and to tell the world the truth about what was becoming of it. God hated lies, which was what the apostate churches trafficked in, all the time, day and night, as if their members could escape their eternal destiny in the agony of hell by merely being bored to death. If there was anybody Roy envied, it was that pastor out in Kansas who had put up the website called www.godhatesfags.com—but then, come to think of it, he didn't. It was the "fags" that were the problem. Like The Other Word for Negro, Roy never used it—not because it was derogatory, but because it was slang. There was the influence of the Princeton University English Department for you. Roy Phipps, son of a seldom-employed coal miner and a dedicated slattern, raised on roadkill and dandelion greens, valedictorian of his class, could not use slang.

The door to the study clicked open. Roy put his coffee cup down on his desk next to the silver-framed photograph of a small group of no-longer-exactly boys in front of an elegant pseudo-Gothic building. He noticed himself and paid no attention. He noticed Dan Burdock and almost smiled. He thought—not for the first time—that he might be pushing his

people too far to make them come out to this street to go to
church. This was a street, after all, that reeked of everything
they were afraid of. This was a street that reeked of money.

The man who had come in was very young and very badly
dressed: Fred Havers. Like a lot of just-about-fat men with no
sense of taste or proportion, he wore suits and shirts a size too
small for him, so that he looked as if he were strangling himself. Still, he was dressed, and at this time of the morning,
too. He was even wearing a tie. It was the first thing Roy
stressed to his people. Self-discipline was the key. Character
was destiny. It was the one thing they didn't know and the
one thing they needed most desperately to hear.

Fred came up to the desk and cleared his throat. He was
still in his twenties, but so badly out of shape that he looked
older than Roy did, if looking older meant looking aged. In
some ways, Fred would never look older than anybody. He
had the face of someone who is permanently, irretrievably
clueless, an expression that veered spasmodically between
dazed surprise and embarrassment. He had managed to get
through the General Studies course at some high school on
the outskirts of Philadelphia without, as far as Roy could tell,
learning anything at all.

"So?" Roy said.

Fred cleared his throat again. "I just got back. You know.
From over there. St. Stephen's."

"And?"

Fred shrugged. "I don't know. Maybe I wasn't looking for
the right stuff. They were praying, is all I could see. And some
of them were just sitting. In the pews, you know, and then the
casket was in the front in front of the altar."

"And?" Roy said again.

"And nothing. That's what was happening. His mother is
there. The guy who died. And so are a lot of men. Gay men,
I think. At least, some of them were. They were, you know,
kind of funny."

Roy took a long sip of coffee. It was impossible to explain
to somebody like Fred that not all homosexual men behaved
like flaming queens. *There* was a piece of slang Roy could
use, at least in the quiet of his mind. He put down the coffee
cup and stared at the far wall, over Fred Havers's shoulder.
His bachelor's degree from Princeton was there, framed. So

was his master's degree from Harvard, in history. If he had done what they all wanted him to do, he would have gone on for his doctorate and be teaching in some history department right now, and probably have had tenure before he was thirty-five. He tried to remember when he had had his first vision of hell, and couldn't. The story he told to new parishioners, and to the media when they bothered to ask, was that he had been lying on a mattress on a floor in an apartment in Cambridge when suddenly the hardwood underneath him had disappeared and he was engulfed by flames. That was true enough, but he had a feeling that it had not really been the first time, only the most dramatic in a series of times when hell had seemed very close to him. It seemed very close to him now.

"What we want to know," he said carefully, "is how they're going to handle this funeral. Is it going to be just a funeral, or is it going to be a platform?"

"I know," Fred said. "I went looking for, you know, a bulletin, but I didn't find one. There was one for next Sunday, but it was all about the loaves and the fishes."

"It wouldn't be in the bulletin. Did you hear anybody talking about the funeral?"

"Nobody was talking at all. Oh, except the pastor, you know that guy—"

"Dan Burdock."

"Right. But he wasn't where I could hear him. He was up in the choir loft, and I didn't think I ought to go there. It was just him and this one other guy."

"All right."

"It's strange in there, though. It's like a Catholic church. And it smelled funny. I got sort of queasy. Are we going to go over there today and picket?"

"I don't know."

"He was gay, that guy who died. His guy friend—whatever you call it—he was there in the church when I went over, kneeling on those kneeler things. So we wouldn't be making a mistake, you know, if we got the signs and went."

"He didn't die of AIDS."

"Do we really know that?" Fred asked judiciously. "Don't they try to lie about it, and put other stuff in the paper to keep it quiet? You know, died of cancer—but they don't say the cancer was caused by AIDS."

"In this case, it wasn't AIDS. It was cocaine. Have you ever taken cocaine?"

Fred blinked. "I've never done anything worse than drink a few too many beers, except maybe one time I had some boilermakers. They've got whiskey in them. Not that I don't know what a curse drink can be, Pastor Phipps. I know that. But it's not cocaine."

"Quite." Fred reminded him of his brothers, that was the trouble. Rock stupid and worse. Roy got up and went back to the window. St. Stephen's was quiet, as usual. St. Anselm's was doing its usual traffic in homeless people.

"All right," he said. "This is what we do. We do not picket. Not today. We send somebody to attend the funeral. Is Didi Billings going to be around today?"

"She's due to come in and do some typing at nine."

"Good. We can make her pass, if we have to. Send her in to me as soon as she gets here. We may have to send somebody downtown to buy her a dress. The funeral's at noon. We should have a decent amount of time to get her ready. I don't want her to be obvious."

"What's she going to do?"

"Listen," Roy said. "I want to know if Dan Burdock pulls anything. I want to know if he makes some kind of issue out of Scott Boardman's homosexuality. And then I want the rest of us ready. We won't picket at the church, but if we have to, we'll picket at the cemetery. And if we do, I want the media there. Can you arrange that?"

"Yeah," Fred said.

"Good." It was true, too. Roy had taught Fred himself, and it wasn't that hard, getting news reporters where you wanted them to go, as long as you weren't competing with a major airline disaster. Roy looked up the street and down it again. Everything was quiet.

Back in his freshman year in college, when he and Dan Burdock had been roommates, Roy had known nothing at all about homosexuality, or about God, either. He had only known that he was untouchable, and that his untouchableness came from a whirling vortex of trivialities he could never quite understand. The way he dressed, the way he spoke, the fact that his ambition was so thoroughly single-minded and so thoroughly ruthless—he had changed his dress and his speech, but the ambition was with him still. He would always remember himself his first night at the YMCA, that summer when he'd come north to earn some money before the start of school. That room, with central heat and a slick linoleum floor, with a bathroom down the hall with running water and a real shower. It had shocked him into speechlessness to realize that down-and-outs in New Jersey expected to have more in the way of amenities than coal miners and sharecroppers in most of West Virginia, and that people in the North believed that there was no one, anywhere, who still had to go out in the cold in the middle of the winter to use a chemical latrine.

It was 1962, and on the streets the girls wore skirts so short they looked like bathing suits, in colors so bright they shone even when there wasn't any sun. On campus once the school year had started, the Princeton boys wore polo shirts and penny loafers they wore until they had to be held together with masking tape. Roy went back and forth from his class-room to his bedroom to the library, over and over again, and only on the outside did he begin to change.

www.godhatesfags.com

He wished he had thought of it. He really did. He wished he could go down the street to St. Stephen's and look Dan Burdock in the face.

Instead, he went back to his desk and started to go through the material he would need if they did decide to go out to the cemetery and picket. People thought it was easy, but it really took enormous planning, especially if he meant to keep his people in line. They had to be kept in line. When they were let loose on their own, they got violent. There were people who thought he meant them to be violent, but he didn't. He only wanted them to be violent if they were not also out of control.

A minute or two later, he stopped, thinking that something had been odd, and he hadn't noticed it. Looking down the street at St. Stephen's. Looking down the street at St. Anselm's. All those homeless people. What was it?

His mind came up blank. His coffee cup was empty. He got up to fill it.

It would come back to him, eventually, whatever it was he had seen, and then he could think of what to do about it.

7

Mary McAllister had met the Reverend Roy Phipps only once, but that had been enough to tell her that she never wanted to meet him again. It wasn't that she hated him, exactly. She had expected to hate him. She had seen him on the news, carrying his signs at the funerals of people who died of AIDS, saying that those people were right now burning in the fires of hell. If there was one thing Mary remembered with perfect clarity from her religion classes as far back as First Holy Communion, it was that no human being could ever know whom God had sent to hell. That was because no person could know what was going on in a person's mind at the very moment of death, when God gave everybody a last chance at repentance. Mary had always suspected that this was a chance everybody took advantage of, so that nobody ever went to hell at all—maybe not even Hitler. She was sure that none of the men she had met so far at St. Stephen's, like that poor Scott Boardman who had just died, was in any danger at all of going to hell. It wasn't their fault that they were confused, or that the people around them had been so cruel to them that they felt there was nothing they could do but band together and fend off the world. In Scott Boardman's case, he had been molested by a priest. He couldn't be held responsible for his hatred of the Catholic Church. If she had been a saint, Mary thought she might have been able to bring one or two of them across the street to St. Anselm's and a life of principled chastity, but she *wasn't* a saint. She wasn't even close. What she did instead was to make a point of being friendly to all of the men she met, and to tell them "God bless you" at every possible opportunity.

Now she pulled the soup kitchen van into the parking lot behind St. Anselm's and tried to get a look at St. Stephen's, but there was nothing to see there but the lighted doorway to the church. Ever since she'd heard that Scott Boardman had died, she had been worried about poor Chickie George, who took this sort of thing very badly. People laughed at Chickie, but Mary knew better. He was really a very sensitive person, very sensitive and deep, and she had learned that if she lis-

tened to him long enough and with enough sympathy, he
would start to tell her the truth. She had always had an intellectual understanding of how lucky she had been—to have had
parents who loved and cared for her; to have had a nice house
in a nice neighborhood; to have had a good education and to
have the possibility of more. Chickie had begun to make her
feel it emotionally. There were times now when she lay in bed
in her dorm room at St. Joseph's and stared at the ceiling for
hours, trying to work it out. She couldn't make the world right.
She couldn't go back in time and give Chickie the kind of
parents she had had, instead of the kind he had had, who
seemed to have been ogres with credit cards. The Lord God
only knew, she couldn't straighten out the economic mess the
world was in and make sure that everybody in South America
had enough to eat. So—what?

She got out of the van and checked the clock over the
church. It was five-thirty. She locked up—you had to lock up,
even in the church parking lot, even in a neighborhood like
this—and tugged at the driver's side door to make sure it was
secure. Then she started across the lot to the back door of the
church. It was cold enough so that she knew she should have
been wearing a coat, but she hated wearing them when she
drove, so she hadn't. Instead, she had a thick wool sweater
and a turtleneck over flannel-lined L. L. Bean jeans. She saw
Marty Kelly's pickup truck and patted it as she walked by it.
It made her feel instantly better, because Marty hadn't been
in church for weeks. Bernadette's diabetes had been acting up.
Sister Peter Rose had told her. Maybe Marty and Bernadette
had come in for Scott Boardman's funeral, because Bernadette
had been close to Scott the way Mary was to Chickie.

Mary had gone out to their trailer park once, to see if they
might need anything, but they hadn't been home—and then,
last week, when she'd tried to call, the phone had been dis-
connected. She hadn't known what to think about that. She
couldn't imagine Bernadette not paying the phone bill, but
with their medical expenses—and no health insurance—she
couldn't imagine them being able to move to someplace better.
It was one of those cases that brought her very clearly to the
understanding that she was not a saint. A saint would have
known just what to do in these circumstances: to seek out
Marty and Bernadette; to check with the trailer park to see if

they'd been evicted; to check with Father Healy and see what he wanted to do. Mary had to admit that she hadn't checked with Father Healy because she hadn't wanted to. Father Healy made her nervous and shy, the way Sister Superior had at St. Anne's Catholic Girls High School.

Mary got her keys off her clip and let herself into the church's back door. The small flight of steps led directly to the basement, which had been "finished" to provide meeting rooms and a cafeteria. She stopped at the statue of the Virgin and made the sign of the cross and a little bow. Sister Thomas Marie, who had taught her religion classes, had been very enthusiastic about the idea that they should all develop a special devotion to the Blessed Virgin, and Mary had chosen the Immaculate Conception to "focus her spiritual life." That was why she wore a Miraculous Medal everywhere she went.

The basement was deserted, not only of people but of things, except for the things that were supposed to be here, like tables and chairs. Mary checked into both the conference rooms and the mudroom, where people were supposed to put their coats and shoes. If she hadn't seen people going in and out the door upstairs, she would have thought the entire church was deserted. She tried the cafeteria and saw that the chairs had been put up on top of the tables so that somebody could mop. The floor did not look as if anybody *had* mopped. What was worse, the rat traps were still all over the place, and probably filled with poison, even though several people had complained and everybody was very nervous.

She went through the cafeteria and out the other side. She was just about to go through to the other stairwell and up to the church proper when she saw Father Healy starting to come down, dressed in black but without his trademark cassock, tucking things into the pocket of his shirt.

"Oh, Father," Mary said. "Good morning. I was looking for the boxes."

"Boxes?"

One of the problems, Mary thought, was that he was so young—not all that much older than she was herself. There were rumors that he had graduated from high school at fifteen and been out of the seminary before he was twenty-five. That might be true or not, but it was true that Father Healy was much younger than most priests were when they got to head an entire parish. It didn't help that he looked even younger than he had to be, thin and dark, with a face still full of acne and scars.

Mary waited until he got to the bottom of the stairs. "Sister Scholastica and Sister Peter Rose," she said. "They did a can collection at the school this week. I'm supposed to come pick up the boxes."

"Wouldn't they be at the school?"

"Sister Peter Rose said to pick them up at the church. Maybe she wasn't thinking. I can check the school, next."

"The sisters are in chapel," Father Healy said. "It's time for their—"

"Office," Mary said. "Yes, Father. I know. Don't you think the Sisters of Divine Grace are a very interesting order? They haven't gone all modern, like IHM. Did you see Marty and Bernadette? Their truck is in the parking lot. I was thinking maybe Bernadette wanted to come in for Scott Boardman's funeral."

There was a small door in the other side of the stairwell that led to a storage closet. Mary opened that, but there was nothing inside but brooms and buckets. She closed it again.

"Maybe they're in the Sunday school rooms," Father Healy said. "Let's go up and check. I've got the key to that if you haven't. And I haven't seen Marty or Bernadette today, but I've been back and forth a lot this morning. Maybe they're in the church."

"I've heard that Bernadette wasn't well. Lately. With the diabetes, you know."

"Last time I heard they were talking about amputating her left leg."

To get to the Sunday school rooms, they had to go back across the cafeteria and out a door on the other side, but not the same door Mary had come in on. Whoever had designed this floor plan must have spent a previous life designing topiary mazes. Mary felt her stomach heave and her forehead break out into a sweat. Bernadette wasn't any older than she was. They had to amputate her left leg?

"That's awful," she managed to say. "That's terrible."

"It is, isn't it?" Father Healy was at the far door. He propped it open and shooed her through. "It isn't unusual, with that type of diabetes. It's a strange disease. Sometimes it can be controlled, and sometimes it can't."

"If it's that bad, Bernadette's never going to get to have children, is she? And she wanted six."

"I don't know how it affects having children. To tell you the truth, I hadn't really thought about it. But you're right. She said the same thing to me. She wanted six."

The hall was dark. Father Healy flicked a switch and it was suddenly light. Mary went down to the first of the classroom doors and waited while Father opened up. In some odd way, what was happening to Bernadette and the Reverend Roy Phipps went together in her mind. They were both things that defied expectation—except, of course, that Reverend Phipps wasn't a thing, even if he did move like a robot. Bernadette should not be in danger of losing a leg. She and Marty should be putting money in the bank every month until they could send Marty back to school. Then Marty would get a better job with health insurance and they could start putting money away again to buy a house. The Reverend Roy Phipps shouldn't sound like a preppie in some ancient college campus movie. He should have a twang, and buy his suits at JC Penney.

There was nothing in the first Sunday school room. They tried the next one. There was nothing there, either.

"Well," Father Healy said. "I guess you'll have to try over at the school."

"Right," Mary said. She put her hands in the pockets of her jeans. The jeans were too warm. Her hands started to sweat almost immediately. "Look," she said. "Do you think he's wrong? Reverend Phipps, I mean, the one who—"

"I know Roy Phipps."

Father Healy seemed to have gone rigid as a board. It made Mary feel a little queasy again. She took her hands out of her jeans and rubbed them against the sides of her legs.

"I just wanted to know. He says they all burn in hell as soon as they die. Just because they're gay and they, you know, they do things—"

"We can't ever know if somebody is in hell."

"Yes, I know, but with these people particular, I mean like Scott Boardman who died, you know, I was just wondering—"

"We can't ever know who is in hell," Father Healy said

firmly. "We can hope that every soul finds a way, even if only at the very end, to reconcile himself to God."

"Yes," Mary said again. It was exactly what she had been telling herself a few moments before, but for some reason it was now completely unsatisfying. She wished she liked Father Healy better, if only because he gave such a strong pro-life witness. Besides, she thought inanely, there had to be something wrong with taking so strong a dislike to her own parish priest.

"Well," she said. "Thank you for all your help. I'll run over to the school and see if they left them there."

"Good idea," Father said.

"I won't be at Mass this morning. I've got to do the transport, you know, so that they all get to eat."

"I'll see you on Sunday, then."

"Yes," Mary said. She was backing away. It was true enough. She would be at Mass on Sunday. She was at Mass on every Sunday, just the way she said a third part of the rosary every day and the Stations of the Cross every Good Friday. She had been doing these things all her life. She couldn't imagine not doing them. It was just that, just like Father Healy's explanation about how people did and did not go to hell, they suddenly seemed to be nowhere near enough.

She got to the door of the cafeteria and went through it. She went through the cafeteria and out into the hall she'd come in through. There was still no sign of light outside, although she could hear the bells ring out quarter to six. She went through the hall and out the back door and looked around the parking lot. After she had the food in the back of the van and the homeless people who wanted to come with her rounded up and organized, maybe she'd go look for Marty and Bernadette.

She was halfway across the parking lot to the back door of the school when the door to the convent burst open and Sister Peter Rose came running out, her long veil flapping, her long habit getting tangled in her legs.

"Oh, Mary," she said. "Mary, I'm so sorry. I just remembered. You don't know where the food is."

"Aren't you supposed to be in chapel?"

"Scholastica will forgive me. It's one of the great good things that came out of Vatican II. Follow your common sense instead of the schedule sometimes. Although of course I don't like a lot of the other things that came out of Vatican II. Oh, never mind me. The food is in the convent pantry, out back, it's right inside the door. I should have told you."

"That's all right. Do you know what? Marty Kelly's truck is in the church parking lot this morning. Isn't that great? He hasn't been here for ages."

"Have you seen him? We've all been so worried about Bernadette."

"No," Mary said. "I haven't seen him yet. I thought I'd get this straightened away and then go look for him. I mean, they must have come in for Mass, don't you think? Why else would they be here so early in the morning? For Mass now, and then for Scott's funeral later."

"Let's just hope it's both of them," Peter Rose said, "and not Marty on his own because Bernadette is in the hospital again."

Mary hadn't thought of that. She looked behind her at the pickup truck and said a quick prayer to the Virgin, because she always prayed to the Virgin first, and because Bernadette was the *kind of* person the Virgin was supposed to be especially protective of. Then it hit her again, in a way, that feeling that this was not enough, that something was missing. It made her feel as if a great gaping hole had been blown through the middle of her body. It made her feel as if she didn't have enough air.

Sister Peter Rose turned and looked back at her. "Mary? Are you all right?"

"I'm fine," Mary said. "I'm just a little tired. I'm coming."

She did come, too, as quickly as she could, forcing herself not to look back at Marty's truck or at the stream of light that came from the front of St. Stephen's. After she was done with this, she would go find Marty and Bernadette. After she had brought the food and the homeless people out to the soup kitchen and run her shift there, she would come back here and find Chickie George and see if she could get him to talk. She had an afternoon of classes, but she thought she could skip them, this once, in order to do the right thing.

Something at the back of her mind was telling her that this was still not enough, but Mary McAllister was doing her best to ignore it.

8

Sister Harriet Garrity had received the invitation to move into
the convent with the Sisters of Divine Grace with as much
politeness as she had been able to muster—but it had not been
much. The problem was, by now, she had the routine taped.
Every time there was a new Superior at St. Anselm's Parochial
School, the invitation would come, usually proffered over coffee in one of the conference rooms in the basement of the
church. Before that invitation, there would be others: to have
dinner with the sisters in their refectory; to stop over for tea
and cake in the convent parlor on Saturday afternoon. Sometimes, Harriet would agree to those, if only to see for herself
if the Sisters had begun to offer some resistance to the patriarchy, or at least to chafe under the burden of its rule. It was
a depressing sight, over there. Sister Harriet's order had given
up the habit in 1969. Sister Harriet herself wore nothing to
distinguish her as a nun but a small gold Eucharistic symbol
on the collar of her plain navy blue wool blazer. She wouldn't
wear a crucifix, because the crucifix was so clearly part of the
problem: God, viewed as male, and only as male. She
wouldn't even wear a cross, because she had reservations
about the entire concept of the crucifixion. As a mythology, it
glorified violence and child abuse. It was a mythology of the
Fathers, and as a mythology of the Fathers, it was a mythology
of death. So much of the mythology of Christianity was a
mythology of death, Harriet had a hard time contemplating it.
Sometimes she sat in her pew at Mass and saw the church full
of the bodies of women and people of color, hacked away at,
destroyed from within. Sometimes she closed her eyes while
Father Healy was saying the consecration and prayed to God
the Mother the way she was allowed to do, out loud, when
she went to the meetings of WomenChurch. There was a time
when Harriet had thought that WomenChurch was the Church
of the future. The legitimate aspirations of women and people
of color would not be held back. They would overwhelm the
hierarchy and shake the foundations of Rome. Now she wasn't
so sure. There were too many women out there like the Sisters
of Divine Grace—too many women willing to aid and abet

their own oppression. That was what made the situation of women like Harriet so very tenuous, and so very dangerous. They were in the belly of the beast, but they could be found out and destroyed at any time.

At the moment, if Harriet was going to be destroyed, she was going to freeze to death. She had opened her bathroom window to look out on the parking lot behind the church. The glass was caked over with ice, so that she couldn't see anything very clearly. Now she could see what she wanted to see—Mary McAllister talking to Sister Peter Rose in the courtyard near the convent—but the cold was going straight through the terry cloth of her bathrobe and making the joints in her fingers ache. She leaned a little farther out to see if there was anything else going on that she ought to know about and caught sight of Marty Kelly's truck. She made a face and retreated back inside. She didn't know what was worse, really, women like Sister Scholastica or women like Bernadette Kelly. Scholastica had the brains, but Bernadette was both a witness and a disgrace. Harriet could just imagine that girl on one of those inspirational shows on EWTN, gushing to Mother Angelica about how the only thing that kept her going in her troubles was her faith in Christ and the comfort of the Blessed Mother.

Harriet closed the window and went back to the bathroom sink. She had already brushed her teeth and washed her face. She never wore any makeup. When she had first entered the convent, they had been forbidden ever to look at themselves in a mirror. For years after the changes that had come with Vatican II, she had found it almost impossible to spend more than half a minute looking at herself in anything at all. Now she looked but did not contemplate. She was a plain, square-faced, square-jawed woman with hair that was almost too thick for her skull. She kept her hair cut short enough so that people could see the turquoise-and-silver earrings she had been given the summer she had spent teaching reading on an Indian reservation in the Southwest. It was the only part of her old life she allowed to be visible around her. The other things—the Equality Now banner from the first women's rights march in New York City; the pictures of herself at the two large demonstrations in Washington against the Vietnam War; the mimeographed flyer from the time the students had occupied the offices in St. Benedict Hall and she had been one of the few teachers to support them—she kept tucked away in a box in a drawer in her bureau, where nobody would ever think to look for them. She had not given up hope. She knew that capitalism was corrupt and that it would eventually have to fail. She expected to live to see the day when socialism rose triumphantly from the ashes of its Soviet betrayal. She looked forward to the moment when the people of the Third World threw off their lethargy and demanded their rightful share of the fruits of the earth. She could see all these things as clearly as if they were a vision of God Herself—but she now thought she would be very old by the time they came to be.

In her bedroom, she put on a white blouse and a blue wool pantsuit. When she had first taken off the habit, she had favored suits with skirts, but after a while she had no longer been able to stand the panty hose. With the pantsuit she was able to wear trouser socks and sensible clogs. The clogs reminded her of the way the women sounded when Women-Church held a celebration, or a retreat—all those women together, worshiping God the Mother, God the Goddess, God as Sophia, the essence of wisdom. Oh, it made Father Healy fit to spit when Harriet went off to WomenChurch, but there was nothing he could do about it. He didn't have any power over her, and the Cardinal Archbishop didn't seem to want to interfere. For now. Harriet was more than sure that the Cardinal Archbishop would interfere if he knew she was giving support to Catholics for a Free Choice, but he didn't know, and Harriet wasn't about to let him find out.

She got her short coat out of the closet in the hall and put it on. Her apartment was on the third floor of the rectory, walled off from the rooms where the priests lived by a set of hastily erected partitions, put up by the archdiocese fifteen years ago, when she had first refused to be banished to the convent. In this front hall there was a grate that hung right over the priests' recreation room downstairs. Sometimes, when she was in a particularly sticky spot, Harriet crouched there and listened to the priests' talking among themselves. Sometimes, she even heard things that made a difference. When she was younger, it would have embarrassed her to be this under-handed. Now she knew that that very guilt had been a tool of the patriarchy, one of the methods by which all men kept all women down. The oppressed had not only the right, but the duty to do whatever had to be done to throw off their oppression. Honor and honesty were the hypocrisies of the ruling class.

At the moment, of course, there was nothing to be heard through the grate, any more than there would have been anything to see through her binoculars, if she trained them—as she sometimes did—on the convent's front parlor window. At this hour of the morning, the nuns would be saying their office and Father Healy would be getting ready for Mass. Father Donovan, the parochial vicar, was off on a month-long course in theology in Rome. Harriet buttoned her coat up to her chin and went out and down the long double flight of stairs. It was cold even in the stairwell. She hated February.

Outside, it was not only cold but dark. The big arc lamps lit up the parking lot, but did nothing for the pathway to Harriet's entrance door. This was, most certainly deliberate. They thought that if they made her live in fear of her own safety, she would give up and go away. Maybe they were hoping for something more dramatic to happen, for her to be the victim of a mugging or a rape. Whatever they were trying to do, it wasn't going to work.

She got to the parking lot and went by Marty Kelly's truck, looking inside as she passed. There was an empty carton from an order of McDonald's french fries on the floor near the gas pedal. Harriet wondered if Marty ate that sort of thing in front of Bernadette, tempting her to throw her diet to the winds and gobble herself into a diabetic coma. In all likelihood, he just didn't think. The soup-kitchen van was still parked near the convent's door, but there was no sign of Mary McAllister. Harriet thought that was just as well. Where had all these people come from—where had all these *women* come from— who wanted nothing more than to go back to the days of pray, pay, and obey?

Harriet let herself into the church's side door. She hated going through the basement. Deep in the body of the church, she could hear the homeless people moaning. Some of them were mentally ill. They sang to themselves all night long, and sometimes they screamed. There was this much she had to charge to the credit of the Sisters of Divine Grace. When it was necessary, they would sit for hours with these people, women as well as men, nonwhite as well as white, soothing them.

When she got to the big double doors that led into the church proper, she stopped and looked inside. None of the nuns were present this morning, but none of the homeless people were agitated, either. Some of the homeless people seemed to be asleep, sacked out on pews. She went to the church's front doors and looked out. Across the street, St. Stephen's was lit up like a stage, but nobody seemed to be going in or out.

"Ah," Father Healy said. "Sister. Were you thinking of coming to Mass for a change this morning?"

Harriet took her mind off St. Stephen's. Father Healy was young enough to be her son, but he was an unpleasant martinet just the same. It was as if the last fifty years of history had never happened.

"You're not dressed," Harriet said. "Doesn't Mass start any minute now?"

"The first Mass of the morning is at seven. That makes it a little more than an hour away. Mary hasn't even picked these people up to take them out to breakfast."

Harriet went back to looking at St. Stephen's. She did not go to Mass at St. Anselm's unless she had to. She preferred to go two parishes away, where they had a Eucharistic minister who was a woman.

"What's happening across the street?" she asked. "They're never lit up like that at this hour of the morning. Especially on a weekday."

"Vigil for a funeral service. That young man, the one who took cocaine. Scott Boardman."

"Oh. Yes. Another victim of the patriarchal church."

"I've talked to Father Burdock. He seems to think there's some danger of a demonstration. By the Reverend Phipps and that sort of person. He's very concerned."

"Isn't Roy Phipps very convenient?" Harriet said. "He's so extreme, he makes you look like a moderate."

"I'm not a moderate," Father Healy said. "I'm a Catholic. I wish you were."

"The people are the Church," Harriet said, automatically.

"You may be the Church, but you're not this Church. And I don't understand why you bother. Why call yourself a Catholic at all? If you no longer believe what the Church teaches, why not just leave?"

"It's my Church as much as it is yours."

"It's Christ's Church. It belongs to neither one of us."

"Then it's really strange that you get to run it and keep me out. The Church has to change. You think it won't, but you're wrong."

"The Church changes all the time, it just doesn't change at the core. And you won't change it. I want you to move into the convent with the other sisters. And I want you to wear something, some article of clothing, that will clearly identify you as a nun."

"The sisters are not sisters of my order. I don't belong in their convent."

"You don't belong in the rectory."

"I do wear something to identify me as a nun. I wear this." She tapped her Eucharistic pin. "I've been in this parish for fifteen years. I was here when you were still in the seminary. I've been doing it this way all that time."

"I'm sure. But you're going to stop doing it this way, Sister, or you are going to leave. I've been patient as a saint for the last three years. I've had enough. You have forty-eight hours to get into some kind of habit. I don't care if it's a sweat suit and a veil, as long as it is a veil, and as long as you've got some Christian symbol on you larger than a Kennedy half-dollar, displayed where the public can see it."

"You can't give me orders like this. Only the archbishop can make these kinds of decisions, and he's—"

"—willing to call you into his office and make it clear that he is supporting me in this in every way possible. I'll arrange it for later this afternoon."

"Sisters in my order—

"The sisters in your order," Father Healy said, "amount to nine women, all of them older than you, and you must be—what?—sixty? Your order is dying. It has no new vocations. It has no young nuns. When you go, it will go with you. If it doesn't go before. Go buy a veil, Sister. Because if you don't, you'll be out of that rectory apartment by the end of next week, and I'll have an ordained deacon in the slot for parish coordinator before you've gotten off the train at your mother-house."

"Marvelous," Harriet said. "The dead hand of the patriarchy strikes again."

"If the dead hand of the patriarchy had been running things around here, you would have been out on your ass years ago. Go buy a veil. Don't think I'm bluffing."

There was a sound from inside the main body of the church, and they both turned. It was not repeated. Probably, Harriet thought, one of the homeless people was having a nightmare. She was feeling a little breathless. People did not talk to her this way. Not even the Cardinal Archbishop talked to her this way.

"Excuse me," Father Healy said. "I'd better go find out what's going on."

If she excused him, it was silently. She had no idea what it was she was supposed to say. She looked back at St. Stephen's and saw that there were now people in the lit-up entryway, Mary McAllister and the most startlingly beautiful man Harriet had ever seen. She had seen him before, she knew, but she didn't know his name. Mary McAllister was holding his hand, even though there was no way in hell he could be anything but gay.

Underneath her, in the basement, there was noise. The sisters had finished their Office and come over to the church. Their voices were muted and giggly. Harriet was suddenly feeling very high, almost as if she'd taken a lungful of laughing gas.

She had nothing to be afraid of. She really didn't. She had been waiting for this for years, and expecting it. She just hadn't recognized it when it first showed up. She was finally going to get what she had always wanted, and when she had it, she was going to be invincible.

There was only one way to gain real authority in the Church, and that was to be martyred for the faith.

9

Bennis Hannaford did not think of herself as someone who had quit smoking, even though it was three months since she'd given up cigarettes. Instead, she thought of herself as someone who was being required not to smoke, both by the person she loved most (Gregor Demarkian) and by her doctor, who seemed to think that she had to either get rid of the coffin nails or die. Coffin nails. It was quarter to six in the morning, and she had spent almost all of the night wide-awake and thinking about death. There was a lot of death to think about. On her desk in her spare bedroom, she had the scribbled message she'd taken when Chickie George had called to tell her about Scott Boardman's funeral. Scott was a man she had known only slightly, because he did graphic design work for her publisher and they ran into each other at parties in New York, but Chickie she knew very well. Chickie was one of those people who exist in every city, the people who know everybody of any importance without being in any way important themselves. She also *liked* Chickie, which was more to the point. She got a little uncomfortable with his act every once in a while—was it really necessary for *anybody* to be that much of a flaming queen?—but he meant well, and there was no malice in him, which was more than she could say for a good many of the straight people she knew. In this case, he also had a point. St. Stephen's was right there on that same street as Roy Phipps's Full Gospel Independent Baptist Church. Roy Phipps's people were always picketing funerals.

"We need all the help we can get," Chickie had said when he'd called. "We need as big a presence as possible. We can't let them outnumber us at Scott's funeral."

Bennis thought it was very unlikely that Roy Phipps could get enough people together to outnumber the men who would be at Scott Boardman's funeral even without Chickie's efforts at organization, but she had agreed to come, and she still thought it had been the right thing to do. The only problem was that she was going to show up so tired, she would barely be able to see. It might even make sense for once to give in and take public transportation. It might make more sense to get some sleep, but at the moment it was impossible. There was more than the message she'd taken from Chickie's call lying on her desk. There was also the formal invitation to her own sister's execution, last scheduled for November and then delayed three more times for a month at a shot.

"It won't be delayed again," Gregor had warned her, when the invitation came. "The governor is fed up, and there isn't a lot more room to move. And she doesn't have the attractiveness factor. Not that a woman's attractiveness counts as much as it used to in these things. It didn't count at all for Karla Faye Tucker."

No, Bennis thought, Anne Marie was nowhere near as attractive as Karla Faye Tucker. If she had been, she might not be in the mess she was in to begin with. Bennis reached to the side table automatically, expecting to find her pack of cigarettes and her Bic plastic lighter, but they weren't there. Then she looked over at Gregor Demarkian and got out of bed. He looked so peaceful when he was sleeping, and he slept so much. Bennis could barely get five hours a night without feeling awful. Gregor could get five hours in the afternoon when he was supposed to be watching football, and once he conked out, it was worth your life to wake him before he wanted to be woken. A freight train could drive across the ceiling, blowing its whistle at full power, and all he would do was turn over and mutter something incoherent about how somebody ought to get the cows off the tracks.

Bennis sat up and swung her legs over the side of the bed. Then she stood up and got Gregor's robe from where he had thrown it over the back of the wing-backed chair near the fireplace. They had to do something about these apartments, knock them together maybe, or expand them. It only worried her that it might be pushing things a bit far, even on Cavanaugh Street, to be that open about the fact that they were— uh—she didn't have a word for it. At least she didn't have a word that would do in this neighborhood. She wondered why that was. It wasn't that they didn't know what she and Gregor were doing. Half the street had been involved in the plot to arrange it. Even the Very Old Ladies didn't really disapprove. They just put it down to These Days, which were so different from The Way It Used To Be that they couldn't be judged by the same standard. Even Tibor never said a word about the two of them, and Tibor was a priest.

"I'd still feel better if we were married," Bennis said, to the air—and then, mentally, she took it back. She would not feel better if she and Gregor were married. She didn't want to be married. She had never wanted to be married. She would only feel better about openly living with him on Cavanaugh Street if they were married, and that was a very different thing.

She tied the belt of Gregor's robe as tightly around her

waist as it would go. Then she padded out of the bedroom and into the living room, where the big plate-glass window looked out over the street. This was Gregor's apartment they were sleeping in. Gregor refused to sleep in hers, because she always had papier-mâché models of scenes in her books lying around everywhere, and in some of them there were trolls. If the apartments had been knocked together, though, she would have been able to get to her own computer without going out into the hall. She could have used Gregor's computer, but he had done something to it again, and you couldn't surf the Web on it. She was going to have to fix that for him someday soon.

The street below her was empty. It was too early for anybody at all to be up. Even Donna and Russ, who had the closest thing to an ordinary respectable schedule of anybody she knew, didn't get up until six. The Ararat didn't open until seven. Here was the real problem with smoking cigarettes, aside from the fact that it made her feel as if her lungs had been ripped out and she would never get enough air. When you didn't smoke, you had no way to waste time. When you tried to waste time, you were far too conscious of the fact that you weren't really doing anything. Of course, smoking a cigarette wasn't really doing anything either. She wasn't making any sense.

She went into the bathroom and shed the robe and her pajamas. She had a pair of jeans in there and a turtleneck. She really needed to go upstairs and take a shower and find clean things, but at the moment she was much too restless. She went back into the bedroom and found a pair of Gregor's socks to put on, because she hated rewearing socks no matter what she was doing. Then she went into the hall and found her clogs. There was one person on this street who was likely to be up at this hour of the morning, because he was almost always up. Bennis didn't know if she had ever seen Father Tibor Kasparian sleep.

She could have run upstairs for her coat, but she didn't. She could have put on one of Gregor's sweaters, for the layering, but she didn't do that either. She did stop in the hallway to listen to the quiet of the house, and to wish, not for the first time, that somebody would rent the top-floor apartment. Ever since Donna and Russ had renovated their town house and moved down the street with Donna's son Tommy, this place had seemed far too empty, and far, far too quiet.

It was freezing cold outside—at almost six in the morning in February, it would be. Bennis darted across the street and down the block. There were people awake, as a matter of fact. There were lights on in the back rooms of the Ararat, meaning that Linda Melajian was already at work and trying to set up. Bennis ducked into the narrow alley next to Holy Trinity Church and came out in the courtyard in front of Tibor's apartment. It could have been the one day in history when Tibor was actually asleep, but it wasn't. All the lights in Tibor's apartment were lit at once. It was as if the man thought he was a lighthouse in a fog, needing to turn the power up high to save a fleet of ships at sea.

Bennis let herself in Tibor's front door—he never locked it; almost nobody on Cavanaugh Street locked anything, which was incredibly stupid, if you thought about it. Cavanaugh Street might be a safe place, but the rest of Philadelphia wasn't. Just inside the door there was a big stack of paperback books leaning precariously to one side. The book on top was Jackie Collins's *Lucky*. The one underneath it was Thomas More's *Utopia*. Bennis straightened the pile a little and went into the living room.

"Tibor?"

"In the kitchen."

Bennis went through to the kitchen. It wasn't quite as much of a mess as it usually was. Lida and Hannah must have been in recently to clean. Still, the oversize kitchen table was covered with books, to the point where it was impossible to find a space to put down a coffee cup. Tibor had managed it only by moving books out of the way and putting them in stacks on other books. Bennis took a copy of Norman Cantor's *Civilization of the Middle Ages* and a paperback of John Grisham's *The Rainmaker* off a chair and chucked them onto the table with everything else.

"I couldn't sleep," she said.

"I can see that. I was out. With the Relief committee. It was depressing."

"I've been thinking crazy things," Bennis said. "Like the fact that I don't know what form of execution they have in the state of Pennsylvania. I don't think it could still be the

electric chair, do you? Does anybody still have the electric
chair?"

"Florida."

"Oh," Bennis said. She got out of her chair and began to
walk around. She remembered the stories about Florida's electric chair. They weren't pleasant. "Gregor says there won't be
a stay this time. That it will really happen. And I was wondering, you know, if I should force the issue. If I should make
her see me."

"Can you do that?"

"I don't know," Bennis admitted. "But I haven't seen her
since it happened, and it's been ten years. And Gregor is really
no help, because he gets all rational and philosophical about
it, and I'm not feeling rational and philosophical. I'm feeling
crazy. It doesn't seem right, to me, capital punishment. It
never did, really."

"Mmm," Tibor said.

Bennis checked out the coffee. It didn't look safe. "And
the thing is, I know, on the day it happens, if it happens, there
are going to be people out there waiting for it. You know what
I mean. There are going to be people out there with signs
wishing she would die in horrible pain and other people with
signs protesting the death penalty, and it just doesn't make
any sense. Why would people come a hundred miles just to
stand in the road in front of the state penitentiary and wish for
somebody to die a horrible death?"

"Sit down," Tibor said. "I have a teakettle. You can have
some tea."

"I've had enough caffeine in the last few hours to last a
millennium. No, seriously. Why do they do that? And then
this afternoon, I have to go to a funeral. Scott Boardman's
funeral—"

"At St. Stephen's," Tibor put in helpfully.

"—and the thing is, the reason I have to go is because a
friend of mine is worried there are going to be pickets. I mean
people picketing the funeral. There's this guy—"

"Roy Phipps," Tibor said.

"Right. Roy Phipps. I suppose everybody on earth has
heard of him. God only knows, he's on the news enough. He
sends out press releases just so the media can show up and
call him names. So, okay, say he's a nut. There are nuts in

this world. But what about all the people who follow him, the people who hold the picket signs and go to his church. Are they all nuts? Has this guy put together all the nuts in Philadelphia in one place? I mean, why do people *do* these things?"

"I wish you would sit down," Tibor said. "You're making me dizzy. And I have only one answer to your question and you do not want to hear it."

"Yes, I do. What is it?"

"Original sin."

Bennis sat down. "You know what Chickie said? That's my friend who asked me to come to the funeral. He said that last week, one of the people from the Phipps organization tried to kill them. The priest or the minister or whatever he is went to the altar and there was this little cake of white powdered stuff right there next to the wine, and it turned out to be rat poison. Arsenic, isn't that what rat poison is? And somebody had just put this cake of rat poison right next to the Communion wine."

"Did they put it in the Communion wine?"

"I don't know. Chickie didn't say. He didn't even tell me what they did about it, you know, after they found it. I guess they didn't turn in the Reverend Phipps, or it would have been on the news. But still. Who else could it have possibly been? And now with the funeral coming up, they have to be especially careful. They're holding a vigil so that the altar is in sight of at least two people all night. It's worse than crazy. And don't tell me it's original sin. I don't believe in original sin."

"It has the virtue of explaining a great deal that is otherwise inexplicable," Tibor said. "Maybe I will go to this funeral with you. Just to make certain you do not drive."

Bennis stood up again. She picked up a copy of J. M. Roberts's *History of Europe* and put it down again. She picked up a copy of something in Latin and put that down again, too. She felt as if she had taken a whole load of methamphetamine and it was just starting to kick in. This was not good news. The crash, when it came, was going to be awful.

"Crap," she said. "I'm right off the wall, aren't I? Do you think that if I went back to the apartment, Gregor would be awake?"

"You could always wake him up."

"Mount St. Helens at full spew couldn't wake him up. He goes to the Ararat at seven, though. What time does he usually get up?"

"You should know that better than I do."

"I don't pay attention. Oh, damn." Bennis ran her hands through her hair. "I hate it when I get like this. I really do. It was a mistake to quit smoking, no matter what any of you think. Smoking could always calm me down. What am I supposed to do now?"

"Warm milk and honey and a hot bath?"

"That sounds really awful," Bennis said. She checked the clock on the wall, the big round L. L. Bean one Donna Moradanyan had given Tibor the Christmas before last. It still wasn't six o'clock yet. She was moving faster and faster, and time had slowed to a crawl.

Bennis went over to the stove and found the kettle. She didn't like tea, but she could at least make some coffee for herself. She filled the kettle at the tap and put it on the burner. Then she took a deep breath and tried to slow herself down.

It would help, she thought, if she knew what it was she was really worked up about—Anne Marie, or the possible pickets at the funeral, or Chickie's story about the rat poison on the altar, or what. Instead, it all went around and around in her head, and she was beginning to suspect that she was worried about nothing but the lack of nicotine in her lungs. Cigarettes, cigarettes, cigarettes, she thought. She used to buy six cartons at a time in North Carolina and then stack them up on the top shelf of her linen closet, above the place where she kept the pillowcases.

Tibor kept a little box of those coffee bags in the cabinet next to his mugs. Bennis got both a bag and a mug and grabbed the kettle as soon as it started to go off.

"The thing is," she said, "sometimes it makes perfect sense, and that's what worries me. There are times when I could smash somebody's face in. But that's the difference. I couldn't sneak around about it. I couldn't plan it."

She put the mug full of coffee and coffee bag at the place she had cleared for herself and sat down in front of it, wondering if Tibor would realize, as she did, that she didn't know if she was talking about the rat poison on the altar, or about Anne Marie.

10

When Father Robert Healy first came to St. Anselm's parish, he had been sure he knew what it was he needed to do. That was three and a half years ago, before Roy Phipps had taken the storefront at the end of the block and put his makeshift "church" there. Father Healy had just finished a five-year assignment as parochial vicar at St. Bridget's in Radnor, where he had gone right after he came back from studying at the North American College in Rome. The Cardinal Archbishop had warned him that he would not like parish life, and the Cardinal Archbishop had been right—but Father Healy had put it down to the fact that he was an assistant, instead of the head of his own parish. Robert Healy had never done very well when he was forced to take second place. Sometimes he tried to think back to what he had been like, growing up, and found to his surprise that he really could not remember anything. He had graduated from a tough Jesuit prep school at the age of sixteen, valedictorian in his class. Then they had made him go to Georgetown for three years to wait, because he wasn't old enough to enter a seminary. He wondered if they had expected him to change his mind, or to go so mad with sex that he wasn't able to think straight enough to pass his theology courses. Instead, he had had three sexual experiences, all with the same girl, which he had liked very much but been a little impatient with, because they were so distracting. Then, as soon as the diocesan seminary would take him, he had packed up his things and come back to Pennsylvania.

Now he moved things around the desk in his office and thought that he was going about it all wrong. This was one more proof that he belonged on the faculty of a theology department, or on the staff of a marriage tribunal or a canon law court, but not in the trenches, where what mattered was how much you knew about people. Father Healy liked people—he liked them quite a lot—but it was like his relationship with that girl at Georgetown: he found them distracting. He also found them puzzling. When he wanted to relax, he sat down with one of Michael Grant's histories of ancient Greece and Rome, and put Bach on the CD player in the rectory living room. He did not watch television. He had tried to watch television once, when Sister Peter Rose invited him to the convent to have popcorn and take in *The X-Files*, but he had ended up entirely confused. As far as he had been able to tell, the message of *The X-Files* was that aliens from outer space were among us, and that they provided the explanation for everything from the tinny taste in well water to witchcraft. The bit about witchcraft had alarmed him. There were no such things as witches—not in the sense of women who made pacts with the devil and could do magic spells—and if there was one thing the reading of history had taught him, it was that religion was very dangerous when it became unmoored from the discipline of reason. That was all they needed now, with the Church under attack from every side—another season of witch-hunts, with stories about exorcisms in the *New York Times*. It was bad enough, the kind of nonsense that was written about the Church and homosexuality, as if a straightforward moral objection to unlimited sexual license turned you into . . . Roy Phipps.

Father Healy moved things around on his desk again. There was a small square television in one corner of the office, and he had put it on as soon as he had come in, because he was feeling so guilty about Sister Harriet Garrity. What was on was not *The X-Files*, but a music video of Christina Aguilera singing "Genie in a Bottle." This, Father Healy understood. He had understood it ever since he was twelve years old and got his first look at the *Sports Illustrated Swimsuit Edition*. It was not true, as some people wanted to make out, that you had to be some kind of sexual oddity to commit to a life of priestly celibacy. Father Healy's sexual impulses were in perfectly good working order. If he had been a scrupulous man, he would have been driven nearly insane by the way the young women dressed on the streets of Philadelphia in the summer— and forget the University of Pennsylvania campus in the spring, where they seemed to have abandoned the custom of women wearing something on the top halves of their bodies even while sunbathing.

What marked him out was not his lack of sexual response, but the fact that he also responded to other things, and always had, even as a small child. He might remember very little about himself when he was young, but he did remember lying on his bed in his darkened room, knowing he was supposed to go to sleep, and feeling the presence of God all around him, thicker and more pressing than any blanket. He had felt the presence of God around him all the time, in those days. He had carried it with him like a mist. When he received his First Holy Communion, he had felt it inside himself, as heat: the real body and blood of Jesus Christ, Our Lord, not a symbol, but a fact. He was much older when he realized that everybody else did not feel what he felt. If they had, they would behave differently, and there would not be many churches but only one. That was when he knew he had to be a priest, the way some people knew they had to be painters or writers or musicians. Next to the feeling he had when God touched him at the moment of the consecration, sex was nice, but not compelling.

There was a knock on the door. Father Healy said "come in," and then wondered if he would be doing better here if he were older—fifty-six instead of thirty-six, experienced at living instead of just at argumentation.

The office door opened, and Sister Scholastica came in. Father Healy relaxed. He hadn't been aware that he had been tense, but now he realized that he had been expecting Sister Harriet at any moment. He didn't think Sister Harriet was the sort of person to let a matter rest.

Sister Scholastica looked at the television and raised her eyebrows. Christina Aguilera faded, and in her place came something called Smash Mouth, singing something called "All Star." Apparently, this was a program that showed people singing things.

"You can turn it off," Father Healy said. "I just turned it on to have background noise."

"From VH-1?"

"I didn't pay attention to what was on." This was not exactly true. Father Healy wanted always to be honest. He might end up on a faculty somewhere, he might even end up a bishop, but he would never be a Vatican politician. "I did like that last song," he said. "She was very attractive. The young woman."

"Right," Scholastica said. She left the television alone. "Do you have a moment? I know it's six o'clock, and we're coming up on Mass, but I'm getting a little worried. Do you know that Marty Kelly's truck is parked in the parking lot?"

"Oh, yes. Somebody told me it was. I'm so glad to have him back. Them. I only hope Bernadette was well enough to make the trip."

"So do I. What worries me particularly is that she might have made the trip and then become ill, because the truck is in the parking lot, but Marty and Bernadette are not in the church. At least, they're not anywhere I could find them. With diabetes as volatile as Bernadette's, she could have fallen into a coma—"

"But wouldn't Marty have come to someone in the church for help? Bernadette wouldn't have brought the truck here on her own, would she? I thought she couldn't drive, because her eyesight was too poor."

"She was nearly blind."

"Well, then."

"The fact remains that I can't find them. I even sent Sister Peter Rose across the street, to see if they'd gone over to the vigil, but they weren't there. It would have made a certain amount of sense. Bernadette and Scott got along when Bernadette was coming here regularly. Or at least, Peter Rose says they did."

"Maybe they went to get something to eat," Father Healy said. "Doesn't Bernadette have to remember not to go too long without eating? Surely there must be places that would be open even this early in the morning."

"I suppose."

Sister Scholastica went to the window and looked out. This was Father Healy's church office, not the rectory one, so the window faced the street and St. Stephen's front courtyard, where the people from Roy Phipps's church sometimes sat in for hours on end. Father Healy drummed his fingers on the top of the desk.

"Are they going to be over there," he asked, "Roy Phipps and his people? You know, with the picket signs."

"What? Oh. I don't know. I wouldn't think so. The man didn't die of AIDS. The Reverend Roy is very focused when it comes to that kind of thing."

"Well. That's good."

"On the order of thank heaven for small favors, I suppose." Scholastica moved away from the window. "I wish I knew where they'd gone. She's not a well woman, no matter how young she is, and I don't like the idea of her wandering around loose in a diabetic coma. If you can wander in a coma. I'm sorry. I'm not making any sense."

Smash Mouth had disappeared from the television screen. In their place, somebody named Melissa Etheridge was singing something called "Angels Fall." She was not as conventionally pretty as Christina Aguilera, but Father Healy liked the sense he got of her much better. This was a woman you could talk to.

"Well," Scholastica said, "I'd better get going. I've been up all night. I'm going to be a wreck in school today. Maybe I'll take one more tour and see if they show up."

"It's probably a good idea."

"It probably is. All right, Father. With any luck, you'll see them both right up front when you process in for Mass."

Scholastica went out, her long habit skirts hissing in the air just above her ankles, her long veil billowing out behind her as she walked. Father Healy got up and walked over to the window himself. There were people on the stone steps in front of St. Stephen's, tight little clusters of men leaning their heads together, looking cold. Everything had seemed so clear to him, when he first got here, so straightforward and sure. Homosexual practice was an objective moral evil. That was true, and it was also true that the Church had to take a public stand against its acceptance in the culture at large. A public stand had to be public. If you took a stand that nobody could see, you might as well not have taken a stand at all. It was like abortion. There was a good reason to have people out there on the streets in front of abortion clinics, praying the rosary, even if their acts did nothing to stop a single child's death. It created a climate of opinion. It made it clear that this act was not celebrated by everyone everywhere, that people all around the world knew it was wrong.

Out on the steps of St. Stephen's, there was movement. Father Healy focused his eyes on the front doors and saw that Daniel Burdock had come out, dressed all in black with a clerical collar on. In all the years that Father Healy had been in this parish, Daniel Burdock had come closest to being somebody who could truly be a friend. He was one of the few that Father Healy respected without reservation, for his commit-

ment to his vocation, for his scholarly erudition, for his un
compromising attachment to all things anchored in mora
principle. The only problem was, Daniel Burdock didn't speak
to him, except to say hello in the chilliest voice possible, i
they happened to pass each other on the street. That was be
cause of Father Healy's insistence on upholding the Catholic
understanding of homosexual practice, which Dan seemed to
think was—

What?

Father Healy turned away from the window and sat down
again. The song on the screen had changed again, this time to
something he knew—The Beatles, all four of them together
looking very young. He rubbed the palms of his hands against
his face until his eyes began to tear. He could hardly have
made more of a mess of things if he had set out from the first
day to sabotage himself, and now he was going to make a
bigger mess of things by forcing a showdown with Sister Harriet Garrity. Surely, there had to have been a way for him to
have said what he had to say to her without sounding as if he
were starting a war. Surely Father Kennedy, at St. Bridget's,
would have known how to—finesse—this sort of thing. Then
again, Father Kennedy had had a parish coordinator, too, and
she had been just as much of an . . . unpleasant person . . . as
Sister Harriet was.

On television, The Beatles had been replaced by Will
Smith, whom Father Healy knew on sight. After the disaster
of *The X-Files* evening, Sister Peter Rose had tried again by
asking him over to see the video of *Men in Black*. Father Healy
got up and crossed the room and turned the television off. In
an hour, he would be able to say Mass, and then things would
be better, by definition, at least until he recessed out of the
church with the altar boy carrying the cross in front of him.
Other priests might hurry through the seven o'clock Mass, but
Father Healy never did. He got lost in it.

He sent up a silent prayer that he might get lost enough in
it today to forget all about Sister Harriet Garrity, then he
headed out the door and down the stairs toward the sacristy.

11

For Marty Kelly, the six o'clock bell was like an alarm clock. He had been sitting in the little changing room just off the sacristy, with Bernadette beside him, for so long he had begun to feel the tops of his legs going to sleep. He had, as well, been noticing things he had never noticed before. The ceilings in this church were much higher than ceilings were other places. That was what made the rooms feel so big. The windows in this church all had thick panes that couldn't be seen through—or they did up here. Marty couldn't remember what it was like in the basement, where the meeting rooms were, because every time he had been there he had resented it. It was the one thing Bernadette ever did that really upset him, insisting over and over that they should take courses together. Bible study, catechism, marriage encounter: Marty had hated them all. He had especially hated sitting at the wide conference tables with a book open in front of him, knowing that anything he could think of to say would be foolish, or worse. It had been like being back in school again, where the only thing he had ever been able to do right was to keep his mouth shut.

Marty got up off the step he was sitting on and went to the door on the other side of the door to the sacristy. It was all a matter of logistics. If he went through the sacristy, he would come out on the altar, and that wasn't what he wanted. Bernadette would have hated the idea of being laid out there, as if she were some kind of pagan sacrifice. If he went out the other door, though, he would go into the church proper just to the left of the Mary Chapel. That would lead him right to the Communion rail, which was made out of marble and set in place, so that it couldn't be removed. When they ended the practice of kneeling at Communion, the churches with wooden rails had taken them out. It had happened so long ago that Bernadette hadn't even been alive, but she had always refused to go to a church without a rail anyway. At least she hadn't been one of those people who dropped to their knees in front of the priest as soon as they got to the head of the Communion line, holding up everybody who was waiting and getting themselves talked about, in whispers, until the end of Mass. Bernadette never did anything obvious like that. It wasn't in her nature.

Marty looked up one end of the narrow hall and down the other, but nobody was in sight, not even the homeless people. If this day was like any other day, Mary McAllister would be rounding them up to take them to the soup kitchen, where they would be given breakfast and kept out of the cold for an hour or two. Eventually, they always wandered off. The ones who weren't crazy were pickled in alcohol. They never knew where they were. Down at one end of the hall, there was a window. Marty was sure he saw a trace of lightening sky. He always thought of February as the dead of winter. He forgot that spring was only a month away.

Marty went back into the changing room and looked down on Bernadette lying on the floor, curled up as if she were still sitting in the truck—but not quite as curled up as she had been. Her body had been so stiff, but now it seemed to be relaxing a little. He leaned down and touched the skin of her face, then stepped back quickly. She felt like polished rock, and she really was cold. He had heard on television that people got cold when they were dead, but he'd never really understood what that meant before now.

He leaned over and got his arms underneath her. It was true. She had relaxed a little. She was still stiff, but not as stiff. She didn't feel rigid.

He lifted her in his arms and waited for a few seconds, to make sure he had his balance. She weighed almost nothing, even as a deadweight. When she'd been alive, he'd been able to carry her around like a bag of groceries, taking her from the living room to the bedroom to the kitchen just because they were teasing each other and it was a game they could play. They had played a lot of games in their time together, and made love often enough to make Marty bored with the pictures in *Playboy*, but what he had loved most was the way they were together in bed when they weren't making love. That was what Bernadette had given him that he had never had: that sense of companionship; those hours of being easy and without the need for defense. It bothered him that he could no longer remember what they had talked about in the dark. It bothered him even more that they might have talked about nothing in particular, but just rambled on, warming in the sounds of each other's voices.

He took her out into the hall, and then across the hall into the side of the church proper. There was a little corner there that was cut off from the people in the pews. The only way they could have been seen was by somebody praying in the Mary Chapel, but the only person in the Mary Chapel was stretched out on a pew and fast asleep. Marty looked at the pews in the center of the church and felt a moment of hesitation. What had happened to Mary McAllister? Usually she had the homeless people up and moving by this time. He hadn't intended to do what he was going to do in full view of thirty people—and especially not these people, who were not right in their minds and might be set off by it. On the other hand, he didn't see what else he could do. If he waited any longer, Father Healy would come down to change. The Sisters of Divine Grace would come over from their convent. He wasn't stupid enough to believe he would be able to get past all of them with Bernadette.

Marty looked out at the pews again. The homeless people were still there, but now he made sure that nobody else was. People knew that Catholic churches were open twenty-four hours a day. They came in at all hours of the day and night, to pray for help or to offer repentance. At least, that was the theory. Marty had never actually known anybody who did something like that. He checked the front of the church, and the back. He squinted long and hard at the great double doors. He looked at the empty stretch of floor in front of the Communion rail. He had never noticed before that the church had so many statues, or that they looked so dead. He made the sign of the cross. Bernadette would have killed him for that last bit. She did not think that statues of the Blessed Virgin were dead.

Somewhere in the back, a light flickered. It happened so fast, he thought he might have imagined it, except that the homeless people seemed to have noticed it, too. The ones that were awake began to move around on the pews. One or two of the ones who weren't moaned in their sleep.

It was now or not at all. Marty knew that.

He hefted Bernadette higher into his arms and started out across the church proper. Several of the homeless people noticed him, but they said nothing. They didn't even come to look at what was going on. Where they came from, they probably saw things like this all the time—people too drunk or stoned to walk on their own; people being carried and lifted from one place to another. Marty didn't think it would occur to them that Bernadette was dead.

He got to the very center of the Communion rail in front of the altar and put Bernadette down carefully on the floor. There was a good thick carpet there, so he didn't have to worry too much about her being uncomfortable. He made the sign of the cross in the general direction of the monstrance, where a consecrated Host was kept for the adoration of the faithful. He wondered if the Church counted the homeless people as keeping the Host company through the hours of the night. It was terrible. He knew so little about religion, even after all the time he had spent with Bernadette. The only thing he was absolutely sure of was that God hated him, and that he must have hated Bernadette even more. There was no other explanation he could find for why the things that had happened to them had happened to them. God's love seemed to be reserved for people like nuns and priests and people like Mary McAllister, who came from big houses in the city or the suburbs and went to colleges like St. Joe's that cost more in one year than most people made in two. He knew that people were not supposed to be born cursed, but he was sure that was exactly what had happened to him.

Bernadette was lying in front of the Communion rail, her body uncurling slowly, almost as he watched. Marty reached into his pocket and took out the gun. He had bought it on the street for two hundred dollars, along with two rounds of ammunition, and he had no idea if it was what the man who sold it to him had said it was. A .357 Magnum. That was what he had wanted. He was only sure it was a real gun, because he had insisted on test-firing it first.

The homeless people hadn't noticed the gun any more than they had noticed Bernadette. They might not have been able to see it. Marty looked at the statue of the Blessed Virgin in the Mary Chapel, and then at the cloth-draped marble altar that was made to look like a banquet table in the palace of a prince of the blood. The church ceilings were even higher than the ceilings in the rooms around it. The cavernous space seemed to be full of wind that blew in and out of his ears in hiccoughing gusts.

"Hail Mary, full of grace," he said to himself.

Then he put the gun in his mouth and blew off the back of his head.

PART ONE

God is expensive, but he has very good taste.
—SHIRLEY CURRY

ONE

1

For Gregor Demarkian, for most of his life, the inevitable end of a successful criminal investigation did not exist. He had been called into court from time to time to testify to something he had seen or heard or analyzed. When he had been a special agent for the FBI, he had been called to court particularly in kidnapping cases. Later, when he was head of the Behavioral Sciences Unit, he had watched other men go to court in his stead. Behavioral Sciences dealt with serial killers, and they went to court far more often than kidnappers did. Gregor had a theory about that, eventually. It was that murderers were almost always entirely self-absorbed. A kidnapper was after money. When he failed to get it, when his plans went haywire and he found himself in custody, his primary objective was to save his skin. If a decent plea bargain would do that, he would take it. Murderers were different. Somebody who killed in the heat of the moment might be willing to listen to reason when he was arrested and in jail, but the kind of murderer who planned it almost never was. That kind of murderer wanted to star in his own movie, to be the focus and center of attention, to have all the world's cameras trained on him. He wanted people to know how shimmeringly brilliant he had been, even though that knowledge would send him to the electric chair or the gas chamber or, as was more and more often the case now, a hospital gurney with rubber restraints and a lethal injection. Gregor sometimes wondered if they liked it, all the way to the end, the ceremony and solemnness of it. He wasn't sure, because this was the part he didn't know about. His objections to capital punishment were moral and practical. He

had seen exactly one execution, and he had never been interested in seeing another. He only thought that the old line from
Dr. Johnson was not entirely accurate. The prospect of hanging
might work wonderfully to concentrate the mind for some people, but for others it only heightened the sense of specialness,
of being a chosen instrument, of being the next best thing to
God.

Now he padded into the living room and confirmed his
suspicion that Bennis was, indeed, asleep on the couch. She
had curled up into a ball against the leather, with one of his
own robes bunched up under her head for a pillow. The television was on and turned slightly on its stand so that she could
face it directly while lying down. The morning news was playing, with another story about the suicide of that young man at
St. Anselm's Church. Gregor frowned slightly—it had been
over a week; the fuss and fumbling had gone on far too long—
and wandered back down the hall to his own bedroom to get
dressed. His hair was still wet from his shower. His neck was
cold. Outside the big living-room window, the world was
mostly dark. Sometimes it seemed to him impossible to figure
out what to do in these situations. He almost never knew what
to do about Bennis at all. Everything he did do was somehow
off—not wrong, exactly, but not really right. He wondered if
he ought to be satisfied that, in the mess this had become, she
had not started smoking again—but he had a feeling that that
had more to do with Bennis's fundamental stubbornness than
with him.

Suddenly, on a whim—no, more on a premonition—he
went back to the living room to check on her again. He was
wearing his boxer shorts and his socks and his shirt and his
tie, but the tie was still hanging around his neck like a scarf.
He was all too aware of the fact that his big window had no
curtain. If Lida Arkmanian happened to come to her window
across the street at just this moment, she would catch him in
his shorts. The trick was that Lida would not come to her
window. She always had her breakfast coffee in her kitchen,
which was on the ground floor in the back. Gregor looked at
Bennis and hesitated. He had no idea what he had intended to
do when he got there. Bennis had not moved. The coffee table
she had pulled up next to the couch was littered with debris,
but it was the debris of somebody who had stayed up all night

to watch the creature features: a coffee cup still half-full; an open bag of Chee-tos, barely touched; a half dozen crumpled paper napkins that looked as if they had been used to wipe up spills. Bennis looked haggard and half-dead, the way she did most of the time these days, but at least she had gotten out of her clothes and put on an oversize T-shirt. A half dozen times over the past three weeks, Gregor had found her still in her knee socks and clogs. He had been able to tell by the dirt on her soles that she had been out walking again.

The invitation from the state was not on the coffee table. That, Gregor realized, was what he had been looking for. In the beginning, when they had first sat down with Anne Marie's lawyer and he had outlined just how final the situation had become, Bennis had carried that damned invitation with her everywhere, as if she needed it to identify who she was. It hadn't helped that the governor of Pennsylvania had gone on the air three times in ten days to assure the people of Pennsylvania that this time justice would be done. Anne Marie Hannaford might have escaped execution over and over again for the past ten years, but she wouldn't escape it one more time. There were no more appeals left to try, no more avenues left to explore. The only chance she had was an order of clemency from the governor's office, and the governor had no intention of issuing one.

"Do you think she's evil?" Bennis had asked him, one afternoon, out of the blue, when they had been wandering through a department store looking for a bright red scarf to buy Donna Moradanyan Donahue for her birthday.

It had been the oddest scene: the department-store aisles flanked by counters and shelves full of things that all seemed to be made of something metallic in silver or gold; Bennis in her shop-for-something-expensive uniform of Calvin Klein coat and two-and-a-half inch stacked-heel boots; himself trying desperately not to meet the eyes of saleswomen who had nothing to do in a store that was practically empty. Before Bennis spoke, Gregor had been feeling guilty. Now that they were officially a "couple," they were expected to buy their presents together—but didn't that shortchange the people they were buying presents for? Surely Donna deserved a present from each of them, the way she had every year before. At Christmas, Gregor had had to restrain himself from running out at the last minute and buying another whole set of Christmas presents. If he hadn't been sure that Bennis—already pumped up beyond belief from nicotine deprivation—would have killed him, he would have done it. But things had been better, then. That was before the new date of execution had been set. Anne Marie's lawyers were still in court. It still looked as if there might be a chance.

Bennis was holding a red scarf in her hands. Gregor would have thought it was just what they were looking for, but he could tell from the way she was fingering it that she didn't like it.

"I don't think 'evil' is a very useful word," he said finally. "I think she's dangerous. I don't think she ought to be walking around loose. I think, under the right circumstances, she would probably do it again."

"I want to know if you think she should be dead."

"I never think anybody should be dead," Gregor said. "No, I take that back. There was one person, just one, whom I thought ought to be executed. I'm putting that badly. In that one case, I thought execution was justified. I suppose what I'm trying to say is, whether or not I think she ought to be dead doesn't mean very much."

"Well, it won't change anything, but that wasn't what I was getting at." Bennis bunched the scarf into a ball and threw it back on the display table. Gregor could see the saleswomen watching her. She was such a prime target: obviously rich, and obviously used to it. He wondered if she was even seeing the scarves anymore, of if they had wandered into a more urgent area of her mind, the part where she had to solve the problems of the universe, now, immediately, without excuses. It was a part of the mind that usually atrophied after adolescence, but the withered organ never disappeared. Gregor knew that from experience, too.

They got to another set of shelves and another set of scarves. Bennis seemed to like this set more. She passed up the solid red one to look at one with red-and-grey stripes. She wound it around and around her hands and nodded slightly.

"Pashmina," she said finally. "You don't usually see it in patterns."

"What's pashmina?"

"A kind of cashmere." She handed the scarf to Gregor.

Gregor noticed that the scarf was both softer and longer than the ones he was used to. Then he looked at the price tag: $278.

"Good God," he said.

Bennis took the scarf from him and headed for the nearest counter. Saleswomen probably got commissions on the things they sold. Whoever ended up with Bennis was going to have a very good sales day.

"What I want to know," Bennis said finally, "is what I should think about it. It's not as if we were ever close. I don't think Anne Marie has ever been close to anyone."

"Yes," Gregor said. "That's the point."

"I know. And there's what she did. Which was horrible. Beyond horrible. But I still don't know what I should think about it. Maybe it's because she's my sister, still my sister, you know what I mean. In spite of everything. Even in spite of the fact that we never really liked each other. Maybe I'd feel the same way about the execution of anybody I'd ever known."

"People do, you know. It's almost impossible for a psychologically normal person to kill someone he can see as fully human. That's why, when there's a movement to stop an execution, there's so much time taken to make the convicted murderer seem human. Think about the Karla Faye Tucker case in Texas. It hurt to see her die in the end because she had become real to so many of us. She wasn't a name and a story. She was a person."

Bennis had found a counter. She folded up the scarf and put it down. The saleswoman was there in a blink, gurgling incoherently. Gregor didn't think Bennis heard a word she said.

"There's something else," Bennis told him. "I thought I might as well warn you. The state of Pennsylvania sent invitations to my brothers and to Dickie Van Damm."

"And?"

"Chris is going to come out and stay with Lida. I don't know about the other two. I don't even know where Bobby is. And as for Teddy—" She shrugged.

"I like your brother Chris. I'll be glad to see him."

"Yes, well, the thing is, he may not be the only person you see. I've got it on good authority that Dickie is going to wit-

ness the execution. That he's going to—be there. In the peanut
gallery. Or whatever you call it."

"Ah."

"If he's there, he won't leave us alone. You must know
that. We'll see him. He'll come out to Cavanaugh Street. He'll
make a nuisance of himself somehow. In person, I suppose I
mean. Anyway, that's what I've heard."

"Ah," Gregor said.

The saleswoman was no idiot. She could see that Bennis
wanted to talk to Gregor and not listen to her enthuse about
the scarf or about the wonders of pashmina. She interrupted
only once—to ask if Bennis would like a gift box—and as
soon as she had a positive answer went about her work with
silent efficiency. The gift box was red and came with a white
satin ribbon. Valentine's Day was only a few days away.

"You know," Gregor said, "I don't think you really have
to worry about Dickie Van Damm. He's a nuisance and a
damned fool, but he's not dangerous to you, or to anybody
except when he's driving drunk. And I've heard he doesn't do
that anymore."

"He hired a driver."

"There, then."

The saleswoman handed back Bennis's credit card and then
handed over the box. Bennis tucked the box under her arm
and walked away. Halfway down the aisle to the back door,
she stopped.

"It's just that it's going to be such a mess," she said desperately. "It would have been a mess under any circumstances,
but you know what he's like. He'll be all over the news. He'll
make a celebration of it. The dim-witted little prick."

"Yes," Gregor said—and now, all this time later, he said
"yes" again, out loud to the air in his bedroom. Then he tight-
ened the belt around his pants and slipped his feet into the
penny loafers Bennis had bought to replace his standard FBI
wing tips. It still felt strange to him that he didn't have to bend
over to tie his shoes. He still didn't understand why the shoes
didn't just fall off his feet, without laces to hold them on.

He went back out to the living room. Bennis was still sleeping. The news was still on. Now it seemed to be about puppy
mills, somewhere in Bucks County. Gregor leaned over the
coffee table and turned it off.

Bennis coughed in her sleep, and moved. Gregor got the throw blanket from the back of the couch and tossed it over her. He didn't think she had actually slept in a bed since that interview with the lawyer, and she didn't look as if she were about to start sleeping in a bed anytime soon.

Ages ago, when Gregor was just out of the Army and engaged to Elizabeth, he had thought he knew what love was. Surely, when Elizabeth was sick, in those last awful years, he actually had known what it was. He would never have been able to stay with her, and to help her, if he had not loved her. Duty would not have been enough. Even so, this time around and with Bennis, he felt as if he didn't know anything at all. She was such a complicated person. There were so many twists and turns and secrets to her body and her soul. He knew he would have been wrong to think that her life had been easy merely because it had mostly been rich—but he thought that that was what he must have thought, deep down, until very recently. Now he wanted to run the palm of his hand over her cheek, to feel the smoothness of it, to feel the heat. Sometimes it seemed to him as if his love for her reduced itself to these things: the visceral; the physical; the couldn't-be-put-into-words. It surprised him, really. He had never been a primarily physical person, but his response to Bennis was intensely so, and so insistently present that he found himself coming to in stores and on street corners with the smell of her wrapped around him like a cloak.

The throw blanket didn't cover anywhere near as much of her as Gregor would have liked, but there was nothing he could do about it but stretch it smooth in the corners. He did that and then planted a kiss on her forehead. She neither moved nor spoke. He backed away into his front hall and got his coat. They'd been through a lot together over the last however many years, and they would get through this.

Still, Gregor thought, I'd be happier if I wasn't about to be the one responsible for the death of her oldest living sister.

2

It was later, sitting in the Ararat over coffee and eggs, that Gregor realized there was something he could do about what was going to happen. He couldn't do anything about the execution itself, about the fact of it or its timing. He couldn't even do anything about Dickie Van Damm, who was supposed to be the grieving widower of Bennis's sister Myra—although he doubted if Dickie could hold a single emotion for the space of ten years, never mind a single thought. His mind flitted back and forth through the scenes at Engine House in the days after Bennis's father had been killed, but he could never make it rest on Dickie Van Damm. Dickie himself was never at rest. He gestured and bopped. He hurried from one end of a room to the other. He talked, nonstop, while pulling at his tie hard enough to strangle himself. He had, Gregor realized with a shock, all the mannerisms that men of his own generation associated with homosexuality—except, of course, that he was not homosexual. The Truman Capote Syndrome, one of Gregor's instructors at Quantico had called it. The memory made the past seem eons away instead of decades. Had they ever thought like that, as a matter of course, without even questioning it? Had there ever been a time when an "enlightened" view of homosexuality was that it wasn't their fault, it was a kind of birth defect they were born with, and people who weren't born with it should be less censuring than kind?

Gregor was sitting in the big window booth, opposite Tibor and Russ Donahue, who was married to Donna Moradanyan. Next to him, Donna's son Tommy was bent over a hot chocolate covered by a mountain of whipped cream. The cup was big enough to be a soup mug, except that it had a handle. Outside, on Cavanaugh Street, the pavements were slick with ice. There was a needle-fine rain falling, the kind that turned to ice in the air.

"So," Russ Donahue was saying, "what I told her was, she should apply to all the places around here, Temple and Penn and that kind of thing, even Bryn Mawr. It wouldn't be that much of a commute. And so she did. And Penn took her right off, early admissions, first thing."

"So," Tibor said. "She will go to Penn."

"Right," Russ said. "And she was ecstatic, at first. But then, right after Christmas, it started to get odd. She's all wound up. She's, uh, decorating. If you know what I mean. You can see what she's done to the front of our house."

Everybody could see what Donna Moradanyan Donahue

had done to the front of the house she shared with Russ and Tommy. It was wrapped in red and white satin ribbons, and had a heart the size of a Volkswagen beetle on its roof.

"She has also decorated the church," Tibor said. "Not inside the church, where it would be a sacrilege, but the front where the sign is. We have now Cupids with arrows pointing to the time of the liturgy on Sunday."

"Now she's going to go decorate your house," Russ said, nodding at Gregor, "just the way she used to do. According to her. I think she's talked to Bennis about it, but I can't, because Donna's the only one who can talk to Bennis these days. I'm all for Bennis's quitting smoking, but you know, Gregor, she's having a really hard time with it."

"She's not having nearly as hard a time with it as I am," Gregor said.

"My mom is going to go to college," Tommy said. "She's already the second smartest person in the world, but now she's going to get a paper that says so so she can show people when they want her to prove it."

"The second smartest?" Russ said. "Who's the smartest, Father Tibor?"

"You."

Gregor lifted his coffee cup and waved it at Linda Melajian, who was on the other side of the room trying to placate one of the Very Old Ladies. Gregor thought the Very Old Ladies had to be at least a hundred years old by now. They looked a hundred years old, and every time there was any news about Armenia they seemed to be able to remember events that took place in the seventeenth century. Even the assassination that had happened last fall had brought up memories of other assassinations, and of coups, and of Turks rampaging through the countryside. Gregor thought that what was really going on was a kind of emotional displacement. What they really remembered was the fear, and the sense of living in a landscape of chaos and uncertainty. There was something about the bad emotions of childhood that no adult could ever completely shake. Gregor was the same way about fires. His childhood had been full of fires, back in the days when Cavanaugh Street had been nothing but tenements cut up into meager cramped apartments, and when the people who lived here had had no money to speak of and no space to breathe. Even after all these years, Gregor could remember the light of the flames flickering in his window from a fire devouring one of the houses across the street. Three of them had gone up in a single year, when he was seven, and Gregor could still remember himself lying as still as possible in the narrow bed in the room he shared with his older brother, as if any movement of his might attract the fire's attention, might make it leap across the street and begin to destroy his own. Then there would be the sound of sirens and screeching tires. The adults in the rooms around him, his parents, his Aunt Vida and his Uncle Michael, the Velaskians from across the hall, would gather in the De-markian living room to look out on what was going on. They would talk rapidly, in panicked squeals, and in Armenian, so that the children might not understand. Maybe that was why Gregor had fought so hard against learning the language with any degree of competency. He'd always thought it was because he'd wanted to be a Real American, instead of the hyphenated kind. Across the street, the houses that had burned down all those years ago—and been left as rubble for decades—were now town houses owned by well-heeled women who spent their winters in fur coats. His parents' old apartment was now one of the storerooms above the Ararat. Gregor waved again. Linda Melajian caught his eye and nodded.

"So," Russ Donahue was saying, again, "that's it. I mean, I thought that when I got married, you know, over time, I'd start to understand her. Not just love her or like her, but really understand her. And instead, she gets more incomprehensible every day."

"Wait till she gets pregnant," Linda Melajian said, pouring coffee into Gregor's mug from her Pyrex pot. She checked everybody else's cup, and everybody else's food, so that she was satisfied that nobody needed anything. Then she marched away.

"I don't think Donna wants to get pregnant just yet," Russ said. "I mean, she does eventually, you know, but I think she wants to finish college first."

Gregor got a clean paper napkin out of the little stack of them Linda had placed in the middle of the table when they first sat down. The Ararat used cloth napkins for lunch and dinner, but for breakfast they used paper. It was a good thing, because Gregor was always trying to find something to write on. He took out his pen—Bennis's pen; she stole his bathrobes, he stole her Bic medium-point pens—and began to draw a diagram that started with the governor's office on top and meandered its way down to the state attorney general and the mayor of Philadelphia. He was just thinking that he had never gotten along with the mayor of Philadelphia—which was rather like saying that Jesse Jackson had never gotten along with Jesse Helms—when he became aware that everybody else at the table had suddenly gone quiet.

"What is it?" he said, looking at his diagram as if it could really tell him something, instead of being the restless doodle it was.

He looked up, and when he did he saw Sister Mary Scholastica standing by their table, wearing what looked like the Count Dracula's cape over her long habit. Her veil was on slightly crooked, as if it had been knocked sideways in the wind. A few strands of hair were coming out of the white-tipped edge of the stiff crown. She was not alone. A small, much younger, much more tentative nun was standing just behind her. Gregor stood up.

"Sister," he said. "Sit down. I haven't seen you in a year. Bennis isn't here. She had a late night last night. I think she's still—"

"I haven't come to see Bennis," Scholastica said. "Oh, I'm sorry. I mean, I do want to see Bennis. I've been wanting to see her for weeks. But now. Now I came to see you. This is Sister Peter Rose."

"Sister," Gregor said.

Sister Peter Rose bobbed and blushed simultaneously.

"Maybe Sister Peter Rose would like to sit down," Scholastica said. "While you and I go somewhere to talk. It really is important. Couldn't we just go and find an empty table—"

They looked around. There were half a dozen empty tables in the middle of the room. Sister Scholastica shrugged.

By now, of course, everybody in the room was looking at them. People on Cavanaugh Street had run into Sister Scholastica before, since she and Bennis were friends, but it was still highly unusual for two nuns in only slightly modified habits to show up at the Ararat at quarter after seven in the morning. In fact, Gregor was willing to bet it was unheard of.

Linda Melajian had already appeared with two clean coffee cups and the coffee. Sister Peter Rose slid into the place Gregor had just vacated.

"We'll go over there," Gregor told Linda, pointing to a table five feet away. He led Sister Scholastica across the room. "I thought you said it was no longer a rule, that nuns had to travel in twos," he said.

"It's not." Scholastica sat down. "I just didn't like the idea of wandering around in the dark on my own. I'm not used to cities, did you know that? Colchester was as close as I'd ever gotten to one before this, at least to live in, and it was hardly Philadelphia. I've got a problem."

"I had figured out that much."

Linda Melajian was there with the coffee and the cup. She had Gregor's half-full cup with her as well. She put it down before Gregor could analyze how she was managing to juggle all these things at once.

"Cream and sugar?" she asked Scholastica.

"No, thank you," Scholastica said. "I drink it black."

Linda Melajian wandered away.

"Well," Gregor said. "What is it? I can't believe you're in any kind of serious trouble. You're one of the sanest people I've ever known."

"Oh, it's not me exactly," Scholastica said. "It's—do you know I'm living in Philadelphia now? I've meant to call Bennis, but I've been too busy. I came in at the beginning of January to replace the principal at St. Anselm's Parish School."

"St. Anselm's? The place where there was that suicide a couple of weeks ago?"

"It's been nine days," Scholastica said. "Exactly ten days. Today makes ten days. That's the place, yes."

Gregor cocked his head. "Don't tell me it turns out not to have been a suicide? I thought it was witnessed by all kinds of people—"

"Oh, it was. By Peter Rose, for one. And Father Healy. As well as by a whole lot of homeless people who were sleeping in the church. Father Healy lets them sleep in the church. The Cardinal isn't sure that he likes the idea. No. Marty Kelly committed suicide. It isn't about Marty. It's about Bernadette."

"Bernadette?"

"His wife. He brought her dead body to the church. She was a diabetic, one of those ones where the disease seems impossible to control. Anyway, he was at work one day and she went into a diabetic coma at home and died. And he—I don't know all the details, Gregor, it's very complicated. But to make it short, he brought her body to the church. And he went into the sacristy, to the changing room where the priests robe for Mass, I think because he knew that nobody would be in there until right before seven. And he wrote a suicide note. And then he came out and put her body in front of the altar and, well, you know."

"All right." Gregor's coffee was still too hot for him to drink comfortably. Scholastica seemed to be drinking hers without noticing how hot it was. "So, there was his wife, Bernadette. Kelly?"

"Right."

"And?"

Scholastica put her hand up to the crown of her veil and tried to adjust it. With these new veils, there was always a little hair showing at the front, and a stiff half-moon at the crown that was almost like a linen tiara. Scholastica's efforts to put the thing right only made the mess her hair was in even worse. She put her hands down on the table.

"The medical examiner's office is going to have a press conference today and announce the results of the autopsies. The Cardinal has managed to acquire an advance copy of the autopsy report."

"Ah. And?"

"Bernadette Kelly didn't die in a diabetic coma. She died of arsenic. A lot of arsenic. And what's almost more important, it's nearly certain that Marty couldn't have given it to her."

Gregor slapped his hand against the table. "They can't possibly know that. Not unless they can pin this man down with certainty at least for several hours, and even then—"

"They can pin him down with certainty. Look, Gregor, it's not just Bernadette, either. It's—I really can't go into all this now. You have no idea. I talked to Father Healy and Father Healy talked to the Cardinal. The Cardinal wants to know if you'd be willing to come down to his office as soon as you can get there."

"Now?"

"Now. Gregor, please believe me. You have no idea how bad this is. That's why I came instead of the Cardinal calling you. He doesn't even want the chance of somebody finding out in advance that he's consulted you. And under the circumstances, I don't blame him. Will you come?"

"Of course I'll come," Gregor said, and then his eye was caught by Tommy Moradanyan, standing on the book seat at Sister Peter Rose's back in such a way that her veil cascaded over him, hiding him completely.

It wasn't really relevant at the moment, but Gregor disliked the Cardinal Archbishop of Philadelphia almost as much as he disliked the mayor.

TWO

1

Like many other people, Gregor Demarkian had long had a love-hate relationship with the Catholic Church. The love was an acknowledgment of cultural achievement. Michelangelo and Bach, Hildegarde von Bingen and Teresa of Avila—it was impossible not to notice that the institution that still called itself Holy Mother Church had been mother to men and women of great talent, integrity, and intelligence over the course of twenty centuries, and still was. Gregor had seen those critiques of religion put out by the various "skeptical" societies that had sprung up over the last twenty years, claiming that all religion was a delusion and all religious people were addle-headed idiots who only believed out of a craven and atavistic fear of hell, but then the people who wrote the critiques seemed to him to be more than a little addle-headed themselves. If you didn't have an axe to grind, you had to accept it. Catholic art, Catholic music, Catholic literature, Catholic philosophy, Catholic architecture: you could go for years studying nothing else, and always be in the company of the best the human mind could produce. It even worked when you were in the presence of imitations, as he was now, walking through the high-ceilinged halls of the archdiocesan chancery. The pictures on the walls were reproductions, but they were good reproductions of good art. The almost-not-audible polyphonic chant was coming from a CD player and not from monks praying as they walked, but it was soothing to listen to. In the days of the old Cardinal Archbishop, Gregor would have been happy to be where he was. He had enjoyed the chancery then, even though he had never been in it except to discuss a problem, potential or actual. When his interviews were over, he would go downstairs and across the way to the cathedral and sit in a pew in the back for a while. In the late afternoon, this was usually safe. No Masses were being said. He hadn't wanted to attend a religious service. He liked to watch the changes in himself, the way the place and the quietness of it rocked against the bleakness of his agnosticism. He had felt the same thing when Bennis had taken him to the Cathedral de Notre Dame in Paris, except that the experience had been even stronger. If there was any sense to the phrase "to wake the dead," this was it. In Notre Dame, especially, Gregor had felt as if he were in the presence of centuries of souls, all still alive, all still alive, all just out of sight—and all, of course, as thoroughly convinced of the reality of God as he was of the impossibility of knowing anything about Him. Gregor sometimes wondered if this would have been different if he had been brought up a Catholic instead of in the Armenian Church. Much as he loved Father Tibor, the services at Holy Trinity, and even Holy Trinity itself, left him cold. He would never in his life be able to shake his childhood conviction that all things connected to it were foreign, and un-American, and second-rate. He supposed Catholics felt that way, too, about Catholicism, if that was what they were brought up with—but not all Catholics, obviously, since Sister Scholastica had both been born one and become a nun.

Gregor's response to Catholicism might be confused, but his response to the new Cardinal Archbishop of Philadelphia was not. He had met the man twice. He had detested him both times, and the second time more strongly than the first. Physically, the man was almost a caricature of a Jesuit and a cardinal, written as a villain by Miguel de Cervantes: tall and thin, with features so narrow it almost seemed as if he had tried to iron them flat. Gregor could have gotten past the man's looks, but he was unable to get past his personality. Ferociously intelligent and just as ferociously well educated, he lacked any of a dozen qualities that might have made him human. Warmth had no place on his face. Humor was something he indulged in only at the expense of other people, and he was able to indulge in it often. It would have been difficult for any man with this man's gifts *not* to have made many of the people around him look stupid, but another kind of man might have tried.

The worse thing, as far as Gregor was concerned, was the fact that the Cardinal saw himself as a man on a mission. He was here to clean up the mess that had been made of the Church in the Archdiocese of Philadelphia, and most specifically the liberal mess. John Paul II had given in on the matter of altar girls, but other loose practices had to go. In the three years this man had been in office, he had put an end to women distributing Communion, to general absolution at the Good Friday penitential service, and to Bible readings in "inclusive language." There was a rumor now that he was about to go after the nuns. They would either get back into habit, and into convents, or lose their right to function in the archdiocese. Gregor could sympathize with the view that said Catholics ought to be Catholics, meaning Christians united with the Bishop of Rome, and not just free-floating believers in anything they chose. He couldn't sympathize with this man's apparent ruthlessness. He didn't have much use for the sort of people who described the Catholic hierarchy as devils in Catholics, but he couldn't shake the feeling that this man was not only vindictive, but someone who enjoyed vindictiveness.

Up ahead of him, Sister Scholastica's veil was waving from side to side as she walked. The young priest who was showing them the way to the Cardinal Archbishop's office had his head bent in her direction, listening. Gregor wished for the third time that he could just find his way on his own. He knew where it was.

They got to the Cardinal Archbishop's door, and Sister Scholastica turned. "Here we are. And on time, too. His Eminence doesn't have a lot of patience."

"I've noticed."

"I don't think you have to worry about patience," the young priest said. "After all, you're doing us an extraordinary favor. His Eminence understands that."

The young priest opened the door and ushered them inside, where a nun sat behind the secretary's desk, at work at a computer terminal. Both the nun and the young priest were as tense as strung wires. In the days of the old Cardinal Archbishop, nobody had been tense. The nun looked up and nodded.

"It's Mr. Demarkian, isn't it? His Eminence has been waiting for you. Good morning, Father. Good morning, Sister."

Sister Scholastica and the young priest both murmured something unintelligible. The nun called in ahead, then stood up to see them through the inner door.

"We're all very glad you came," she said to Gregor, nodding slightly.

Inside the office, the Cardinal Archbishop was standing at the large window looking down on the cathedral. Gregor tried to rid himself of the impression that the man had done that deliberately, in order not to be caught having to stand up. The Cardinal Archbishop seemed to him vindictive, not petty. The young priest hurried ahead of them and said,

"Your Eminence, this is Gregor Demarkian."

"Mr. Demarkian and I have met," the Cardinal Archbishop said. "At the awards dinner for the Spirit of '76 Foundation, the last time, am I right?"

"Absolutely right," Gregor said.

The Cardinal Archbishop turned slightly. "Father Doheny, Sister Marie Claire, if you would please—"

"Oh," Father Doheny said, backing quickly toward the door. "Oh, of course. I wouldn't think of invading your privacy—"

Sister Marie Claire moved more slowly. Gregor found himself wondering irrelevantly if she minded it much that she had the same name as a notoriously prurient women's fashion magazine.

When the two were gone, the Cardinal Archbishop motioned both Gregor and Sister Scholastica to the chairs in front of his desk. "I'm sorry to get you out so early in the morning," he told Gregor, "but we are about to have what is surely going to be a major crisis here by the middle of this afternoon. Has Sister told you anything about the autopsy report?"

"Only that Bernadette Kelly died of arsenic poisoning, and that for some reason her husband is not likely to have been the one to have administered it."

"Yes. That's the core. That's what started the further investigations. I must say I'm impressed with the police department for keeping what's been going on as quiet as they have. But of course that can't continue. In this country, the press has extraordinary access to the internal workings of government on every level."

"Yes," Gregor said.

"Do you know of a man named Scott Boardman?"

"No," Gregor said.

"Mr. Boardman was a parishioner at St. Stephen's Episcopal Church and a homosexual. St. Stephen's is directly across the street from St. Anselm's. Later on the same morning that Martin Kelly brought his wife's dead body into St. Anselm's and killed himself, Scott Boardman was buried out of St. Stephen's."

"They thought it was a cocaine overdose," Sister Scholastica said. "They just assumed it was. Except it wasn't. It was arsenic, too. I'm sorry, Your Eminence."

"Sister is understandably distressed," the Cardinal Archbishop said. "We all are. Of course, the truth about Mr. Boardman's death would have been known eventually—"

"I'm surprised it wasn't known right away," Gregor said. "There's a law in this state that requires an autopsy after any suspicious death, and a drug overdose would have been treated as a suspicious death almost by definition."

"They did do an autopsy," Scholastica said. "They just—"

"They allowed the funeral to go ahead even though they didn't have the results of all their tests," the Cardinal Archbishop said. "Mr. Boardman was well-known to the authorities. His habits were particularly well-known. And he had, apparently, been hospitalized several times for cocaine poisoning."

"He was a mess," Sister Scholastica said.

"There was also some concern," the Cardinal Archbishop went on, "that if the funeral were delayed, rumors might spread that Mr. Boardman had died of AIDS. Nobody wanted the kind of situation that would cause, not even the medical examiner's office—"

"Roy Phipps has his church on the same street," Scholastica said. "He pickets. You know what I mean—"

"So they let the family rush the funeral," Gregor said.

The Cardinal Archbishop sighed. "It wasn't the family. The family had disowned him. It was Daniel Burdock, the pastor at St. Stephen's. The family was Catholic, of course. The newspapers will have a field day with that one."

"Is that what you're worried about?" Gregor looked from the Cardinal Archbishop to Sister Scholastica and back again.

"Because if it is, you know, I really can't help you. I have a good deal of expertise in poisons. And I'm useful in matters of motive and in unraveling certain kinds of complications in a criminal investigation. But I've got no influence with the press. I can't even affect the things they say about me."

"The press isn't what we want you for," Scholastica said. "I'm sorry, Your Eminence. Twenty-five years of practicing interior and exterior silence, and now I can't shut up."

"I have two worries." The Cardinal Archbishop ignored Scholastica as thoroughly as he ignored the pen holder on his desk. "One is that the pastor at St. Anselm's, Father Robert Healy, is an open opponent of Dan Burdock's treatment of homosexuals and homosexuality at St. Stephen's. Dan is an interesting man in many ways, but he is a radical in theology on matters of sex and has made St. Stephen's a haven for the sort of homosexual man who will be satisfied with nothing but the unqualified blessing of the Christian Church on homosexual conjugal unions. In order to protest that stand, Father Healy has preached several outspoken sermons, and given several uncompromising statements to the press, about the activities across the street from his church. And on one occasion he held a—a—"

"It's called a pray-in," Sister Scholastica said. "It's sort of like a sit-in, except you kneel and pray instead of sit and sing."

"Quite." The Cardinal Archbishop looked pained.

"It's really not anything at all like what Roy Phipps does," Scholastica said. "It wasn't even on St. Stephen's property. It was right in St. Anselm's Church. Mind you, I think it was a very bad idea, but that doesn't mean—"

"You're still talking about public relations," Gregor pointed out.

"No," the Cardinal Archbishop said, letting out a sigh. "I'm talking about motive. I'm afraid that there's a very good chance that the arsenic used to kill both Scott Boardman and Bernadette Kelly came from St. Anselm's Church. It was bought three days before the two young people died by Father Healy himself, wearing full clerical dress and dealing with a store clerk who happened to be a parishioner and knew him on sight. At four o'clock this afternoon, when the Philadelphia police commissioner holds his press conferences, the entire city is going to know that one of my priests is the prime suspect in two very nasty murders, one of them almost certainly a hate crime. An hour later, when CNN gets done with this, the entire country is going to know as well. I don't want your expertise for public relations, Mr. Demarkian. I want you to prove that Father Healy isn't the Jeffrey Dahmer of the Archdiocese of Philadelphia."

2

Twenty minutes later, Gregor found himself standing on the pavement outside the cathedral with Sister Scholastica at his side, wondering how he had gotten to where he was without buttoning his coat. It was worse than a cold day. It was raw as a wound, and gusts of wind blew down the street as if it were a tunnel. February was not his favorite month. It needed something like Valentine's Day, full of bright colors and silliness, to break it up. In this part of the city there was nothing, not even storefront decorations, to break the gray dullness of a morning without visible sun. He stepped back a little and looked up at the cathedral's great mock-Gothic facade. In Europe, church architecture had gone beyond the spires and pointed arches. You could find cathedrals built with Renaissance magnificence or with all the madness of the baroque. Even in England and Ireland, there was variety, and history, in church art. In the United States, it was as if time had stopped five centuries before the country had even come into existence. Successful cathedrals here—like successful religions—were always deliberate anachronisms.

"Gregor?" Sister Scholastica said.

Gregor dragged his mind away from speculating on what the actual building of this place had been like. If the contractor hadn't been one of those legendary Good Catholic Laymen of that long period before Vatican II, Gregor wouldn't have been surprised to find that he'd gone mad in the process. Scholastica's veil was whipping back and forth in the wind. Her face was red with cold.

"Sorry," he said. "I was just thinking what it must have been like actually to build this thing. To be the contractor."

"Oh. Yes. Well. I know he's not a very pleasant man. His Eminence."

"He's a son of a bitch. Sorry."

"Thank you for the apology, but I hear worse these days in the fourth grade. And yes, he is that, I know that. But he's a blessing, Gregor, he really is. He came in here after that awful mess, with the priests and the boys and, oh, all that—"

"You weren't here then," Gregor said.

"I know, but I heard about it. The order runs six elementary schools and a high school in Philadelphia. We have a lot of interest in the place. And it was bad, Gregor. You must have seen what it was like in the press, but it wasn't just that." Scholastica flapped her hands in the air, seemed to realize what she was doing, and blushed. Her hands and arms went back into the folds of her cape.

"So," Gregor said. "He was good about straightening out the scandal."

"You know, I look at it all, and it's not fair, really. I mean, yes, those men did those things, and they shouldn't be forgiven. But it was 1962. The way the Church responded wasn't underhanded or devious or even cavalier. We didn't know about child sexual abuse in those days. Churches and schools, Catholic or not, they all did the same thing. They brushed it under the rug, they transferred the adult, and half the time they blamed the child. And they kept it secret, too, but not to save the adult. It was all considered so much the child's fault that nobody wanted him branded—branded with that kind of misbehavior. I can remember it happening to a girl in the elementary school I went to. She was about eleven, and she was caught with her uncle doing, you know, things. And forever afterward, we all thought she was a slut."

Actually, Gregor remembered the same kind of thing, from his own childhood. Especially if the victim was a girl, even a very young girl, the assumption seemed to be that she had gone looking for it.

"So," he said, "he was good for the scandal. And I'm glad. But I don't have to like him."

"No," Scholastica agreed. "You don't have to like him. I'm just trying to let you know he has his points. The archdiocese settled the lawsuit, and part of the settlement was that a lot of the people involved were either removed from active apostolate or transferred out of the chancery. Not only the priests who did the, uh, the deeds, you know, they went to therapy, and at least one of them went to jail. But other people. People whose only real fault was being in the wrong place at the wrong time and having known what was going on. Secretaries. Schedulers. Of course, the man who was archbishop at the time was long dead. But the old archbishop, the one who came before this one, really couldn't cope. We thought for a while that the archdiocese was going to collapse, or have to go into some form of bankruptcy. Everything just fell apart. And then he died. And I hate to say it, but it was good for the Church in Philadelphia that he did."

"All right," Gregor said. "I'm really not arguing with you. I just find this man cold, and condescending. And I don't like being condescended to."

"Nobody does. Will you help us out in spite of that?"

"I've promised to."

"Yes, I know. I was hoping you weren't just being polite. Father Healy is—well, he's very young and he's very conservative and he's very stiff, but he couldn't have done anything like this. Believe me."

"You don't hold to the theory that any one of us could be a murderer under the right circumstances?"

"The right circumstances in this case would be a fit of rage and a handy mallet. He wouldn't buy rat poison and plan for days." Scholastica cocked her head. "Do you believe it? That all of us could be murderers if we met the right circumstances?"

"The fit of rage and mallet kind of murderers, yes," Gregor said. "The other kind, no. It takes a peculiar kind of personality to plan a death, or several."

"I think calling it 'peculiar' would be something of an understatement." Scholastica looked around. "I really do have to get back to school. I've left Peter Rose in my place, and she'll be all right for a while, but she's still very flighty in some ways. She was on my teaching staff in Colchester when, you know, when we met. She was just out of the novitiate. She drove me to distraction."

"It's been a long time."

"It surely has. Do you want to share a cab? In the old days, nuns were expected to take public transportation, but His Eminence must have considered this a special occasion. He gave me money for a cab."

"Then you use it," Gregor said. "I want to walk around for a while and think."

Scholastica looked dubiously up and down the street, at the neighborhood, at the weather. "Well, if you want to," she said.

There was a cab coming just then, and Gregor waved it down. "It will be fine," he said. "I'll help out. I'll go see Father Healy this afternoon. Don't worry so much about everything. It doesn't matter what I think about the Cardinal Archbishop."

"He's one of those people," Scholastica said, settling on the cab's backseat. "You always want to give him his full title."

He was one of those people who seemed to have been born with their full titles, Gregor thought, but he didn't say it, and a moment later the cab had pulled away from the curb and Scholastica was gone. Gregor turned around and around on the sidewalk, as if, by spinning very slowly, he could confuse his own mind about what he had known he was going to do from the moment he had first entered this neighborhood. Then, when that didn't work, he crossed the street at the light and made his way to the cathedral's front steps.

Once, about a year ago, Bennis had taken him to Sacre Coeur in Paris. The Church of the Sacred Heart. It sat high on the top of a hill above Montmartre, as white as powdered sugar, as if it had been bleached. To get to it, you had to climb the hill and then a steep flight of wide white steps, to go up and up, up and up, until even athletes in perfect shape began to find it hard to breathe. Gregor had thought at the time that there was something to this. If God was supposed to be up there, somewhere, then it made sense to make people climb to get to him. Bennis had only wanted to buy a small crystal rosary in the gift shop, where they had special ones made and blessed at that church. She had climbed without thinking about it, and without being affected by the atmosphere of the place, one way or the other. Where Gregor was caught by moods and mysteries, Bennis was a blank. When she had discovered, later, that there was an alternate route around the back that required no climbing at all, she had been furious.

The steps of the cathedral were nowhere near as steep as the ones at Sacre Coeur. They weren't even as steep as the ones Gregor had seen on ordinary parish churches in some places where the landscape was uneven enough to force the architect to make accommodations. Gregor went in through the great Gothic double doors and blinked into the dark of the vestibule. Like any parish church, there was a small table along the wall at the left with bulletins piled on it, and racks along the wall holding pamphlets on everything from praying the rosary to Natural Family Planning. He walked past all this to the inner doors that opened onto the long rows of pews and the elaborate marble altar. He saw the holy water font and did not touch it. He was sometimes drawn into churches to think, but he was never able to take part in any of the rituals that defined them, not even the most minor ones.

He passed through the inner doors and made his way down the center aisle to a pew in almost the exact middle of the church. A Catholic would have genuflected. He did not. A Catholic would have knelt for a while on the padded kneeler and said a Hail Mary, or some other prayer, learned in childhood, meant to change the tone and tenor of the mind and make it fit to come before the seat of God. Gregor only sat down and looked at the people around him, the old women saying rosaries, the young men bent over the backs of pews as if they were in agony. Elizabeth would have understood this—Elizabeth his wife, dead of cancer now over five years. It was one of the things about her that Gregor had never been able to fully understand, that she believed in God as simply and as straightforwardly as she believed the sun would rise in the mornings and set at night. Gregor realized that he knew a number of people like that. Lida Arkmanian. Hannah Krekorian. Even Donna Moradanyan Donahue. He didn't know what they thought about religion, or how they would resolve the great moral questions of their time, but he did know they believed. He was sure Tibor believed, too, although, Tibor being Tibor, that was more complicated. He wondered what it was like, to know something so clearly, and without hesitation.

After a while, he became aware of the fact that the pew was not padded the way the kneelers were, and that his back had begun to hurt from pressing against the back of it. He stood up. More people had come in while he was sitting there, thinking incoherently. He wondered if they were tourists, come to view the cathedral as an artifact, or ordinary parishioners. He remembered how surprised he had been when he had realized, for the first time, that St. Patrick's Cathedral in New York was, for some people, a parish church. It had to be getting on in the morning. Didn't most Catholic churches have Masses on and off all day?

He left the pew by the center aisle again. There was a light glowing in the sanctuary. That meant that at least one consecrated Host, considered to be the actual body and actual blood of Jesus Christ, was resting in the—ciroborum? It was incredible, what he almost knew as a result of thirty years of looking into murders.

Out on the sidewalk, the street seemed bare of taxis. He had to wait at the curb looking at nothing for long minutes, feeling the wind get under his still-open coat. Maybe he didn't believe because he was not constituted to believe. Maybe belief was like an ear for music, and some people had it and some did not. That was the way he would have described Bennis's approach to religion. His own, though, took in a heavy dose of fear. Religion was dangerous, and not only religion itself, but antireligion as well. There was something about the people who took it all so seriously, who believed that it was a matter of life and death whether you believed that the Host was really the Body and Blood or just a symbol, who believed that they would rather die than have a church take up shop next door, who believed to the point of obliterating the self, whether in the good of religion or the evil of it—there was something about those people that scared him to death.

It would be one thing if the world was made up of believers like Donna Moradanyan Donahue, or Sister Scholastica, or Father Tibor.

The unfortunate thing was that so much of the world seemed to be made up of believers like the Cardinal Archbishop of Philadelphia.

THREE

1

This morning, Edith Lawton did not get out of bed when Will did, or go down to breakfast. She heard the door to the spare bedroom open and close. She heard the sound of Will's heavy work boots on the carpeted stairs. She even heard the sound of the water being run in the bathroom for his washing up and his shower. He must have left the bathroom door open. The walls in this house were thick, made of plaster six inches through. Usually, she couldn't hear anything at all through them, and certainly nothing as minor as running water. She lay in her bed and closed her eyes and willed herself not to turn on the light. She didn't want him to know she was paying attention to the things he did, because she was convinced—convinced—that that would only make him more stubborn. The bedrooms were at the back of the house. If they hadn't been, she would have had a streetlight shining through her window to make shadows on the ceiling. Instead, she had to imagine her own shadows, the way she imagined music inside her head, to pass the time. By the time she heard the front door open and close, the heavy solid-core door banging into the frame, the metal latch catching to lock automatically as Will went out in the cold, she was so tense her muscles felt as if they were made of porcelain.

Now, over three hours later, sitting in her sunroom office, she was tense again, but for an entirely different reason. Not ten seconds ago, she had heard the thunk of the mail as it came through the slot in the front door. This street got its mail earlier than almost any other in this section of the city. She knew that it was lying out there in the little foyer space in front of the front door, spread out across the round rug she had placed there to take the dirt from people's shoes. She knew, as well, that if she left it there, Ian would pick it up when he came in, and that would be anytime now. Nine-thirty. She checked the clock and it was almost nine-fifteen. Ian said there wasn't going to be any sex, but Edith knew he was lying. He always was. Now that she had become squeamish about doing it in her own soft bed, they did it on the floor in the master bedroom, with her bare back pressed into the scratchy green carpet and her head hitting into the wood underneath it. They did it on the couch in the living room, with the shades drawn only halfway. They did it in the kitchen, on the tile, until their nakedness was etched with tile lines and they looked as if some artist had plotted a pattern to break them up into collages of themselves. Edith would have thought that they would slow down, once Will caught them, but the opposite was true. They never seemed to be able to get enough sex now. They never seemed to want to do anything with each other but get naked and go at it. Edith wondered if Ian did as she did, sometimes, and, right at the moment of climax, imagined Will bursting in on them once again.

Edith went on making her way carefully through the letters that had been posted to her website. She had erased the one Bennis Hannaford had sent, but Bennis Hannaford was apparently not the only one who knew that there was something called Christian Humanism that had come before Secular Humanism. The trouble was that she herself had not known. She clicked through the essays on the page she called *Getting It Out of My System*, found the offending piece, and flushed. It wasn't fair, really. She must have read a thousand essays by self-important media pundits that were just shot full of holes, but nobody ever called *them* on it. They didn't lose their jobs. They didn't lose their chances. They just went on being "real" writers, and here she was, sitting in a sunroom in Philadelphia, unpublished except for her column in *Free Thinking* magazine and her deal with Freethinker Press—and that didn't count. When she was honest, she admitted it. She brushed hair out of her face and tried to forget that she was, at the moment, embroiled in a huge argument with the two women who ran *Free Thinking* magazine, and that if that went on much longer, she wouldn't be published there anymore either.

She pushed her chair away from her worktable and stretched. She clicked at her mouse again and got rid of her own Web page. She ignored the rest of the e-mail. She didn't want to read another word about how Christian Humanism was just another name for the Renaissance, and anybody who had ever had so much as a freshman college course in Western Civilization should have known this.

Even "freethought" organizations weren't really all that impressed with "freethought" writers. When they held conventions, their stars were always people from the outside: Barbara Ehrenreich, Katha Pollitt, Richard Dawkins, Wendy Kaminer. Edith felt a wave of heat roll over her and took her hands away from her head. She had started to get hot flashes. She hated them.

The mail was out there on the carpet. It wasn't going to go away while she sat there. Edith got out of her chair. She hated the thought of going through the dining room, because the copy of *Vanity Fair* was still there, still marked at the place where Bennis's picture was. She solved this by looking above it, out the window to the side, and catching a glimpse of a police car parked somewhere down the street, its lights flashing slowly but its siren silent. It did not faze her. Ever since that fool man, with his dead wife and his religious faith that had done him no good but to make him crazy, had shot his head off at the altar in St. Anselm's, there were police cars in this street all the time. It was almost comforting. This was Philadelphia, after all. They could always use a police presence. Edith made a mental note to write a column about faith healing, something everybody hated, something she couldn't be made a fool of for writing. Then she realized that she was standing there in front of the mail slot with the mail at her feet, and that all the news was bad.

"First rule of real life," Bennis Hannaford had told her. "When they want the piece, they don't send mail in your stamped, self-addressed envelope. They don't even use e-mail. They get on the phone and call."

What was lying on the carpet in front of the mail slot was a little pile of her self-addressed stamped envelopes, four of them, from *Redbook, Mademoiselle, Good Housekeeping* and *Ladies Home Journal*. Edith picked them up and turned them over in her hands. She didn't know if it was good news or bad news that there was no other mail. The bad news was that the mailman had had no other letters to distract him. He had seen these and probably knew what they were. The good news was that she couldn't miss one between the gas and the electric bill, where it would fall out and into the hands of Will when he came back from work.

She opened the first one and found a printed rejection slip. It started "Dear Contributor." She opened the second one and found the same. She opened the third and fourth ones and barely paid attention. This was, she thought, all Bennis Hannaford's fault. If Bennis had really been interested in helping her out, she would have introduced her to some people, or made a few phone calls to the right people in the right offices, so that Edith's proposals would not have been coming in over the transom blind. Instead, all Bennis had ever really done was give her the kind of advice she could have gotten for herself out of *Writer's Digest*, and most of that was clearly worthless. Edith didn't believe for a minute that it was necessary to do as much research for a proposal as you would for an article. It was, in fact, just branding yourself as an amateur. When Bennis Hannaford proposed an article, she just got on the phone and asked.

Edith looked down at the paper in her hands and began ripping it all apart. Then, when it was a mass of shreds in her hands, she suddenly felt as if she were willing to do anything but stay in the same house with it. She didn't even want it in her own garbage cans out back. She opened the front door and stepped into the street. The police car was still there, parked in front of St. Anselm's again. It would be wonderful if it turned out there was more going on down there than just the aftermath of a suicide. Maybe the priest had been caught interfering with little boys, like the priests who had been part of the lawsuits had. Maybe one of the nuns was pregnant and had had an abortion. It was all hypocrisy and lies, religion was, but it was slick hypocrisy and lies. You had to work hard to expose it for what it was. She saw a policeman going down a little walkway to the side of the church, the one that led to the convent, the rectory, and the school. Then she nodded slightly to herself and went down the sidewalk to the trash can at the curb.

She was still throwing scraps of paper into the void when

Ian came up, driving, of course, because he drove everywhere. She stopped for a moment to notice how much more impressive his car was than Will's ordinary Jeep. Money mattered, and Edith had never thought it didn't. Ian waved to her and pulled his car into the narrow driveway at the side of her house. Will still wasn't using it. Edith had no idea why. She threw the rest of the paper away and went around the side to meet him.

"What were you doing?" he asked her, when he got back to the street. "You looked like you were doing the trash paper equivalent of sowing the land with salt."

"I was just throwing out some junk mail," Edith said. "What do you suppose is going on up there now, at St. Anselm's?"

Ian looked up the street along with her. "They're investigating a violent death," he said. "It takes time. Even with what is clearly a suicide."

"*Was* it clearly a suicide?"

"Well, something like six people saw him blow his head off. That's a pretty good indication, I'd say. I think you're going to have to let this one go. I'm all for crusading against religion, but sometimes you just don't get any kind of lucky."

"I wish Will would be all in favor of crusading against religion."

"As far as I can tell, Will isn't much in favor of anything. Are we going to go inside, or do you want me to stage a seduction right here on the street in broad daylight? It's cold as a witch's tit. My dick would probably freeze right off."

It *was* cold. Edith hadn't noticed. She looked into the trash can and saw that the scraps of paper had disappeared from sight. They were down there in the muck of other people's rotting food and soiled Kleenex tissues. She looked back at St. Anselm's again and then at Ian. He wasn't really a very good-looking man. Seen in full daylight like this, it was clear that he was one of those people who had done well but not well enough. He had money but not the—authority—of celebrity.

"Well?" he said.

Edith turned slightly so that she could see Roy Phipps's place, with the white cross on the front door and the smaller one over the front window. Ian was doing a great deal better than she was, even if he wasn't doing as well as Bennis Hannaford. He had things she could only dream about.

"How far do you think someone would go, to make the Catholic Church look bad?" she asked him. "I mean, think about Roy Phipps. He thinks the Catholic Church is the Whore of Babylon. How far do you think he'd go to discredit it? The Church, you know. So that it didn't have so much influence."

"Edie, please. The kid shot himself in the head. Let's go find a convenient spot and screw like rabbits."

She didn't move. She wasn't a rabbit. Her breasts felt heavy and ugly and dull.

"I think I'd go a fair way," she said. "It's so destructive, really. On abortion. On gay rights. On everything that matters. And with all the fuss they're having over there, you can't help wondering. Not that it won't get covered up. This is Philadelphia. The Pope could burn a witch in front of Independence Hall and the papers would hire six theologians to explain how it really was an act of great Christian love."

"Edie."

Ian was the only one who had ever called her Edie. In the beginning, she had liked it—the nickname she had not had in junior high school, the badge of belonging. Now it just made her feel tired, or as if she were being forced back into a childhood she hadn't liked much to begin with. She turned her back to St. Anselm's and headed for the house.

Sometimes she thought that this anger she had was not really connected to anything. It wasn't about Bennis Hannaford, or the Catholic Church, or even Will and Ian. It was just there, as it had always been there, all her life, rising up in her in sharp stabbing peaks, making her blind. It wasn't fair, that was what she thought, but now she couldn't pin down what it was that wasn't fair. Bennis Hannaford, who had been born beautiful and rich and talented and intelligent all at once. The Catholic Church, which could go on spewing hate and irrationality from one end of the earth to the other and still get dozens of new converts every hour. If there was any justice in the world, it would be Edith herself who was in *Vanity Fair*, and all the churches would be empty.

The front door had swung shut while she had been outside. Edith got her key off her belt and opened up. The foyer was dark. The entire house was dark.

If she had to screw like a rabbit, she might as well do it in the dark.

2

Mary McAllister had spent the last hour looking everywhere for Chickie George, in spite of the fact that it was the middle of the workday and he was supposed to be at his desk in the St. Stephen's Rectory. Now it was nearly ten o'clock, and she was fed up, almost as fed up as she had been when she first got off work at the soup kitchen. She had a full schedule of classes later this afternoon. She was fighting with both her roommate and her boyfriend. Even the rosary she had said in church this morning while Peter Rose packed the van hadn't helped, and that was the most disturbing thing of all. Mary McAllister had always been able to lose herself in the rosary. Sometimes she even felt as if the Blessed Mother was in the room with her, listening to her, pleased that she was saying it right. When she was very little, the Blessed Mother had always been in the air above her head. These last few months, she had been right there beside her, close enough to touch. Today there had been nothing. It had been frightening to stare at the polished wood back of the pew ahead of the pew in front of her, and to see only that and nothing else.

Now she swung around the stone walk that led from St. Stephen's back courtyard and stopped when she came to the church's front doors. She knew there was no longer any reason why she should not enter, or even take part in a service if she had a reason of courtesy to do so, but she always felt uncomfortable at the idea of being in a church that was not a Catholic church. She felt especially uncomfortable in this one, because she knew that the Reverend Burdock supported not only gay rights but abortion. The gay rights part seemed perfectly natural to her. In a church full of men like Chickie, there was very little else he could have done. In spite of the fact that the Catholic Church officially believed that it was possible for any gay man to live a celibate life according to the word of God, and Mary always tried very hard to accept anything the Church taught as true, in this one instance she secretly felt that somebody in the Vatican was seriously confused. Nobody could meet Chickie George and not understand, in an instant, that whatever it took to heal him would be a lot more complicated than just saying "no" to sex. Not, Mary thought, that he needed to be healed of his homosexuality. It wasn't that. It was just that he needed to be healed from *something*.

She ran up the church's front steps and looked through the doors. She really had come a long way on this subject since she'd first started to come to St. Anselm's. Back in Wellesley, Massachusetts, where she had grown up, she had never doubted for an instant that gay men were sinners who needed to learn some self-discipline so that they could lead normal and not so dangerous lives. It seemed odd to her that her ideas on abortion had not changed in the same way. Instead, she had become ever surer of her original position. She had started out thinking of abortion as wrong. She now thought of it as a holocaust, the deliberate slaughter of children, no different from taking a sword to a football stadium full of infants in their high chairs and hacking away at them until they were nothing but pieces of flesh and oceans of blood on the ground.

She went through the front doors and into the church's vestibule. She went through the vestibule and into the church itself. Chickie was up near the front, fussing with what seemed to be a bouquet of flowers too large for the vase he had put it in. Gladiolas, Mary thought irrelevantly. Then she went up to the front.

"Chickie?"

Chickie turned around. When he wasn't pulling his full-blast act, he was an incredibly handsome man, slight and straight, with a face that looked as if God had revised it over and over again until it had reached perfection. Sometimes Mary wanted to grab him and say: *see what you are? see what you are? don't playact the way you do.* But of course it was impossible. As soon as he knew she was looking at him, he took it all back on again, the swish, the exaggeration. Mary sighed a little.

"Duckie," he said. "How are you? I'm having the *most* awful time with these flowers."

"They're beautiful. I think you need a bigger vase."

"I may need one, duckie, but I'm not going to get one. These were given by Mrs. Van De Kamp. It's her vase. And you know nobody around this place is ever going to offend Mrs. Van De Kamp."

"Maybe you could take out a couple and put them to the side or something."

"Maybe I could. Although I wouldn't put it past the old cow to come and sit in a front pew and count the things. What's up with you, duckie? You look absolutely miserable."

"I am absolutely miserable. Don't ask me for real reasons, though. I don't have any. I just seem to be in a worse and worse mood lately."

"Is it all that fuss across the street?"

"With Marty and Bernadette? That didn't help, I suppose. But no. Not really. I'm just—out of sorts, I guess. Not satisfied with anything."

"Maybe it's time for your fifteen minutes of fame."

"I'll skip that, if you don't mind. I can't think of anything I'd like less than being famous. That will stand up on its own now if you'll let it."

Chickie stepped away from the vase. It stood up on its own. "I suppose I shouldn't tamper with it. It isn't up to my usual standard, though. Gladiolas are such a perfect flower. Do you know they come in autumn orange with black streaks, like tigers? Why do people like Mrs. Van De Kamp always have to buy pink?"

"Maybe she likes pink."

"All her taste is in her mouth, duckie, and she hasn't got much there. Last potluck, she brought a green bean casserole made with cream of mushroom soup. I nearly died."

"Don't die. Make me some coffee and help me feel like there's some point in going to class this afternoon."

Chickie walked around the flowers one more time, sighed, and stepped back again. "I suppose there's nothing else to do here. It's a shame, though. The people who have money never seem to have the faintest idea what to do with it."

The was a small door at the back of the church that opened onto the courtyard. The rectory was just across the miniature quadrangle, and made of stone just like the church was. St. Stephen's always reminded Mary of a college, one of those ritzy little places the children of rich people went if they didn't want to enter the fray at Harvard. She let Chickie lead her through the passageways in the rectory to his office and settle her in a big wing chair. Then she settled back and watched him get her coffee. Chickie always made real coffee. He did not use instant, or freeze-dried, or even those little coffee bags they sometimes gave out at the university cafeteria. He had a grinder right there next to his desk, and four different kinds of roast in bags beside it, and a real percolator with a glass bubble on top so that you would know when the coffee started to bubble.

"So," he said, "I hope this isn't about what's-his-name, the boyfriend."

"Ned."

"Ned. What a name. Ned. I hope you've been listening to your Uncle Chickie, though, and not letting yourself get talked into anything you don't want to do. You have, haven't you? Because it's like I told you, I've let myself get talked into enough sex I wasn't interested in having to know by now that—"

"No, no, it's nothing like that."

"He hasn't been—pressing?"

"Well," Mary said, "he's always pressing, to one degree or another. But nothing unusual. No, it's not that. I'm just all messed up lately, that's all. I don't seem to be satisfied with anything. And then there's something going on over at the church. My church. I don't know what it is, but I can feel it in the air. Do you know how that goes?"

Chickie nodded, the mask momentarily gone. A second later, it was back. "Yes, I do," he said. "It's happening here, too. Dan Burdock has got some kind of bee up his ass—excuse me. I don't remember where I am sometimes."

"It's all right."

"I hate being out of the gossip. I'm never out of the gossip. All I can think is that Dan is the only one who knows, and he's not saying anything."

"Do you think they could be connected? What's going on over there and what's going on over here? I don't see how they could be."

"Maybe it has something to do with the pray-in," Chickie said. "Rick Luca had this idea that we should all dress up in prom gowns and go over there and pray in with you, but I don't think Dan is going to stand for it."

Mary bit her lip.

"What?" Chickie said. "You think that's funny? Let me tell you, I'd look worlds better in a prom gown than that cow who was queen my senior year in high school. I mean, I know mammary glands are supposed to be attractive on a woman, but there really is such a thing as overdoing it."

Mary laughed. "Not something I've ever had to worry about."

"Listen, duckie, you've got the kind of body that would look perfect in Balenciaga. Don't knock it. Do you want a whole cup of this stuff or only half? I made it a little strong."

"A whole cup. The thing is, though, the pray-in may be part of it. Part of what's going on, I mean. Because there isn't going to be one this year."

Chickie put the coffee cup down on the little round table next to Mary's chair and raised his eyes to heaven. "It's a miracle! God has answered me! The heavens have opened, and a voice has come from the clouds—"

"Oh, hush," Mary said. "No voice came from the clouds. It came from the chancery. Or at least that's what I heard. The Cardinal Archbishop put his foot down. No pray-in this year. No pray-in ever again."

"The son of a bitch, really? Excuse me again. There I go—"

"It's okay, really. You should hear some of the things Ned says."

"Well, if he says them around you, he's a clod. And don't think I don't mean it."

He did mean it. The mask was gone again, lickety-split, and back just as quickly. Mary drank more coffee. Sometimes she wondered if Chickie had friends far closer to him than she was, with whom he could drop the mask for hours at a time. It frightened her to think that he might never drop the mask except when he was alone. It said something about his life that she did not want to look at.

"You know," she said, "I think it might have been Sister Scholastica. The new principal over at the school. She just hated the idea of that pray-in, the first time she heard about it. And she's not like Sister Harriet Garrity. She's still in a habit. She's very traditional, really. People have to take her seriously."

"I take Sister Harriet Garrity seriously. I won't tell you as what."

"Well, everybody takes her seriously as that. But it's true, you know. Nobody would listen to Sister Harriet about the pray-in because, you know, what would you expect her to say. And she doesn't have the Church's interests at heart. But Sister Scholastica is so committed, really, and so—I don't know. Mainstream, I guess. So the Cardinal listens to her. Sort of. Do you suppose, if there's no pray-in, Reverend Phipps will come anyway?"

"He will if he knows there's a television camera in the vicinity."

"Mmmm." Mary stood up. The coffee in her cup was gone. The way she felt, she wouldn't need another for a week. Chickie had been right to say he'd made the stuff very strong. Mary stretched a little and got her bag from the floor. "I'd better go. Thanks a lot, Chickie. I needed to be cheered up. I've got Intellectual History of the Middle Ages this afternoon. It makes my head ache."

"It would make my head ache, too. Are you sure you're all right?"

"I'm fine. Really. I hope you are. You've been looking very tired these last couple of weeks."

"I've been thinking. It wears me out. But you take my advice, you hear me? Never go to bed with anybody unless you really, really want to. Don't do it just because you feel sorry for this Ned person. Especially don't do it because you feel sorry for this Ned person."

"I promise to wear my largest and bluest Miraculous Medal every time Ned and I are out on a date. Thanks again, Chickie. I'll talk to you on Saturday."

"Drive carefully."

"I'm not driving. I took the bus."

Out in the courtyard, the day seemed to have gotten darker, and colder, and to have begun to verge on wet. Mary cut diagonally across the quadrangle and went out the side gate. Then she went around the front of the church and crossed the street so that she could go into St. Anselm's. At this time of day, there was no Mass. The next Mass would be at twelve o'clock. She had already been to Mass, and to Communion, at seven. Now it occurred to her that she might not have been right to go to Communion at all. She was feeling so—dead—inside these days. Her praying wasn't doing her any good. She spent a lot of time at Mass just daydreaming, and then when she came to she couldn't remember what she had been daydreaming about. Surely there was something about all that that rendered her—unfit—for Communion?

She dipped her fingers with holy water from the font and crossed herself. She came up the middle aisle and genuflected in front of the altar. She slid into a pew halfway down the line of them and knelt carefully on the padded kneeler. She had been in dozens of Catholic churches in half a dozen states, and every one of them had been close to identical: the pews, the kneelers, the fonts. It had startled her, the one time she was in France, when she realized that very old churches did not have kneelers, or even pews that were set in place like the ones she was used to at home. She had tried to imagine herself a medieval woman, going to church to stand and kneel, unsupported, on a stone floor, but the picture had not fit. She could no longer imagine herself anywhere, because the picture did not fit anywhere. At some point when she wasn't paying attention, she had been set adrift in space. Now she was no one and nothing, weightless and loose, tossing in the wind without an anchor.

Mary sat back in her seat and turned her attention to the statue of the Virgin that stood watch over the huge bank of candles in the niche they called the Mary Chapel.

"All right," she said, in her head, although she could hear the words as clearly as if she had spoken them. "You're supposed to have all the answers. What do I do now?"

3

For Sister Harriet Garrity, the issues surrounding the execution of Anne Marie Hannaford were problematic. On the one hand, she was a woman, oppressed by definition, and, due to the fact that she was anything but conventionally attractive, one of the victims of the vicious lookism that pervaded every segment of American society. On the other hand, she was the daughter of one of the great hegemonic capitalist oppressors of the Reagan period, and from all the evidence she was not a rebel trapped in the patriarchal fold. Harriet didn't think she had ever seen such a thorough case of false consciousness. Anne Marie hadn't given a lot of interviews over the past ten years, but the ones she had given were monuments to hierarchical thinking. It was just so obvious that the woman thought herself better than just about everybody she met, and that she was convinced that the only reason she had been convicted in the first place was that the jury was full of lower-class Blacks and Latinos acting out a fantasy of revenge on their "betters." She had actually used the word "betters" at one point in one interview, and the very sight of the word had made Harriet flinch. Still, there was principle involved here. Harriet knew the death penalty for what it was, judicial murder, the legal construct that allowed the ruling class to murder the troublesome members of the classes beneath them before those troublesome members could gain disciples and become agents of change. She didn't think it would be possible for her to pretend that this particular judicial murder was not happening. No matter how much she might dislike Anne Marie Hannaford personally—from a distance, of course, since she had never met the woman face-to-face—Harriet couldn't imagine herself staying home while the state of Pennsylvania pumped poison into the woman's veins. Besides, it might all be a trick. Journalists had been gotten to before, and most of them didn't even need to be gotten to. They bought the patriarchal line without ever thinking to question it. In real life, Anne Marie Hannaford might be nothing at all like the woman she seemed to be in interviews. She might be a sister under the skin, or someone who had struck a blow against repression and now just didn't know how she was supposed to behave. Harriet knew from experience how hard it was for women to own their anger, or excuse themselves for acting in their own interests, and without permission.

The Action Alert from the Seamless Garment Network was lying across the green felt blotter in the middle of her desk, along with the Urgent Memo from the Gay and Lesbian Support Advisory, which had to do with the priest-pedophilia case, and especially with the men who had once been victims and in many ways were victims still. There wasn't much she could do about the execution of Anne Marie Hannaford, but six of the men who had been victims of the priest pedophiles worshiped right across the street, and she had already talked to

Father Burdock about what she might be able to do to help them out.

She was supposed to be outlining the needs of the Special Committee for the First Communion breakfast, but she was finding it impossible to concentrate on how many dozen bagels should be plain and how many should be raisin. The whole idea of the First Communion breakfast made her sick to her stomach, and especially so since she had lost this round of the policy war to Sister Scholastica and her traditionalist nuns. The idea of sending tiny girls down a church aisle dressed in white veils and white gloves as if they were brides appalled her almost as much as the execution of Anne Marie Hannaford did—because it was an execution of its own in a way. What the Church was trying to murder was self-respect, and a sense of empowerment. It wanted those things for boys, but what it wanted for girls was only docility and acquiescence. Pray, pay, and obey—that was the old formula, for all Catholic laypersons and for all Catholic nuns. There was a war going on, just the way those Christian idiots said there was, a war for the soul of the country and a war for the soul of the Church. Harriet Garrity had enlisted on the side of Truth, Justice, and the Legitimate Aspirations of Women.

She took the Action Alert and the Urgent Memo and pushed them out of the way. She turned to her computer and looked at the First Communion schedule sitting there on the screen, with the major events highlighted in red. She rubbed her head and wished it didn't ache so much. It had been aching since early this morning, and not even four ibuprofen taken less than an hour apart had done anything to make it better. That was because Father Healy's deadline was coming up on her as fast as a freight train, and she still didn't know what to do about it. She had no intention of getting into a habit. None of the women in her order wore habits anymore. She had no intention of leaving St. Anselm's, either, if only because she didn't have the faintest idea where she could go. Five or six years ago, there were plenty of jobs in parishes and chanceries for nuns with professional training and management skills, but since the appointment of this Cardinal Archbishop, those things were drying up, at least in this archdiocese. She thought of herself being transferred to some college somewhere, or stuck off in a backwater where her only influence on the course of events would come from journal articles in little magazines and the letters she would write to the newspapers, which wouldn't bother to print them. She would be no better off than she had been when the nuns in her order *had* worn habits, and been held to a rule that forbade them to "singularize" themselves. If Harriet had been truthful about herself, she would have had to admit that she was a very ambitious woman. She knew she would have made at least as good a priest as Father Robert Healy. She would have made a better one than half the priests she'd served under in her career, whose only real qualification for the priesthood had often seemed to be that bit of flesh they had hanging between their legs. If she had been a man, she would have been a bishop before she was forty. She would have been a Cardinal very soon after that. She might even have been Pope. As it was, she often felt so stifled she could barely breathe, and then she wanted to blow up at somebody, smash something, do something, anything, to get out of this box without air that she'd lived in for so long she couldn't remember what any other kind of life was like. Maybe, she thought, that was because there was no other kind of life for a woman. All women lived in boxes, and all women died before they could get completely out. If they didn't die of exhaustion from the struggle, then the system killed them, the way it was about to kill Anne Marie Hannaford, the way it murdered the countless women who fought against helplessness for birth control and abortion and reproductive rights. Harriet looked guiltily at her computer monitor, but it still showed nothing but the First Communion schedule: rosary before Mass; Mass; scapular enrollment ceremony; breakfast. She rubbed her temples and sighed. She left the Action Alert about the execution openly on her desk, but she never left anything about Catholics for a Free Choice anywhere anyone could find it. She didn't even go to their website without erasing the cookies they sent and making sure the Web address wasn't left for somebody to see it on her Internet travel history. The Seamless Garment Network would annoy the hell out of the Cardinal Archbishop and drive Father Healy to distraction, but they couldn't do anything about it. The Cardinal Archbishop was one of the most vocal opponents of capital punishment in the American Church. The Gay and Lesbian

Support Advisory was more problematic, but since there were
so many people in it who had been on the innocent victim
side of The Scandal, the Cardinal Archbishop wasn't likely to
use it against her. Catholics for a Free Choice, on the other
hand, could get her bounced—not only out of St. Anselm's
Church and the Archdiocese of Philadelphia, but out of her
order, and maybe out of the Church as well. Harriet wasn't
really entirely clear about the sort of thing that made it possible for the Church to pronounce a formal anathema.

At the moment, she wasn't clear about much of anything, so
she got up from her chair and went out into the hall. Her office
was in a long single-story annex that connected the church and
the rectory, along with the offices of all the other people who
held administrative posts of any kind in the parish. Sister
Scholastica had an office in the parochial-school building, but
she also had one here, because she was not only the school
principal but the parish's delegate to the Archdiocesan Office
of Education. Sister Thomasetta had her office here, too. She
was the new comptroller, brought in by Father Healy only a
year ago, to replace the nun of Sister Harriet's own order who
had held that position for fifteen years. Sister Thomasetta,
needless to say, was a Sister of Divine Grace and wore a habit.
All the other people who worked in the offices were laywomen, of the type Harriet thought of as Daily Communicants,
and most of them did go to Mass every day at seven o'clock
before they checked in for work. Harriet had only begun to
realize how much change Father Healy had brought with him.
Her own office was now the only one that did not have a
picture of the Madonna on the wall, or a holy water font just
inside the door. In the old days, Harriet couldn't remember a
single time when the women in these offices had prayed the
rosary together, or spent their lunch hours studying Catholic
doctrine. Now it happened every noon, and there were copies
of *The Catechism of the Catholic Church* on every desk top.
Copies of *The New American Bible* had disappeared. Copies
of *The Ignatius Bible*, which boasted that it was the only trans-
lation in English that had not given way to inclusive language
at all, were everywhere. It was as if a sea change had happened
in this parish while Harriet wasn't looking. The waters that
surrounded her were cold as ice, and the air was darker than

any ordinary darkness could be. She had said a lot of things about the way the Church was marching back into the Dark Ages, but she had never really believed them. In the back of her mind, she had always been sure that progress was inevitable. Now it frightened her to realize that she might have been wrong. It might really be possible for the Church to go back, and it was going back, returning to a time when it would have ground a woman like her into powder. In a world of devotional rosaries and First Friday Devotions and weekly confessions in a dark curtained box, she would be invisible.

She stopped in front of Sister Scholastica's office door and saw through the window that the office was empty. She went down the hall to Sister Thomasetta's and found the door open and Thomasetta pecking away at a computer keyboard. Harriet didn't think anything looked as odd as nuns in full habit pecking away at computers.

"Can I help you?" Thomasetta asked, not bothering to look up.

"I was hoping Scholastica was over here, that's all," Harriet said. "I was hoping not to have to go all the way over to the school."

"Well, you don't have to. Sister isn't there, either. She's been out all morning."

"Out? Where?"

"The chancery."

"Why would she go to the chancery?"

Thomasetta shrugged. "How am I to know? The Cardinal Archbishop calls, and Sister goes. Oh, and I think she was stopping to see friends afterward. At any rate, she took Peter Rose to the chancery with her and Peter Rose is back, but Scholastica isn't, and she isn't likely to be until after lunch. Would you like me to leave a message?"

"No," Harriet said. "No, that's all right. It's about the First Communion breakfast. I can get to her later, or Father Healy would know. What time is it exactly?"

"Ten-thirty-two-oh-six."

"Thank you." It figured, somehow, that Thomasetta would know the time down to the fraction of the second. Harriet left Thomasetta's office door and went down the hall again. She passed Scholastica's office and tried the door. It opened easily. Like many traditionalist nuns, Scholastica almost never locked any personal space, because she didn't think of herself as having personal space. Harriet went down the hall to her own office and sat.

The difficulty was this: Harriet had no idea why Scholastica had gone to the chancery, but she was sure it had to be about something important, because the Cardinal Archbishop did not waste time on trivialities. She was equally sure that it was going to be something important that concerned her, because at the moment she was the biggest problem the Cardinal Archbishop had. She had to be, because Father Healy was making waves, and the Cardinal Archbishop knew she wouldn't take being bullied lying down. She might even be in a fairly strong position, if only because this Cardinal Archbishop hated publicity more than he hated any other thing. That was entirely natural, considering the damage the child sex abuse scandal had done to this archdiocese when it had finally broken in the papers and been spotlighted on CNN. And *60 Minutes*. And *The CBS Evening News*. Even so, if she didn't know what was coming, she might easily make mistakes. This man was not the fool the old cardinal had been. He was more like Cardinal Richelieu.

Harriet got up and went back into the hall. It was empty. Everybody working on this floor was in her office, minding her own business. Harriet walked down the hall to Sister Scholastica's office. Nobody looked up to see her pass. She went into Sister Scholastica's office and shut the door. The door's window had a curtain that could be pulled across it for privacy, just as the window in her own office door had. Harriet pulled it closed. The door itself had a turn lock. It wouldn't keep a burglar out, but it would stop the casual visitor or the wandering nun looking for something she thought she might have left on Scholastica's desk. Harriet locked up and went to sit down in Scholastica's chair. Scholastica wasn't due back until after lunch. Lunch at the convent was an hour and a half away. Harriet had plenty of time.

It might have been easier if she had known what she was looking for, but she didn't. She found Scholastica's discipline in its little cotton bag and took it out, a set of knotted cords that a nun used to strike herself on the back while she was praying the Miserere. It was supposed to be done lightly, over clothes, but Harriet had known sisters who used it on their bare backs until they bled. Her own order had given up the practice when they had given up the habit. She found Scholastica's Little Office and was surprised at how annoyed she felt that it was so obviously used. Nobody had to pray the Little Office anymore. They prayed the Divine Office together. That should have been enough conformity for anybody. The top of the desk was full of things that nuns were once enjoined from having: pictures of friends and family, a small gift-wrapped box of chocolates from which only one piece had been taken, Scholastica's old varsity cheerleading letter.

Harriet was just tapping into the computer files—so very easy, because all the Sisters of Divine Grace used either Ave Maria or Benedicamus Domine as their passwords—when somebody came to the door and tried the knob. Harriet stopped still, and everything inside her stopped as well. She was so rigid, she might have been an extension of the steel on the chair. When the door wouldn't open, whoever was there knocked, twice, very loudly.

"Scholastica?" Harriet didn't recognize the voice.

"Is it locked?" someone else said—Thomasetta, Harriet was sure. "How very odd. Sister never locks up."

"Maybe she did it absentmindedly," the first person said, and now Harriet did recognize the voice. It was Mary McAllister. "It doesn't matter. I'll come back later. I just wanted to ask her something about that pray-in—"

"Oh, I wouldn't worry about the pray-in," Thomasetta said, her voice fading slightly. She and Mary must be walking away. "I've had it on good authority that there isn't going to be a pray-in this year, and like everybody else around here I'm very relieved. I mean, really, with that idiot right down the road—"

Harriet sat up straight, and stretched, and forced air into her lungs. It was all right. She had not been caught. She would still be able to get out of here without being found out if she would only hurry.

The problem was, now that she was in the files, she did not want to hurry. She had always been outside the gossip loop in this parish. People didn't tell her the things they automatically told each other. They saw her as an outsider and a threat. So far, the things she had seen were not very important, or very interesting, but she was sure there had to be something, somewhere, that would allow her to—

What?

She grabbed the desk clock and turned it so that it faced away from her, so that it would not panic her.

She didn't think she had felt this free, or this exhilarated, since the day she entered the convent.

FOUR

1

For most of the time that Gregor Demarkian was with the Federal Bureau of Investigation, he thought of murderers at one remove, as if they were objects in a window, on display for purposes of evaluation. It was only near the end, when he was head of the Behavioral Sciences Unit, that his attitude had begun to change, and then the change had been gradual. The truth was, homicidal maniacs were not very interesting. He could never understand why millions of people paid good money to read novel after novel about some detective chasing after a serial killer, when most serial killers made as much sense, and had as much relation to the human spirit, as rice pudding. The exceptions were very rare, and never, in his experience, as fascinating as Thomas Harris's Hannibal. The ordinary run of murderer wasn't much better, though. He got too drunk or too stoned to think straight, and then he let loose at the first thing that annoyed him and killed it. If that happened to be his girlfriend, or his best buddy, or his girlfriend's baby, he landed in jail. If that happened to be the store clerk and two of the customers in a convenience store he was trying to rob, he ended up strapped to a gurney while the prison doctor administered a lethal injection. Maybe that was why his opposition to the death penalty had grown, day by day and year by year. There wasn't enough ceremony to it anymore. It had become a kind of prophylactic, almost a medical procedure. The murderer was a bunion. The doctor was suited up in hospital green to take the bunion off.

Of course, most people, making the analogy, would have said that the murderer was a cancer, but Gregor couldn't see it. Most murderers were either so hapless and so stupid it was embarrassing to listen to them, or so mentally ill they didn't know what was going on in front of their noses. The idea of Jeffrey Dahmer in jail made Gregor's head ache. The man had talked to furniture. Ted Kaczynski had talked to trees. Literally. Had the country gone completely insane?

Maybe what it really was was the death of hope. There had been a time when most Americans truly believed that the criminal could be rehabilitated. They wanted punishment. They wanted revenge. They also expected regeneration. Now they only wanted closure. The murderer had ceased to be a human being in any substantive way. He was simply evil, through and through, without so much as a pocket of untainted air, like a solid chocolate Easter bunny. Was he really comparing murderers to chocolate Easter bunnies? It was cold out here. The wind was stiff and constant. He should have taken a cab. Instead, he had decided to walk, to give himself time to think, and now he was thinking things like this.

The problem, really, was that Bennis's sister Anne Marie was one of the rare exceptions. She was not an undiagnosed paranoid schizophrenic hearing voices and cutting throats in the back alleys of a small American city. She was not a terminally stupid drifter with even less education than brains and no discernible self-control. She was a deliberate killer, the kind who thought and planned, the kind who knew what she was doing and thought she had been right in doing it. It had been eight years since Gregor laid eyes on her, but he was sure she hadn't changed her mind about that. He could still see her sitting at the defense table during the first appeal, her hands folded in front of her, her face set in stone and as much like a gargoyle's as anything on the facade of the Rheims cathedral. She believed she had been right to do what she did. She believed she had only been caught because of accidents and coincidences. She believed, most of all, in herself, and she would go on believing in herself, right down to the moment when she was strapped onto the gurney with an IV feed in her arm. If Gregor had believed that personality was genetic, he would have been afraid for himself, and for Bennis—but then, maybe Bennis had received a different set of genes, from her mother instead of from her father, and that was all that was needed to take care of that difficulty.

It was worse than cold out here. It was freezing. There were thin, slick films of ice on the rounded edges of the sidewalks. Gregor checked his watch and saw that it was almost eleven. He was sure that had to be enough time for Henry to have done what he'd asked him to do. If it wasn't, maybe he could wait in Henry's living room while the details were ironed out. He was only a couple of blocks away. He had been circling this neighborhood for half an hour, trying to give Henry enough time. Under the circumstances, he didn't want to seem as if he were pushing. Still. He shoved his hands into the pockets of his coat, then took them out again to raise the collar of his coat higher on his neck. He was always telling Tibor and old George Tekemanian to wear their hats, and he had no idea what had happened to his. He turned right at the next corner and then right again. He started left along Baldwin Place with his hands back in his pockets. All the houses on this street were made of dead brown stone and jammed right up next to each other. They looked like hundreds of other houses across the city of Philadelphia, and they were probably equally expensive. After decades of losing out to the expensive suburbs of the Philadelphia Main Line, the city was becoming fashionable again—at least with singles and couples without children. The living-room windows had heavy curtains hanging at the sides of them. All the curtains were drawn back, their owners preferring to sacrifice privacy for a chance at sunlight. Gregor suddenly realized why it was the neighborhood depressed him. Nobody had decorated anything here. The houses were blank and unadorned, almost regimented, so that they looked as if they had put on uniforms. He made a mental note not to complain so much about the way Donna Moradanyan Donahue decked out the fronts of the houses on Cavanaugh Street. At least it gave the street a bit of color.

He got to Henry Lord's house and looked up at the black front door. The door was shiny as well as black, meaning it must have been painted recently. Gregor had no idea why this should matter. He seemed to be nervous about seeing Henry, although he had known the man for so long now that he might have known him forever. Thirty years, Gregor thought, as he pressed the doorbell and got a detailed mental picture of Henry at the University of Pennsylvania in his sophomore year. Gregor had been a senior. They hadn't liked each other much.

The door opened, and Henry, much balder and paunchier and redder-faced than he had been, came out. Gregor reminded himself that he had liked Henry very much once Henry had gotten out of school and joined the Bureau. That was a good thing, because he needed Henry now if he was ever going to be able to help Bennis out. It was interesting to remember, though, how much those things had mattered when both he and Henry had been young: being from the Main Line or not; attending the Assemblies or not; belonging to the country clubs or not. Henry stepped back, and Gregor wiped his shoes on the mat and stepped inside.

"You gave me a very interesting morning," Henry said. "And I thought I was going to lie around the living room being bored on my day off from work. How are you?"

"I'm fine."

"How's Bennis?"

"Fairly crazy, about this. I suppose that's to be expected."

Henry closed the front door and motioned for Gregor to follow him down the long hall that seemed to run the entire length of the house. It ended at a small third flight of steps that led to the kitchen, which was large and overequipped and very newly decorated. Copper pans hung from the high ceiling on a grid held by four coiled metal wires. The grid had been lowered so far, and Gregor was so tall, he worried about hitting his head on a swinging paella pan. The kitchen table was round and large enough for a family of eight. Henry and Julia's three sons were grown and off in law schools in Cambridge and Palo Alto. The table had been set, too, with a blue-and-white-checked tablecloth and matching cloth napkins. Henry waved Gregor in the direction of the empty chairs.

"Interesting setup," Gregor said.

"Julie's been decorating again," Henry told him. "She misses the boys. I think she wishes one of them would settle down and give her grandchildren, but I'd just as soon they waited until they were out of law school and had a hope in hell of making partner somewhere. You should see what she did to the master bedroom. You want coffee?"

"Please."

Henry got two cups and two saucers and laid them out in the middle of the table. Gregor reached for one and realized that the decorative borders were the same color and pattern as the tablecloth and the napkins. He shook his head slightly and reached for the coffeepot Henry was handing to him. Then he thought about Donna Moradanyan Donahue decorating on Cavanaugh Street and wondered if this was something about women he did not yet understand. Would Bennis start decorating his apartment as soon as she hit the right kind of crisis? Would he be required to know something about how to buy paint?

"I seem to be a little distracted," he said. "Believe it or not, it's already been a long morning. Were you able to find out what I needed to know?"

"Absolutely. It helps to be a judge, whether you believe it or not. You would have made a great judge."

"It helps to have a family from the Main Line. What did you find out?"

Henry poured his cup nearly half-full of cream and put the coffee in on top of it. "You do know, don't you, that there's no chance of stopping the execution this time? The governor is not going to commute this sentence. At all. No arguments."

"Yes," Gregor said. "I know that. I think even Bennis knows that."

"She did make an appeal for clemency," Henry pointed out.

Gregor shrugged. "I think that's only natural. She would have had to."

"I suppose. Anyway, with that understood, I'm happy to report that the governor and the prison administration both want to bend over backwards to make sure that Miss Hannaford receives every humanitarian consideration before the execution. To untangle the language, they don't want to show up on the evening news in a story about how they refused to let a condemned woman see her own family. Tom Ridge has gotten very touchy about the death penalty. You know that group, Seamless Garment?"

"I've seen them on the news."

"Well, between them and the Cardinal Archbishop of Philadelphia, the governor is not happy. So Anne Marie will get all the visits she wants right up until the last second, and then they've issued invitations—"

"I know," Gregor said. "Bennis got one. So did Dickie van Damm."

"Isn't it interesting, the way everybody always calls him

Dickie?" Henry reached for the sugar and used it, liberally. Gregor thought that he must have been making something on the order of a coffee milk shake, only hot. "Anyway, anyway, to get back to the point, the kicker in this is the qualifier. Anne Marie can have all the visits *she wants*. She has to want them."

"And she doesn't?"

"It's not quite that simple." Henry took a sip from his cup, made a face, and began to shovel in more sugar. "Have you talked to her at all since she's been in jail?" he asked. "I don't mean seen her in court or that kind of thing, but talked to her, face-to-face."

"No," Gregor said. "I never did talk to her much, even before she went to jail. Maybe a dozen times over the space of six weeks during the investigation. I did see her at the appeal."

"That's what I thought. What about Bennis, has she seen her in the last ten years?"

"No."

Henry finally had his coffee as sweet as he wanted it to be. He drank a third of the cup in a single gulp, and then placed the cup carefully, and exactly, in the saucer. "I talked to her this morning, briefly. And I talked to her lawyer. Her present lawyer. She goes through lawyers the way other people go through toilet paper. Do you mind, Gregor, if I go on record here as saying that this is a very bad idea?"

"What is?"

"Bennis having an interview, ever, never mind in the next couple of weeks. She's—what she is, Gregor. She is not a pleasant woman. And she no longer has anything to lose."

"Does that mean she's willing to see Bennis?"

Henry sighed. "Nobody listens to a word I say. It's pitiful, really. That's why I stay on the bench. At least the lawyers have to pay attention while they're in the courtroom."

"*Does* that mean she's willing to see Bennis?" Gregor repeated.

Henry sighed again. "Not exactly. Or maybe I should say, possibly, but not right off. Like I said, it isn't that simple. Right at the moment, she doesn't want to see Bennis. She wants to see you."

"What?"

Henry reached under his sweater into the breast pocket of

his shirt and brought out a business card, one of his own, its white back scribbled over with the kind of thick black ink that could only have come from a fountain pen.

"She wants to see you," he repeated, "at eleven-thirty in the morning at the prison on Thursday. Her lawyer will pick you up and drive you there. You'd better be ready early. It's a long drive. Oh, and you'll like the lawyer. Right up your alley. Temple B.A. Temple Law. Fastest rising associate at Richland, Cooper, Shelby and March."

"He must walk on water."

"If I were you, I'd hope he could walk through fire," Henry said. "I don't know what it is you think you're doing, Gregor, but this woman is bad news. I could tell that much in less than five minutes on the telephone. If she gets her nails into Bennis, she'll do a lot of damage that will last a long time."

It's Bennis's sister we're talking about here, Gregor almost said—but then he didn't, because he knew just what it was Henry Lord was trying to say.

He also knew that the one thing he couldn't do, and keep Bennis Hannaford in his life, was to try to arrange her life for what he thought was her own good.

2

Half an hour later and fifteen blocks away, it occurred to Gregor Demarkian that he ought to do something about Sister Scholastica's problem. He thought of it as Sister Scholastica's problem, because if he had thought of it as the Cardinal Archbishop's problem, he would never have gotten himself started. There really wasn't much of anything he could do at this point. Until the medical examiner made his public statement, until the police investigation was out in the open, he had nothing to work with but the Cardinal's paranoia, and that would get him no farther than Father Tibor's kitchen, frustrated and blocked off from information at every turn. Philadelphia was a Catholic town in many ways, as Pennsylvania was a Catholic state. More orders of nuns had their motherhouses in Pennsylvania than in any other state of the union, and the Catholic Church wielded enormous power in city politics. Even so, there was only so far that you could push that, and Gregor knew it. The medical examiner's office would hold off on their press conference for a couple of hours. The police would probably hold off on an arrest for a day or two, to give the archdiocese a chance to marshal its troops and prepare for attack. The public prosecutor might even be willing to strike a better deal than he would have been for an ordinary defendant, as long as the crime wasn't child abuse and as long as he thought he could get away with it. Beyond that, any request for special handling would be ignored, and any demand for it would be met with active hostility. Gregor knew that. What worried him was that the Cardinal Archbishop might not know it. Being a man used to giving orders and having them obeyed, he might give a few, and not react too well when they were ignored. And that—

"Would screw things up," Gregor said. He looked around to see if he had said it out loud or not. Nobody was paying any attention to him, so he assumed not. There was a little convenience store at the corner. Gregor stepped inside and bought copies of the *Inquirer* and the *Star*. The television news might still be full of the deaths of Marty and Bernadette Kelly, but the papers had drifted off to other things, mostly having to do with Al Gore. Gregor tried, for the ten millionth time, to figure out why that man could make his eyes glaze over just by appearing in a newspaper photograph, but got no better answer than he'd ever had and decided to give it up. The counter in front of the cash register was crowded with candy and Slim Jims. As he folded up his papers, the old man standing next to him began laying out money for lottery tickets: instant tickets, daily tickets, the Pennsylvania Big Game, Powerball. There was at least three hundred dollars in cash on the counter. Gregor could see the holes at the tips of the man's shoes. He got his papers and got out of there. He wasn't one of those people who wanted to end all state lotteries as a matter of public morality, left-wing or right. He didn't think gambling was a tool of the devil, and he didn't think most people didn't know what their limit should be. On the other hand, there were other people—He buttoned his coat up to his chin and got out of there.

He walked five more blocks, made a turn, walked five more blocks, and made another turn. By then, he knew where he was going. He could see the church spires rising up over the buildings ahead of him, two of them, next to each other. Of course, they weren't really next to each other, he reminded himself. They faced each other across a street. It was only from a distance that they looked sort of like twins. No, that wasn't true either. Even from a distance, he could tell that they weren't made of the same material. One was that grey stone that seemed to scream "Episcopal Church" all across New England and the mid-Atlantic states, as if the Episcopalians had once owned a monopoly on stone quarries. The other was deep red brick. That was a cliché, too, Gregor thought, the red brick of Catholic churches and schools and convents built at the end of World War I. You could probably write a history of society and immigration in Philadelphia based on something like that, although he had no idea where he would start. His own little corner of immigration history was mostly out of sight, lived by a group of people whose numbers had never become large enough to make an impact on the city.

He turned another corner, and then he was on the right street, only a block away. From this close, the two churches looked huge, imposing, and blank. At this time of the day, they both seemed to be deserted. Gregor looked up at their spires to see if they told the time, and found out they did, but different times. It was either quarter to twelve, or five after. He sighed a little and kept walking, wondering if there was anything to this process of soaking up atmosphere and allowing your intuition to flower. He suspected there wasn't. He just walked around aimlessly and then, when he was tired of that, he got down to work.

He stopped right in front of St. Stephen's Episcopal Church, where the glass-framed announcement board hung on a wooden frame at the end of the walk, and looked across the street at St. Anselm's. That had a glass-framed announcement board hung on a wooden frame, too. He looked at the grey stone walk that led to the church's grey stone front steps, and then across the street at the ordinary pavement that led to St. Anselm's brick ones. Both churches had their small patches of front yard framed in wrought iron, though, and both had leaded side windows that came to pointed arches at the top.

"They did it on purpose," somebody said in his ear.

Gregor turned and found himself faced with the most elegantly good-looking young man he had ever seen, tall, slender, almost perfectly made. For a split second, he thought he was looking at a statue. Then the man's demeanor changed—Gregor could have sworn it wavered and reconstituted itself in front of his eyes—and suddenly he was all swish and mannerisms, exaggerations and camp. Gregor blinked.

"They did it on purpose," the man said, his voice now several notches higher than it had been. "The Catholics, I mean. In 1918. This used to be one of the most socially prominent Episcopalian churches in the city, so of course they took the lot over there as soon as they could get it, and just went hogwild. They're incredible climbers, Catholics are, don't you think?"

"I don't know," Gregor said.

The man held out his hand. "I'm Chickie George. You're Gregor Demarkian. I've seen your picture in the papers."

Swish. Not swish. Camp. Not camp. It was like watching television while somebody flipped channels. Gregor took the man's hand and shook it.

"Are you the pastor here? Or do I say priest?"

"Well, Dan's a priest, technically, yes. I'm just a parishioner, and I do some work on church business when we need a hand, which we usually do. We don't ever seem to have any money, and whatever we do have we must spend on the building. I mean, nothing else explains it. Most of the time I'm a freelance art director. I do food."

"You do food?"

"Well, yes," Chickie George said. "There's a reason why the food in magazines all looks like it could hang in the Metropolitan Museum of Art and when you make the same recipe at home it doesn't. I do presentations. Then the photographer comes in and ruins the whole thing with execrable lighting, but there's nothing I can do about that but take a Prozac and get over it. Have we had a murder here? That's what you do, isn't it? You investigate murders."

"Sometimes," Gregor agreed.

Chickie looked up the street. "I suppose it's too much to hope that somebody had finally decided to ice Rapid Roy, isn't it? My hope has always been that one of his lunatic church members would just lose it one day, and there would be Roy, all over the ground in pieces. Probably be the best he ever looked in his life. Sort of like Jackson Pollock."

"I'd heard he had a church on this street," Gregor said. "But I don't see a church."

"That's because there isn't one. They've got a row house down there. Actually, it's two row houses knocked together. Beautiful spaces, really, you could do something with them. But they haven't."

"How do you know? Have you been inside?"

Chickie George snorted. "If I'm going to commit suicide, I'm going to have some fun doing it. Give me sex, drugs, and rock and roll any day."

"So how do you know they haven't done something you might approve of with the interiors?"

"Because I can look in the windows and see the art. Christ dying on the cross, badly painted and as bloody as the victim in a slasher movie. Blood and death, that's all they think about. And I used to think the worst of that kind of thing was those awful pins that said 'My Boss Is a Jewish Carpenter.' "

"Do they wear pins?"

"If they did, they'd say 'All Fags Burn in Hell.' Do you know the Richard Pryor routine about the word 'nigger'?"

"What?"

The swish was gone again, as gone as if it had never existed in the first place. Gregor found himself standing in front of a very serious young man, with as much force of personality as the Cardinal Archbishop of Philadelphia, and maybe as much determination.

"Richard Pryor," Chickie George said, "went to Africa. And when he came back, he worked this thing into his routine. You can hear it on the *Live on the Sunset Strip* video. About the word 'nigger' and the way black people use it among themselves and think they've reclaimed it. That when they use it it doesn't mean what it means when white people use it. Except it does, you see, and when they use it they're really perpetuating it. So Pryor was trying to get people to stop using it, for black people not to call each other 'nigger' among themselves. If you see what I mean."

"I think it's pretty clear."

"Yes. Well. I think we ought to do the same thing. The 'Gay Community.' Excuse me if I can't say that with a straight face. I don't mind 'gay,' but 'community' drives me bananas. Anyway, I'm beginning to think that we should stop using them. 'Fag' and 'queer' and all of that. That we're never going to get rid of Rapid Roy and his friends until we do."

"Ah," Gregor said.

"It's too bad somebody hasn't murdered him, really. Death is what turns him on. Sometimes I think death is the only thing that turns him on."

"I've never seen him."

"Stand on the street long enough and you will. Especially if you stand here. He'll throw up pickets before you know what's happened to you. It's cold out here. If you want to come inside, I could give you a cup of coffee. We always have excellent coffee, and French pastry. We don't settle for cheese Danish from the supermarket at St. Stephen's."

"Thank you. I'm supposed to be meeting someone for lunch. I just wanted to get a look at the neighborhood."

"Because of that mess that happened across the street, I suppose. Well, have a good time with it. And if you see our boy Roy, shoot first and ask questions afterward."

"Right," Gregor said.

Chickie George turned away and began walking up the stone path to the church's front doors. Gregor watched him go, not sure which Chickie he was seeing now, the swish one or the real one. What an odd young man, Gregor thought.

Then he turned away himself and crossed the street to St. Anselm's.

FIVE

1

For almost three years, Dan Burdock had known that there would come a day when he would have this particular request sitting on his desk. The only thing that surprised him, now that it had come, was that he was so calm about it. That was a good thing, because Aaron Wardrop was watching him, very intensely. If he showed the least sign of distress, this interview would change character in no time at all. Dan was no stranger to the shifting emotional landscapes of true believers. Ever since he had come to St. Stephen's, he had imagined himself in the role of Sane Older Friend, the one who wants to hold the hero back from doing something foolish, the one nobody listens to until it is too late. The ones like Chickie George were bad enough—and Scott Boardman. Everybody said that Scott had been trying to commit suicide most of his life. Dan thought all that crowd were, the ones who went trolling in the bathhouses at four o'clock in the morning, the ones who kept score in five figures, the ones who thought that if you did it stoked to the gills on vodka and methamphetamine, it didn't really count. Except, Dan thought, that wasn't really true about Chickie. Or might not be.

"What?" Aaron said.

"I was thinking about Chickie George," Dan said. "About how I always think of him as being like Scott, you know, because of the camp. But I don't think he is."

"This isn't about Chickie George, Dan. Why don't we try sticking to the subject."

Dan looked down at this desk again. Aaron, of course, did not go trolling in the bathhouses at any hour of the day or night. He would consider it beneath his dignity, and he was far too fastidious to put up with the dirt and mess. This form had been fastidiously done. It was so perfect, it might have been produced by a professional printer.

"You must have run this through the scanner," Dan said. "I've never seen one of these so flawlessly done."

"I was just being careful. Under the circumstances."

"Under the circumstances." Dan pushed the paper away, off the felt blotter, onto the polished hardwood of the desk. "So what do you want me to do, Aaron? Say yes? Say no? Give you a fight with me or a fight with the bishop or a fight with the city of Philadelphia? What's the point?"

"The point is that Marc and I have been together for twenty-three years, and now we would like to make it official."

"Quite."

"That really is the point, Dan. I'm not saying there aren't other points, but that's really the important one and has been for the past six or seven years. We would like to make it official. We think we should have the legal right to make it official—"

"But you don't."

"But we don't," Aaron agreed. "So we're looking to do the next best thing. We're looking to have our church, this church, where we have given of our time and our money and our devotion for a decade—We're looking to have our church validate our union. That's it. It's not hard, Dan."

"When Scott died you were warning me not to do anything too—obvious—that might jeopardize my position here."

"I know. At the time, I thought, Marc and I thought, that we would want to do this quietly. Just a small gathering. Nobody would have to know. We've changed our minds."

"Why?"

Aaron shrugged. "I don't know that it's only one thing. Marc has always been more intense about this than I am. He's always taken more risks."

"Well, this would be a risk, all right. Forget the bishop, for the moment. Forget the media. Think of our friend Roy down the road. Do you really think you and Marc would be able to have this ceremony without a lot of unwanted company?"

"What makes you think it would be unwanted?"

"What the hell does that mean?"

"That means I'm arguing your side of this issue, Dan. At some point, we've got to be honest about it, about ourselves, with other people. If we're not honest about it, we only feed into people like Roy. We don't want anything camp. Marc isn't going to dress up in a white gown like Dennis Rodman, and neither am I. We don't intend to put on a freak show. We just want what any other two human beings who have been together as long and as faithfully as we have been together would have by right. We want to get married. And since we can't actually do that, we want the closest thing we can get. Why is this so hard?"

The question was so ridiculous, even Aaron couldn't ask it and go on looking him straight in the face—and Aaron could do anything. Dan had seen him negotiate with sharks. Still, Aaron walked away, to pretend to be looking at the stained-glass window. Dan looked down at the form again, the answers typed out instead of handwritten in pen, the questions printed slightly bolder and numbered in green. The odd thing was, although he was upset, he wasn't upset for the reasons Aaron probably thought he was. The idea of performing a marriage for two gay men didn't bother him. He was sure that, twenty years from now, that would happen in the Episcopal Church as a matter of course. It would happen because it *had* to happen. It was the only right thing that could happen—the only way this problem could be resolved in a way that was consistent with Christian love. There were bishops in the church right this moment who agreed with him, and more than a few laypeople. Spong had ordained a sexually active gay man in Newark. One of the new women bishops was rumored to be a lesbian. If she wasn't, she had a lot of sympathy with gay "issues." Dan made a face and rubbed his hands against his forehead, as if he were wiping off sweat. There was no sweat. If anything, he was far too cold. He hated the words that were used in cases like this. Issues. Community. Outreach. Maybe he would have felt better if he had been a priest in the Diocese of Newark. Maybe he wouldn't have, because as much as he admired Spong's stands on a lot of things, he did not like Spong's relentless skepticism.

He looked up to find that Aaron had crossed the room from the window and was standing right next to the desk.

"Well?" Aaron asked. "Will you do it?"

"Of course I'll do it. That's why you brought it up in the first place. Because you knew I'd do it."

"We guessed, yes."

"Have you got a date picked out for when you want it done?"

"The end of the month, we thought. We aren't interested in having any sort of big reception, if you know what I mean. It's not the way either of us operate."

Dan nodded. "What about banns? Do you want us to publish them?"

"That's up to you."

"What about announcements? Do you want to put one in the paper? The *Inquirer* would probably take it. I don't know about the *Star*."

"I thought you were interested in keeping this quiet."

"Not exactly." Dan got up and took the form with him. There was a filing cabinet on the other side of the room where he kept "official" papers like this, but of course the whole parish was now run on a computer. If he gave this form to Mrs. Reed, she would copy it laboriously into her files, and then it would disappear, the way all forms disappeared, so that if they should desperately need it again, they would have to go through her elaborate system of classification to find it. He hesitated over the filing cabinet, then walked past it and into the outer office. Mrs. Reed was already off to lunch, or somewhere. None of them quite knew what she did or where she went, only that since she had come there had never once been a problem with scheduling or the budget. Dan put the form down in the center of her desk, where she would be sure to see it, and then looked for a moment at the small framed photograph of her two daughters and their children. Somehow, he couldn't imagine her any younger than she was now, with her hair streaked grey and held back in a knot on the nape of her neck, with her shirtwaist dresses and her string of pearls. Years ago, the marriage form had asked for the bride's name and the groom's. Now it asked only for the names of the "communicants." Dan didn't know if that was lucky, or what.

He went back into his office. Aaron was sitting in the big leather chair, his legs stretched out in front of him. He would have looked better if he had been smoking a cigarette. It was that kind of pose. But men like Aaron Wardrop didn't smoke cigarettes anymore.

"There," Dan said. "It's done. We'll see what Mrs. Reed has to say about it."

"She won't blink an eye."

"Probably not."

"Maybe you ought to take the rest of the day off and see a movie. It's a weekday. Nobody will be expecting you around here. Except that you always are here."

"I'm fine," Dan said. He reached into his trouser pocket and found a tube of soft mints, half-eaten. He took it out and offered one to Aaron.

Aaron hesitated. Dan could see his ambivalence as if it were a physical thing. There was something wrong with the atmosphere in this room. A woman would have gnawed away at it. A gay man like Chickie would have made fun of it. Aaron didn't know what to do with it. At some other time, Dan might have helped him out. Now he only waited, almost desperate for Aaron to be gone. That was in the air, too.

"Well," Aaron said. "That's it, then. I'm somewhat at a loss for words. I expected more of an argument."

"Why?"

"I don't know. Loyalty to the institution, maybe. A wish to protect the Church from controversy. A natural hesitancy. Something like that."

"The Anglican Communion is not a stranger to controversy."

"Right," Aaron said. "Never forget Henry VIII."

Dan smiled, and said nothing, and waited. The air in the room had become thick with something like a miasma, the residue of emotions left unfelt, of positions left untaken. Aaron shifted his weight uneasily from one leg to the other and back again. He was in such perfect shape, his discomfort looked deliberately chosen, as if it were a dance move.

"All right," he said. "That's it, then. I've put down the first Saturday in March. That should give us all enough time."

"For what?" Dan asked.

"For deciding how we want this to play on the evening news."

Somebody else might have accused Aaron of being in it for the publicity, but Dan did not, because he knew that there was going to be no way to keep this *off* the evening news. Instead, he waited patiently while Aaron decided to get out, looking more uncertain and uncomfortable by the minute, the way people do when they expect to have a fight and get acquiescence instead. Except that Dan wasn't really acquiescing. That was not what was going on here. It was much more complicated than that. Aaron backed out of the office door and looked around, probably to make sure that Mrs. Reed was still gone. She must have been. Aaron said nothing to anybody, not even to Dan. When he had backed away far enough so that he was clear of the door, he turned around and began to hurry out of sight.

Dan waited until he heard steps on the stairs. Then he got out of his chair and went to the window on the other side of the room from the one Aaron had been looking at. He didn't want to look at stained glass, at a mosaic of St. Stephen being stoned to death in Jerusalem. He wanted to see the street and the traffic and the weather and the things that were really real.

Unfortunately, there wasn't much to see. This was never a very busy street. There weren't any businesses on it. Anyone who wanted to have a cup of coffee or buy a paper had to go around the corner where the plate-glass storefronts were. The only time this neighborhood ever really heated up was on Sunday, when the churches were all having services at once and the asphalt was choked with cars whose owners couldn't find enough places to park. If he strained sideways, he could see just far enough to catch the white cross on the sign in front of Roy Phipps's place. Sometimes Roy had his people out on the sidewalk with signs, for no reason Dan could tell. Sometimes they were gathered there on their way to a demonstration at a gay bar or the local offices of the Gay and Lesbian Support Advisory. Today, there was nothing, just dead air. Roy Phipps might have been nothing but another neighbor with a job in a bank and a car that needed to go to the mechanic's place almost every month.

Dan retreated back to his desk, sat down again, and sighed. Before Aaron had shown up today, he had almost made up his mind to announce his homosexuality from the pulpit this Sunday. He was still unhappy that he had withdrawn from his initial impulse to announce it at Scott Boardman's funeral. Now he didn't know if he could do it without putting Aaron and Marc's enterprise in jeopardy, and he didn't know what was more important. His head was throbbing so badly it felt as if it were going to split open at the seams.

He had no idea how long he sat there, thinking nothing, totally blank. The next thing he was aware of was Mrs. Reed, back from wherever she had gone, standing in his open doorway. She looked as placid and thoughtless as she always did. If she disapproved of what went on at St. Stephen's, if she longed for a more traditional version of religion, she never gave any indication of it to anyone in the church.

"That police lieutenant called," she said. "He's coming over here in about half an hour. I couldn't put him off. He said it was important."

"That's all right," Dan said. "They have to do what they have to do. Can I ask you a personal question?"

"You can ask me anything you like."

"Have you been an Episcopalian all your life?"

Mrs. Reed blinked. "I'm not an Episcopalian at all. I'm a Methodist. I've been a Methodist all my life. Does that create some bar to my employment here?"

"Not at all."

Mrs. Reed seemed to be on the verge of saying something else, and then thought better of it. "The lieutenant was very urgent. That was why I didn't put it off, even though you weren't around for me to check. I hope you aren't put out by it."

"I'm not put out at all."

"Well, then. Thank you, Father Burdock. I'll get back to my typing."

Mrs. Reed went out and shut the door behind her. When she was in her office, the door between their two rooms never remained open. Dan rubbed his forehead again and thought that it had all seemed so simple when he was in the seminary, what he wanted to do, what he had to do. It had just been a question of making a decision, and never for a moment allowing himself to look away from the decision he had made.

It hadn't occurred to him, then, that loneliness could be like a black pit on the surface of the moon, cold and dead and silent, going on forever, so that all he had to look forward to were the sounds of himself making the bed creak in the night, and of his own voice calling out the words of the Matins prayer in an empty kitchen.

2

If there was one thing the Cardinal Archbishop of Philadelphia did not like, it was having to rely on someone—anyone—to do things for him. He had learned to accommodate the need in small things. He could let Sister Marie Claire type his letters and take his phone calls. He could let Father Doheny handle the negotiations about the electric bill and the talks with the reporters about upcoming archdiocesan celebrations and the schedule and curricula for the parochial schools. It was things like this, things that involved money, or reputation, or the future, that he could not let go of, even when he knew he should. He knew he should let go of this. He even tried to tell himself that he would have let go of it, if he had been able to, but it was a lie, and he was not good at self-deception. There was something a monastery taught you, especially a Carmelite one. When you entered, you took on the discipline of never again looking into a mirror, but you looked at yourself, all the time. It was incumbent on the man in his position to meet with major donors. The donors expected the courtesy. It was part of what they got in return for handing over their money. Even if it hadn't been, though, he would have wanted to be there when the deal was done. He could never trust the people around him to do what was right when it needed to be done. He could never feel sure that the important things would be handled if he didn't handle them himself.

In this case, of course, the problem was that the important things might not be handled if he *did* handle them himself. He was not in the mood for this now. He didn't have the patience. Worst of all, his nerves seemed to be strung so badly they were about to snap. He had too much on his plate today to coddle Andrew Sean O'Reilly, the King of Discount Furniture, the man who Put Philly on the Home Furnishings Map. He had two strains of music running in his head, in that way that meant nothing he could do would get rid of them. One was the "Hosannah" from Bach's B Minor Mass. The other was the jingle from Andy's furniture ads. The ads ran every fifteen minutes all night long from the end of the eleven o'clock news to the start of the network morning shows on every local station. It was as if Andy had decided to make himself famous in the only way he knew how, by making and starring in his own movie, except that it was a movie that lasted only thirty seconds. The Cardinal Archbishop thought his head was going to split open. It hurt that badly. If he had been able to do anything he wanted to do, he would have retreated to the chapel, put the Bach on so loudly they would have been able to hear it at Avery Point, and dropped out of sight for a week. Except, of course, that that wasn't what he would do if he could do anything at all. What he would really do was to let Andy O'Reilly know exactly where he stood in the grand drama that was Western Civilization, and in the even grander drama that was the One, Holy, Catholic, and Apostolic Church.

Out on the street, a wino had started to walk on the edge of the sidewalk near the parked cars. Any minute now, the Cardinal Archbishop knew, he would begin to urinate on the tires. There was a cultural statement for you. You could think what you wanted about it, but it had a lot more directness— and a lot more honesty—than Andy O'Reilly's ads.

The door to the office opened and Father Doheny stepped in. "Your Eminence? Mr. O'Reilly's here. Finally. I put him in the conference room."

"In a minute," the Cardinal Archbishop said.

"When I was young, laypeople weren't late for appointments with cardinals. Not even if they had a pile of money."

"You can't be thirty years old," the Cardinal Archbishop said. "Mr. O'Reilly has us by the short hairs, and he knows it. He's behaving accordingly. You should never overestimate human nature. Celebrate it, when it exceeds expectations, but never overestimate it."

"In this job, I end up underestimating it, I think. I'm certainly getting a bad impression of what its normal state is."

" 'I come not to call the righteous, but sinners to repentance.' "

"He was God. He had a better grip on some things than I do."

"True," the Cardinal Archbishop said. He dragged himself away from the window and rubbed his temples. There was a small bottle of ibuprofen in the filing cabinet. He went there, got it out, and swallowed two caplets without water. The worst thing would be for him to go into the conference room in this mood, with his head pounding.

"Have you left him alone in there?" he asked Father Doheny.

Father Doheny shook his head. "Sister is in with him, pouring him coffee and murmuring at his every word. He's one of those people. Give him a nun in a traditional habit, and he goes totally to pieces."

"And Sister Harriet thinks we want her back in a habit because we want to—what's the word?"

"Disempower. We want to disempower her," Father Doheny said. "The word isn't in Sister Marie Claire's computer dictionary, so she's decided it's a mistake. Whenever Sister Harriet uses it in a letter, Sister Marie Claire circles it in red pen."

"And lets Sister Harriet see it?"

"Not yet, but I'm waiting."

The Cardinal Archbishop put the ibuprofen back into the filing cabinet. "I suppose we'd better go," he said. "It seems to me to be a terrible way to spend the afternoon. Are we going to run through that press conference?"

"Probably. You know Andy."

"I can't tell if that's a good thing or a bad thing."

"I wish I could understand what it is that people like Andy want," Father Doheny said.

The Cardinal Archbishop felt his mouth twisting into a grimace. "Self-respect," he said shortly. Then he shook his head, to soften his tone, because it wasn't Father Doheny he was disgusted with, but himself.

The conference room was on the other end of this floor, in the corner where an office would have stood, but larger than any office in the building. It had windows on two sides and a thick pile carpet on the floor. The furniture consisted of a teakwood table, matching chairs, and a long low sideboard meant to serve as a place to park coffee and refreshments during meetings of boards and committees. There was coffee there now, in a big electric samovar to keep it warm, as well as china cups and saucers from the best set in the storeroom, and two large crystal plates piled high with cookies. Sister

Marie Claire had worked for a Cardinal before. She knew what was expected when significant donors came to call.

Andy O'Reilly was standing next to the conference table, balancing a china coffee cup on a china saucer. Sister Marie Claire was standing, too, and Andy wouldn't feel right about sitting as long as she was. He was a short, wiry, gnarled Irishman, the kind played in the movies by James Cagney and Michael J. Pollock. He had looked forty on the day he was born, and he would look forty forever afterward. He would also never stop moving. For the Cardinal Archbishop, watching Andy O'Reilly was physically painful. He jumped around constantly. When he was sitting down, all his muscles seemed to twitch at once.

Andy saw Father Doheny and the Cardinal Archbishop come in, and put his coffee cup down on the conference table. "Your Eminence! Father! I was just talking to the Sister here about the terrible state of the parochial schools!"

Andy O'Reilly was the only person the Cardinal Archbishop had ever met who spoke in exclamation points. Sister Marie Claire made ready to go.

"Mr. O'Reilly was expressing his great concern that our parochial schools give their students a solid grounding in religion," she said. "I've told him I couldn't agree more."

"Quite," the Cardinal Archbishop said.

Father Doheny went to the sideboard. "Why don't you take some coffee and cookies with you, Sister? I know you're not hungry now, but in another hour or two—"

"That's very kind of you, Father, but I'm due at the refectory for a late lunch at any moment. If His Eminence doesn't need anything—"

"I'm more than fine, Sister," the Cardinal Archbishop said.

Sister Marie Claire bowed slightly, then floated out as they watched her.

"That's the real thing," Andy said, when the door clicked shut behind her. "Nuns in habits, looking like nuns. Not these women with blue suits on that look like lesbian social workers. Not that they really are lesbians. If you know what I mean, Your Eminence."

"Quite," the Cardinal Archbishop said again.

Father Doheny was beginning to look nervous, and the Cardinal Archbishop didn't blame him. Even with the ibuprofen, even with his headache receding into memory, he was still being too stiff, and the last thing he wanted was to be too stiff to the kind of donor who wanted most desperately to be able to feel that he was in on the inner workings of his archdiocese. He gave himself a mental order to unlink—did those ever work?—and gestured to Andy to sit down. Then he sat down himself.

"Well," he said.

Andy got himself a cup of coffee and a saucer full of cookies, stacked high. He had to be one of those people who could eat endlessly without gaining weight.

"Look," he said, sitting down and spreading out his things on the table. "I'm glad you got in touch with me. You know? I had no idea things were in the bad state they're in. It always sounds in the papers like you've got the whole thing taped."

"We've got *some* of it taped," Father Doheny said.

"There are different problems that need to be solved," the Cardinal Archbishop said. "One was, of course, the legal and ethical situation pertaining to the actions of the priests involved in the criminal behavior—"

"It wasn't criminal behavior then, was it?" Andy said. "Back in what, 1960 or whenever it was. It wasn't criminal behavior then."

"I think it was criminal behavior," Father Doheny said. "I think it was just handled differently at the time than we would handle it now."

"And nobody is ever going to know if those people were telling the truth," Andy said. "It's easy, I think, to file a lawsuit against a big institution like the Church. It pays, too. What did the archdiocese end up paying out? Millions of dollars, wasn't it?"

"Twenty six and a half million dollars over a period of ten years," the Cardinal Archbishop said.

Andy banged his fist on the table, triumphant. "There, then. What did I say? And they could all have been lying. They could have made it all up. And they probably did. That whole bunch of them going to that gay church and getting their names in the papers. The Episcopalians have always had it in for the Catholics. I know you've got to honor the deals the old Archbishop made, Your Eminence, but if you ask me, his biggest mistake was caving in on the question of guilt. He should have stood his ground. They couldn't have proved a thing. Not after all that time."

The Cardinal Archbishop had a sudden vision of himself, sitting in a high-ceilinged room in an office building in the Vatican, only an hour after the Holy Father had told him he was going to receive this appointment, watching two black-cassocked priests lay out for him the extent of the evidence that existed to prove that the priests accused were indeed guilty, and guilty over and over again.

His headache seemed to be coming back, fighting with the ibuprofen for pride of place in his skull. He said, "I'm afraid stonewalling on guilt would not have been possible. There was more actual evidence than you realize. Much more than was ever allowed to come out."

"But how could there have been?" Andy demanded. "After all this time."

"There was evidence *from* the time. Doctor's reports. And—letters."

"Letters?"

"From three of the priests involved to some of the boys," Father Doheny said.

"Oh, Jesus Christ," Andy said.

The Cardinal Archbishop rubbed his temples. He did it very carefully, because part of him was convinced that if he did it the wrong way, it would make his reemerging headache worse. "The only mistake the old Archbishop made," he said, "was in agreeing to financial arrangements the Archbishop was not equipped to handle. Those arrangements are now in place, and we cannot, for a number of reasons, change them. The result is that the archdiocese desperately needs money, and not the kind of money we generally need. To be specific, we need something on the order of a million dollars a year, over and above our usual intake."

Andy Reilly blanched. "A million dollars a year? For how long? Can't the Vatican put in some of that?"

"If Rome wasn't putting in some of what we need," the Cardinal Archbishop said, "we would need twice as much. And we need it for ten years."

"Jesus Christ," Andy said again.

The Cardinal Archbishop felt a sudden rush of mean-spirited satisfaction. Andy O'Reilly had been caught up short.

This was entirely out of his league, and he was scared to death. The satisfaction receded almost immediately, to be replaced by a hot shame he was sure must have shown on his face. He hadn't become a priest to despise his parishioners. Andy O'Reilly was out of his chair and pacing around.

"I can't give a million dollars a year," he said. "I don't know anybody who can."

"We aren't asking you to give a million dollars a year," the Cardinal Archbishop said. "We're asking you to put together a committee to raise it. Ten or so men, perhaps, with enough stature to contribute, say, fifty thousand dollars each—"

"I can do fifty thousand," Andy said. "At least, I can do it this year."

"—who could mount a long-term effort to cover what we need. Because quite frankly, if we don't find some way to cover it, this archdiocese is finished. We'll be bankrupt in six months. We'll be absorbed into another archdiocese within a year."

Andy sat down again, abruptly. "A committee," he said.

"We thought you'd be a good person to head it," Father Doheny said. "You know a lot of people. You belong to a lot of organizations. You're active in the church. And you're known to be a successful man. We thought there would be a number of other good Catholic laymen who would want to be part of anything you were part of."

The Cardinal Archbishop blinked. Andy O'Reilly seemed to be swelling up in front of his eyes. "It's very kind of you to say so," he said. "Very kind of you. I have always tried to be a good Catholic and a supporter of the Church."

"And you've succeeded," the Cardinal Archbishop said.

"And I guess I could put together a committee. I don't know if we could really raise a million dollars a year. But I could put together a committee."

"That's all we're asking, really," Father Doheny said. "We realize you can't guarantee us results. We're only hoping for somebody willing to try, and with a decent chance of making a success of it. You seemed to us to be the obvious choice. You're one of the most committed laymen in the cathedral parish."

Andy had brought a briefcase in with him. The Cardinal Archbishop hadn't noticed it. Now Andy picked it up off the floor and put it on the conference table, and the Cardinal Arch-bishop was shocked to see that it was an exquisite Mark Cross number, made of black leather and probably costing the earth. It was totally at odds with the image Andy presented in his television ads, and with the image he had been careful to present here—the JC Penney suit, the Timex watch whose metal wristband was just a little too large for his wrist. Andy folded his arms across the briefcase and put his chin down on his hands.

"You should run it like the Knights Templar, or whatever it was," he said. "A club of ten, and make it a club. Men who are on the inside. Who get information nobody else has. Like those secret societies are supposed to be."

"Secret societies?" The Cardinal Archbishop was confused.

"You know," Andy said. "Like Opus Dei. Or the old Jesuits. The Pope's army. Except this time we'll make it the Cardinal's army. And we'll meet here. Because they'll want to be part of it. They'll want to know that they belong. Don't you see?"

"No," the Cardinal Archbishop said.

"I see," Father Doheny said. "It's a very insightful idea."

"Yeah." Andy stood up. "The Church is under attack. She needs an army to defend her. We'll be that army. You give me about a week, okay? I've got to work out who to ask. Then we can get started. There's just one thing."

"And what is that?" the Cardinal Archbishop said.

"If there's more to this scandal, I want to know about it before I read it in the papers. We all will. We can't be blind-sided by press reports about issues you know are sitting in the closet waiting to fall out. If we're not informed, we can't help."

But all they have to do to help is to raise money, the Cardinal Archbishop thought. What do they think they're going to do with privileged information? But then it struck him, because he was not a stupid man, that what they were going to do with it was simply to have it, to be the people who knew when nobody else did, to be the people who could hint to their less fortunate colleagues that they were privy to all the inner workings of the chancery and of Rome. Suddenly, the Cardinal Archbishop's distaste for Andy O'Reilly was overwhelming. The arrogance, the conceit, the soul so lacking in anything of value that the only thing it could think of when Holy Mother Church was in grave danger was how to use that danger for its own advantage. He expected that kind of thing out of newspaper reporters, and the president of the local chapter of the American Humanist Association, and the writers who fed stories to the tabloid television shows. For some reason, he had been convinced that no "real" Catholic could be anything like this, that the people who knelt in the pews in front of him as the bread and wine became the Body and Blood of their Lord Jesus Christ felt as he did, about Christ, about His Church, maybe even about their own souls.

He looked sideways at Father Doheny, and nodded slightly. Andy O'Reilly caught the look, and the nod.

"What is it?" he asked. "Is there more of the scandal still in the closet? Is there something else about to come out?"

"Not about the scandal, no," Father Doheny said. "There is something else."

"I think I'll leave you to explain it," the Cardinal Archbishop said. "I'm wanted at the convent." He stood up and held out his hand to Andy O'Reilly, who kissed his ring and came close to kneeling while he did it, but stopped just short.

"You won't be disappointed, bringing good laymen into your confidence," Andy promised. "We've got the Church's best interests at heart."

The Cardinal Archbishop had no idea if that was true or not. He only knew he did not want to stay around here to find out. He didn't want to be in this room any longer with the creature this man was. He nodded to both Andy and Father Doheny and went out, walking so quickly that the folds of his cassock beat against his legs like streamers in the wind. He was sick to his stomach, and what frightened him was that he might have to stay this way, for months, for years, until life would become one long exercise in nausea. Take up your cross and follow me, the man had said, but the Cardinal Archbishop of Philadelphia was sure he couldn't have meant anything like this.

3

For Roy Phipps, the decision to watch the medical examiner's press conference on what the news stations were calling "the

Kelly killings" wasn't even a decision. Since the first he had
known about what had happened up the street, he had been
nearly obsessed with it. It had been bad enough on the day it
happened, when the street was full of police cars and ambu-
lances, and there had been nothing he could do to find out
what was happening. He had sent Fred Havers into the crowd,
but Fred was not an actor. Catholicism scared him. He looked
on St. Anselm's as the home of the devil, with a cloven-footed
old goat seated right out in the open on a throne on the altar,
and parishioners dancing naked to the accompaniment of a
jingling tambourine. Of course, there was no Mass going on
at the time. Father Healy was standing right out on the sidewalk where both Roy and Fred could see him. So were a dozen
nuns, in habits, and the stocky, angry woman who was ad-
dressed as "Sister" but wore ordinary suits. Fred still found it
hard to believe that something was not going on in the sanctuary, even while the police were coming in and out. In the
end, he had gone, because Roy asked him to, but Roy had
watched him. He hadn't gone any farther than the edges of
the crowd, and even then he had held his arms stiffly at his
sides, trying not to touch or be touched, as if Catholicism were
a disease that could rub off on him. Whore of Babylon. Mark
of the Beast. When the Antichrist came he would come in
glory, and his instrument would be the Pope in Rome, and all
men would bow down and worship him.

"Somebody died," Fred had said, coming back, and then,
"somebody committed suicide."

That was all, and Roy had known better than to try to get
something more out of him, or to send him back. There were
members of Roy's congregation who would love to be sent
off as spies, but for that very reason they would have been
unsuitable. Even Fred himself stuck out a little too much on
this city street. There weren't supposed to be real rubes and
hayseeds anymore. That was all supposed to have been taken
care of by movies and MTV. When Fred was growing up,
though, his parents hadn't had a television, and the only movies they had approved of had been the Disney animated features from the nineteen fifties. Then there had been home
schooling, and church Sundays, and Bible college. It wasn't
hard for Roy to understand how Fred had come to be Fred. It
only angered him sometimes, the way they all angered him,

all the members of his congregation. Their lack of education was appalling. Their lack of sophistication would have been comical if it weren't so dangerous. Their superstitions were tangled knots of confusion that couldn't be hacked through with a sword, no matter how many sermons he gave on the sin of credulity, no matter how often he railed against astrology as a tool of the devil. They were committed to him, but he thought they wouldn't have been, if they could have found someone who frightened them less. Then again, maybe not. They were used to living on fear. They were afraid of everything. Maybe a man they couldn't fear would be, as well, a man they couldn't respect.

Roy kept the television on the second floor in a special room that only a few people were allowed access to, and then only when he gave them explicit permission to come in. It was important that they understand how spiritually dangerous television was. This was true not only of the obviously bad channels, like Playboy and HBO, but of the ordinary broadcast ones as well. There was enough heresy on the evening news to send a hundred souls to hell. A hundred souls probably went, too, because they had learned to doubt from Dan Rather and Peter Jennings. Doubt, Roy always told them, was the worst possible thing. Doubt was the worm eating into the apple of your soul, eating out your spiritual eyes, until you couldn't see the majesty of God standing right in front of you, but thought you were alone. The problem was, they were not only stupid, but opaque. He had no way of knowing how much of what he was saying sank in and was taken to heart, and how much just passed over them like so much wind. He was sure most of them either didn't have televisions at all, or had those specially sealed sets sold by Home Life that played videotapes but did not get channels. He was sure most of them didn't have cable. He had to stress, over and over again, that even "Christian" programming wasn't necessarily Christian. Kenneth Copeland praying for prosperity, or Benny Hinn working up a sweat while he "healed" one poor deluded soul after the other—the devil could heal; the devil could perform miracles; the devil knew what backsliding Christians wanted to hear— all that kind of thing was just as dangerous as watching a sex show or listening to one of those book channels where the author had written another book on how the Bible wasn't true.

Sometimes, when things got rocky enough, Roy took them on archeological expeditions in the city: finding the evidence of the flood on the streets of Philadelphia. Most of all, he reminded them of the worst thing, the greatest danger, the vice that was waiting inside each and every one of them, looking for an opportunity to come out. That was another piece of evidence that Roy Phipps wasn't stupid—although nobody who had ever met him thought he was. Only television reporters, who saw him leading his pickets at AIDS funerals or carrying signs that told the truth about gay men and hell, and who didn't talk to him, made him out to be an uneducated rube. Roy Phipps was smart enough to understand the television reporters, and to understand the men like Fred Havers, too—the men who understood nothing about themselves, who didn't know that random sexual arousal was the mark of original sin, that every man felt it, that it didn't mean anything. As long as Fred Havers and the other men like him thought it *did* mean something, it would be possible for Roy Phipps to do God's work on this earth.

The television was set on a wheeled cart at the front of the room, meant to look tentative and temporary. Metal folding chairs were set up in front of it in rows of four across. The scene was supposed to remind people of a movie theater, or maybe a meeting in a town hall—but most of these people would never have been to such a meeting. Most of them had never voted before they joined Roy Phipps's church. Roy stood off to the side and watched them file in: Fred himself; Doug Frelinghuysen; Carl Schmidt; Peter Gessen; Nick Holt. All the members of Roy's inner circle were men. Only men could be lectors in the church, and only men could serve on its administrative board. Women, St. Paul had said, ought to be silent in church. Roy had translated this to mean that they should have no hand in the running of it, although he had been forced to hire a woman as his secretary. It seemed to be impossible to find men who could type. The men of the inner circle were all one of two types. Either they were like Fred, and just a little too heavy, with suits that were always a size too small, or they were like Carl Schmidt, and far too thin, in that painful-to-look-at way that spoke of too many childhood meals missed and too little in the way of basic nutrition even now. They arranged themselves on chairs throughout the room, not one of them sitting directly next to any other, or directly ahead or behind. They must all have gone to considerable trouble to be here, in the middle of the day, when they all had the kinds of jobs that paid by the hour and expected their warm bodies in place at all times.

Roy stood at the front of the room next to the television set and watched their faces. Mostly, they were blank. Fred Havers cleared his throat.

"Three minutes," he said. "It's three minutes before they start the press conference. Don't you think we ought to turn that thing on in case they get started early?"

The other men moved around in their chairs. There was no way to tell if they were agreeing or disagreeing. They were deliverymen and truck drivers, mechanics and repairmen. They were used to impassivity, and just as used to taking orders. Only Fred wore a suit with any regularity, and that was because he worked for the church.

"In a minute," Roy told them. "We won't miss anything if we miss the first minute. I wanted to ask if anybody had done anything about what we talked about last Sunday."

The men moved around in their chairs again. They knew he was referring to their private meeting last Sunday, and not what he had talked about in his sermon or discussed in the Bible class afterward. Most of them looked embarrassed. Then Doug Frelinghuysen raised his hand.

"Mr. Frelinghuysen," Roy said.

Doug looked uncertain of what to do next—stand, perhaps, the way teachers had once made students stand next to their desks to give an answer, in an era far too long ago for Doug to be able to remember it. In the end, he stayed where he was.

"I went to the meeting of GLAHCOT. On Monday night."

"GLAHCOT?"

"The Gay and Lesbian Ad Hoc Committee on Tolerance. Ad Hoc. That's what it said on the flyer. It's run by those people, you know, the Gay and Lesbian Support Advisory."

"Very good," Roy said, biting back the lecture on "ad hoc" that sprang so quickly into his mind. Lectures like that sprang into his mind all the time. If he gave them all, he would never do anything else. "Now," he said. "Can you tell us what went on there?"

Doug Frelinghuysen nodded. "It was a new members meeting. They had a table with food, you know, and stuff to drink. And they went around meeting everybody."

"And?"

Doug Frelinghuysen blushed. "And I had to leave early. That's what you told us to do. If we were in danger of getting into any trouble."

"You were in danger of getting into trouble?"

"You know." Doug Frelinghuysen blushed again, this time so red he looked as if he had painted his face with oils and then let them dry against his skin until they cracked. "There was this guy, you know," he said. "And he was, you know. Getting friendly. He was asking me to go out to a bar with him. There was stuff like that going on all over the room. People hitting on each other. And, uh, people kissing."

Some of the men in the room visibly blanched. Roy kept his temper.

"So," he said. "While you were there, did you hear anything of interest to us? Any talk of a demonstration, or some news about a public action. Anything of that kind?"

"They weren't doing that stuff," Doug Frelinghuysen said. "They were just, you know. Eating. And kissing. And. Stuff."

"Yes," Roy said. It was harder to keep his temper than ever, but it was important not to lose it too often. He needed his anger for strategic moments, when it would matter. He turned his attention to the rest of the men. "Well?" he said. "Any of you?"

"I bought the *Advocate*," Carl Schmidt said. "I don't know if it did any good. It was full of personals."

It was also full of articles about fundamentalists, including one about this very church. Roy had seen this week's issue of the *Advocate*. He counted to ten in his head, the way he had to do so often, and looked over the rest of the small crowd. They were staring at the floor, every one of them. He had sent them on a mission, and they had failed even to start it. If he pressed them, they would take on that pouty resentment they got so often at work. They were in their thirties and forties, but they were still children in the ways that mattered most. They were still people whose decisions were made by authority figures who did not believe they were mature enough to run their own lives.

Roy went over to the television set and turned it on. He

had preset it to the right channel, and the first thing they all saw was the bland, blond prettiness of the KPAL anchorwoman, trying to look serious under a hairdo that would have embarrassed a toy poodle.

"It's always women on the news shows now," Carl Schmidt said. "You ever notice that? It used to be only men, and now it's always women."

The other men murmured in what might have been agreement, and might have been noise. Roy turned the volume up and took a seat in the empty front row. The picture wavered, and the next thing on the screen was a bank of microphones on a table with no one behind it. The anchorwoman's voice in the background was hushed, as if she were calling a tennis match.

"Listen to me," Roy said. "If we're going to carry this off, you're going to have to do your part. Go out to those meetings. Read the newspapers and magazines, but go out to those meetings. Go down the street and sit through the service at St. Stephen's. Keep your ears open. Listen. You don't have to be stealth bombs. You don't have to tell anybody who you are. Just go. Those meetings are open. Anybody can go to them. Go and come back and tell us what was said."

There was a low murmuring throughout the room, but Roy knew there was no way to tell what it meant. He turned his attention to the set, where a heavyset man carrying a large sheaf of papers had appeared behind the microphone, looking grave. That would be the medical examiner. Roy had never seen him before. He wished he'd brought a cup of coffee with him when he'd come upstairs. By now, this man had to know what had really happened to Marty and Bernadette Kelly. He might even know more than that. Roy wasn't worried.

The trick was always to stay one step ahead, and he was out in front by light-years.

SIX

1

Gregor Demarkian had made it a point, through all the years of his retirement and "consulting," always to work with police departments. The reason for that was twofold. First, it was simply easier. Father Tibor sometimes gave him mystery novels to read, but they always ended up making him feel impatient. In the real world, spunky housewives and nosy librarians did not solve crimes, no matter how bright they were. They didn't have access to the necessary resources. Long before the Bureau had established the Behavioral Sciences Unit, law enforcement had become mostly a matter of technology. Fingerprints, footprints, tire tracks, fiber analysis, the chemical analysis of poisons—all these things were vital for any case that was going to get anywhere in a court, and they had been joined, in recent years, with even more esoteric tools like DNA analysis and voiceprints. No housewife, no matter how spunky, was going to be able to do a DNA scan in her kitchen, and no nosy librarian was going to be able to know Who Done It if she didn't also know that the voice on the answering machine belonged to the Sweet Sister-in-Law rather than the Vituperative Ex-Wife, who was trying to mask her own voice while incriminating her rival. Of course, in real police cases, the characters in the drama almost never stacked up like that, and the murder was almost never the kind that required this sort of investigation. Instead, some idiot with more alcohol in his system than brains in his head went haywire one late Friday night and shot up his girlfriend, or some other idiot hyped high on cocaine got into a fight outside a bar about the color of his running shoes and stabbed the first person who came to hand, or some yet bigger idiot decided to hold up a convenience store and panicked when the clerk didn't bow down and worship him at the first opportunity, which resulted in five people dead and three more wounded before a single dime ever came up out of the till. *Hill Street Blues* was the only thing Gregor had ever seen or heard of that tried to portray crime as it really was, and it only got away with it because it spent most of the time concentrating on the private lives of the cops in the station than it did on the crime. Even Ed McBain, whose realism was close to meticulous, dressed up his books in unusual crimes and unusual circumstances, and the other "realistic" writers Tibor had given him were about as realistic as an Oliver Stone screenplay. Gregor almost preferred the books about little old ladies and their cats. At least they didn't pretend to be anything but what they were. If "crime novels" had really been about real crime as it really existed, nobody would buy them.

The other reason Gregor liked to work with police departments was that it kept him out of trouble. Here was something else that was unrealistic about crime novels. In real life, an amateur who tried to investigate on his own would end up in court on an obstruction charge. If he did anything that might even conceivably compromise the police investigation, he might even find himself in jail. Cops did not take kindly to interference from outside, even when that interference was well within the law. They didn't want the Federal Bureau of Investigation "helping" except when they asked it to. They didn't want the cops of some other jurisdiction getting in their way. They didn't want anything but to be left alone unless they asked not to be, and they were likely to treat an interloper the way antibodies treated a virus. First they would isolate him. Then they would try to kill him off. Gregor preferred to be asked in. That was why he called himself a "consultant" for police departments, and why he had always steadfastly refused to get his private investigator's license. He didn't want to be Philip Marlowe. He didn't even want to be Raymond Chandler. He only wanted to have interesting work to do that didn't take up so much of his time that he no longer had a life. Having waited until middle age to chuck workaholism for living, he did not intend to backslide into an obsession about procedures.

In many places, simply having an invitation from the local Catholic Archbishop would be enough to get him an invitation from the police department involved. That would have been true in Philadelphia only fifteen or twenty years ago. Now things were stickier. There weren't as many Catholics as there had been, and, more importantly, not as many of them were cops. Then there was what Gregor was rapidly beginning to think of as the Personality Problem. The first thing he had discovered, making a few phone calls to set up this meeting, was that the Philadelphia police didn't like the new Cardinal Archbishop any more than he did.

He checked his watch. He was cutting this very close. He shouldn't have spent so much time at St. Anselm's, or walked from there halfway to here. He watched a couple of uniformed officers come out the front doors and head away from him on the sidewalks, both wearing thick coats that were designed to look as much like their uniforms as possible. Then he went through the front doors himself and presented himself to the officer at the desk.

"Gregor Demarkian," he said. "I'm here to see John Jackman—"

"Right here."

Gregor looked up and saw Jackman coming toward him, dressed in a suit so well made and so conservative he could have been a banker. What he was, instead, was the deputy commissioner of police of the city of Philadelphia, an appointment he had held now for exactly six months. Gregor had first met him when he was a detective lieutenant in Bryn Mawr. Since then, Jackman had gone from township to township and from township to city, moving carefully and without hesitation toward the only thing that mattered to him. It didn't hurt that he was Black, and very photogenic, and Catholic into the bargain. Gregor hardly thought he could have done better if he had been allowed to put in specifications with God. At the very least, if they ever decided to make a movie of his life, they would have to get Will Smith to play the part.

The uniformed officer at the desk was a woman. Jackman said good morning to her and took Gregor firmly by the elbow.

"Third floor," he said, and he pulled them both toward the elevators. "I've got somebody waiting for us up there. How are you? How is Bennis?"

"I'm fine. Bennis is Bennis. The execution is set for the end of the month."

"Shit."

"That won't get you the commissioner's job before you're fifty."

"I've revised my plans and made it fifty-five." They were at the elevators, but they didn't have to wait. Jackman pushed the button, and the doors opened, automatically, as if he had been able to hold the car until he wanted it. He tugged Gregor inside and pushed the button for the third floor. "What were you doing over at Henry Lord's? Trying to find a way to get a stay?"

"No," Gregor said. "Not that. We think a stay is probably impossible this time. Bennis wants to talk to her. She doesn't want to talk to Bennis. I was trying to see if I could arrange something."

"Shit," Jackman said again.

The car stopped, and the door slid open. The third floor was slightly less utilitarian than the first, but there was still an air of basic practicality about it. Build solid and build cheap. It was the best of the three possible ways to build a municipal building. The worst was to build cheap, period. The iffy one was to build expensive, with marble and fountains and the kind of thick pile carpet most people only dreamed of having in their bedrooms. On the one hand, you built a monument. On the other, you ended up on the evening news in a story about the waste of the taxpayer's money.

Gregor glanced up at the large round clock that was the only decoration on the wall behind the receptionist's desk. "We're going to be late," he said.

"It doesn't matter. I've got the press release. And a full ME's report. My office is this way."

Jackman's office was down a hall, then down another hall, and in a corner. Gregor was sure it was not as large or as well appointed as the corner office given to the commissioner himself, but he knew Jackman well enough to know that the man could wait. There was a man sitting on a chair near a low round coffee table, watching a television set that had been wheeled in from somewhere else. When Gregor and Jackman came in, the man looked up, looked back at the set, then stood.

"How's it going?" Jackman asked.

"All hell's breaking loose." The man was white, and not quite young, in spite of the fact that his pasty face was still pocked with acne. He turned to Gregor Demarkian and held out his hand. "Garry Mansfield," he said.

"Garry's a homicide detective," Jackman said drily.

Garry had his eyes trained on the television set again. "This is not going to be good," he said. "People have been way too bored in this city for way too long."

Jackman waved Gregor in the direction of the chair on the other side of the coffee table and pulled his own chair out from behind his desk to sit down. Gregor was watching the set carefully, but the scene was too confused to evaluate. Obviously, the press-release part of the program was over, because now the reporters were asking questions. They all seemed to be talking into air instead of microphones. Gregor would hear half a question, and then the voice would disappear.

"Maybe we'd better turn this off," Jackman said after a while. "This isn't getting us anywhere. Were there any surprises?"

"You mean with the press release?" Garry shook his head. "He read it verbatim. And he's trying not to speculate. But you know how it is. Everybody will be speculating in a minute or two. The evening news shows are going to be ridiculous."

"Are you the detective in charge of this case?" Gregor asked.

It was the kind of thing Jackman should have told him in the elevator, or when they first came into the room. Instead, they seemed to have been talking in code. But Garry Mansfield was nodding.

"It depends on which case you're talking about," he said. "I'm in charge of the Marty and Bernadette Kelly case. The Scott Boardman case belongs to Lou Emiliani."

Gregor raised his eyebrows. "There's the first thing. I knew this mess was going to be full of inaccuracies. The Cardinal gave me to understand that there weren't two cases, but only one connected one."

"There probably will be in a day or two," Garry Mansfield said. "But Boardman died first, at least as far as we knew—"

"We'll get to the times later," Jackman said. "That's driving everybody up the wall."

"Yeah, well, whatever," Garry said. "Boardman was the first case. He died over at that church, St. Stephen's, in some office they have over there. You'd have to ask Lou. But nobody thought much of anything about it. I mean, the man practically breathed coke, morning, noon, and night. Somebody like that has a few convulsions and dies, you figure it's cocaine poisoning. You don't get all worked up about it."

"When I talked to the cardinal, he said that there had been an exception made to allow the family to prepare the body for burial before the final autopsy reports were in."

"Ask Lou," Garry said again. "From what I understand, it was more complicated than that. Anyway, Boardman came first that we knew about, and that got assigned a detective, and then Marty did his little jig in St. Anselm's, and I got assigned to it, so it's still two separate cases. But it won't be for long. You read the press release?"

"No," Gregor said.

"I'll give you a copy. It's very cagey. The Boardman thing is just a line on page three, but it's not like nobody's going to notice."

"I'm surprised there's anything about the Boardman 'thing' at all," Gregor said. "And, for that matter, I'm surprised about the press release. Why take so much trouble to attract publicity? Doesn't the medical examiner's office usually play it more closely than that?"

Jackman stood up. "He's covering his ass, that's what the problem is," he said, starting to pace. "He screwed up on the Boardman thing, and now he's covering his ass. Don't get me started, Gregor, I'm serious."

"You should have heard the language he used," Garry said.

"At this rate, he won't make commissioner before he's sixty," Gregor said.

Jackman sat down again. "You remember the sex-abuse thing, a couple of years ago, with the old Archbishop and all that jazz?"

"Trobriand Islanders remember the sex-abuse thing," Gregor said.

"Yeah, well. The commissioner," Jackman stared at the door, as if he expected the commissioner to burst in at any moment. "The commissioner," he repeated, "seems to think we look like we're picking on the archdiocese. And he doesn't

want to look like we're picking on the archdiocese. And that's
especially true because Boardman was one of the plaintiffs in
the sex-abuse case. So, the bottom line is, the commissioner
wants to hire you."

"I think I've already been hired by the archdiocese."

"Did they pay you any money?"

"Of course they didn't pay me any money."

"Well, then," Jackman said, "you weren't really hired. So
go over to the precinct with Garry here, and listen to Lou
Emiliani, and come on board. You'd rather work for us than
for that son of a bitch anyway. And we won't tie your hands."

"Unless you say no," Garry Mansfield said pleasantly.

Gregor leaned forward and turned off the television set. It
had gone to a commercial for Pampers, which was the kind
of thing he could never watch without getting confused.

2

Gregor had expected that the precinct that housed the police
who covered St. Anselm's and St. Stephen's would be one of
the better-kept ones in the city. The neighborhood was one of
the more expensive ones, and all the houses Gregor had been
able to see when he walked around the two large churches,
hoping to get some sense of direction, had been well kept and
devoted to the use of a single tenant. He had failed to reckon
with the perversity of Philadelphia street life. New York was
supposed to be changeable, but next to this, New York was a
model of consistency. No wonder so many of the really rich
people here had moved out to the comfort of the Main Line.
There was this street with the two churches on it, and the row
houses with their polished front doors and gleaming windows.
Two streets over, the row houses looked as if they were dis-
integrating into sand and the one vacant lot was full of garbage
and people who huddled over a fire they had made in a tin
can. Junkies and drunks: even when Gregor was growing up
here, fifty years ago, there had been junkies and drunks, but
they had called the junkies "hopheads." In those days, it had
all been marijuana and cocaine. If heroin happened, it happened out of sight, and drugs in general were restricted to the
musicians who blew through after a week or two in New York

or Detroit. That was one of the great attractions of going to
hear jazz on Saturday nights. All the fraternity boys from the
University of Pennsylvania tried it. If they were really rebels,
they actually bought themselves a joint and smoked it in the
alleys in the back before they joined their girlfriends at their
round tables and tried to pretend that it didn't matter that they
were the only white people in the room. Maybe because Gregor had never been a fraternity boy, or had a hope in hell of
becoming one, he *hadn't* tried it. He had been in the Army
before he smoked his first marijuana cigarette, and then he
hadn't liked it much, and hadn't gone back to try it again.

Still, he had come into the black neighborhoods of this city
to hear music when the only place you could hear real jazz
was in the storefront cabarets that were supposed to be "for
coloreds only"—except that this was Philadelphia, so nobody
had been willing to come right out and say it. God only knew,
there had been enough in the way of neighborhoods that were
"for whites only," although nobody had been willing to say
that, either. And then, as now, the real skids were always the
most integrated parts of town. Alcoholism was color-blind.
The old men sleeping off the shakes on park benches and
heating grates were any color at all, or no color, and they were
so far beyond caring that even an official policy of apartheid
would not have mattered. Gregor wondered how the South
Africans had managed that, or if they had even bothered to
try: the community of bums. Could you have a community
among people who could barely speak without slurring their
words, or who wanted nothing more than another bottle of
booze and oblivion?

Garry Mansfield was leading him up the stairs of the precinct house. At the top, standing in the half-opened front
doors, was a man who looked like he might have been Black
or Hispanic or Asian or all three. He was in an ordinary business suit, but he was all cop. Gregor wondered if they gave
them walking lessons the way they gave those to debutantes,
except instead of walking with books on their heads they'd be
required to walk holding a steel baton stretched out behind
their backs, so that they would learn to strut properly.

"What's the matter with him?" the man at the top of the
stairs said.

Garry Mansfield looked Gregor over. "He's got the urban

blue. Hey, Lou. We got here as fast as we could. Jackman can talk the ass off a cooked chicken."

The Black/Hispanic/Asian man must be Lou Emiliani. Maybe it was time for them all to stop trying to pin each other down by ethnicity. It was getting too confusing. Gregor held out his hand.

"Gregor Demarkian," he said.

"Lou Emiliani," Lou Emiliani said. He stood back and propped the door a little farther open, so that they could pass by him and into the precinct house itself. It was, Gregor saw, filthy in the way these places got. He was sure it was cleaned often enough. It was probably washed down in Lysol twice a day by a cleaning staff that had nothing else to do but try to make the place as antiseptic as possible. The problem was that some kinds of dirt did not come out, not ever, not even if you destroyed the building and reduced it all to dust.

In the big front room, an old woman in a coat that didn't quite come down to her knees was standing at the big front desk, tapping her hands against the surface as she tried to explain something to the desk sergeant. On the other side of that counter, three men were handcuffed together and sitting against the wall in wooden chairs. Gregor had no idea what had caused the police to handcuff them in the first place, but at the moment they were closer to sleep than to violence. Big-city police departments like this were usually unbearably noisy, full of confusion, full of complaints. This one was almost eerily quiet. The only sound Gregor could hear was the old woman talking, her voice rising and falling almost as if in song.

"Cambodian," Lou Emiliani said helpfully, seeing that Gregor was puzzled. "We've got a lot of them in this precinct. They're decent enough, but they just don't learn the language."

"Well, for Christ's sake," Garry Mansfield said. "I mean, what do you want? They're old ladies. They watched their families get shot up by machine guns in the old country and they come here, they're starting over, they're supposed to be grandmothers, instead they're cleaning toilets in some building downtown. I mean, Jesus."

"I don't think you call Cambodia the old country," Lou Emiliani said.

"I don't think you bug some old lady when she's lost her

old family and she's in a new country and she's only trying
to catch a break."

"I don't bug the old ladies," Lou Emiliani said.

They had gone through the big front room and into a narrow corridor. They were stopped in front of a steel door with
a fire window in it. Gregor pushed the door open and looked
inside, at a bare-bones imitation of a conference room. This
was where arrested prisoners would be brought to have a private word or two with their Legal Aid attorneys.

"Gentlemen?" Gregor said.

The two men both looked at him. Neither one of them could
be much more than thirty. They had forgotten he was even
there.

"Oh," Garry Mansfield said.

Lou Emiliani pushed into the room and looked around.
"Just a minute," he said. "Marsha was supposed to bring in
the file."

He disappeared down the corridor, and Garry and Gregor
went inside to sit down. Gregor tried to remember if he had
ever been in the precinct house in an unadulteratedly rich
neighborhood, and supposed he must have. He had once
worked kidnapping detail for the FBI, and in general it was
rich people whose family members were kidnapped. He
couldn't remember those precinct houses being much different
from this one. Even the suburban police stations, if the suburb
was large enough, weren't much different. The differences began to show in rural districts, where crime was almost nonexistent and the police sometimes felt as if they had only been
hired for show.

Lou Emiliani came back in, carrying a thick manila folder,
and shut the door behind him. "Here it is," he said. "Marsha
got held up by a shoplifting. What is it, these days, with the
hookers? Is business bad or something? Why are they all shoplifting?"

"They aren't all shoplifting," Garry Mansfield said patiently.

Lou Emiliani ignored him. He flipped open the manila
folder and stared down at its first page, although Gregor knew
that there couldn't be much of anything there that would make
any difference to what he had to say. Gregor had looked
through a lot of manila folders in his time. Unless they had

been especially arranged for a press conference or a meeting, they were generally incomprehensible.

Lou Emiliani pushed the folder away. "Look," he said. "I'm glad you're here, okay? I don't know what Garry thinks, but I'm glad Jackman's bringing you in. Somebody has to deal with the son of a bitch."

"I thought we were going to stop calling him that," Garry Mansfield said. "Jackman said that if we kept it up we were going to slip one day and do it on the air, so you said—"

Lou ignored him. "It's not that I'm against the Catholics. You have to understand this. All right? I've been a Catholic all my life. And I know what they were thinking, those guys in Rome, when they sent him here, after all the trouble. So. It's not that. It's just that I can't deal with him. I can't deal with him."

"Nobody can deal with him," Garry said.

"I take it we're back on the Cardinal Archbishop," Gregor said.

Lou Emiliani stuck his fingers under his collar and came out with a silver chain with a crucifix and a Miraculous Medal hanging on it. Entwined around the metal were the brown cloth strands of the scapular of St. Simon Stock. Lou tucked it all back out of sight.

"I think the best thing you could do," he said, "is to be our point person with the archdiocese. You deal with him."

"Why don't we talk about this young man," Gregor said. "This Mr.—"

"Boardman," Garry Mansfield said.

Lou brought the manila folder back to him and closed it. "It was my fault, more than anybody else's. It didn't occur to me that he died from anything but bad cocaine, or too much cocaine. It looked like that kind of death. And you know what autopsies are. They can't test for everything. They only find what they go looking for."

"Back up a little," Gregor said. "This Mr. Boardman was how old?"

"Scott," Garry Mansfield said.

"He was twenty-eight," Lou Emiliani said. "Gay. Out, but not very comfortable with it. Not camp, not even a little. If you hadn't known he was gay, you would never have guessed it."

"Oh, Jesus," Garry Mansfield said. "Here we go again. What was he supposed to look like so you could guess it? What, you think the gay guys paint their hair green?"

Gregor ignored him. "If he wasn't comfortable being out and he wasn't distinctively gay, why was he out at all?"

"He had to be," Lou said. "He was one of the plaintiffs in the sex-abuse scandal. The way those things work, the defense attorneys made his life an open book. And it wasn't a secret. He got caught in the garage doing it with another kid in high school. So his father kicked him out. His mother was still in touch, though."

"And he came to St. Stephen's?" Gregor asked.

"I think it took longer than that," Lou said. "He was in art college when he got kicked out. He must have finished. Anyway, by the time he died he was a graphic artist, got a lot of work on coffee-table books and book-cover stuff in general. Got a lot of work from New York. Some of the men at St. Stephen's said he was thinking of moving there."

Gregor nodded. "All right. Eventually he came to St. Stephen's. Was he in a relationship?"

"No," Garry Mansfield said.

"He screwed around," Lou said. "He'd get stoked up on coke and hit the bars. In the beginning it was just sort of off and on. He'd coke up on the weekends and be clean the rest of the week, or he'd at least be clean enough. But the last six months or so, that changed."

"He was zonked all the time," Garry said. "We all saw him. He was all over the neighborhood. Half the uniforms in this precinct must have rolled him into the emergency room at least once, or rolled him home."

"Nobody arrested him?" Gregor said.

"What for?" Garry Mansfield said. "He wasn't dealing. Hell, if he got a significant stash, he'd just hole up until he did it all himself. He was a mess. He didn't need to go to jail. He needed a hospital. There just aren't any hospitals."

"Let's not debate the drug war," Lou Emiliani said. Then he sighed. "I know it's wrong to jump to conclusions. We shouldn't have assumed anything. But it wasn't just us. It was Jackman and the commissioner both. Here's this guy, he's been stoking himself to the gills on coke for six months, it was only a matter of time before he killed himself. Now he goes into convulsions in a church office and kicks—what would you think it was?"

"Back up again," Gregor said. "This was, when? That Scott Boardman died?"

"January 30," Lou said. "Just about six o'clock in the evening."

"And he wasn't alone? Somebody saw the convulsions?"

"A whole mass of people saw the convulsions," Lou said. "Reverend Burdock, for one. Oh, and that guy, what's his name. George."

"Chickie," Garry Mansfield said.

"Yeah, Chickie. That one, you can tell that he's gay."

"Oh, Jesus," Garry Mansfield said.

Lou brushed it away. "We weren't thinking about arsenic," he went on. "We weren't thinking about murder. Not any of us. What we were thinking about was Roy Phipps. You know about the Reverend Roy Phipps?"

"In detail," Gregor said.

"Yeah. Well. What we were all worried about was, we figured if we didn't give them the go-ahead to get the funeral arrangements made and that kind of thing, old Roy would think Boardman died of AIDS, and then we'd be stuck with another demonstration. The asshole has picketed five of the last six funerals at St. Stephen's. It's creepy as hell. So we didn't get completely stupid. We got the whole autopsy done. We just released the body to the undertaker a little ahead of schedule, so the family and the church could, you know, get things in gear."

"Before the chemical analysis tests came back from the lab, is what he's trying to say," Garry Mansfield said.

"One thing at a time," Gregor said. "The body was released to the family. It was embalmed?"

"Yeah." Lou looked depressed.

"The family had it embalmed? The mother did, or did the father have a change of heart?" Gregor asked.

"It was the people at the church." Lou slid down in his chair. "Reverend Burdock and those people. Guy named— Aaron something. He made the arrangements."

"Aaron Wardrop," Garry Mansfield said.

"Was that acceptable to the family?" Gregor asked.

Lou straightened up again. "Look," he said. "You don't

have to tell us that we cut a lot of corners. We cut a lot of corners. And we shouldn't have. But the thing is, this guy, this Phipps, is not a joke. He's never pulled anything violent yet, but that doesn't mean he won't, and the people who trail around after him are not the most stable eggs in the carton. So we were a little spooked. And the mother—well, the mother couldn't have taken him home. The father wouldn't have allowed it. He didn't even come to the funeral. She doesn't have any money to speak of. She couldn't have buried him herself. I mean, what the hell. We were just trying to be decent to everybody involved and head off an incident in the process."

Gregor nodded. "So you released the body for burial earlier than you should have. And the body was embalmed. And the body was buried? Yes?"

"Yes," Lou nodded.

"Where?"

"Martyrs Cemetery," Garry Mansfield said. "The Episcopal diocese owns it. I think Dan Burdock arranged it."

"If the body was buried, it can be disinterred," Gregor pointed out.

"Yeah." Lou got out of his chair. "And isn't that going to be a can of worms. When Roy gets finished with that, we won't know what hit us."

Gregor drummed his fingers on the table. "The autopsy found arsenic, isn't that right? How did the autopsy find arsenic? Why did the medical examiner go looking for it?"

Lou Emiliani was pacing. "There wasn't enough cocaine to account for the convulsions, according to him. So it bothered him. So he put all the stuff aside. And then, when the Kelly thing hit, and she was full of arsenic, it hit him that arsenic causes convulsions if you take enough of it. So he ran a few more tests, and—bingo."

"Enough arsenic to cause convulsions," Gregor said.

"Yes," Lou Emiliani said.

"Enough to cause convulsions and death before it caused significant vomiting," Gregor said.

"Enough to kill a herd of elephants," Lou said.

Gregor almost got out of his own seat. "In a church office at six o'clock in the evening with other people in the same room?"

"I think they were in the next room over," Lou said, "but yeah. That's the idea."

SEVEN

1

At first, Bennis Hannaford thought the call was going to be just one more annoyance. Usually, when people called from the *Inquirer* or the *Star,* it was because some reporter somewhere had come up with one more good idea about how to get her to talk about Anne Marie. They all wanted to see a feature with a headline like "Hannaford: The Famous Novelist Talks About Her Notorious Sister." Lying on the big double bed in her own bedroom, fully dressed except for the fact that her clogs were lying on the carpet under the window, Bennis didn't see the point of getting up to answer the phone. She was screening all her calls these days, anyway. She had to. As the execution got closer and closer, more and more people came out of the woodwork, looking for a piece of her. There were editors in New York who wanted nothing more than to have her write a "memoir" of the murders, and agents who wanted it even more badly. There were ghost writers by the legion, apparently of the opinion that even a woman with fifteen best-selling novels to her credit would need a little "help" when it came to writing something like this. But she had no intention of writing something like this. She knew that her books gave the impression of being full of self-revelation. It was an illusion. The reason Bennis had always liked fiction was that it allowed her to hide almost entirely behind the antics of characters she had invented and could control. What was worse, what she wanted to hide was the mess they all now wanted her to reveal: the chaotic terrorism of that big house in Bryn Mawr. Sometimes, in the middle of the night, she woke up thinking she was fifteen again, home from boarding school for Christmas vacation. If Gregor was there, she was all right. She felt his body beside her and that woke her up, completely. For some reason, she never imagined that he was one of the countless men she had seen fit to traffic in during the years when she'd been "free." Sometimes, though, Gregor was not there. He was traveling, or she had worked so late that she hadn't wanted to go upstairs and disturb him. Then it took her minutes to realize that she wasn't at home again, and she would lie very still, holding her breath, to hear if her father were prowling in the hallways. That was what Bennis remembered most about being home. Her father never slept, and his wakefulness was always pitilessly, viciously angry. Her mother was the only one who could calm him. Her mother was the only one he would not wake.

When the voice came over the answering machine, Bennis was thinking that, if she hadn't promised Gregor, she would be smoking right this minute. Surely, that would be the thing it made most sense to do, in these last days before Anne Marie died: smoke, and in the evenings, drink. The odd thing was that, now that she had quit smoking, she couldn't drink, either. All her favorite drinks suddenly tasted foul. Even Benedictine tasted foul. The only thing that didn't seem to taste awful without a cigarette to mask it was Drambuie, which actually tasted better, but she couldn't drink too much of that at once. It was meant to be taken in small glasses, after dinner, as dessert.

When the voice started talking, Bennis recognized it, but she couldn't place it, and she missed the name. The next thing she heard was ". . . from the *Inquirer*," and then she just shut off her brain. The voice sounded familiar because it was one of the reporters who had been hounding her. She didn't have to deal with it. She drifted off into a memory of Anne Marie's fifteenth birthday dinner, with them all seated at the long table in the dining room and a cake sent in from some caterer in the city.

"Fifteen years old and ugly as sin," her father was saying, and then the voice on the answering machine went, ". . . so I thought you'd better look at it, because whoever this woman is, she really has it in for you."

Bennis sat up in bed. The answering machine turned itself off. She tucked her legs under her almost-yoga style and reached for the phone and the machine. She pressed rewind and play. Outside her big bedroom window, the thin branches of a single spindly tree twisted and snapped in the wind.

"Bennis," the voice on the machine said. "This is Dick Coggins, from the *Inquirer*. I'm sorry I didn't catch you home. It's been a long time since we talked. I'm faxing you a copy of a submission we got this morning from a woman named Edith Lawton. We're turning it down, but it concerns you, and if you ask me, it's really nasty, so I thought you'd better look at it, because whoever this woman is, she really has it in for you."

The fax machine started its staccato burping. Bennis got up and watched the first page as it came out. She remembered Dick Coggins. He was on the op-ed page. He'd tried, once, months ago, to get her to write a piece on the execution, but he'd had the incredible good taste to take no for an answer and not come back for more. The page came all the way out, and she picked it up.

"The Death Penalty Reconsidered," by Edith Lawton.

Bennis sat back down on the bed.

There was, of course, nothing odd about the idea of Edith Lawton submitting an op-ed piece to the *Inquirer*. Edith wanted to be a writer, and submitting pieces was one of the ways one got oneself started being a writer. Bennis herself had suggested that Edith try the op-ed pages. The editors there read what they got and expected to publish at least some blind submissions. If you made it into an important paper, like the *Inquirer* or the *New York Times*, you got read by people who could matter to you in the long run. All in all, op-ed was a good way to get yourself taken seriously on the cheap, if you could do it well. Another page came out of the fax machine. Another page started printing. How had she known, as soon as she saw the title and the by-line, that this was going to be a hatchet job? It was more than Dick Coggins's warning. She would have known even if he hadn't warned her. She thought of herself and Edith in that little coffee place out near Independence Hall and felt sick to her stomach.

The third fax sheet came out and a fourth started. The fourth came out and a fifth started. The printing noise went on and on, and as it did the world got darker, outside and in. I ought to turn on the light, Bennis thought idly, but she didn't move from where she was. Now the spindly tree outside her window looked as if it were about to disappear. Across the street, the people in the town houses had started putting on their lights. Really, Bennis thought, I've got to make up my mind. Either I have to stop helping people who ask me for help, or I have to accept the fact that some of them will be ... Edith Lawton.

The fax machine stopped spitting paper after the sixth page. Bennis got up and got the pages from the table and the floor around it. The table was too small, and faxes were always ending up on the carpet. She sat down on her bed again and turned on the light. It wasn't night, not really. It was only latish afternoon. She thumbed through the pages, catching her own name dotted across them like pats of butter. She caught three factual errors about the history of the death penalty and two about death-penalty law. Trust Edith, Bennis thought. She can never be bothered to check.

"Of course, on a human level, it's more than understandable that Bennis Hannaford would want to put her sister's life above any abstract principles. But the exercise, in someone who has made a reputation on being the moral watchdog of her generation ..."

"It is ironic that the case where Bennis Hannaford should so desperately seek an exception should be the one case where no exception should be given ..."

"It is incumbent on the rest of us to judge by the facts, and not by the emotions. It will be hard to do, because Bennis Hannaford is a consummate manipulator of emotions ..."

"God, but she's such a chunky writer," Bennis said, out loud.

Then she realized that she was staring at the answering machine, where the red lights were steady and unblinking. Gregor was gone. He had been gone all afternoon, and he had phoned an hour ago to tell her he wouldn't be back for dinner.

Bennis got up, folded all six pages of the fax into quarters, and stuffed the wad into a pocket of her jeans. She slipped on her clogs and went out of the bedroom and down the hall into the living room. Her apartment and Gregor's were exactly the same. The only apartment in this building that wasn't the same was old George Tekemanian's, on the first floor, which had been extensively remodeled by his nephew Martin and his wife. She went through the living room to the foyer and out the front door. She ran down the stairs so quickly, she almost fell twice. She didn't stop in at old George's apartment, even though she usually did. She went right on outside, into the cold.

She was wearing a white cotton turtleneck under a flannel shirt—not exactly perfect for February weather—but she was also running, and she didn't really realize how cold it was until she was standing on the step in front of Donna Moradanyan's town-house door, ringing the bell. If Lida Arkmanian had seen her, she would have had a fit. Lida was always convinced that Bennis was trying to kill herself by exposure to the elements. Bennis tried to remember what day of the week it was, and found she couldn't. She tried to remember what Donna did at this time of the afternoon, and couldn't remember that either. She had no idea what she would do if Donna was not home. Then Donna opened the door, and Bennis breathed a sigh of relief.

"Oh, thank God," she said. "Gregor is off somewhere. If you'd been gone too, I think I would have exploded."

"What's the matter?"

Bennis pushed past Donna into the town house's recently renovated foyer. The space was full of decorations for Valentine's Day, ready and waiting to be put up on the street. Bennis took the fax papers out of her pocket and handed them over.

"Dick Coggins from the *Inquirer* sent those to me. They came in today. To him, I mean. They came in to me about five minutes ago."

Donna frowned. "Edith Lawton. Isn't she the one who went on the Net and said that you were phobic about oral sex?"

"That's the one."

Donna flipped through the fax pages and winced. "Oh, for Pete's sake. This is awful. Are they going to publish this?"

"No."

"Oh, thank God." Donna looked around guiltily. "I can't say 'thank God' around Tommy anymore. He tells me not to take the Lord's name in vain. It's very disconcerting having a genius for a son. Do you want some coffee?"

"I want a tranquilizer, but coffee will do. Unless you're going out. I'm sorry to just burst in on you. I hate to say I haven't the faintest idea what your schedule is these days. And I'm not thinking straight about much of anything."

"It's okay. I don't have a schedule today. Russ is picking Tommy up after school and taking him to hockey practice, and then after that they just pick up McDonald's. Only don't tell Linda Melajian about that. She'll think they hate the Ararat and they're abandoning her. I really can't believe Lawton wrote this. How could she have written this?"

"Once she figures out they've turned it down, she'll submit it someplace else. The *Star*. Someplace. Or she'll use it on her website or for that column she writes for that freethought newspaper."

"Freethought? Oh," Donna said. "Now I remember. She's the one who makes some kind of career out of atheism. Why do you suppose she does that? I mean, what's the point?"

"Tibor makes a career out of religion," Bennis pointed out.

"That's not the same thing. Do you think she's trying to start some kind of organization, like that woman, what's her name—"

"Madalyn Murray O'Hair."

"That's the one. I've got a lot of coffee. Come on back."

Donna went off down the hall, waving the pages of the fax in the air as if they were a fan. Bennis took off her clogs and followed. All the floors in Donna's town house were either hardwood or marble. Walking on them in clogs made you sound as if you were setting off heavy artillery. It was incredible how much better she felt, now that she was here. Edith Lawton would not have her op-ed published in the *Inquirer*. She might have it published in the *Star*, but that would be later, and she could deal with it when it came up. It was terrible, the way she lacked perspective, when she was left on her own. She pushed her clogs up against the wall under the coat rack and went down to the back, where the kitchen was.

Donna was bringing tins of cookies down from the top of the refrigerator.

"Do you want some of these?" she asked. "Lida and Hannah are having some kind of Bake-Off. Or something. Are you still upset?"

"A little."

"She's an idiot, Bennis. That's all. And she doesn't even write very well. Sit down and have something to eat. Gregor has got himself involved in another murder. Think about that."

"What murder?"

Donna went over to the television set that sat in a corner of the breakfast nook and turned it on. "I don't know exactly, I wasn't paying any attention, but it will be on if we watch long enough. You really shouldn't worry about it, Bennis, you know you shouldn't. She's just a—gnat. You've dealt with gnats before. You always win."

The television was turned to ABC, which seemed to be showing some tabloid talk show about girls who had decided to get pregnant at twelve so that they'd have somebody to love. Bennis reached into the closest of the cookie tins and found a heap of *loukoumia*.

Donna was right, of course, Bennis thought. Edith Lawton was a gnat, and there was no reason for her to spend her time worrying about her. In the course of her long career, Bennis had run into a dozen such gnats, every one of them desperate "to be a writer," every one of them as self-destructive as hell. If they got a break, they sabotaged it. Once they sabotaged it, they went looking for someone to blame for their failure, and Bennis was always not only handy, but an easy target, the one person they could not help but bitterly resent. Or something. Donna had thrown the pages of the fax on the table. Bennis picked them up and looked through them. The tissue-thin paper had begun to crinkle. The printing had begun to smear.

It was easy to say that it had happened before and it would happen again and she should not worry about it, but she was herself, and she worried about everything. Mostly she worried that someday she would not be able to stand it anymore. She would break, and in breaking she would become somebody else, the very bitch people like Edith Lawton wanted her to be, something cold, like a block of ice. Sometimes she felt as if she were freezing to death even now.

She wondered what Gregor would make of that.

She got up and went to the television and started flipping through the channels with the remote. She hoped that Gregor really was involved in a murder again. It would be a relief, to fret about a murder that did not belong to her.

Donna got down a tin of baklava and put that on the table, too.

"Try CNN," she said. "Even if they don't have the news

of the murder, they'll have the latest about Hillary Clinton. Why does that woman make me so insane?"

Bennis switched to CNN, and sat down to eat baklava by the fistful.

2

Father Robert Healy wasn't sure what he was supposed to do next. He had been warned that, once the press conference had happened, he was unlikely to be left alone. Even if nobody knew that he was the chief suspect in these two killings, that he had bought the poison himself and laid it out in traps in the church basement, they would know that the deaths had happened here, and they would come to see. People had been telling him for years that he was out of touch. For the first time in his life, he had begun to agree with them. It hadn't seemed possible to him that people would behave in the way the Cardinal Archbishop had warned him they would behave. Why would people—not policemen, but just people, not even Catholics—who had nothing to do with these deaths, who had never known any of the victims and did not know him, come to this church just to . . . look? Look at what? It was a beautiful church, of course, exquisite in its way. It had been built by people who had been trying very hard to measure up to the sort of display that had been committed across the street. They had done very well for their time and place. The ceilings in the main body of the church were high and arched in that way that made them seem to rise to the very majesty of heaven. The paintings and the statuary were not the usual Catholic kitsch, but brought from Europe and made by artists who had taken themselves and their work seriously. The pews were hand-carved and polished. Father Healy was proud of this church as his first real parish, proud of its people as well as its art, but he still couldn't understand why a lot of gawkers would want to come from the other side of town, just to stare at it. He especially didn't understand why they would want to come to stare at him, but they did.

The first thing he had done was the first thing he had thought of to do. He had gone to the private chapel that the rectory shared with the convent and got down on his knees.

This place was not as majestic as the church, but nobody knew about it but the priests and the nuns, and it was empty. He had gone to the kneeler in front of the Blessed Virgin and knelt there. Whenever he was in trouble, he went to the Blessed Virgin first. Some people said they could feel Jesus standing at their sides or hear the voice of God whispering in their ears, but for Robert Healy the only aspect of the immortal that had ever been present to him had been Mary. He took out the plain black wood rosary that he carried in his pocket and began to pray the Sorrowful Mysteries. He had no idea if it was the right day of the week. If you did a third part of the rosary—the five-decade short rosary, instead of the fifteen-decade long one—you were supposed to say the Glorious Mysteries on Sunday, Wednesday, and Saturday, the Joyful Mysteries on Monday and Thursday, and the Sorrowful Mysteries on Tuesday and Friday. He found he had no idea what day of the week it was, but that the Sorrowful Mysteries somehow felt right. The Scourging at the Pillar. The Crown of Thorns. Next to the sufferings of Christ, his own were less than trivial. Even if he were arrested and tried and wrongly convicted, even if he were executed in the bargain, his sufferings would be no closer to the Passion than a tapeworm is to a kangaroo on the evolutionary scale. Even so, the thought of execution made him cold at the very pit of his stomach. The cold spread to his legs, and he thought that he had frozen here on his knees. He closed his eyes and stretched out on the floor with his arms flung out at his sides, in the form of a cross, the way they had been taught to do in seminary. He began to say the Hail Mary out loud. The words rose into the air around him like smoke. In a while, they began to cover him. The Agony in the Garden. The Scourging at the Pillar. The Crowning with Thorns. The Carrying of the Cross. The Crucifixion. Death and agony in the desert. The mountains shuddering. The earth cracking apart. The graves giving up their dead. There were people out there who knew nothing of this, who hadn't even heard the story. He thought that if he could get them by the hands, he could show them the truth of it, unfolding out before them, a Passion play that never closed. Christ had died one dark afternoon in Jerusalem, but he was dying still. Christ had risen one Sunday morning, but he was rising still. The Church was a living body, with Christ as its head. If he remembered that, nothing else could touch him.

Hail Mary, full of grace. The Lord is with thee.

He had reached the last bead on his rosary and begun the Salve Regina, in Latin, because that was how he had learned to pray it in Rome. He was at peace. The jangled agitation of the last few hours had left him. He lay for a few more moments in the position in which he had prayed, just to go on feeling the Blessed Virgin alive and watching over him, then he got up.

There was still light coming in from the windows, but not very much of it, and it might have been from a lamp. He had no idea what time it was. He was due to say the vigil Mass at seven, but if he had been in any danger of missing that one of the Sisters would have come to get him. He left the chapel and went down the stairs to the first floor. Looking out the front door, he could see that there were still people milling about in front of the church, going in and out. Maybe, if he did nothing at all about them, and just celebrated Mass as usual, they would stay for the Mass and listen. God had done stranger things. He could manage to convert a few rubber-necking fools who had only come to church in the hopes of seeing someone keel over from arsenic poisoning.

He walked around to the side of the building and looked up at the clock on St. Stephen's spire. It was only five-thirty. He walked over to the side of his own church and slipped in the door there, near the shrine to Mary. The body of the church really was full of people, just like one of the nuns had told him it was. They were mostly subdued, as if, now that they'd gotten there, it had suddenly occurred to them that they shouldn't treat the place like a circus tent. Most of them were not praying, though, and most of them were not sitting down. Instead, they were wandering around the aisles and looking at the paintings. They were going right up to the Communion rail and leaning over it to get a better view of the monstrance and the altar.

He started to withdraw again, then realized that he was not alone in this part of the church. There was someone kneeling in front of the statue of the Blessed Virgin here. This must be the day for people to need Mary—but then, in his experience, every day was the day for people to need Mary. He started to leave, discreetly, so as not to distract this woman in her prayers, when the woman stood up and crossed herself, and he realized it was Mary McAllister.

"Father," she said.

"I didn't mean to bother you," he said.

"You didn't bother me. I didn't even know you were there." They were both whispering. Mary looked out over the church. "It's awful, isn't it. The way they treat this place as if it were a movie theater. And you know what's going to happen. After the scandal and all that. Have they been bothering you?"

"Not so far, no. I was thinking that if some of them stayed for Mass, we might be able to convert them."

"I'll bet half of them are fallen-away Catholics," Mary said. "Except for Edith. Did you know she was here?"

"Edith who?"

"Edith Lawton." Mary gestured into the church. "She lives down the block. You know who she is. She's some kind of professional atheist or something and she writes for that strange little newsletter, all about how awful the Catholic Church is, except she always gets it wrong."

"*Free Thinking*," Father Healy said, suddenly remembering.

"That's it. I don't know if you read it, but it's around here all the time. She comes and puts big stacks of it in the foyer every time it comes out."

"And we leave them there, for people to pick up?"

"Sure, sometimes. Why not? We've got something called the Campus Freethought Alliance at St. Joe's, and they're always throwing their newsletter all over everything. People think it's funny. Besides, it's good for the Church."

"Good for the Church? Why?"

"Well," Mary McAllister said, "you know, secularism is so big today, and there are all the problems in the world, and the scandals in the Church, that people might think there's something to it. But it doesn't take more than two paragraphs to realize they don't know what they're talking about. They get everything wrong. Trust me. Read this stuff for yourself."

"Maybe I'll pick up a copy the next time there's one in the foyer," Father Healy said. "Which one is she, Edith Lawton?"

"The one in the turquoise sweater standing in the front pew on the left. Don't you hate turquoise?"

"I've never really thought of it." Edith Lawton seemed to be a pleasant-looking woman on the cusp of middle age, or maybe just into it, but with good luck in genes. Father Healy shrugged. "She doesn't look at all impressive."

"She isn't impressive. And I can't believe she came here today. Like some kind of vulture. Except, of course, Sister Harriet had to suck up to her—excuse me, Father."

"What do you mean, Sister Harriet had to suck up to her?"

Mary McAllister winced. "I don't think I've ever heard a priest use that term before. Anyway, I don't really know. They were standing with their heads together in the foyer when I came in today. I'm not sure what they were talking about, except that it had something to do with the 'legitimate aspirations of women.' That's the phrase they used."

"Which you accidentally overheard."

"Well, Father, I tried to overhear more, but I couldn't do it without being obvious. And Sister Harriet doesn't trust me as far as she can throw me. She says I'm a male-identified woman. Whatever that means."

"It means your aspirations are actually legitimate."

Mary McAllister laughed, loud enough so that some people turned their heads to look at her. Father Healy had a short feeling of panic, sure that he would be found out and inundated by people wanting to know what he thought had happened to Bernadette Kelly, but he must have been in a shadow. Nobody noticed he was there.

"Anyway, Father," Mary McAllister said, "I couldn't just stand there, because Father Burdock was waiting with some things he needed doing for the Joint Charities fund drive. And Sister Harriet seems to have disappeared, so we're both safe at the moment. Did you need something, or were you just coming in to look at the sightseers before you had to face them at Mass?"

"I was looking for Sister Scholastica," Father Healy said.

"She's gone off to do some errands. She's not expected back until Mass. I think she's even having dinner out. Is it important for you to get in touch with her?"

"No, not really. I just wanted a shoulder to lean on, so to speak."

"Because if it's important, I think Sister Peter Rose knows how to get in touch with her. She's got a cell phone."

"Nuns with cell phones," Father Healy said. "Nuns in full habit with cell phones."

"Sister Scholastica says that she's not really a nun. She's a religious Sister, because nuns take solemn vows and the Sisters of Divine Grace only take simple vows. Do you get all that?"

"Yes," Father Healy said, "but it doesn't matter. What about you? Are you all right? You were praying up a storm when I came in. Is there something wrong at school, or at home, that I could help you with?"

"Not exactly. It's just—did you ever feel that something was missing? I mean, that something was just not there, so that even though your life was just perfect, it just wasn't enough?"

Father Healy blinked. "Well, yes," he said. "Of course I did."

"You did?"

"Do you get this feeling a lot, or did it just sort of show up this morning and hit you on the head?"

"I don't know. It's been going on for a couple of months, I guess. Maybe from the beginning of the year. And I'm getting to be impossible to live with, really. I'm not satisfied with school. I'm not satisfied with the homeless shelter. I'm not satisfied with my boyfriend, and that's really unfair, because he really does try and he's good to me. And half the time I'd rather stay home, except when I do I'm all dissatisfied with that, too. Even my mother says I'm irritable all the time, and all I do is talk to her on the phone."

"Ah," Father Healy said. "Well."

"I'd better let you go, or they'll figure out you're here and just inundate you. Sister Scholastica told Sister Peter Rose that they might have to protect you from being harassed while you're celebrating Mass. It bothers me that people are so awful all the time."

"It bothers me, too," Father Healy said. "Do you know which way Sister Harriet went?"

"So that you can go in the other direction?" Mary McAllister laughed. "I think she went over to her office. At least that's the way she was headed. Maybe you'd better go over to the convent and talk to Sister Peter Rose. Sister Harriet never wants to go over there."

"True," Father Healy said.

"See you later," Mary McAllister said.

Father Healy looked out over the church again, and found his eyes fixed on Edith Lawton. He hadn't known that copies of *Free Thinking* were being given out in his own church foyer, but he had seen the magazine, or newspaper. It was hard to know what to call it, since it was in the shape of a large newspaper like the *New York Times*, but on better paper than newsprint. And Mary McAllister was right. It got everything wrong. It got everything so wrong, it was hard not to think that the editors felt it was too much of an effort to look things up in the dictionary.

He looked at Edith Lawton again—not impressive, not at all. She lacked even the casual sophistication of the Philadelphia suburbs, and her face was as round as a chipmunk's—and then he turned away and went back out of the church. He considered it a grace that no one had noticed him, and gave thanks for it. He would consider it an even greater grace if he managed to get back to his own bedroom without running into anybody he would rather not see. If things were like this when all anybody knew was that Bernadette Kelly had died of arsenic poisoning and Scott Boardman had died of arsenic poisoning, too, what would it be like when the details of this case became too clear for anybody to misunderstand?

He looked at Edith Lawton again and decided he was treating her like a rare animal in a zoo: the village atheist, in captivity. He went out the side door he had come in and felt better for being in the cold air. He thought of himself laying down the rat poison in the boiler room in the church basement and felt a little sick to his stomach.

It was odd how the smallest thing you did, the most innocent thing, could look so damning when it was cast in the wrong kind of light.

3

There was a clock in the window of the newsstand across the street from the small restaurant where Sister Scholastica had had an early dinner, and it startled her, when she saw it, that it was only six o'clock. Like most nuns in traditional orders, she was used to having dinner early, just as she was used to having breakfast early. When you woke up at four and went

to bed at nine, you did almost everything early. The one great
exception, for the Sisters of Divine Grace, was lunch. Lunch
had to be provided at the times most convenient for the students at St. Anselm's school. Because of that, Scholastica
sometimes found herself dizzy with hunger at eleven o'clock,
because it had been so long since she'd eaten and because she
had never been able to choke down more than a piece of toast
when she first woke up. Of course, they prayed the Office and
went to Mass before they actually sat down to breakfast, but
that didn't seem to matter. Scholastica's internal clock did not
adjust. Early morning was early morning. She didn't want to
eat in the early morning.

The friends who had taken Scholastica to dinner were really
only one friend and a husband—a woman who had been in
Scholastica's high-school graduating class, and who had suddenly decided, five years ago, that it was time to have children.
Scholastica had done the math a couple of times—Genevra
would have been forty when the first baby came along, and
forty-three when she had the second one—but the age question
didn't bother her as much as the way Genevra responded to
having children in her life. Maybe there was some truth to the
things some people said about women waiting too long to have
children. Genevra was wound tight as a drum, so hyperactive
that the smallest noise seemed to make her jump out of her
skin. She was never satisfied with the children, who were, in
their turn, unruly and sullen. Scholastica had spent the whole
meal not saying the things she wanted to say. Even the parents
of her own students didn't want to hear her ideas on child
rearing, on the rather strange assumption that a woman who
spent all day with people under the age of twelve couldn't
possibly know what they were like because she'd never given
birth to one from her own personal womb. They had gone to
an Arabic restaurant, and the children had refused to eat anything that could be had from the menu. They wanted Mc-
Donald's. If they couldn't have that, they wanted to tell
everyone in the room how gross the food here was, and how
if they even touched it with their little fingers, it would make
them puke. The little one had perfected a high-pitched whine
that could have cut through glass. By the time they had
reached the small cups of mud-thick coffee, Scholastica was

wishing she had begged off this evening even if it meant appearing to be rude.

Out on the sidewalk, the children tugged at Genevra's arms. The older one, the boy, sat down on the sidewalk and would not let himself be pulled up.

"I'm sure everything will be all right," Genevra's husband Tom was saying. "It's not like the scandals. It doesn't have anything to do with the Church. It isn't the fault of the Archdiocese of Philadelphia that some kid murdered his wife and walked into a parish church to commit suicide."

"I'm not going *anywhere*," the older child said. "And you can't *make* me."

"Well," Scholastica said.

"You really don't have to take the bus," Genevra said. "We can afford to put you in a taxi. Even without my working full-time."

"I keep telling you," Tom said. "I don't need you to work full-time."

"I don't want to go in a taxi," Scholastica said. "Really. I've been riding in taxis all day."

"With something like this, the trick is to make sure the police are efficient," Tom said. "That's the biggest danger. That they're going to screw it up, you know, and drag it out. I mean, it ought to be obvious to anybody what happened. The wife was so sick she got too much for him. The kid killed her, then he felt guilty about it. It happens all the time."

"You can't make me *either*," the younger child said, but she didn't sit down on the sidewalk. She had that odd fastidiousness some girls did even from infancy. She didn't want anything near her to have anything to do with dirt.

Scholastica looked up the street and thought she saw a bus far in the distance. A little flag went up at the back of her mind that said: see? prayer can be very effective. She put her arms under her cape and wrapped them around her body. The wind was cold and stiff and made the hem of her habit whip around her legs.

"Well," she said again.

"I keep telling Tom it's not a question of if he needs me to work full-time," Genevra said. "It's the future. We're going to want to send them to private schools. We're going to want to send them to college. What am I going to be making, if I take too much time off?"

"You're not taking any time off," Tom said. "You've just got a reduced schedule."

This time, Scholastica was sure of it. There was a bus. Her cape had a collar. She flipped it up against what would have been her neck, if the folds of her veil weren't hanging in front of it. Sometimes she regretted choosing a life that did not allow her to have children of her own. She never regretted choosing one that did not allow her to marry. The bus stopped three blocks up. Scholastica moved closer to the bus stop sign and leaned a little into the street, to make sure the driver would see her.

"Think of it," Tom said. "You'll get to meet Gregor Demarkian. The Armenian-American Hercule Poirot."

"I met him years ago," Sister Scholastica wanted to say, but that would have taken explanations, so she didn't. The bus pulled to a stop in front of her, and she leaned over to give Genevra a standard nonpeck on the cheek.

"I'll call you next week," she promised. Then she smiled at Tom and hurried up the steps into the bus, her token in her hand. The other nuns at St. Anselm's had told her that there were drivers who would not take fares from nuns in habits, but the idea of accepting that kind of favor made Scholastica extremely uncomfortable. She had the token in the stile before the driver could say anything at all. Then she smiled at him, with more warmth than she had managed for Tom, and went to the back of the bus.

There were some favors that were so universal, and automatic, that Scholastica had given up worrying about them. It was the end of the day, and rush hour. The bus was packed. A young man in his twenties got up to give her his seat, and she thanked him and sat down. The old woman she sat down next to patted her arm, and said, "Bless you, Sister." Scholastica wondered, idly, what it had been like to be a nun in the days when people knew what it was nuns did, and how important it was that they did it. These days, people had the money to write checks for what they wanted. It wasn't the case that if the nuns didn't work for almost nothing, their children wouldn't be able to go to Catholic school.

The bus lumbered, and Scholastica closed her eyes. This

was why she hadn't wanted a taxi. She needed the time to unkink. For some reason, she had the prayer on the Miraculous Medal running through her head: O Mary, conceived without sin, pray for us who have recourse to you. It hummed through her brain like bees on telephone wires at the start of the summer. The first time she had ever received a Miraculous Medal had been right before her First Holy Communion. She could still remember the old nun who had taught religion at her elementary school, leading the whole class over to the church where the medals were sitting in a big box near the Communion rail. There were brown scapulars, too, hanging from the hands of the statue of Mary in the little wall niche next to the candles. The nuns in her elementary school had been Sisters of Divine Grace. She wondered if that was usual. Did girls always enter the same orders their elementary school teachers came from? The method was working. She was relaxing. She was at peace for the first time all day.

She was so much at peace, she nearly fell asleep and missed her stop. She saw the lit windows of Cardman's Books at the last minute. She would have jumped to her feet, but in her long habit it was nearly impossible. As it was, she knocked her veil off center, letting her hair, as grey now as it was red, spill out. She smiled sheepishly at everybody around her and tucked it back in. There was something that was good about the old habits with their collars and their wimples. You'd practically have to be decapitated to have your hair spill out. Scholastica went for the back door, pulling the bell cord on her way. When the bus screamed to a stop, she went out by herself, feeling like a black thing in the night. There was something about habits she could get behind. The Sisters of Divine Grace should change theirs from black to something colorful, like the sky-blue that used to be worn by the Sisters of the Immaculate Heart of Mary. Scholastica was tired of looking like the Ghost of Christmas Yet to Come.

She actually had four blocks to walk to get to St. Anselm's. She could have transferred to another bus, going in the right direction, but it hadn't seemed to her worth the effort. The cold was waking her up. Her nerves were no longer on edge. She turned right and hurried along the crowded street toward the floodlights that illuminated the spires of both St. Anselm's and St. Stephen's. When she got to St. Stephen's, she noticed that something seemed to be going on there, as usual. The notice board at the end of the walk said something about a "reading circle." Scholastica liked to read, but she had never liked the idea of sitting in a circle and talking about a book. In her early days in the convent, she had resented most the habit of having a Sister read aloud at meals and recreation. To this day, she couldn't stand the sound of audio books on the convent van's radio.

She crossed the street and went down along the side of St. Anselm's, to get to the convent entrance. She let herself in the wrought-iron gate and looked around at the courtyard. The school was dark. It would be, at this time of night. The convent was mostly dark, too. It couldn't be much later than twenty minutes to seven. She went down to the annex where the offices were and tried the door. It was locked. She let herself in with her key.

Whoever had been last to leave this place had not been very careful. There were lights on in the hall, and in at least two of the offices. Scholastica left the lights on in the hall and turned the office lights off automatically. "Let me inform you," her novice mistress had once said, "of the concept of the kilowatt-hour." She got to her office and tried her door, but that was locked as well. She got out her keys and opened up, wondering who had bothered with the lock, and why. She had told Thomasetta long ago that there was nothing in her office that needed to be protected like money in a vault.

She knew as soon as she opened her door that there was something out of place, but because of the way the light was coming in from the door she couldn't tell what it was. Her first thought was that there might have been some vandalism. That would explain why her door was locked. Somebody had gotten in and made a mess. She reached for the light switch and flipped it up, wondering if she was about to find graffiti spray painted across her cabinets.

Instead, she found Sister Harriet Garrity, slumped across the top of her desk, her body weighing down manila file folders stuffed thick with papers and stuck all over with colored Post-it notes. Her face was blue. Her neck was raw and caked with brown blood, as if something had torn at it, trying to rip out her throat. There was vomit everywhere, and as soon as she saw it, Scholastica knew what it was she had first noticed as wrong. It was the smell, that was what it was. The room had been shut up, maybe for hours, with the heat on, and now there was a smell so sweet and intolerable and thick she almost threw up herself.

She reeled backward, out of the room, and dropped to her knees. She was so dizzy, she didn't think she could breathe. She put her head down between her knees and then all the way to the floor. The floor felt cold and good against her skin. She would have to get Father, she thought. She would have to get Gregor Demarkian.

But right now, all she wanted to do was scream.

EIGHT

If Gregor Demarkian had had a cell phone, John Jackman would have been able to get in touch with him anywhere in the city; and the newspapers would never have had any reason for WPLD to show a picture of Cavanaugh Street looking as if a bomb had gone off there. Instead, Gregor had meandered home from his last interview with the Philadelphia police, stopping at one store to pick up a box of dark chocolate Godiva raspberry crowns for Bennis and at another to buy a copy of the latest Nora Roberts for Tibor, and then walking up one street and down another looking in windows. He saw a sequined and beaded evening scarf, so obviously not made of real silk that it was painful to look at. He saw a giant ostrich costume made out of fake red feathers, left over from New Year's Eve. Eventually he got a cab, but the driver had the radio turned to a foreign language station. It wasn't a foreign language he understood. He had a copy of the *Philadelphia Inquirer* and read that instead. There was something very wrong with the water mains near city hall. The mayor was concerned. A study showed that drug use was down among the teenagers of Philadelphia, but since the study had been done by asking those teenagers whether they took drugs or not, he didn't put much credence in it. He did think over a little of what he had heard about the deaths of Scott Boardman and Bernadette Kelly, but until he had a chance to see the scenes and go through the papers for himself, he didn't expect to have much of a handle on it. He did worry, a little, about this business of being consulted both by the Church and the police, but he didn't worry about it long. John Jackman was right. The Church was not paying him, and had not offered to pay him. The Cardinal Archbishop had only asked him to help. He would never have helped in any way that would have concealed the truth, if the truth was not what the Cardinal Archbishop wanted it to be. This was why he never took consulting fees from individuals or private organizations. Real conflicts of interest came at the end, when there was no way to escape the fact that your client was hip deep in culpability.

The cab turned the corner onto Cavanaugh Street, and for a moment Gregor thought he was looking at another of Donna Moradanyan Donahue's extravaganzas. This time, instead of just wrapping Holy Trinity Armenian Christian Church in red and white crepe paper, she had put up lights. There were lights everywhere. They illuminated the front of his own small brown brick apartment building. Donna Moradanyan *had* made something of an extravaganza of that. There was a gigantic heart, studded with red-and-white twinkling Christmas lights, that reached from the windows of the empty top-floor apartment to just above the windows on the first floor. It was good that it was hollow in the middle, or nobody would have been able to see out. How far away was Valentine's Day?

The cab slowed to a crawl, and Gregor suddenly saw why. The street was full of police cars—three black-and-whites and an unmarked that only a little old lady who never watched anything but *Barney* reruns could mistake for an ordinary person's car. There were television people, too, although not as many of them as there might have been. Gregor saw one sound truck and a reporter with a mike being set up in front of hot lights. His stomach lurched. Cavanaugh Street was the safest place in the city of Philadelphia. That didn't mean it was invulnerable. And there were accidents, too, although this didn't seem to be one. Gregor scanned the vehicles anxiously, but not one of them was an ambulance.

He took a wad of bills out of his pocket and threw them into the front seat. "Let me out here," he said. "Keep the change."

He was at least two blocks away from his own building. On the street, it was cold, but that made it easier. He looked at the little knots of people near him and saw nobody he knew. He looked at his own building and saw nothing in the way of a police line. At last he spotted Bennis, standing on the steps in front of their own building's front door, talking to a tall black man who had to be John Jackman. He pushed past a couple of other people, including a cameraman for WPCT who was swearing at a minicam, and made it to the clutch of cops standing around the bright yellow fire hydrant as if they were dogs waiting to take their turns. Who had decided to paint fire hydrants yellow?

"Bennis," he said, reaching the steps.

Bennis turned. "Oh, thank God," she said. "Here he is."

"Where have you been?" John Jackman demanded. "Aren't you on a mobile? What's the matter with you?"

"Of course he isn't on a mobile," Bennis said. "He barely has e-mail."

"Will you tell me what's going on?" Gregor said.

John Jackman tugged his arm. "Let's go. My car. We've been looking for you for an hour."

"That's what all this is about?" Gregor looked from one end of the street to the other. "You sent three police cars with their lights flashing just to find out where I was."

"We've got a major problem," Jackman said.

"And what are you doing here?" Gregor let himself be pulled toward the unmarked, unprotesting. "Does the deputy commissioner make a habit of paying personal visits to consultants on homicide cases? What are you doing?"

"Wait," Bennis said.

She ran down the steps and across the sidewalk and caught Gregor just as John Jackman was about to push him into the car. She gave him a quick peck on the cheek, and said, "Take care of yourself. And say hello to Scholastica for me."

Gregor pecked air and half fell backwards, because Jackman was pushing him.

"We've got a problem," Jackman said again. "I don't know where you've been, but we've had a bulletin out for you on every radio station in the greater metropolitan area. What's the matter with you? Don't you even listen to music?"

"The cab driver was listening to salsa," Gregor said.

Jackman's driver turned around. "You want to go straight to the church?" he asked.

"Straight," Jackman said. Then he turned to Gregor. "We've had another murder."

"And that's it?" Gregor demanded. "That's why you staged

a major siege on Cavanaugh Street? What were you thinking?"

"It's not about the dead body," Jackman said.

"Then what is it about?"

Jackman threw himself back on the seat and stared at the car's upholstered ceiling. "Look," he said. "Shut up and wait until we get there. You'll see what it is soon enough. What do you know about the Reverend Roy Phipps?"

"Not a lot."

"Well," Jackman said, "you will."

PART TWO

The first born from the dead
—COL. 1:18

ONE

1

Gregor Demarkian would have spent the ride across the city making John Jackman explain what was going on, but he didn't have a chance. Almost as soon as they were off Cavanaugh Street and out in real traffic, Jackman was leaning over the front seat, talking frantically into the shortwave radio. Gregor found himself thinking that it would be a good thing if the deputy commissioner's car was fitted out with a shortwave in the back—and then how idiotic it was that Jackman wanted to go into administration. What was this man going to do behind a desk, with no real contact with ongoing investigations? Jackman was one of the most totally committed officers Gregor had ever met. Even as a rookie, still in uniform and studiously ignored by the men who considered themselves "real" detectives, John Jackman had been unable to approach a crime scene without bonding with it. Some people loved their families. Some people had hobbies they couldn't live without. John Jackman loved the half-panicked miasma that surrounded a newly found body, the barely controlled chaos that seeped into the bones of everybody responsible for bringing order to the scene. It always looked so well organized on television shows, so much a matter of training and skill and remembered organization. In real life it was a nagging, edgy fear that you would do something wrong, that you would step sideways when you should step back or drop a piece of paper you didn't even know you had in your pocket and contaminate the crime scene forever.

Most of Philadelphia was quiet, and well lit. Whatever crisis John Jackman had on his hands, its urgency had not seeped into the rest of the population. They passed through the kind of neighborhood where the bars would open as soon as the law allowed and stay open until the law required them to close. Gregor remembered how shocked he had been, in college, to discover that there were men who would sit down on a barstool at eight o'clock in the morning and have a couple of beers before going in to work. He tried to figure out if they would be passing anywhere near the University of Pennsylvania campus, but he had never been particularly good at directions. He didn't know where he was. The houses in this neighborhood were shabby, and mostly cut up into apartments. The one small park they passed looked like it needed to be raked. There were dead leaves and broken bottles on the ground, even though this was February.

Then they turned a corner, and Gregor was suddenly able to see light, far too much light, right ahead of them. He leaned toward the front just as John Jackman slumped backward, but the scene was too far away to make sense, and too bright. He sat back himself and asked,

"What's that ahead of us? It looks like somebody's setting off fireworks on the ground."

"It's St. Anselm's and St. Stephen's," Jackman said.

Gregor slid forward again. Now that he knew enough to look for the spires, he had no trouble finding them, but the scene on the ground still made no sense. He made out the Channel 6 Action News van, mostly because its ABC logo seemed to be lit by a spotlight and facing right toward him. After that, all he could get was an impression of people, hundreds of people, far more than there should have been.

"I don't get it," he said. "What is that, rubberneckers? Why don't you have your people clear the area?"

"It's not rubberneckers. It's a demonstration. And a counterdemonstration."

"A demonstration of what?"

Jackman tapped the driver on the shoulder, and he sped up, just a little. They were three blocks away, and those blocks were clear. It was only when you got to the corners where the churches stood that you ran into a solid wall of people. Past the Channel 6 Action News van, Gregor got sight of what seemed to be a man in a white bedsheet, wearing a gold foil crown on his head and gold-painted . . . wings.

"Wings," he said cautiously.

Jackman pulled him back and leaned forward himself. "Yeah, wings," he said. "Wings and halos. They told me about the wings and halos. Shit."

"Do you want me to pull up to the side entrance so you can go around to the back and avoid the crowd?" the driver said.

Jackman shook his head. "Let us out here. The whole point is to get ourselves on television. Let the good people of Philadelphia know that their police are on the case, right to the highest levels. Do we know if the Cardinal has arrived yet?"

"No," the driver said.

The car pulled up to the curb. John Jackman got out, and Gregor followed him. They were now less than half a block away. Gregor could see other news vans, and the tight crowd of demonstrators in their white sheets and gold wings that seemed to be clogging the street between the two churches. This was not a spontaneous demonstration, at least not entirely. The demonstrators had professionally printed signs, the kind you usually had to put orders in for weeks in advance. GOD HATES SIN one of them read. Another read YOU WON'T BE GAY IN HELL. As they got closer, Gregor realized that at least some of the sound they were hearing was music. The angels were singing.

"What's that music?" he asked Jackman.

"How the hell am I supposed to know?" Jackman said. "It's probably something Rapid Roy wrote all by himself."

"That's who these people are? They're connected to Roy Phipps?"

"Right. They've got a full gospel something or the other church down the street. You know the kind of names these places have. They annoy Dan Burdock a lot."

"Dan Burdock is the pastor at St. Stephen's," Gregor said.

They had pushed far enough into the crowd for Gregor to see that there were, indeed, counterdemonstrators. It took him a moment to place the man at their head, but then he did: Chickie George, the man he had met when he'd come to look over St. Stephen's and St. Anselm's after he'd talked with the Cardinal. Chickie George's sign was not professionally made, and it showed. The cardboard was too thin to make for an effective sign. The letters, drawn hastily with a black felt-tip pen, wavered slightly. Their message, however, was unmistakable: Queer Nation.

"I didn't realize St. Stephen's had this big a congregation," Gregor said.

"It doesn't." They had reached the line of uniformed officers standing near St. Anselm's front walk. Jackman pulled over the first one he saw, shouted in his ear, and got something that looked like directions. He grabbed Gregor by the arm and pulled him along. "They've got a cordon up on the other side of the block," he said, shouting a little to get heard over the singing. "It's not doing any good. They're coming through the side doors of the church and then out the front."

"Who are?"

"Half the gay men in the city," Jackman said.

Now that they were right in the middle of the demonstration, Gregor could feel how wrong it was, and not only wrong but ugly. Everything in this place was anger. Even the nuns standing on St. Anselm's front steps looked angry. Roy Phipps's people exuded a will to violence so clear and so malevolent, Gregor could taste it. Chickie George was not significantly calmer, and some of the men around him were murderous.

Gregor tugged at Jackman's sleeve. "You'd better get these people away from each other," he said urgently. "They're going to explode."

Jackman whirled around. "We can't," he said desperately. "Don't you get it? We can't touch anybody until they start something serious. We just settled a huge lawsuit over gay-bashing. And you know what happens if we touch Roy. Roy knows how to use the courts. We can't do a damn thing."

It was then that the angels started chanting. "Burn in hell," they said, and then, louder, "Burn in hell. Scott Roger Boardman is burning in hell."

Out in the middle of the crowd, Chickie George reached down and grabbed the nearest angel by the crotch. The angel whirled around and hit Chickie in the side of the head with his YOU WON'T BE GAY IN HELL sign. Chickie dropped his own sign and doubled over. Blood was spurting out of his ear. Two more angels dropped their signs. One of them kicked Chickie in the rear. The other aimed a ham-fisted punch to his midsection, and Chickie went down.

"Here we go," Jackman said.

Somewhere in the lines of police, a whistle went off. The uniformed cops began moving in. It almost didn't matter. It was almost too late. By now everybody was kicking and screaming and gouging, the angels and the gay men both. A very young woman and a nun in habit came racing off the steps of St. Anselm's and into the crowd. A man in a clerical collar and black clothes came racing off the steps of St. Stephen's. They all converged on Chickie George at once, only to be met by one of the angels, a big one, shoving them out of the way with his arms and kicking out at Chickie with his boots. They were big boots with weather spikes in the soles of them. When they hit Chickie's clothes they tore them and the flesh underneath them. There was blood everywhere.

Jackman grabbed two uniformed patrolmen and pushed them in Chickie's direction. He followed them. The young woman from St. Anselm's had got hold of the angel's sign and was using it to hit the angel over and over again in the side of the head. The angel didn't seem to notice. He wasn't bleeding. Other people were. Two or three of the angels were down. So where several of the gay men. You couldn't move in the street without stepping into blood.

Jackman got to Chickie George with Gregor right behind him. He got hold of the angel and dragged him off, throwing him into the arms of two waiting patrolmen who wrestled him to the ground. The sheet tore and flapped. The angel was wearing the uniform of some gas station somewhere. Gregor leaned over and saw that Chickie was conscious and breathing. He was not in tears.

"We've got to get him out of here," the young woman said. She was in tears.

"Wait for the ambulance," Gregor told her, having to shout over what now seemed to be a full-scale riot. "He's been hit in the head. You shouldn't move him."

"I'll kill that man," the young nun said. "I don't care what the Ten Commandments say. I'll kill that man."

Chickie George rolled over slightly and smiled. "You go, Sister." His voice sounded like a radio speaker more than halfway to dead.

The man in the clerical collar looked up. "There's the stretcher. Okay, Chickie, you're going to the hospital."

Jackman came back to them. "Listen," he shouted, "we're going to give the ambulance guys time to get this guy out of here, then we're going to teargas. You've all got to get out of the street. Get back inside. Do it now."

"I want to go with Chickie," the young woman said.

One of the ambulance guys grabbed her by the wrist and motioned her to follow him. John Jackman herded the rest of them toward St. Stephen's through the only break in the crowd any of them could see.

"Oh, no," the young nun said. "I've got to get back to the other side."

Jackman kept pushing her along. There was no time. She could get back across the street sometime later. Down the block somewhere, there was the sound of glass breaking. Gregor had a sinking conviction that he knew what it was.

"That's going to be Roy Phipps's church, isn't it?" he asked Jackman.

"Let's just hope that's all it is," Jackman said.

There was another break in the crowd—caused, Gregor saw, by two patrolmen who were clearing their path—and they all pushed through St. Stephen's front gates and up to the church's front steps. The street was full of people, and they were all crazy. Men like the ones who attended Roy Phipps's church forgot that gay men were at least as much men as they were gay. Some of them might be small and delicate, but most of them were tall, broad, strong and, on top of that, they worked out. There was no way to tell who was getting the better of this fight. The cops were pulling up a van with a loudspeaker on it. Some of the people lying in the street were recognizable as angels, but some of the angels must have lost their costumes. Some of the gay men were making an effort to strip them off.

"Now hear this," the loudspeaker said. "Vacate this area immediately. I repeat. Vacate this area immediately."

"Let's go," Jackman said, pushing them all those last few feet to St. Stephen's front door.

Gregor turned back at the last moment, and that was how he happened to see it, the image that would forever afterward define this riot in the history of Philadelphia.

There was a gay man with a feather boa wrapped around his neck, pummeling an angel with his sign, over and over again about the head and shoulders. Another angel, already on the ground, reached up and touched the boa at its lower tip. A second later, the boa exploded in flames, and the gay man was on the ground, his shirt on fire, his pants on fire, his skin turning black in the unnatural light.

"Jesus Christ," Jackman said.

Then he pushed Gregor all the way back into St. Stephen's foyer and ran out to the aid of the man on fire.

2

It took nearly two hours to clear the street. There were too many people injured on the ground to use the tear gas after all. That left nothing but phalanxes of uniformed cops to clear the area, and nobody wanted to leave. For the first half hour, Gregor sat in St. Stephen's foyer and watched the action. Every once in a while, Dan Burdock—the man in clerical black—would come out to bring in one of the gay men that Jackman had convinced to leave the fray. Most of them were bruised. Many of them were bleeding. Of course, the angels were doing no better.

Most of them were bruised and bleeding, too, and, unlike their gay opponents, most of them didn't have sense enough not to fight with the police. Police vans came and went. Gregor found himself surprised that there were that many pairs of handcuffs in the entire city of Philadelphia. The young nun who had been with the young woman at Chickie George's side came out and tugged him by the sleeve.

"Mary called from the hospital. I mean she called across the street, and they called me."

"And?"

"Chickie's going to be all right. He's got four broken ribs, but it isn't anything serious. He doesn't even have a concussion."

"What about the man who was set on fire?"

The young nun looked away. "I don't know. I don't even know if she knows about it."

Well, Gregor thought. She probably didn't know about it. It happened after she'd left. Out on the street, all sorts of things seemed to be happening, but none of them made any sense.

Some of the angels had never moved from their original positions. They were kneeling on the sidewalk by St. Stephen's front gate, frozen solid.

Jackman came in one more time, with one more gay man, and Gregor grabbed him. "Look," he said. "I can cross the street and do what I came to do. What's the point of keeping me in here?"

"How about making sure that none of my officers hits you over the head by accident?"

"So walk with me."

Jackman looked outside. It was no calmer now than it had been a few minutes before, but Gregor didn't think he had expected it to be. What it really looked like was the night scene in an early Fellini movie. It was full dark, and there were all kinds of lights everywhere: the streetlights, the lights from the churches and the other buildings on the street, the lights the police had put up to "illuminate the area." In all this artificial light, the battlers looked more animated than real, like the characters in one of those New Age video games where verisimilitude mattered more than plot. Even their bleeding looked fake.

"All right," Jackman said.

Gregor felt him grab him by the arm and tug. He went willingly. He wanted to be out of this foyer, but he wasn't stupid enough to think he could cross this street at this moment without getting hurt, unless he had some kind of protection. Coming out into the air, he was surprised, again, at just how cold it was. For a while, in the middle of the riot, he hadn't noticed the cold, only his own fear and the feeling that it would be easy for it to turn to panic. Jackman dragged him across the street to St. Anselm's front walk. They both said hello to the uniformed patrolman standing there, his entire purpose to keep people out of St. Anselm's unless they belonged there and could prove it. Up on the steps that led to the front doors, it was quieter. Jackman stopped for a moment and looked back over the scene.

"What a mess," he said. "Do you know this is going to be a disaster?"

"It is a disaster," Gregor said.

"For the department. Because you know what's going to happen. No matter what we do, no matter what happens out here, it's all going to be our fault. Everything. We didn't get here fast enough. We got here too fast. We didn't move in fast enough. We moved in at all. We were unnecessarily rough with . . . pick your favorite party."

"I don't think it could have been helped," Gregor said.

Jackman shrugged. "It doesn't matter. Reason and logic don't matter. Fairness and truth don't matter. When the dust clears from this thing, we're going to be up on the carpet in front of one of those special commissions, and it will be a damned miracle if I don't lose my job."

Gregor would have said something comforting, except that he couldn't think of anything. It was entirely possible that what Jackman had said was true, and for some reason it was enormously depressing, even more depressing than the scene on the street. He scanned the crowd one more time and found Roy Phipps, standing on the sidelines, dressed in an ordinary business suit and not moving.

"He doesn't seem to be taking part in this riot," Gregor said.

"He's a very smart man," Jackman said sourly. "Thirty demonstrations and six riot situations since he got to Philadelphia, and we haven't been able to arrest him once. The body is supposed to be in some kind of office annex behind the church. We can go through and out the back."

They went through and out the back, moving as quietly as they could, because in spite of what was going on outside, there was a priest at the altar celebrating Mass. Maybe, Gregor thought, it was because of what was going on outside. He wondered where the worshipers had come from. Some of them were nuns, and that was easy enough to understand, but some were ordinary lay people. Gregor couldn't imagine they'd come through that crowd outside with all the fighting going on, but some of them must have, or else seen the mess in the street and come in by the side. Most of the lay people seemed to be workingmen and women still in working clothes: mechanic's uniforms, nurse's uniforms, waitress's uniforms.

"Daily communicants," Jackman said shortly, and Gregor had to remind himself that Jackman's full name was John Henry Newman Jackman and that he'd been brought up Catholic and educated at Catholic schools. "You'd be surprised how many there still are," he said. "Daily communicants, I mean. People who go to Mass every day and receive Communion every day. You'd think all that would have gone out with Vatican II."

They went out the side door near the statue of Mary and into the courtyard. That was lit up, too, but the lights were concentrated on one small place on the first floor of a long, low annex. Behind them, out in the street, a sudden surge of sound rose up and broke and then died abruptly. Jackman ignored it.

"I can't know what it was," he told Gregor. "I don't even want to speculate. There's the Cardinal Archbishop."

The long low building—the annex, Gregor supposed—was cordoned off, with a uniformed patrolman at the door and a bustle of tech men in white smocks milling around inside. Just outside it, though, there were two low benches, side by side. The Cardinal Archbishop was standing next to one of those, leaning over to talk to Sister Scholastica, who was sitting.

"The Cardinal Archbishop of Philadelphia, Roy Phipps, and the Gay and Lesbian Alliance of Greater Philadelphia, all in one night," Jackman said. "I ought to be canonized."

"You're not dead yet," Gregor told him.

Sister Scholastica caught sight of them and stood up, her veil whipping out behind her as soon as it was free of the bench. "Oh, Gregor, I'm so glad you're here. I really am. You have no idea—"

"Mr. Demarkian seems to be working with the police," the Cardinal Archbishop said stiffly. "Possibly it would be wise if you refrained from making statements until you have an attorney present."

"Oh, Your Eminence, don't be silly. Hello, Mr. Jackman."

"Mr. Jackman is the deputy commissioner of police," the Cardinal Archbishop said.

"I found the body," Scholastica told Gregor. "Sister Harriet Garrity's body. She wasn't, you know, a Sister like me, from my order. She was the parish coordinator. She didn't wear a habit or anything like that. She didn't live in a convent."

"How did you find her?" Gregor asked.

Scholastica sat down again. "She was in my office. I was out this afternoon. I had dinner with friends. And then when I came back I decided to look in my office to see if I had any messages. Because Thomasetta, you know, she's supposed to make copies and bring them to the convent, but it gets hectic and she doesn't always remember. And so I went to my office and opened the door and there she was."

"You're sure she was dead?"

"She was cold as stone, Gregor, and she was—she was blue." Scholastica looked at her hands. "I didn't like her, that's the trouble. I never liked her. She was one of those women, you know, officious and self-righteous and always so politically correct, and I've only been here a few weeks, and she was already driving me crazy. I don't know. Maybe I just feel guilty."

"You came back when?"

"I don't know. Five-thirty. Maybe six," Scholastica said.

"And these offices close when?"

"Oh, at five, like any other offices. Except that I'm not usually here after four, you know, because of the school day."

Gregor looked at the tech men in their white coats, and at the annex. "So the office closed at five, and you showed up half an hour to an hour later, and she was cold. I'd have to ask the medical examiner, but I think that means she must have already been dead at five. Shouldn't somebody have noticed that she was in your office?"

"The door was locked," Scholastica said. "I had to use my key to get in. I don't know."

"And people wouldn't have found that suspicious?"

"Well," Scholastica said, "you can ask Thomasetta, or Peter Rose, but I don't think so. I think they would just have thought that somebody did it accidentally. Because you can set the door to lock automatically when you go out, and sometimes people jiggle it wrong or they slam too hard when they leave the office and it sets itself. It doesn't matter, really. There are dozens of keys that could open it. It's not really a problem."

"Do you think it's odd that nobody would have opened it?" Gregor asked.

"Oh, no. Not really. Everybody knew I was going to be away today. There wouldn't be any need to make a big fuss about it. They all knew I had a key. Thomasetta would just have put my messages in my mailbox and gone on home." Scholastica rubbed her eyes. "I acted like an idiot. I started screaming at the top of my lungs. Reverend Mother General is going to be very disappointed in me."

"Reverend Mother General will have nothing to reproach you for," the Cardinal Archbishop said. Then he turned to Gregor and John Jackman. "A little while ago, I went into the church and looked out at the problem in the street. The demonstration seemed to me to have devolved into a full-scale riot. Would you say I was correct to think so?"

"Yes, Your Eminence," Jackman said. "I would say you were correct to think so."

"And this riot was caused by whom?" the Cardinal Archbishop said.

John Jackman blinked. "I don't know how to answer that. Riots aren't caused like that. They're the result of a chaotic situation—"

"But the chaotic situation was brought on by the decision of the Reverend Roy Phipps to stage a demonstration in front of St. Stephen's Church in response to the news that Sister Harriet had been murdered."

"Wait," Gregor said. "Did Roy Phipps stage a demonstration in front of St. Stephen's because a nun from this church had been murdered on this church's grounds?"

"Yes," John Jackman said.

"And the violence," the Cardinal Archbishop said. "That was also caused by the Reverend Roy Phipps? And not by, what do they call themselves—"

"GALA," Sister Scholastica said helpfully. "It's short for the Gay and Lesbian Support Advisory. I think they didn't want to be GALSA."

"GALA," the Cardinal Archbishop repeated.

John Jackman took a deep breath. "Well," he said, "if you want to get technical, one of the GALA people made what might be termed a pass at one of Roy Phipps's people, however—"

"It wasn't a violent pass?" the Cardinal Archbishop said.

"Ah, violent, no. Physical, though, yes." Jackman squirmed.

"You'd better just tell him," Scholastica said. "He won't stop asking until you do."

Jackman stared up into the night sky. "This man, Chickie George, his name is—"

"He worships across the street," Scholastica said. "He's a friend of Mary McAllister's."

"Yeah, well," Jackman said. "He grabbed this other guy's, uh, private parts."

"Hard?" the Cardinal Archbishop asked.

"How the hell should I know?" Jackman said. "I mean, excuse me, Your Eminence."

"You'd know if the other man experienced pain," the Cardinal Archbishop said. "I take it you were an eyewitness to this incident."

"So was Mr. Demarkian here," Jackman said defensively.

"You must have noticed if the other man doubled over in pain," the Cardinal Archbishop said. "Or if he cried out in agony. Or began to tear up. Or if he was only startled and upset."

"Oh." Jackman nodded. "Just startled and upset. He, uh, he sort of blushed."

"Very good." The Cardinal Archbishop nodded. "So what we had here was this man, Chickie George, delivering the same kind of pass that hundreds of men experience every afternoon on their walk through Penn Station. An imprudent act, perhaps, but not an act of violence. This Chickie George, he was the one Miss McAllister accompanied to the hospital?"

"That's right," Scholastica said. "You remember. She called. Thomasetta came out and told us."

"What Sister Thomasetta came out and told us," the Cardinal Archbishop said—and then, just then, Gregor realized that the man was furious. Worse than furious. Angry to the point of explosion. "What Sister told us," the Cardinal Archbishop repeated, "was that as a result of this perhaps stupid but wholly symbolic act, Mr. George is now in the hospital with multiple contusions and several broken ribs. And in the wake of what was done to Mr. George, another man, also a member of GALA, was set on fire."

"It's already on television," Sister Scholastica said apologetically. "Thomasetta came out and told us about that, too."

"I think," John Jackman said cautiously, "that I'd really like to know what the point is here. If you wouldn't mind."

"The point," the Cardinal Archbishop said, "is who started the violence, and it was not the counterprotestors from GALA. If nobody wants me for anything here at the moment, I am going to go back to my residence. The archdiocese will issue a statement about this matter sometime tomorrow afternoon."

"Marvelous," John Jackman said.

"Your Eminence?" Scholastica said.

The Cardinal Archbishop bowed slightly in the direction of all of them at once or none of them at all, turned on his heel, and walked off in the direction of the church. John Jackman threw himself down on the bench and dropped his head into his hands.

"This is incredible," he said. "This is worse by the minute. They're going to have to fire the whole department and start from scratch."

In the annex, the tech men were beginning to bring out more than they were bringing in, and a couple of them were just standing around waiting. Gregor tugged at Jackman's sleeve.

"Let's go in there and do what we came to do," he said. "Then we can work out the future of the Philadelphia Police Department."

TWO

1

Usually, it was Bennis who fell asleep on the couch, and Gregor who went looking for her when he didn't find her in bed. This morning, Gregor woke to find himself staring at his own living-room window and, across the street, at the lit window of Lida Arkmanian's second-story reception room. Something was going on down there that involved red crepe paper and silver balls, but he wasn't sure what. Since the room was lit up but completely uninhabited, he didn't think he was going to find out anytime soon. He sat up and looked around him. He was still wearing the clothes he had had on the night before, including his jacket and tie, and his tie had a note pinned to it. "Didn't want to disturb you. Going off to read," the note said. Gregor unpinned it—Bennis had to be crazy, pinning something to him with a straight pin—and put it down on the coffee table on top of the notes he had been making about the death of Sister Harriet Garrity. He hated to admit it, but he was much happier to be looking into a murder that had just happened, almost right in front of his nose, than he had been at the thought of looking into two like the deaths of Scott Boardman and Bernadette Kelly. Cold trails were always bad news, of course, but it was worse than that. Over time, people edited their own memories. They took out what shamed them and put in what they wished they had done. Cold trails almost always involved hot lies and even hotter self-delusions, and there was no reasonable way to untangle them. Even if you solved the case, and built enough into the foundation so that a decent prosecutor could get a conviction, you always ended up with a picture of what had happened that was more than a little false.

He went down the hall to his bedroom and looked inside. Bennis was asleep under both his blankets and all three of his quilts. The blankets were Hudson Bay Point king-size at three hundred and fifty dollars a pop. The quilts were down-filled from L. L. Bean and cost more than Gregor wanted to think about. Bennis had bought them all when she'd realized that he liked to sleep under nothing but a top sheet, "as if," as she put it, "you didn't have anything on yourself at all." Then she'd gone out and bought eight thick, hard foam pillows to go with them.

At the moment, Bennis was not only sleeping under his blankets and his quilts, she was sleeping in his pajama tops as well. His pajama bottoms were draped over the back of the chair in front of the computer. Gregor got a clean set of clothes out of the wardrobe, considered putting on his robe, and decided against it. If Bennis woke up, she would want the robe. He had never met another woman who so disliked wearing her own clothes, and so much insisted on wearing his. Of course, his experience with women was somewhat restricted. There had been a few girls in college and the Army, and then he had married Elizabeth and stayed married to her for almost thirty years. Maybe it was a generational thing. Maybe women of Bennis's generation always wore their lovers' clothes. He rolled the word around in his mouth a couple of times—lover, lovers, love—and wished it didn't feel so out of place. Then he decided that it might have been worse. He was so big and Bennis was so small, there was only so much she could get away with borrowing. If she'd been a larger woman, he might not have had any clothes left at all.

He took a shower, came out, and shaved. In the mirror he looked tired, but he always looked tired. He had one of those Armenian faces that looked as if it had seen everything on earth, twice. It was Tibor who ought to look like that. He got into slacks and a shirt and a sweater, but he was very careful not to put on a tie. Bennis's nagging was finally getting to him. He had become embarrassed about wearing a suit when he was only going down the street to have breakfast at the Ararat. He came out of the bathroom and walked back down the hall to his bedroom. Bennis was still asleep, and now that he gave the room more attention he could see that she would probably stay that way for some time. There was a stack of new paper next to the computer. Either she was working on a book, or she had some other project that required her to work late into the night. Bennis being Bennis, even if she had nothing to do, she would find something that required her to stay up most of the night. Gregor put on socks and shoes and thought about leaving her a note. He walked out of the bedroom without doing it because he couldn't think of a thing to say. It was too bad he hadn't been willing to let Bennis buy him that leather jacket she saw at Brooks Brothers. His long coat felt much too formal. The leather jacket, though, had cost almost as much as a small car. He had no idea how people could buy things like that without feeling guilty.

Going downstairs, he stopped on the first floor at old George Tekemanian's apartment and knocked, but there was no answer. Old George was probably already down at the Ararat. Gregor went out onto the stoop and looked around. His own building was just about decorated, but Donna's town house was wrapped solidly in red and white crepe paper and hearts. The lights were on in front of the church. Tibor wouldn't turn them off until he got back from breakfast. If Tibor wasn't back from breakfast, Gregor couldn't be too late.

Gregor went down the block to the Ararat. There was a newspaper dispenser on the street next to Ohanian's Middle Eastern Foods. He stopped there and got a copy of the *Inquirer*, which had managed to get a picture of last night's riot into print, although not the one of the man burning up. He winced a little and folded the paper under his arm. Ohanian's was open, to the extent that Mary Ohanian was running the cash register in case anybody needed to pick up gum or lottery tickets on the way to work. Gregor sometimes thought Armenians were bigger gamblers than anybody in the world except the Hong Kong Chinese, but that might just have been his skewed perception from living on the street. He went past Ohanian's to the Ararat and inside. Old George Tekemanian and Tibor were sitting together in the long booth built into the wall next to the window, doing something with sock balls.

Gregor waved to Linda Melajian and went to sit down. "What's that?" he asked them. "Is that new? You had another machine for making sock balls, didn't you?"

"This is new, yes," old George Tekemanian said. "From my nephew Martin. I had another one he gave me, but this one is digital."

"A digital machine for making sock balls?"

"You can decide which direction to ball them in," Tibor said, "and you can do more than one kind of ball. And you can secure them with a plastic thing."

"Why would you want to?" Gregor asked.

Old George Tekemanian shook his head. "Krekor, Krekor. If the people who made these things asked themselves that question, they would never make anything. I like this one because when you make the sock ball you can shoot it out. Like this."

Old George Tekemanian flicked a switch. A sock ball came roaring out of the end of the little machine and hit Linda Melajian in the leg, making her jump. Coffee flew up out of the coffeepot and landed on her shoes.

"You do that again, I'm going to pour coffee on your head," she said when she got to the table. "That's the third time he's got me today. You want some actual breakfast, Gregor, or do you just want to stick with coffee?"

"Two eggs sunny-side up. Side of sausage. Side of hash browns. Toast."

"You sure you don't want the fruit plate?" Linda said.

"Yes," Gregor told her, "I'm sure. And I'm equally sure I don't want you writing Bennis a note with the calorie and cholesterol counts for my breakfast. What's with the two of you, anyway? I'm not going to change my mind."

"We're just trying to stop you from having a heart attack before your time." Linda turned one of the coffee cups over and poured it full. "Never mind us," she said. "You know what women are like. We were put here by God to spoil every man's fun."

"I take it you broke up with what's-his-name," Gregor said.

Linda made a face. "I don't break up with men anymore. I just spend the first date figuring out how they're going to screw me up. I'll be back in a minute."

She marched off. Tibor shook his head. "I don't like it when they get that way," he said. "You know, with the men thing. They're never in a very good mood."

Gregor pushed a little pile of sock balls down the table to

old George and opened his paper. He should have turned on the news or logged on to the Internet. Their information would be much more recent, and probably much more complete. It was all well and good to say that we should do everything we can to preserve our daily newspapers, but the fact remained that "news" was what was new, and the faster you could get it to the public, the more successful you would be. The television stations were faster, that was all. In a few years, the Internet would be faster still. Gregor looked through the first four paragraphs of the story, decided that there was nothing egregiously wrong in any of them, and pushed the paper away.

Tibor picked it up. "I saw it on the television last night, Krekor," he said. "They interrupted the *Rosie O'Donnell Show* to have the bulletin. It was a disgraceful thing, don't you think? And you were there."

"I was there to see a dead body that had nothing to do with the riot," Gregor said, "except that it did, except that I could never figure out what. Do you know this man, this Roy Phipps?"

"I've met him," Tibor said cautiously.

"And?"

Tibor shrugged. "He's not popular with the clergy in Philadelphia, Krekor. They see him as an interloper, coming here from out of state with—what's the word?—with attitudes that do not fit here. But he's not what the papers and the television stations make him out to be. He's not stupid."

"No," Gregor said. "I'd heard he wasn't."

"But he's a very bad thing," Tibor said. "He gives all of religion a bad name. He gives all of Christianity a bad name. There are people out there who know nothing but what they see on television. What are they going to think when they see a man like that?"

Gregor took a long sip of coffee. It was so hot it nearly scalded his throat. "According to John Jackman, Phipps and his people decided to demonstrate last night after word got out that there had been another murder by arsenic in the neighborhood. The woman who was murdered was Sister Harriet Garrity. Was that on the news last night, too?"

"Yes," Tibor and old George Tekemanian said at once.

Old George Tekemanian's nephew Martin had a wife who had made it a rule that old George was not allowed to watch anything on television that was too "exciting." Old George was not paying any attention to her unless she was in the room with him and able to get hold of the remote. Gregor let it pass.

"Let me try to explain this as well as I can," Gregor said, "because I'm having a very hard time making it make sense. Sister Harriet Garrity was found dead in Sister Scholastica's office at St. Anselm's Parish complex by Sister Scholastica herself around six o'clock—"

"Our Sister Scholastica?" Tibor asked.

Gregor nodded. "Our Sister Scholastica. She's been assigned as principal to St. Anselm's Parochial School. Yesterday evening, she had dinner with friends, and when she got back to St. Anselm's she decided to stop in to her office and see if she had any messages. The door to her office was locked. She unlocked it and found Sister Harriet, blue and just beginning to stiffen with rigor. She had a fit. She found Father Healy. Father Healy called the police. So far so good?"

"Perfectly sensible," Tibor said. "Sister Scholastica is a very sensible woman."

"Things get less sensible very fast," Gregor said. "When Father Healy called the police, the call went out on the police band, which Roy Phipps's people were monitoring."

"Why?" old George Tekemanian said.

"I don't have any idea," Gregor said. "But they were, and they heard it. They sent somebody up the street to see if they could find out anything more, and they managed to get hold of the information that it looked very much like Sister Harriet had been poisoned—"

"Had she been poisoned?" Tibor asked.

"I would guess so, considering what she looked like," Gregor said, "but we'll have to wait for the autopsy. Back to the point here. They found out that Sister Harriet was assumed to have been murdered by poison. They then put two and two together and got forty-six. They decided that since both Scott Boardman and Bernadette Kelly had been poisoned, and Scott Boardman had been poisoned at St. Stephen's, then all the poisonings were being caused by the people at St. Stephen's—"

"Why?" Old George Tekemanian looked confused.

"—and," Gregor said, "that there was therefore some kind of police plot to protect the gay members of St. Stephen's parish from the adverse publicity that would result if the public knew that one of them was the prime suspect in a series of murders. So—"

"Pfaw," Tibor said, slapping his hand against the booth table. "This is ridiculous. It is not even coherent."

"I agree," Gregor said. "But that's the story Phipps gave to the police.'

"Listen," Tibor said. "I have met this man. He is a fanatic. He is a demagogue. He is not stupid. He is especially not this kind of stupid. This is the cover story of a mentally retarded sociopath."

"I agree," Gregor said again. "But again, it's the story he gave to the police, and he's sticking to it. What I can't figure out is why. Why the demonstration and why the story."

"Is there someone at St. Stephen's who is suspected of the killings?" old George Tekemanian asked. "I thought it was only the girl at the Catholic church, and then they thought her husband had done it, because she was so very ill and he hurt to see her suffer."

"No, no," Tibor said. "There was another one. At St. Stephen's. You had to listen carefully, but it was there."

"Right," Gregor said. "There was Bernadette Kelly. Her husband brought her body to St. Anselm's Catholic Church, then shot himself. There was Scott Boardman, who died in a parish office at St. Stephen's."

"But is one of the people of the parish of St. Stephen's suspected of killing them?" old George asked.

"Nobody is suspected of killing them," Gregor said. "We don't even know where Bernadette Kelly died, yet. She didn't die at St. Anselm's Church. We don't know anything about the death of Scott Boardman at all."

"But this Sister Harriet Garrity," Tibor said. "She died in Sister Scholastica's office?"

"Oh, yes," Gregor told him. "The vomit was still on the floor next to the desk. Autopsies can always bring surprises, but I don't think this one will. I'd say it's better than ninety-nine percent certain that she died where she was found."

"I'd say it's better than ninety-nine percent certain that you're not going to get to eat this in peace," Linda Melajian said, arriving at the table with a large oval plate full of food. Behind her was Bennis, in jeans and clogs, her wild black hair pinned up into a knot on top of her head. "I didn't suggest it to him," Linda said to Bennis. "You know what he's like."

Bennis picked up the plate and moved it to the other side of the table. "I'll eat this," she said. "Bring him the fruit platter."

"I don't want the fruit platter," Gregor said. "And I won't eat it."

"If you get to tell me to quit smoking, I get to tell you to go on a diet. Linda, do you have any grits? Could I have two sides and some extra butter?"

"Oh, for God's sake," Gregor said.

Bennis speared a sausage and looked at every side of it, as if it could tell her something she didn't already know. Then she put it down again and let Gregor take the plate from her. "I don't see how you can eat that stuff," she said. "The fat practically oozes out of it."

"I don't see how you can eat grits, with or without butter," Gregor said. "It's good to see you actually awake in the morning. Unusual, but good."

"Oh," Bennis said. She stood up and reached into the back pocket of her jeans, coming up with a wadded mess of what looked like fax paper. "I wanted you to look at this," she said. "I wanted to know what you thought I could do about it. And don't tell me I can't do anything, because I'm not going to listen."

Gregor opened the papers and looked at the title just as Linda Melajian came back yet another time, with yet another pot of coffee. "Reconsidering The Death Penalty," the papers read, "by Edith Lawton."

Gregor shook his head, and said, "Why does the name Edith Lawton sound so familiar?"

2

It was late, much later than he had expected it to be, by the time Gregor left the Ararat. Ohanian's was all the way open when he came out, and Lida Arkmanian was already getting into a cab for her twice-weekly trip to the serious department stores. She was wearing her three-quarter-length chinchilla coat, and taking with her poor Hannah Krekorian, who had all the fashion sense of a psychotic duck. But then, Lida and Hannah had always been this way, even when they were all growing up together on this street, and instead of town houses the blocks were filled with tenements. Lida was the most beautiful girl in school, the one who always knew what to wear and what to do and what to say. Hannah was the quiet little lump in the corner of the dance floor. As Gregor passed them, they waved, and he saw, glinting in the start of the winter morning, the gold of the cross Lida always wore around her neck. Hannah wore one, too, and so did all the older women on this street. When Gregor was growing up, it had almost been part of a community uniform, for the men as well as for the women. Gregor tried to remember if old George Tekemanian wore one, but old George tended to wear shirts buttoned high up on his neck or turtleneck sweaters his niece-in-law bought him at Neal's. The women, though, definitely did. The very old ones wore theirs outside the high collars of their dresses, as if they wanted very much to have them seen. Gregor stopped where he was, in the middle of the sidewalk, and looked up the street to Holy Trinity Church. Bennis stopped with him, shoving her hands into the front pockets of her jeans.

"I'm freezing," she said. "I forgot to wear a coat."

"You always forget to wear a coat. If I wasn't stumbling over it all the time, I'd think you didn't have a coat."

"Whatever. Maybe we should go inside."

"I'm thinking."

"About Edith Lawton?"

"About religion," Gregor said. He walked a little farther up the block and stopped again. Holy Trinity was a very traditional church. All Armenian churches were. You wouldn't find an Armenian-American community building a Crystal Cathedral. Gregor crossed the street and then crossed again, heading always for the church. It seemed to him that Armenian people, or at least Armenian-American people, were—what? He had been about to think "more liberal than other Americans," but that wasn't true. In a lot of ways, they were a lot more conservative. They believed in marriage and family and putting children before career, for men as well as women. They believed in working hard and doing without to get ahead, and they were very antagonistic to the idea of welfare. Their church had held the same doctrines and practiced the same rituals, word for word, for over a thousand years. And yet—and yet. Gregor stopped when he got to the sidewalk in front of Holy Trinity and looked at the building. It was made of rough stones and set back from the street, small but sturdy-looking, built in the 1920s by people who had had very little money to give to its construction, but who were not willing to live without what they felt it could give them. And yet, Gregor thought again.

Next to him, Bennis wrapped her arms around her body and shivered. "Do you at least want to tell me what we're doing?" she demanded. "I'm turning into an icicle."

"I'm thinking about religion," Gregor said. "Would you say that Tibor is a very religious person?"

"Of course Tibor is a very religious person. He's a priest."

"I don't think that necessarily follows," Gregor said. "What about Lida? Would you say she's a religious person?"

"I guess. Why?"

"I would say she was a religious person," Gregor said. "She believes in God. She goes to church every week. She really does think somebody is watching over her. What about Hannah Krekorian?"

"All those women are religious," Bennis said. "At least in the way you've defined it. And the older women, too. But I wouldn't count on Howard Kashinian."

"I never do," Gregor said. He looked the building over one more time. He could remember being very young and being brought here by his parents, at a time when the church was shabby and in desperate need of repairs. Later there would be a boom or two and the work everyone had done for so long would begin to pay off, but then there was still no money. He would sit in his pew at the long service and count the holes in the plaster walls and the chips in the gold paint in the molding that sat hip high on the iconostasis. He remembered looking at those pictures and wondering what they meant, because in spite of all the Sunday school he'd attended, nobody had ever told him. He still didn't know what most of them meant. He only knew that they represented the saints of the Church, and that a great many of them seemed to have died violent and agonizing deaths.

"Gregor?"

"I'm going inside. Do you want to go inside with me?"

"At least it's got heat," Bennis said. "Do you want to pray? I didn't think you did that."

Gregor led the way up the walk and in the front doors. Unlike St. Stephen's and St. Anselm's, there were no high ceilings, except in the vault of the church itself. Nor was there much of anything in the foyer. The Armenian Church in America was not large enough or rich enough to put out dozens of pamphlets on the spiritual life. Gregor went through into the church itself, which was dark. In Catholic churches, the altar was exposed to the people, and often, just behind it, the Host was displayed for adoration. In Armenian churches, as in most churches in the Eastern tradition, the altar was hidden behind the iconostasis, whatever the priest did was supposed to be a mystery.

Gregor sat down in the very last pew on the left. Bennis sat down next to him, let her clogs drop to the floor, and tucked her legs up under her. With anybody else, Gregor might have protested. He had begun to think this was the only way Bennis was comfortable sitting down.

"So," Bennis said. "What is this? You're getting religion in your old age?"

"I don't think I've ever gotten it or not gotten it," Gregor said. "I don't think about religion much. Do you?"

"Um, no. Why would I?"

"Well, Bennis, people do. The people I've met in the last twenty-four hours think about religion a lot. Not just Roy Phipps. The Cardinal Archbishop of Philadelphia. Your old friend Sister Scholastica."

"It's what they do," Bennis said reasonably. "I mean, it's their profession. They've got to think about it a lot."

"You don't think ordinary people do that?"

"Oh," Bennis said. "Well, yes. Of course they do. Some of them."

"Exactly," Gregor said. "And I can't really figure out why. I've got three dead bodies, all in churches. Four, if you count Marty Kelly, and I'd think you'd have to. Yes, he committed suicide, but he committed suicide because his wife died and his wife is one of the three bodies in churches. If you see what I mean."

"I thought it was pretty clear that Bernadette Kelly had died somewhere else," Bennis said. "I mean, I thought that was the whole point of the press conference."

"The whole point of the press conference was to get the information out in a way that the media wouldn't be able to understand its importance. It failed. But back to Bernadette. She was killed elsewhere, too. But something about her death had to have something to do with a church. Otherwise, she wouldn't have ended up in one."

"Maybe she only ended up in one because her husband was religious."

"She was the one who was religious," Gregor said. "I got that much out of Sister Scholastica. She was religious. She brought him along with her. Scholastica thinks he brought her to the church because he thought he was bringing her where she would want to be."

"All right."

"No," Gregor said. "Not all right. The most important thing, in any of these cases, is to be able to think your way into the mind of the killer. It's not that it ever works perfectly. It doesn't. And it's a good thing. Sociopathic murderers are bad enough. We don't need sociopathic policemen. But in this case I just don't get it. Do you ever look at that thing up there?"

"What?" Bennis said. "The iconostasis? I look at it all the time."

"And?"

"And what? It's an interesting example of Byzantine icon making. Interesting but not particularly good. Lida was talking about going to Armenia to find better ones, now that you can travel there."

"It's the saints I'm thinking of," Gregor said. "Doesn't it ever make you wonder how many saints of the early Church died bloody and horrible deaths?"

"Not really," Bennis said drily, "I was raised a debutante Episcopalian."

"What's a debutante Episcopalian?"

"A woman with old Main Line money who shows up every week at the Episcopal church to show that she's still in the *Social Register*. We weren't really big on saints dying terrible deaths. But I don't think most people on Cavanaugh Street are either, and they take religion a lot more seriously than my family did."

"Do you know what the rule of thumb is in murder cases?" Gregor asked. "Love and money. That's why people kill. Love and money. For a long time I thought serial killers were an exception to that rule, but they're not. They've just displaced their love, most of them, onto third parties. And even the mass killers, the school shooters, are running on love and money—on status, which is the kind of thing teenagers have as the coin of exchange. Am I making any sense here?"

"Not a lot."

"Let's just say that I don't like the idea that I'm investigating people I don't understand," Gregor said. "It bothers me. It bothers me beyond belief. Do you think there's something about religion that causes people to go off the deep end?"

"Well, Gregor, it's not just religion. I mean, think of Edith Lawton. A professional atheist. As fanatical about being an atheist as Roy Phipps is about being whatever he thinks he is. There are fanatics of everything. Politics. Religion. Anti-religion. Beanie babies."

"Do you think anybody has ever killed for a Beanie baby?"

"I have no idea," Bennis said, "but I'll bet that there are people out there who have wanted to kill because somebody insulted Beanie babies. Would you say that comes in on the love side? Maybe that's all this is. Somebody is killed because they—I don't know what I was going to say. Because they insulted the Church, maybe. Or because keeping them alive would mean the Church was harmed. How's that?"

"Not bad," Gregor admitted. "We'll concentrate on Sister Harriet Garrity, of course, because we're in on the beginning of that one. The markers are still out there for anybody to see. But I wish I had a better handle on the people."

Bennis unfolded her legs and slipped them back into the clogs she had left resting on the floor. "I don't think you should have all that much trouble with the people," Bennis said. "Even Roy Phipps is just a petty dictator with ambitions. What worries me is that it will turn out that he wasn't the one who did it, and none of his people did either."

"Why does that worry you?"

"Because, so far, he's practically the only one of these people I'd want to have done it. At least, as you've described them. Everybody else, except Roy and his church pickets, sounds very nice."

"The Cardinal Archbishop of Philadelphia?"

"That's different," Bennis said. "I wouldn't want to give Edith Lawton the satisfaction. If it turned out that the Cardinal did it, she'd have an essay up on the Web and in that amateurville freethought magazine in no time at all, proving beyond the shadow of a doubt that the Catholic Church has never been anything but a murderous, hypocritical engine of oppression from the day it was founded until now. And getting half her facts wrong in the process."

"Right," Gregor said.

"I'm going to go back to the house and get on the Net. If you come with me, I'll give you some baklava."

"You made baklava?"

"Lida did. Also some grape leaves. They're in the fridge. Oh, and that stuff, the meatballs with the crusts on them. That's in the fridge, too. With microwave instructions."

"Marvelous. Lida doesn't even trust us to know how to heat something up in the microwave."

"She's right. You want to come?"

"No," Gregor said. "Don't worry about it. I want to stay here and think. You go eat baklava at eight o'clock in the morning, and I'll be back later."

"If Tibor finds you in here, he's going to declare it a miracle," Bennis said. Then she shimmied down to the end of the pew and onto the carpet runner that muffled the sounds of her clogs on the floor of the center aisle.

Gregor did just what he'd said he was going to do. He sat where he was and tried to think. He didn't really believe that there was something peculiarly evil about the effects of religion. People were people, and human nature was human nature. Most of the religious people he knew were perfectly sane, and Bennis was right. There were fanatics of all kinds out there. Lots of them didn't even believe in God.

He closed his eyes and imagined the scene in Scholastica's office the night before, with Sister Harriet Garrity just being taken down from the chair behind Scholastica's desk, and the little half-hardened mound of vomit next to her on the floor. There was no sign anywhere of anything she might have eaten or drunk, no plate, no cup, no glass. Gregor was still convinced that she had died in that room. If she had, then she almost surely must have ingested the arsenic in that room. The only other possibility was that she'd taken it in one of the other offices on that same floor and been able to walk the few steps to Scholastica's office before the poison really hit. But that didn't make a lot of sense, either. The door was locked. Somebody must have come in with her, or watched her die and come in after her, and that would have to be the person who killed her. Gregor couldn't think of a reason why anybody else would want to lock that office door.

He got up and slid down to the end of the pew nearest the center aisle. The church was dark. The windows were stained glass in deep reds and purples, letting very little light in even on the brightest days. The only lights that were glowing were the small ones on the sidewalls that always reminded him of Christmas bulbs. What did Sister Harriet Garrity have in common with Scott Boardman? What would Bernadette Kelly have in common with Scott Boardman? Gregor could think of a million things that Sister Harriet and Bernadette Kelly had in common with each other. The key would have to be in the other connection.

He was already out of the church and on the sidewalk when it suddenly struck him: why the name Edith Lawton was so familiar and where he had seen it before.

There was an Edith Lawton on the list of subjects for questioning that the homicide detectives had drawn up the night before, before they allowed anybody in the church to go home.

THREE

1

Edith Lawton knew she was in trouble, but through the long night since the riot and the discovery of Harriet Garrity's body, she hadn't been able to think straight. She hadn't been able to sleep, either, which was worse. There were people who could get along on almost no sleep, but Edith wasn't one of them. If she got less than eight full hours, she felt fuzzy all day. If she got less than five, she was walking into walls. This morning, she was sure she had had less than three, but all she could really remember was lying alone in her bed with the lights off, listening to Will moving around in the living room. In the old days, she would have told him what was wrong and asked him to straighten it out for her—or, really, to rearrange the facts so that they would begin to make sense. Now, of course, she couldn't say a thing. She didn't even want him to know that she had been questioned by the police, or that she would be questioned again. She had no idea how long she would be able to keep that from him. The police would probably come here, one of these days. Either that, or they would find Will where he worked, and ask him about her then. He would tell them all about Ian. Then the police would talk to Ian. Eventually, the news would hit the papers or the television stations or both. If she became a serious suspect, her face would be everywhere. Then what would she do? There was a cold place at the pit of her stomach that said this was not the kind of publicity she could afford, if she expected to make something of her life someday—and then she felt ludicrous, because by the time you were fifty you should already have made something of your life. Still, she could see it, everything that could go wrong from here on out. Once you got a reputation, you could never get rid of it. And if it all came out—Ian, for instance, and all her attempts to get published in places that didn't want her, and the fact that Will was going to file for divorce—

It was cold in her bedroom. The pipes needed to be bled. The boiler was acting up. Something. She kept thinking that these murders were like winning the lottery. She didn't expect to be arrested, but she might be exposed, and that would be . . . shameful. The sort of thing that happened to trailer trash. The sort of thing that didn't happen to people who were real writers who got their pictures in *Vanity Fair*. She had written a beautiful essay once on the stupidity of the lottery, but the fact was that she was afraid to win it. She didn't want to be one of those people with their pictures in the *Inquirer* and the *Star*, holding oversize checks, never to be taken seriously again. There had to be a reason why so many of the people who won the lottery were convenience-store clerks when they won it, and never did much else with themselves ever afterward.

Now it was much later, nearly noon, and Edith didn't know what to do with herself. The *Inquirer* had turned down her op-ed. She had sent a copy to the *Star* and hadn't heard back yet. She didn't want to work. She was too tired, and too jittery, to make any sense. She kept going from the papers to the television to the front windows to the papers again, and coming up blank. Earlier in the morning, there had been cleanup crews on the street, hosing down the last of the mess from the riot. Now there was nobody. The only sign that there had been trouble was the fact that one of the windows on one of the town houses nearest St. Stephen's Church was broken, but it could have been broken by anything. Every once in a while, she pressed her face to the window glass and tried to see farther up or down the street, but she never got anything but the fog of her breath on the pane.

If she hadn't been known to be an atheist, she wouldn't be in this much trouble. She knew that was true. The police were all believers. That Gregor Demarkian—who was a friend of Bennis Hannaford's—had a best friend who was a priest. It would be so convenient for all of them if they could just pin these murders on her. It was too bad for them that she had never bought any arsenic and never been known to talk to any of the victims, except this last one, who was on the street all the time. If she managed to escape the worst sort of publicity, she could see how to make something of this. It would make a good essay for *Free Thinking*, or for her site on the web: the prejudice visited on unbelievers; the mortal peril of the freethinker in a believer's society. It might even get some wider play in the freethought press. She had never had the chance to be a martyr before. It gave her an odd sense of exhilaration.

The exhilaration was followed by another wave of nervousness. She couldn't stay in the house anymore, by herself, talking to no one. She was going to go crazy. What did it mean that she couldn't think of a single person to call? She got her coat off the newel at the bottom of the stairs, picked up the little change purse with her keys attached that fit into her pocket, and stepped outside. She should have brought a hat and gloves.

There was a little corner store at the end of the block opposite the one with the churches on it. Edith went there first and looked through the papers, even though she subscribed to all the ones in town. She finally bought a York Peppermint Patty and went back out onto the street. Going back up the block, she passed Roy Phipps's town house "church" and saw that it looked the way it always had. Nothing was broken, and there was no indication that half the church's members had spent the night in jail. That was material for a column, too—what the Phipps people had done during the riot, how violent they were, how dangerous—but Edith had the depressing feeling that she had said it all before. She wandered past her own house and to the walk in front of St. Anselm's. She looked across at St. Stephen's and thought she had done *that* before, too. She'd written an essay on how enlightened and forward-looking churches like St. Stephen's were, and then she'd been taken aback when Dan Burdock had let her know that he thought that Jesus had really risen from the dead.

She went up the steps into St. Anselm's and looked around. There was a noon Mass coming up, and there was a fair-sized group of people at the front near the altar, saying the rosary together. Edith went back out and around the side. The courtyard was deserted, but a big van was pulling into the parking lot. As she watched, it settled into a space, shuddered a few times, and stopped running. The driver's side door opened and a very young woman with long red hair hopped out. Edith walked in that direction. The van belonged to some kind of homeless shelter. The young woman was somebody she had seen around.

"What are you doing here?" the young woman said, suddenly, when Edith wasn't expecting it.

Edith froze. She hadn't realized she'd gotten so close to the van, or that the young woman had noticed her. "I'm not doing anything," she said. "I'm just—walking around."

"This area is supposed to be sealed off," the young woman said. "Nobody is supposed to be here unless they have business here. The police lines are still up at Sister's office."

Edith wrapped her arms around her body. "There wasn't anything sealing it off. I was in the church, and then I came out and walked around. There weren't any barriers up. Nobody stopped me."

"What were you in the church for this time? If we don't watch out, there'll be a million gawkers here all day. We won't be able to get anything done."

Edith shook her head. "Do you work here? You don't look like you work here. You don't look like a nun."

"Nuns aren't the only people who work here."

"You're wearing jeans," Edith said. "Does the Church let you wear jeans when you work for it?"

"Her," the young woman said automatically. "The proper pronoun for the Church is 'Her.' "

"I don't think so," Edith said. "It's not a her. It's an it."

"Are you always so delicately attuned to the sensibilities of people from cultures other than your own?" The young woman slid the van's side door shut and went around the back to open up there. "I've got to get these boxes into the basement. I'm running late by two hours."

Edith went around the back of the van and looked inside. The backseats had all been shut down and the empty space was full of cartons that seemed to be full of cans and other food, pasta, cookies, peanut butter. The young woman propped the van's back door open with her shoulder and took one of the boxes out.

"I'm Edith Lawton," Edith said.

"I know who you are," the young woman said. "If you're going to hang around, will you help me out with this? Go open the door to the basement."

Edith looked dubiously at the door to the basement. "Won't it be locked?'

"The keys are on my belt. All you have to do is unhook them."

The keys were on one of those snap-spring key rings. The young woman jutted out her hip, and Edith got them off.

"You could tell me your name," she said. "If it wouldn't be too much trouble."

"My name is Mary McAllister," the young woman said, "and you already know it. Or you should. You've asked three times before."

"Sorry."

"Get the door."

Edith got the door. Mary McAllister went inside. Edith pushed against the door until the spring caught and held it open. Mary McAllister had disappeared down a hallway. Edith went in the only direction she could go, and found herself in a large open room with an industrial-grade carpet on the floor. The room was decorated with children's crafts, crosses and lambs cut out of construction paper. They gave Edith the creeps.

"The thing is," Edith said, "I wouldn't have done it. Killed her, I mean. I wouldn't have killed that nun because she was, you know, she was one of the good ones."

"One of the good ones." Mary straightened up. She had been bent over a table, sorting the food in the box into different piles. "What do you mean by one of the good ones?"

"Oh, you know," Edith said. "One of the ones who think. Who live in the real world. Not like the ones in the habits who think they're still in the sixteenth century."

"Right," Mary said. "I've got to get another box. Carry boxes if you want to hang around and talk."

Edith didn't know if she wanted to hang around and talk. She only knew she didn't want to go home. She followed Mary out into the parking lot and took the box she was handed. It was heavy.

"What's this for?" she asked. "Is the church having a picnic?"

"It's from the food bank," Mary said. "We do the food bank down at the homeless shelter mostly. There isn't much need for it in this neighborhood. But there's some, and there are always people who would rather come here than get their stuff somewhere there's likely to be a drive-by shooting, so once a month we do a distribution from the church. Watch out for that box. It's got jars in it."

It felt like it had rocks in it. Edith wondered how old Mary was. Eighteen? Nineteen? She was stronger than Edith had ever been. The box she was carrying was bigger, and she was balancing it on her shoulder. Edith followed her across the parking lot and down the steps into the basement again. Mary put her box down next to the table. Edith put her box down next to Mary's box.

"We used to make up bags for people to take," Mary said. "Then I realized, that was stupid. They're like everybody else. They like some things. They don't like other things. Now we put the stuff out and give everybody a bag to fill and they can put whatever they want in it that will fit. I wish we could make it two bags for everybody. We never have enough food."

"The Church should sell some of its art and give the money to the poor," Edith said virtuously. "That's what they'd do if they really believed all that crap they put out."

"Is that so?"

"The Church is full of hypocrites," Edith said. "You must know that. You can't miss knowing that. You're not stupid."

"Everything is full of hypocrites."

"The history of the Catholic Church is nothing but tyranny and oppression. It's been the enemy of humankind from the word go. It stifles science. It promotes superstition. Every place it's in power, it holds back civilization until its power is destroyed. Think about it. The last time the Church had control of society, it was called the Dark Ages."

"No it wasn't."

"What?"

"The Church didn't have control of society in the Dark Ages," Mary said patiently, looking up from a pile of pasta packets. "The Dark Ages are the period between the fall of Rome and the rise of Charlemagne. They were dark because nobody had control of everything. All of Western Europe was overrun by warrior tribes. Nobody could keep a government or a city or a society going for very long before another invasion happened, so nobody could keep agriculture going or run schools. It would be like trying to do those things in Kosovo or Bosnia now. The Church wasn't in charge of society during the Dark Ages. You're thinking of the Middle Ages."

"The Dark Ages and the Middle Ages are the same thing."

Mary moved down the table to the jars of peanut butter. "Look," she said, "you need to get hold of a halfway decent history of Europe. The Dark Ages and the Middle Ages are not the same thing. You don't know what you're talking about. You never know what you're talking about. Doesn't it bother you to get things wrong all the time?'

"I don't get things wrong all the time," Edith said. "You've just been fed a biased view of history. The Church doesn't want you to know the truth, and so it tells you a lot of lies."

"The definitive history of the period is Cantor's *Civilization of the Middle Ages*. Cantor teaches at Columbia, and he's not a Catholic. Go look it up."

"You've never been taught to think," Edith said. "That's your problem. The Church doesn't want you to think, so it teaches you with rote and drills and then you can't make up your mind for yourself. You've been brainwashed."

"I at least know that the Middle Ages and the Dark Ages are not the same thing," Mary said. "Now, if you don't mind. I have to unload these boxes, and then I have to go back for another set. I've spent all morning at the hospital with a friend who is not in good shape and I have to get across town and to class before three. I'm in no mood to put up with your nonsense. Come back and talk to me when you're able to say a complete declarative sentence without getting six facts wrong."

"It's not my facts that are wrong," Edith said, hearing the high thin rise in her voice that was the start of something like hysteria. "I'm not the one who's mired in fear and superstition. I don't go to bed every night begging some fantasy who doesn't exist not to send me to hell."

"Good," Mary said. "Neither do I. I've got to hurry.'

Edith stepped back. Mary strode out of the room into the hall. Edith followed her. The closer she got to the open basement door, the colder it was. She stepped outside and looked around. Mary was at the van, hoisting another large box onto her shoulder.

"It's not me who's mired in fear and superstition," Edith said again, but her voice came back to her on the wind. There was nobody else who could hear it. She was shaking, but that might be the cold. Her head hurt. There were a million things she wanted to do right then, but none of them were looking up the Dark Ages in a book by somebody named Cantor. Mostly, she just wanted to scream.

What she did instead was to walk away from the basement door and from the parking lot, to the side path that went around to the front of the church. By then, her muscles were twitching uncontrollably. If she hadn't been keeping strict hold on herself, she would have looked like a Parkinson's patient. She went around to the front of the church and headed up the street to her own house and her own living room and her own coffee. When she got there, she thought better of it and kept going.

If she walked long enough, she would come to a bus stop. She could get on and go somewhere to shop, or to the library, or to a museum. If she rode long enough, she might even be able to calm herself down. The only thing she knew for sure was that she couldn't stay here, on this street, any longer this day.

Maybe, she thought, I need to find a hotel room.

2

Roy Phipps had been in jail before. In fact, he had been in jail often, but never more than overnight, and never in any facility more serious than a municipal holding tank. Even in those places where most of the police and most of the populace agreed with everything he said and wished him well, he ended up in jail, because one or another of the people who followed him got overly enthusiastic or way out of line. They cared, he knew, when they ended up behind bars. It frightened them in a bone-deep way that it could never frighten him. They lived so close to the edge that they were always worried about falling off—but Roy wasn't. It had been years since Roy worried for a moment about sinking back into the lower middle class, or worse. God was on his side. More importantly, celebrity was on his side. This was the truth about America: people would forgive you anything as long as you were famous. Roy had made it a point of becoming famous, just as he had made a point of never veering a single inch from the revealed word of God. It all worked together. The truth will make you free.

Now he stood patiently at the desk and let the woman officer count out his personal things, naming each one, as if it mattered if she spoke the list aloud.

"One black leather wallet," she said. Her voice had the flat-bottomed drone of central Pennsylvania. "Fifty-four dollars in bills. Seventy-six cents in change. One American Express gold card. One driver's license. One bank card."

"Reverend Phipps doesn't believe in credit cards," Fred said. "He says it's the way Satan seduces us into slavery."

The woman looked up. Then she looked down again and went on counting. "One copy *The Pocket Bible*, King James version. One set of keys on a cross-shaped key chain."

Fred looked at the floor, and the ceiling, and the walls. Roy could see that he was so ashamed he could barely breathe, and he seemed to be coming out of his suit, bursting the buttons as they stood. The suit was wrinkled, the result of a night in the tank and the fact that Fred had bought it at JC Penney's. Roy didn't know why the suits always bothered him so much, but they did. It seemed to him that he had been better than this, even in the days when he had had no money and had had to bus dishes to make his walking-around money.

Of course, maybe he hadn't been. The trouble with memory was that it played tricks on you. That was what had happened to him the one time one of his brothers had come up to see him in Philadelphia, when he had just started to make a name for himself as a preacher. He would have said, before that, that he knew his brothers' faces as well as he knew his own. He saw them in his sleep. He saw them in his *nightmares*. Then this huge hulking man had appeared in the doorway to his church, and he hadn't had the faintest idea who it was.

"That's it," the woman officer said. "Will you sign this, please, attesting to your agreement that your property has been returned to you."

Roy took the paper she handed him and bent over it. He

never signed anything without reading it. That included things like this, which were just copies of things he had signed before. The officer looked annoyed. Fred shifted his weight from leg to leg. Roy thought about protesting the use of the phrase "in the same condition"—nothing was ever in the same condition; wear and tear and misuse damaged all things—but then bent down and signed. There were times and places to make scenes. This was not one of them.

He handed the paper across the desk to the officer. The officer handed him his things. Roy put them back one by one in his pockets. It was quiet in this police station at this time of day, although out here the neighborhood was no longer very good. Last night, when they had come in, the place had been pandemonium.

"I sent Carl out to get a cab," Fred was saying. "It didn't work too well. Cabs never seem to like to stop for Carl. So I sent him home."

"We don't need a cab," Roy said.

"I thought maybe you'd rather ride than walk," Fred said. "I mean, you know, in case they've got press people around here, with cameras. And that kind of thing. I thought maybe you wouldn't want for it to be on television, you coming out of jail."

"It's been on television before."

"Well, yeah, I know. But I thought that was different. The protests, I mean. It wasn't like this."

"What's so different about this?"

"Well," Fred said.

They had come out onto the front steps. The day was cold but clear, not quite as dark as it had been in the last few weeks. Roy snapped up the collar of his coat and drew his scarf more tightly around his neck. It really wasn't a very good neighborhood. Some of the buildings were either abandoned or close to it. They had windows boarded over with plywood and trash on their front steps. The gutters were clear, but that was only because the police station was there and the garbagemen didn't want to annoy the cops. Roy pulled on his gloves and headed down the stairs.

"I don't see why this arrest should be any different than any other," he said. "Why do you think it is? Because the homosexuals behaved like the animals they are and made the blood flow in the streets?"

"No," Fred said. "No, that wasn't it."

"Then what was it?" Roy had them headed to the left, back to their own quiet street. "Have the newspapers been blaming it all on me? There's nothing new in that. They always blame it all on me. I never start the violence. They always say I do. So what?"

Fred started looking around again, up and down and sideways. Then he reached under his own coat and brought out a newspaper. "This," he said, handing the paper over.

It was the Philadelphia *Star*, and the biggest picture on the front page was not of the riot, but of Roy himself, in a studio shot taken for publicity purposes maybe five years ago. The headline read: *Controversial Pastor Chief Suspect In Church Poisonings Case.*

Roy handed the paper back. "This is interesting," he said.

"It's all over everywhere," Fred said. "It's on the television. They're all saying you killed that woman at the church yesterday. And the other two. You know."

"And then what?" Roy asked. "I started a riot to cover it all up?"

"Something like that."

"It isn't true, you know," Roy said. "The police aren't interested in this angle. The papers are making it up."

"How do you know?"

Roy looked over his shoulder in the direction of the police station and the holding tank. "Because they didn't ask me about it. They didn't make me get a lawyer. They didn't demand that I come in for questioning. If I were really their chief suspect, they would have done all those things. Do we know how this woman died?"

"It was poison," Fred said, surprised. "We knew that last night."

"Do we know what kind of poison. Are they sure that it was arsenic yet?"

"Oh," Fred said. "I guess they are. I mean, I assumed they are."

"But nobody has said so."

"No," Fred agreed.

They reached the corner, and Roy stopped, waiting for the

light. "This woman who died," he said. "She was a nun. But not one of the usual nuns. She was the one who didn't wear a habit. The one who was—" Roy tried to think of a word for it, but there wasn't one. "The one who was in favor of abortion," he said finally, but he didn't like that. From what he remembered, the woman had never said anything in favor of abortion. It was just her . . . general demeanor. "The feminist one," he said finally.

"Oh," Fred said. "Well, yeah. It's like I told you yesterday. She was the one who wore the suit who went on television that time and said that we were un-Christian. You remember. She sort of—"

"I remember. So she was a liberal at least, and maybe a radical. She had a lot to do with the gay people at St. Stephen's."

"Well, yeah," Fred said. "You said that last night."

The light changed. They crossed the street. Roy sighed. "I know what I said last night," he said patiently. "What I'm trying to get at is what the papers have confirmed. What have they said about her? That she was a liberal? That she was a radical? That she knew a lot of the gay men at St. Stephen's?"

"Oh," Fred said. "I don't know."

"Didn't you read the papers this morning? You brought me one. Didn't you watch the news?"

"Well, yeah," Fred said. "But I wasn't thinking about her. I was thinking about us. You know. The people in the church. There's a lot of bad stuff out there about us."

"There will be. They'll hate us. It doesn't matter," Roy said. "Tell me what you did notice. What about the murder itself? Where was she found? What was she doing?"

"Oh, she was found in somebody's office at St. Anselm's. I don't think she was doing anything. I think she was dead."

Yes, Roy thought. Of course she was dead. Of course she was. His head hurt. Surely there had to be a better way than this to do what he had been put on earth to do. If God had to choose him as an instrument, why couldn't He choose a few secondary instruments with the brains He gave to chickens? They were coming up on another light and another crosswalk. Roy stopped again.

"All right," he said finally. "Here it is. We've got to get hold of a certain amount of information. For one thing, I want to know who it is the police really are treating as their prime suspect. For another thing, I want the autopsy report before it hits the street. Don't we have somebody in the medical examiner's office?"

"Jeb Brandish," Fred said. "He sweeps up."

"That's all he has to do, that and listen. The other thing I need is some information on this Gregor Demarkian. Where he lives. How he lives. Who he lives with. Is he gay, do you think?"

"I don't know.'

The light changed again. They moved again. "I've read a few things about him in the papers, but I don't know either. I never paid much attention. On the other hand, I do seem to remember some woman. Send somebody to check that out. Maybe they're living in sin."

"Gotcha," Fred said.

"The best thing would be to find him on the record with something completely discrediting," Roy said. "Or at least something we could use to charge bias. Some anti-Christian statement. Some atheist organization. Something."

"You mean like the ACLU?"

"Not really," Roy said. "The police department isn't going to fire him just because he belongs to the ACLU. If he does. I was thinking of something like American Atheists, or the Council for Secular Humanism. The chances are he doesn't belong to either, though. He used to be with the FBI. He'd know better than to join organizations that could compromise him."

"Right," Fred said.

Now they were coming up on St. Anselm's by the side. Roy looked into the parking lot and saw that it was nearly empty. The noon Mass had to be over. He picked up speed and turned left at the corner, down their own long and almost-pristine-again street.

There was a lot of activity going on at St. Stephen's, people going in and out. Roy stopped and looked at the bulletin board, but it was too far away for him to read. Underneath it, though, there was a sign made of red letters on white posterboard that said: PRAY FOR TOLERANCE. 6 PM.

"What's all that about?" he asked.

"They're doing some kind of service for the guys who got

beat up last night," Fred said. "Carl was wondering if you wanted to picket it. You know. I said I'd ask."

"We should think about it. It's the kind of thing we picket. There may be a serious police presence after last night."

"Right," Fred said. "That's what I told Carl."

Roy turned away and started down the street again. "We've got guys who got beat up," he said. "We should do a service, too. But it wouldn't attract the same kind of attention. There's something else about Gregor Demarkian."

"What?"

"He might not have joined any of those organizations, but somebody close to him could have. Somebody he's connected to, publicly. Check into that."

"All right."

"And while you're at it, check out Edith Lawton. Check out—" Roy stopped.

He could spend all day telling Fred what to check out, but in the end he would have to do at least some of the checking himself. Fred wasn't up to it, and Fred was the cream of his own particular crop.

Up the street, the front windows of their church gleamed in the sun, untouched by last night's madness.

God would always take care of His own.

3

The call from the Cardinal Archbishop came at five minutes to one, and when it did, Dan Burdock had an almost-irresistible desire to refuse it. He did not, like some people, have reason to dislike the Cardinal, at least not personally. As far as he knew, he had never met the man. The problem was that he was so immensely tired, physically, mentally, and emotionally, he couldn't imagine himself coping with what he was sure was going to be an unpleasant call. If it wasn't unpleasant for the obvious reasons—it was the Cardinal, after all, who gave interviews to the papers once a year calling homosexuality an "objective evil"—Dan had the feeling it would be unpleasant for the peripheral ones. He didn't think he would ever want to say it, but the truth was that he was sick of the entire *issue*. He didn't even understand why it had to be an *issue.* Some people were gay, and some people were not. Why should that be any business of his? Why should that be any business of *anybody's*? What was it, exactly, that made so many people feel that they had to Take A Stand at every possible opportunity, until the world was full of stands on matters so trivial, they made the mind numb? If he ever had the chance, he was going to quit this job and move out to Wyoming or Montana, where he could live with a television set and a computer and no contact with his neighbors at all.

Mrs. Reed was hovering in his doorway. Dan thought that, under the circumstances, Wyoming might not be the very best choice. He rubbed his eyes. He had been rubbing them since late last night. They were as raw as hamburger.

"Father?" Mrs. Reed said.

"Call me Dan," Dan said automatically.

"It's the Cardinal Archbishop of Philadelphia," Mrs. Reed said. "I do understand that you're very tired, Father, and it's no wonder, with that disgraceful man and the disgraceful mess he made last night, but it is the Cardinal Archbishop of Philadelphia. I will tell him you're out, if you'd rather I do that, but I thought—"

"No," Dan said. "It's all right. I'm going to—transfer it to the cell phone, will you? I've got to walk around. I'm asleep on my feet."

"Of course I will, Father."

"Oh, and while you're at it, do you think you could call the hospital and find out when they're going to be letting Chickie out? Aaron thinks we should do something in the way of a homecoming. I think we should have somebody there with a car. Whatever—"

"Mr. George is being released this afternoon," Mrs. Reed said. "That Miss McAllister from across the street is picking him up. He called this morning to let us know."

"Oh," Dan said. He got up and took the cell phone out of its leather case. The leather case was from Coach. It had been a gift, but he couldn't now remember from whom. "Is Chickie coming here? If he isn't, do we know when he will come?"

"Miss McAllister is taking him to his apartment so that he can change," Mrs. Reed said. "Then I believe she's bringing him here."

"Right," Dan said, then he thought: trust Chickie to have

made the kind of friend willing to do all that for him. He got the cell phone open and put it to his ear, and then put it down again. There was nothing on it but a dial tone. "I'm going to take this thing and walk," he said again.

"I'll put the Cardinal Archbishop through," Mrs. Reed said.

She went out, and Dan went out after her. She sat down at her desk, and Dan walked past her into the hallway and down the stairs. He was going around to the choir balcony in the church proper, where he had been going on and off all day, compulsively, as if merely being there would somehow straighten out the mess his mind had become. It was beautiful, this church. It had been built to be beautiful, and to show the rest of Philadelphia that the people of this parish were solid. The Anglican Communion was not a Calvinist stronghold, but there had always been a streak of predestination in it. God had His elect, and you could know them by their exalted positions in the community of the people of God.

The cell phone rang in his hand just as he was starting up the stone steps to the balcony. He flipped the switch that put him on just as he was entering the balcony. From where he stood, the church below might have been empty. He got only the soaring height of the ceiling and the gleaming pipes of the organ. He headed toward the railing that would allow him to overlook the church.

"Dan Burdock," he said.

"Father Burdock." The Cardinal Archbishop's voice was unmistakable. If you heard it once, even on television, you knew it forever afterward. "This is Aidan Kennedy."

"Yes, Your Eminence," Dan said. "I recognized your voice."

He also couldn't imagine anybody calling this man "Aidan." He got to the very front of the balcony and sat down, so that he could watch everything that was happening in the church. At the moment, nothing much was. There were still a few people left over from the night before, but the wounded had mostly been dispatched to emergency rooms and their own apartments. Aaron was working on collecting bail and fine money in another part of the church complex. The few people who were straggling through were mostly cleaning up. Dan fished around in his trouser pocket for his roll of soft mints, pulled it out, and ate two.

"I don't know if that's good news or bad," the Cardinal said. "I suppose it means I should never say anything compromising over a cell phone."

"Excuse me?"

"If I have a recognizable voice."

"Oh." Dan blinked. "I'm sorry, Your Eminence. I'm very tired at the moment."

"Yes, I would expect. I shouldn't think any of us slept very well last night. Has there been any damage done to your church?"

"Physical damage, you mean? Not a thing. They didn't even knock over the gate, and they've done that a couple of times before."

"There have been riots a couple of times before?"

"No, no," Dan said. "Not riots. Just demonstrations. That's what Roy and his people do. They demonstrate. They picket AIDS funerals."

"Yes, I've heard."

"We have a fair number of AIDS funerals here," Dan said. "Although not as many as a few years ago, thank God. Sometimes they picket if they think one of the gay men is acting as reader. Sometimes they picket just because they don't have anything else to do. I don't know, your Eminence. They're a fact of life around here."

There was the sound of papers shuffling on the other end of the line. Two men had come into the body of the church with rags and spray cans of Pledge and started to polish the pews.

"I wanted you to know," the Cardinal Archbishop said, "that I've spoken to Father Healy, and the pray-in for the conversion of homosexuals has been canceled. Under the circumstances, it seemed to be the only responsible course of action. I didn't want there to be even the possibility that something we did could set off Mr. Phipps and his, uh, parishioners."

"That's good," Dan said. "I'm glad to hear it. Was that what you called about?"

There was the sound of papers shuffling again. Dan wondered if this were nervousness, or if the Cardinal meant for him to get the impression that whatever the object of this call was, it was official enough to require being written down like a script.

"No," the Cardinal said finally. "If it had been just that, I wouldn't have bothered you on what I knew to be a very bad day. I'm calling to ask for a meeting."

"What?"

"I'm calling to ask for a meeting," the Cardinal said again. "I would like the two of us to sit down and talk. In private. At a time and place comfortable enough for the both of us that we would not be constrained for time."

"But—*why*?" Dan said. Then he blushed, even though the Cardinal couldn't see him. He'd sounded like a ten-year-old, or worse. He'd sounded like an overemoting actress in a soap opera whose plot was headed for a major crisis. "Excuse me, Your Eminence. I'm sorry. It's just that—"

"It's just that this is highly irregular. Yes. I realize that. Tell me, there was nobody left dead last night, so I suppose your people are all right on that score, but what about serious injuries. Wasn't one of your parishioners seriously injured?"

"A couple of them were."

"And aren't you going to have a service, a Mass, a memorial, to pray for those who were injured?"

"Well, yes," Dan said. "We're doing a couple of things, really. A small one tonight. And then the day after tomorrow, we're going to do something more formal, invite the families, that kind of thing—"

"Yes, of course. We would do something like that, too, in similar circumstances. That's what I want to talk about. The larger service you intend to hold. Do you think you could come here for dinner this evening? Is that convenient for you?"

"Dinner," Dan said.

"We could make it later in the evening," the Cardinal Archbishop said, "or, of course, I could come to you, or we could meet on neutral ground. The problem is that it's almost impossible for me to travel in privacy. I've got too many people watching me. And if we met in a restaurant, half the city of Philadelphia would know within the hour. Of course, if you'd rather not come here, I'd be more than willing—"

"No," Dan said. The two men who were polishing the pews were nearly obsessive about it. They polished and repolished. They were going to take all night. "No," Dan said again. "It's not that, it's tonight. We've got something on tonight. Could it be tomorrow or—"

"I'd rather it be sooner than later. How about four this afternoon?"

There was really no reason why he should not go at four that afternoon. There was only the fact that the very idea of it made him tired.

"Four would be fine," he heard himself saying.

"Excellent," the Cardinal Archbishop said. "Would you like me to send my car?"

"Wouldn't that defeat the purpose?" Dan said. "Your car isn't exactly any more anonymous than you are."

"I could send a different car. Let me do that. You sound ready to drop. Would you like to be picked up at your rectory or your office?"

"The office," Dan said.

"Wonderful. Thank you very much, Father Burdock. I'm very sorry about that nastiness you were forced to endure last night. Let's hope that Mr. Phipps is chastened enough by his arrest to lie a little low for the next few weeks."

"He isn't."

"The car will be there promptly at three-forty-five. I'm looking forward to seeing you."

"I'm looking forward to seeing you, too, Your Eminence," Dan said, but the phone had gone to dial tone in his hand. There was nobody at the other end of the line. Dan flicked the switch that turned the cell phone off, folded it up, and put it in his pocket. Then he looked at his roll of soft mints, still in his other hand, and put those in his pocket, too.

He couldn't see the Cardinal Archbishop for dinner because he was leading a service here. He didn't want to see the Cardinal Archbishop at four o'clock because—why? Because, Dan thought, there had been a tone in that man's voice as dangerous as any he had ever heard in Roy Phipps's.

He leaned over the balcony rail, meaning to call down to the two polishers in the pews, and then thought better of it. They were all doing odd, obsessive things today. It wouldn't hurt the pews to have them polished. He straightened up and headed back to the stairs.

Maybe he could take an hour and sack out in his living room, so that he wouldn't show up at the chancery so whacked-out he was walking into walls.

FOUR

1

Gregor Demarkian couldn't decide if he liked fax machines or not. They were one of the few of the new machines he had no real trouble with—although lately, being around Bennis as much as he was, he had become far more relaxed on the computer. They also had the virtue of being able to get him large amounts of material in a very short time without the waste or expense of traveling through the city. Garry Mansfield and Lou Emiliani hadn't bothered to make him get into a cab, or to make their department pay a messenger. They had both just got on their fax machines and sent him everything they had, reams and reams of it, so that, by late in the morning, he had found himself surrounded by flimsy paper: toxicology reports, search reports, interview transcripts, expert advice. What worried Gregor was that, having supplied him with all this information, Garry and Lou would now expect him to make something of it. It certainly seemed as if there ought to be enough to make something of something. At the very least, he ought to have a clue. Instead, he was just as bewildered as he had ever been, and the information that was now coming in about the death of Sister Harriet Garrity wasn't making things any clearer. All three victims had eaten arsenic. None of them had eaten anything else in common, at least in the period for which the autopsy would be valid—although that wasn't as sure as it could be. It didn't take much arsenic to kill a person. If they had ingested it in something very small, like a gel-cap pill, the elements might not always show up in the autopsy reports. All of them had known the same people, more or less, or at least been in close proximity to them, and all of them had been connected, to one extent or the other, to the arch-diocesan priest-pedophilia scandal. Beyond that, he had nothing. The police had nothing. Maybe there was nothing to be had. He was being asked to come to a logical solution to a series of crimes that amounted to ducks being shot off a conveyer belt at the marksmanship booth at a carnival.

The taxi pulled up in front of St. Anselm's side gate. Gregor got out, paid the fare, dropped a better tip than he should have in the front seat, and looked around. He couldn't see the main street from there, but St. Stephen's looked calm enough, if a little busier than it had the first time he had been there. He went through the gate and around the back of the church to the parking lot and the convent. The offices were still sealed, and would be for three days, in case the police suddenly found they needed to investigate something they hadn't thought of before. A uniformed policeman was standing on the convent steps, looking cold.

"Mr. Demarkian," he said, when Gregor walked up. "They're in there. In the front room. The, uh, the parlor."

"Thank you," Gregor said.

The patrolman looked uncomfortable. "You figure this is okay?" he asked. "With the Church, I mean. It's okay to question the nuns?"

"Of course it's okay to question the nuns," Gregor said.

"I guess." The patrolman stepped out of the way so that Gregor could get through to the door.

Gregor didn't bother to ask if he were Catholic. Of *course* he was Catholic. Gregor let himself in the front door and headed for the parlor, easily visible a few steps to his left.

Garry and Lou were there, sitting uncomfortably at the edge of a couch. Lou, at least, was also Catholic. Sister Scholastica was there, too, which Gregor had not expected, and as he came in he raised his eyebrows at her.

"It's the rule of the order," she said, standing up to take his coat. Garry and Lou practically leaped to their feet. Gregor revised his estimate. Garry Mansfield, too, was probably Catholic. He looked at the other nun, the very young one, and nodded.

"This is Sister Peter Rose," Scholastica said. "The order says none of us can be alone with a layman or even with a priest, except for Confession or spiritual counseling. And that's man, not in the generic sense. If you know what I mean. Actually, if the police department insisted, we'd oblige. But they didn't insist, so . . ."

"No, no, no," Lou said. "It's perfectly all right, Sister. We understand."

Sister Scholastica put Gregor's coat on a coat tree and sat down again. Lou Emiliani sat down, too. Garry remained standing. Sister Peter Rose looked up, and said, "We met, you know. In Colchester. When all that happened. I'd just taken tertiary vows. Sister thought I was a flake."

"I never said you were a flake," Scholastica said.

"You never *said* it," Peter Rose said. Then she turned to Gregor again. "It's true, you know. I am a flake, at least a little bit. I should have realized she was up to something. Even Thomasetta noticed there was something very odd. It just never occurred to me."

"Thomasetta?" Gregor said.

"You met her last night," Garry said. "Older nun. She was on duty in the main office when Sister Harriet first came looking for Sister Scholastica."

"I remember," Gregor said.

"The thing is," Sister Peter Rose said, "it didn't make sense, not really. I mean, Sister Harriet never came looking for Sister Scholastica. She phoned up and demanded that Sister come visit *her*. If you know what I mean. She was just so—she thought that we were all terrible for wearing habits, that was one thing. And she wanted everybody to know she had an important position in the parish, as parish coordinator, and that she wasn't just another parochial-school nun. Although what's more important in the life of a parish than running the school, I don't know. Oh. Except for celebrating the Eucharist, of course."

"Of course," Gregor said. "And you—you work in the office?"

"Oh, no, not usually," Sister Peter Rose said. "I teach second grade. And I serve as vice principal, you know, which means I'm supposed to mete out the discipline when it's necessary, but I'm not very good at that—"

"She's a marshmallow," Sister Scholastica said.

Sister Peter Rose blushed. "I'm a marshmallow. It's true. And most of the kids who get sent to me are just boys who have too much energy, and they're bored. It's terrible what we do to boys, trying to make them sit still in a classroom for six hours a day."

"But you were in the office yesterday," Gregor said.

"Yes," Peter Rose agreed. "I was. It's First Communion, you see. They're all going to make their First Communions right after Easter. And they had practice—"

"Practice?" Gregor said.

"How to walk in lines and how to kneel the right way and that kind of thing," Peter Rose said. "And, you know, singing. Only, Mrs. Giametti was doing the practice. She's the head of our CCD—"

"CCD?" Gregor asked.

"Confraternity of Christian Doctrine," Scholastica said. "A fancy name for catechism for children in public schools."

"The public-school children and the St. Anselm's children are all going to make their First Holy Communions together," Peter Rose said, "and Angelina—Mrs. Giametti—wanted to drill our children so that she was sure they'd all be in sync when the time came. So I sent them over to the church with her, and I came over to my office to get some paperwork done. Did I tell you that the vice principal has an office?"

"I think he would have expected that," Scholastica said.

"Yes, well." Peter Rose blushed. "Anyway, I was there. When she came in. And she was looking for Scholastica."

"She told you she was looking for Scholastica?" Gregor asked.

"No, she didn't tell me anything at all. I don't think she ever saw me. She went right past my door without saying hello."

"Then how do you know she was looking for Scholastica?"

"She asked Thomasetta," Sister Peter Rose said. "Thomasetta didn't like her much. And she didn't like Thomasetta much. You know how it is. But she asked Thomasetta, and Thomasetta told her that Scholastica was out."

"This was when?" Gregor asked.

"About ten-thirty."

"What did she do then?" Gregor asked. "Did she leave? Did she ask questions?"

"Thomasetta said something about where Scholastica was and where she had been, and then Sister Harriet walked down the hall and passed me again. And then she must have gone into Scholastica's office—"

"Must have?" Gregor shook his head. "You mean you didn't see her?"

"No," Peter Rose admitted, "but I didn't really have to see her. There are only two places to be down on that end of the hall. Either she went into Scholastica's office, or she went out the fire door and down the stairs."

"Why are you so sure she didn't go out the fire door?"

"Because it screams like a banshee," Scholastica said. "We have it oiled and oiled, but nothing seems to work. The hinge probably ought to be replaced."

"So, the hinge didn't scream," Gregor said. "How do you know she didn't just stand in the hall for a while?"

"I don't," Peter Rose said. "But it doesn't make any sense, does it? Why would she just stand there, not even moving. And besides—"

"Besides?" Gregor cocked his head.

"She was in there fifteen minutes later," Peter Rose said. "She must have been. Nobody came in from that end, because I would have heard the hinge. And nobody came in and down the hall from the other end, because they would have had to pass me. But Mary McAllister came in at just about quarter of, and she wanted to put some things on Scholastica's desk, and when she went down to the office, the door was locked."

"I never lock my door," Scholastica said. "None of us do, except sometimes by accident, because there's no point to it."

"There are duplicate keys all over the place," Peter Rose said. "And don't say it's possible that Scholastica locked the door herself by accident, because it was open when I came back that morning and it was open not five minutes before the first time I saw Harriet in the hall. I saw it coming back from the bathroom."

"But you're sure it was locked from the inside?" Gregor said.

Scholastica shook her head. "Inside, outside, it doesn't matter. The keys work regardless."

"Why didn't somebody use the key to get in so that—"

"Mary McAllister," Lou Emiliani said.

"Mary McAllister," Gregor repeated. "Why didn't somebody use a duplicate key to get in when Mary McAllister wanted to leave the things on Scholastica's desk? What things, by the way?"

"Some papers about the food drive. Mary works with a homeless shelter downtown, and she does food distribution here. Our parochial-school kids collect canned goods and non-perishables. Sometimes, there's a special call—for peanut butter, for kidney beans, for cranberry sauce. Things that are especially needed or that somebody wants. Mary had the special-needs schedules for next month."

"And she took them away with her?" Gregor asked.

"She just went down to the main office and put them in Scholastica's box," Peter Rose said. "She didn't want to take the time for Thomasetta to go find the key and open up. Except, you know, that she was bothered by it. The locked room. She was, and I wasn't. And she didn't really have any reason to think there was something wrong. I should have known right then that Harriet must have been inside. It just didn't occur to me."

Gregor stood up and began to pace, but very slowly. It was hard to move, because the room was small and too full of furniture. "So what you're saying," he said finally, "is that Sister Harriet Garrity went into Sister Scholastica's office at ten-thirty yesterday morning and locked the door behind her. Why?"

"I don't know," Peter Rose said.

"Probably to get a look at my computer," Scholastica said. "It's got a password on it, but we all use the same ones. Benedicamus Domini. There are a couple of others. It wouldn't have taken her much to go through them."

"What would be on your computer that Sister Harriet Garrity would want?" Gregor asked.

Scholastica and Peter Rose looked at each other. Scholastica took a deep breath. "Well," she said, "nothing, really, but Sister might have hoped there was. We've been having a lot of, well, friction, since I got here in January."

"Friction about what?"

"About the First Holy Communion Mass, for one thing," Scholastica said. "I'm all for the traditional event, with girls in white dresses and veils. She was all for something more 'relevant,' except that wouldn't have been the word she would have used. More 'feminist,' maybe. Anyway, we had a fight about it, and I won that round. She might have been looking for embarrassing information to use the next time we had a run-in."

"And there was no such information?"

"Good grief, Gregor, I've been here less than two months." Scholastica laughed. "Not that there isn't enough embarrassing information in my past, but Harriet wasn't going to find out about it in my office. She might have discovered that I've been less than strict about the academic requirements in the case of one or two of the kids, but that isn't anything Father Healy didn't know about. Besides, she was the one who was always saying that grades were a tool of white-male hegemonic oppression."

"All right," Gregor said. "What happened after ten-forty-five? Did Sister Rose see her come out of the office?"

"No," Peter Rose said. "She was in there as late as one o'clock without ever coming out to the extent of using the fire door or passing my office."

"You were in a position to know that throughout that whole time?"

"Yes. There's a rosary at twelve, but I didn't go. I had a lot of work to do."

Gregor thought about it. "So," he said. "She was in that office at least until one. What happened at one?"

"I ran over to the convent to have some lunch."

"And then?"

"Then I taught my class until three. Then I made sure everybody had their coats and their backpacks. Then I made sure everybody got on the bus."

"You didn't go back to your office?" Gregor asked.

"No," Peter Rose said.

"Fine. What about Sister Harriet Garrity? Did anybody else see her at any time during the rest of the afternoon?"

"No," Lou Emiliani put in. "We've asked everybody in the place. Nobody saw her after Sister Thomasetta and Sister Peter Rose saw her at ten-thirty. Somebody even went looking for her and couldn't find her. Ah—"

"Sister Bridget," Garry Mansfield put in. "She had phone duty. Somebody was looking for Sister Harriet from something called GALA."

"Gay and Lesbian Support Advisory," Scholastica put in.

"It's an advocacy organization that deals with gay community issues. It was practically the only thing Harriet belonged to that the Chancery didn't scream about, although they probably would have liked to. GALA did a lot of work on behalf of the plaintiffs in the pedophilia suit."

"Did anybody look for Harriet in Scholastica's office?" Gregor asked.

"I doubt it," Scholastica said. "I mean, why would they? Although we could always ask."

"Ask," Gregor said. "Just in case. What about time of death? Do we have that yet?"

"Later on this afternoon," Lou Emiliani said. "But you know what that's like. We won't get anywhere near a narrow enough band to pin down something like this—"

"I know, I know." Gregor sighed. "But we can always hope. You're sure that nobody could have come past you and into Scholastica's office between ten-forty-five and one?"

"I'm positive," Peter Rose said.

"And you didn't hear any sounds coming out of the room? You didn't hear thrashing, or a scream?"

"I'd hope I'd do something about a scream," Peter Rose said. "I didn't hear anything unusual. What could I have heard?"

"There might have been nothing to hear," Garry Mansfield put in. "It would all depend on just how much—"

"I know," Gregor said. He walked over to the coat tree and took his coat down. "I think," he said, "we'd better go have a talk with Father Healy."

2

Gregor Demarkian had spent enough time around the Catholic Church, and around priests of other denominations, to understand that he was unlikely to find Father Healy standing at the altar of his church at any odd hour of the day, but as soon as he came out of the office building he veered in that direction anyway. Garry and Lou still weren't used to him. They veered when he veered, but they were clearly very surprised. He let himself in the church's side door and walked out to the center aisle. It was a high-ceilinged, mock-Gothic building, and, like most of the churches in the era in which it was built, very ornate. The backs and ends of the pews were carved into rolls and swirls. The marble of the Communion rail was sculpted into a smooth raised curve. The altar was marble, too, and it looked nothing at all like the ersatz tables so many Catholic churches went in for these days. For one thing, there were cracks and discolorations, the kind of small thing that went wrong with expensive buildings when their owners didn't have quite enough money to keep them up. Gregor walked down the aisle to the back of the church and looked back the way he had come. He walked back up to the altar and paced back and forth in front of the rail. The church was nearly empty of people. The few who were there did not look up.

"What are you doing?" Lou demanded. "Father Healy is in the rectory."

"I just wanted to check something," Gregor said. "Bernadette Kelly was found here, at the front, near the altar?"

"Right in the middle of the center aisle," Garry said.

"What about her husband? Where was he when he shot himself?"

"Same place." Garry looked around. "You can't tell, can you? They really cleaned it up."

"There was a mess?" Gregor asked. Then he waved this away. "Of course there was. Don't pay any attention to me."

"There was blood all over everything," Garry said. "The front pews. The carpet. The Communion rail. Head wounds bleed the worst. They must have gotten professionals in to do this kind of job. It's impressive."

"Mmmm." Gregor paced back and forth in front of the altar again. His first question was answered. There was enough room. Marty Kelly had not been cramped. He looked around at the people in the pews. They were bent over the pews in front of them, their eyes closed, prayer. "The time," he said. "It was just before Mass?"

"An hour before," Garry said.

"But the report you gave me said that the Church was full of people," Gregor said.

"Father Healy lets the homeless people come in here and sleep," Lou put in. "There's a shelter around here somewhere, but it gets full fast in the winter. And some of these people would prefer not to go there."

"It's nicer here," Garry said. "And you know, the shelter feels like an institution, and a lot of these people, especially the women, they've spent most of their lives in institutions. I'd think they'd want to go back, but they don't."

"Jail is jail," Lou said. "No matter what you call it. And even if you're crazy."

"But there were nuns here, too, weren't there?" Gregor asked.

"Oh, yeah," Garry said. "They do things. Bring flowers for the altar, that kind of thing. And that girl, Mary McAllister, she was here, too. She gets the homeless people before Mass and brings them out to the soup kitchen. Unless they want to stay for Mass. Then one of the nuns stay in the pews with them to look after them, you know, and somebody takes them over to the soup kitchen for the second breakfast sitting."

"The place sounds like an airport," Gregor said. "Did Marty Kelly know all this when he brought his wife here that morning? Did he expect an empty church?"

"I don't know," Garry said. "There's a lot we don't know about Marty Kelly. Do you think he would have come if he'd realized there would be a lot of people here?"

"I wouldn't have," Gregor said. "And there's another thing. Are you sure he brought her here? She couldn't have been somewhere on the grounds, out of sight? I know about the forensic evidence from the truck, but that doesn't really prove anything. She must have been in that truck dozens of times."

"She was dead better than ten hours when we found her," Garry said. "If she died on the grounds, you'd think somebody would have run across the body. Or somebody would have smelled something. She had to have vomited. Somewhere. With arsenic—"

"Yes, I know," Gregor said. "There was no vomit found in the truck?"

"None," Garry said.

"And none in her home, either, I would presume," Gregor said.

"She and Marty lived in this trailer park," Garry said. "Except it wasn't what you'd think. She kept that trailer as neat as anything. As neat as this church. Everything polished. Everything washed."

Gregor was startled. "You're sure that wasn't done afterward? Somebody could have been cleaning up after—"

"Not like this, they couldn't have," Garry said. "It was more than just clean. It was bone clean. You know how those places get. The cooking smells are into everything. The stains. This was spotless."

"Spotless," Gregor repeated. He walked back and forth in front of the altar again. "Where did he bring her in?" he asked. "From the side over there, the way we came in? He couldn't have brought her in the front."

"We think he brought her in the side, yeah," Garry said. "But nobody saw him. He could have come in from the basement."

"You've checked?"

"More than once."

"Okay, walk me through this," Gregor said. "Let's say he brought her in the side door. He walked through into the church and he saw it was full of people, but nobody was at the altar. And the homeless people—would they have been mostly sleeping?"

"I'd guess," Garry said. "A couple of them weren't. Or said they weren't, afterward. They said they'd seen him shoot."

"Okay. So. He brings the body of his wife into the church, he walks to the altar—across this front part?"

"That's right," Garry said.

"And he lays her body down in front of the Communion rail. According to the report, that would be almost exactly in the middle, in front of the middle aisle. Then what did he do?"

"He shot himself," Garry said.

"Just like that?" Gregor asked him. "He laid her down, he stood up, he took a gun out of his pocket, and he blasted away?"

"Oh," Garry said. "Well, yeah, pretty much. He didn't talk to anybody, if that's what you mean. He put her down. Then, according to one of the Sisters who were here, he sort of looked around. Then he took something out of his coat and shot himself in the head."

Gregor rubbed his eyes. It was incredible, how little feeling he had for this man or his wife—well, no. That wasn't what he meant. He had so little feeling *of* them, was more like it, he couldn't imagine what they had felt or hoped or wanted. What was worse, he had the impression that Garry Mansfield was just as clueless as he was. He shook his head.

"He brought her here," he said, "because she was very religious, and he wanted her to be where she would have wanted to be herself. He shot himself—why? Because he was despondent at her death? Because he felt responsible for her death?"

"We interviewed his mother," Garry said drily. "She's a barfly from way back. Totally pickled. The only thing she was completely clear about was how much she hated her daughter-in-law's guts. But don't get your hopes up. She couldn't have managed something as elaborate as an arsenic poisoning if her life had depended on it."

"This was out in the trailer park? The same trailer park?"

"Right," Garry said. "Out in Wilmot Township. Which is one hell of a long drive from here, even in the middle of the night with practically no traffic. And don't ask me why they lived in the same place his mother did, because I don't know. She seemed to think they were persecuting her."

"Maybe they were trying to get her off booze," Lou said.

Garry snorted.

Gregor sat down in a pew. He always felt strange, sitting in pews very close to the altar in a church. It was as if he thought that if he were going to be so near what mattered, he ought to be standing, or kneeling. But he never knelt, even when he came to liturgy at Holy Trinity on Cavanaugh Street, to please Father Tibor.

"Okay," he said. "Let's straighten this out. Bernadette and Marty Kelly were poor. True enough?"

"True as it gets," Garry said.

"What about Scott Boardman?" Gregor asked Lou.

"Middle class," Lou said. "Not poor, not rich. Had a decent enough profession. Got a lot of work. From a working-class family. Nothing significant in the bank. But, you know, there was the settlement money. From the pedophilia suit. I don't think any of the men got a lot, but it came in every month."

"What about Harriet Garrity?"

"She was a nun," Garry said. "I thought nuns weren't allowed to own any property."

"She could have a family that owns property," Lou said. "Rich people become nuns."

"I'll check it out," Garry said. "But I don't see it, do you? She dressed like a bag lady."

"She didn't dress like a bag lady," Lou said. "She was just being modest."

"She dressed in sacks," Garry said.

Gregor waved them quiet. "Love and money," he said. "That's what we've got to concentrate on. Love and money. And none of them had access to any money, as far as we know."

Garry frowned. "That's not exactly true," he said. "Sister Harriet was the parish coordinator. I don't know what that means, exactly, but she might have had access to the parish budget. And I'd bet the budget around here isn't small."

"What about Scott Boardman?" Gregor asked.

"He didn't officially have access," Lou said, "but he might have been able to get it unofficially. He volunteered a lot over there. He did office work. If you know how to tap into the computer files, you could do anything. And St. Stephen's was the administrator for Scott Boardman's reparations payments. Him and about five other guys, I think. That probably came to something."

"All right. That leaves us with Bernadette Kelly. And there, I take it, we come up blank."

Garry and Lou looked at each other and shrugged.

Gregor stood up. "Gentlemen," he said, "we've got three bodies, each one of them murdered almost identically, as far as we can figure out. We've got no connections. Do you realize that? We don't have a single thing to hold these three people together except that they attended the two churches located on this corner. And last I heard, that was not a credible motive for murder."

"Maybe it is," Lou said. "Maybe we have one of those serial killers you used to chase, and he's targeting parishioners."

"And he starts doing that by following Bernadette Kelly out to a trailer park in Wilmot Township?—wait."

"Wait what?" Lou asked.

"Arsenic," Gregor said.

Garry and Lou looked at each other again.

Gregor headed for the side door they'd come in by. He felt good for the first time since he'd started looking into this— not because he had the solution, but because he finally knew that a solution was at least possible. Solutions were not possible in all cases. There were perfect murders, and he had had the misfortune to be on the team investigating one or two. Life not only wasn't fair. It often didn't make sense.

Outside, he turned down the path that led around to the back and the rectory, moving quickly because his coat wasn't buttoned, and he was cold. He had to talk to Father Healy, and after that he had to sit down with some scratch paper and think. Bennis would want him to think on the computer, but at least this time he wasn't going to listen to her.

The wind was whipping through the courtyard, icy and stiff. His hands were cold. His nose was numb. Only his mind was warmed up and working.

Arsenic, he thought, solved the problem of place.

FIVE

1

Father Robert Healy had had a very hard time sleeping the night before, so hard a time he thought he might not have slept at all. What he remembered clearly was getting up in the dark and the silence to look at his clock. It was three in the morning, and so deathly still he might have been waking in his own grave. It was also deathly cold. He found himself wishing that he had chosen one of those old-fashioned windup clocks that ticked to put on his bedside table. It seemed less important to him, then, that he not be woken by the sound of ticking than that he not feel so thickly encased in isolation when he did wake. He tried closing his eyes and praying silently. He tried opening them and lighting the candle in front of his small statute of the Virgin, as if it might be possible for him to will her to speak. Under ordinary circumstances, he considered most of the traditional prayers to Mary—except, of course, for the Ave—to be embarrassingly overwrought and sentimental. In his room with the candle lit, with his narrow bed and its black horsehair blanket, they seemed to be only reportage, a documentary description of the apocalypse. *To you do we cry, poor banished children of Eve. To you do we send up our sighs, mourning and weeping in this vale of tears.* He could remember himself in third or fourth grade, squirming and impatient under the eyes of old Sister Benedicta, while his confirmation class recited the Salve in unison. If he'd been born twenty years earlier, he would have learned that prayer. He would have been happier.

Now, watching Gregor Demarkian come up the rectory walk with the two police detectives he recognized from the

night before, Robert was mostly worried that he would fall
asleep in the middle of a question and embarrass himself even
more than he had already been embarrassed by events. The
Cardinal Archbishop had been clear as a bell. He was the chief
suspect in three murders, including the murder of Sister Harriet
Garrity, which had almost certainly happened by arsenic, like
the two others. He had bought the arsenic. He knew all three
victims. He was known to be on rocky terms with Sister Harriet—but really, Robert thought, it was hard to take that seriously. *Everybody* was known to be on rocky terms with
Sister Harriet. The woman made a vocation out of being on
rocky terms. It disturbed him more that anyone thought he
might be responsible for the death of that poor young man
across the street, whom he had hardly known except to say
hello to once or twice. Only a crazy person killed somebody
he didn't know, or, worse, killed to bring the wrath of God
down on the people he thought God ought to condemn. Robert
was sure he had never suggested, or even thought, that the
wrath of God should come down on the gay men at St. Stephen's. He had only wanted to be clear in his support of the
Magisterium. He had only wanted his position to be impossible to misconstrue.

The detectives all had their coats open, even though it had
to be below zero outside. They all had their heads down, but
Robert thought that might have been the wind. He looked
around the rectory foyer and realized with a certain amount
of resignation that it, like the rectory living room, was full of
bad art. There was a painting of the Sacred Heart of Jesus that
might as well have been done by numbers on a velvet field.
There was another of the Virgin and Child that made the Virgin look like a saccharine sheep and the Child look like a
stuffed toy. He never noticed those things when he was in the
rectory by himself—if he had, he would have gotten rid of
them—but they always impressed themselves on his consciousness as soon as he had company.

He opened the door before they had a chance to knock and
stepped back to let them in. "Mr. Demarkian," he said. "And
Detective Mansfield. And Detective—Emilio, isn't it?"

"Emiliani," Emiliani said.

"Emiliani. I'm very sorry." He took the coats they were
shrugging off—all but Demarkian; Demarkian seemed deter-

mined to keep his coat—and put them over the banister at the bottom of the stairs. There was a closet, but it was full of junk that nobody knew what to do with. He gestured them in the direction of the living room, and they went. Mansfield and Emiliani went directly. Gregor Demarkian stopped at every piece of art.

"It's really very bad stuff," Robert found himself saying. "I ought to replace it with prints of decent work. The Church has such a wealth of truly fine art. But I never get around to it."

"It was here when you came in?" Demarkian said.

"Oh, yes. It was here when my predecessor came in, too. Father Corrigan put it up. Which is funny, actually."

"Why?"

"Well," Robert said carefully, "because Father Corrigan was one of the priests who later, uh, well, was caught up in the pedophilia thing. He admitted to . . . interfering . . . with two altar boys who were underage at the time of the contacts."

"How underaged?"

"One of them was eight," Robert said. "The other was ten. They're grown men, now, of course. But I'm surprised you don't know. All this was in the papers for weeks a few years ago. I thought everybody in Philadelphia knew."

"I knew about the scandal," Gregor Demarkian said. "I didn't know a lot of the details. It's not the kind of thing I follow closely. Do you think it should have been less likely for Father Corrigan to commit child abuse if he liked bad art?"

"What? Oh, no. No, that wasn't what I meant. It's devotional art, you see. That's the Sacred Heart you were looking at it. There are special novenas to the Sacred Heart, and a special devotion called the First Fridays, where you make a point of going to Confession and saying special prayers on the first Friday of the month for nine months running, and receiving Communion. The people who have this kind of art in their houses are the kind who are committed to those sorts of devotions, very traditional, very conservative people, really."

"And you thought people like that would be less likely to commit child abuse?"

"I don't know what I thought," Robert said. "Maybe I was just stunned by the hypocrisy of it. All the sweetness-and-light piety. It's funny the way it works, isn't it? When there's trouble like that, it's never the holy terrors like the Cardinal Archbishop who commit it. Didn't you want to have a seat in the living room?"

The detectives already had seats in the living room, on opposite sides of the couch, facing the big, garish painting of the Last Supper. Da Vinci might have painted the original, but whoever had copied it for this print had had the artistic version of a tin ear. Robert sighed slightly and then, because it had become obvious that Gregor Demarkian did not intend to sit down, sat down himself in the wing chair.

"Well," he said. "You wanted to ask me about Sister Harriet."

"Not right away," Gregor Demarkian said. "I wanted to ask you about Bernadette and Marty Kelly. You knew both Bernadette and Marty Kelly, didn't you?"

"Oh, yes," Robert said. "Well, I did in a way. With Marty, it was only in passing. But with Bernadette, I knew her rather well. She did a lot of volunteer work at the church. And she was nearly a daily communicant, until the last few months at the end. Diabetes, you know."

"Yes," Gregor Demarkian said. "I do know. When you say she volunteered in the church, do you mean she had some semiofficial position? Did she work here on a regular basis?"

"Oh, no," Robert said. "There was nothing like that. She just pitched in with our projects, with the soup kitchen and the homeless shelter and that kind of thing. She had her own job to go to, after all."

"Bernadette Kelly didn't have a job," Detective Mansfield said confidently. "That's in the record. She was unemployed."

"When she died she was, yes," Robert said, "but that was because of her medical problems. They became so severe those last six months or so, she wasn't able to work. But she had a job before then, for years. She was a receptionist at Brady, Marquis and Holden."

"What's Brady, Marquis and Holden?" Demarkian asked.

"It's a law firm," Detective Emiliani said. "A big one. Weren't they the one that handled the, uh—"

"The pedophilia scandal, yes," Robert said. "Or rather, they handled part of it. They represented several of the individual parishes. There was another firm that represented the archdiocese as a whole. It was very complicated. But yes, you see, that's how Bernadette got the job. My predecessor got it for her. Father Dunedin. He tried to get her a job as a secretary, but of course that didn't work out."

"Why didn't it work out?" Demarkian asked.

Robert shrugged. "Well, you know, Bernadette was a remarkable person. She had very good sense, and she was very devout. She had great practical intelligence. She knew what was wrong with the lottery. She and Marty owned that trailer of theirs. She decided they would, and six months later she did it. She was aiming for a house. If she hadn't gotten sick, she would have made it. She could calculate the interest on a credit card in her head. But it was like watching an idiot savant. Other than money—even with numbers, if it didn't have to do with money, she was dead. She just wasn't very bright."

"And Marty Kelly? What about him?"

"Well," Robert said, "it's one of those things. He dropped out of school at sixteen. He was always in trouble. He was always doing drugs. He probably did some stealing. He was lucky not to get caught, and he was lucky to fall in love with Bernadette. She refused to go out with him if he didn't go back and get his high-school diploma, and then she refused to marry him if he didn't register at the community college. She brought him to church. She got him off all drugs except two beers with the game on the weekends. She turned him around. When it first happened, you know, I wasn't really very surprised. I could see that Marty might not be able to face his life with her gone. She made a different person of him."

"You don't think she might have been ready to leave him?" Demarkian asked.

"No," Robert said. "Bernadette was the most committed Catholic I've ever known. If Marty was beating her up, she might have left him. If he was acting up, she might have left him. But it would have taken the marital equivalent of thermonuclear war. I know she died from arsenic, but if you're thinking Marty killed her, you're wrong. Marty could no more kill Bernadette than I could fly."

Demarkian nodded, and Robert found himself thinking that he liked this man. That surprised him. He had expected to feel tense and under pressure, but instead he felt the way he always did when he gave interviews, like when the press came to ask questions about the outreach programs that Mary McAllister and the nuns had made such an important part of parish life. He stretched out his legs and sat back. If he wasn't careful, he really would go to sleep.

"Let's talk about Sister Harriet for a minute," Demarkian said. "She was the parish coordinator. What does the parish coordinator do?"

"She coordinates the parish," Robert said, and smiled. "She keeps the schedules straight. Mass linens sent out to the laundry. First Communion breakfast not in conflict with the Senior Citizens' Celebration. Rosaries and scapulars ordered for First Communion. Bibles ordered for Confirmation. Mass schedules made out so that both I and the parochial vicar say Mass every day and all the Masses that are supposed to be celebrated are celebrated. That kind of thing."

"What about money?" Gregor asked. "Did she have anything to do with the money?"

"I'm not really sure what you mean," Robert said. "She had something to do with money, of course, because she had to make sure there was enough money in the budget to buy the rosaries and that sort of thing. But she didn't deal directly with the parish finances. That's Sister Thomasetta's job. She's the comptroller."

Demarkian paused in his pacing—he was all over the room, from one wall to the other, from one painting to the other, from the windows to the couch and back again—and said, "What about her background? Did she come from a wealthy family?"

"I have no idea," Father Healy said. "I never asked her. I'm sorry, but at least in the old days the nuns weren't supposed to tell you about their backgrounds. Not that I was around in the old days, of course, but most of the Sisters here are very traditional, and I try to be sensitive to, well, you know—"

"Yes, I do know. What about Bernadette Kelly? Did she come from a wealthy family?"

"Oh, no," Robert said. "I know Bernadette's family—well, her father, anyway. Her mother died when she was eight. Diabetes, too. Her father worked in a factory most of his life. Then he got laid off in the early eighties and clerked in a liquor store for a while. Her brother is a mechanic somewhere in Delaware. They're very good people, very solid people, but they've never had much money."

"Hmm," Demarkian said.

On the couch, the detectives stirred. "You're barking up the wrong tree here, Mr. Demarkian," Detective Mansfield said. "There isn't this kind of connection."

"We ought to check, anyway," Demarkian said. "The books on both churches—has anybody bothered to ask if there were any irregularities in those books?"

"We're a little early in this case to have gone in for audits," Detective Emiliani said.

Robert leaned forward. "If you want to know about us, I can tell you right now that there are no irregularities in our books. If there had been, Sister Thomasetta would have noticed. And she would have told me. Or she would have told Sister Scholastica, and Sister Scholastica would have told me. Sister Scholastica is her superior. But Sister Thomasetta did a complete internal audit when she was appointed comptroller back in September. And she's a very competent woman."

"I'm sure she is," Demarkian said. "Let's try one more thing. What about the settlement that was made with the men who sued the church in the pedophilia scandal? Is the parish part of that settlement? Do you make a monthly payment into a fund, or to the archdiocese, for the restitution payments or the legal fees?"

Robert thought about it. It was shameful, but there were whole segments of parish life he knew very little about. Parish priests were supposed to be hands-on administrators, in charge of every aspect of running their parishes, but he had known from the beginning that his talents in some areas were slight. One of those areas was budgets and finance.

"I'm not entirely certain," he said, "but I believe that we were assessed a single payment several years ago, and that we now pay a portion of that to the archdiocese every month. We don't deal directly with the litigants in that case or with their attorneys or with the court. The suit was against the archdiocese principally and only peripherally against the parishes. I think they referred to the suits against us having 'nuisance value.' "

Demarkian shook his head. "It doesn't make any sense," he said. "It really doesn't make any sense. Does it make sense to you, Father, that somebody would kill Bernadette Kelly and Harriet Garrity?"

"Bernadette is a puzzle," Robert said drily, "but there was probably a waiting list for Sister Harriet. I'm sorry. I don't see any reason to disguise the fact that she and I were not exactly friends. No matter what His Eminence says."

"Forget His Eminence," Detective Mansfield said. "We've already had an earful about how people felt about Sister Harriet. Not exactly a world champion at winning friends and influencing people."

"No," Robert agreed.

"I think we can leave you to your life for the moment," Gregor Demarkian said. "You've probably got work to do. So do we. Would you mind doing me just one favor?"

"What favor is that?"

"Do you mind telling me the last time you saw Sister Harriet alive?"

"Oh," Robert said. "That's easy. It was at Mass that morning. Seven o'clock Mass. She was there, and then afterward she was downstairs for coffee and doughnuts. We do that after weekday morning Mass so that the people who come on their way to work and want to receive Communion can get something to eat. You're not supposed to eat for an hour before you receive Communion."

"And was Sister Harriet her usual self? You didn't notice anything different about her? She wasn't particularly upset?"

"Well, Mr. Demarkian, she was particularly upset, but that wasn't much of a surprise. We'd just told her—I'd told her, on instructions from His Eminence, that I concurred with entirely—she'd been told that she would have to adopt some sort of distinctive habit if she wanted to go on working in this parish. I don't mean the long dress and that sort of thing that the Sisters of Divine Grace wear, but something, you know, that would make it clear she was a Sister. The Holy Father has been explicit about this. Members of religious orders are supposed to wear simple but distinctive garb. They aren't supposed to be running around in sweatpants and blue serge suits."

"I see," Demarkian said. "And Sister Harriet didn't want to adopt a habit?"

"She would rather have eaten cow dung."

Demarkian shook his head. "That doesn't get us anywhere, either, does it?" he said. "Thank you, Father. We really will let you get on with your life now."

Robert nodded politely, and stood while the two detectives got up and made their way to the foyer and their coats. He felt suddenly very light-headed, as if he had just jumped from a tall building and the bungee cord hadn't taken hold until the last second. He was so exhilarated, he thought he was going to be sick.

"Well," he said. "Well. I'm glad to have been of help. Really. More than glad."

It was true, too. He was glad to have been of help, especially since it had cost him so little, and meant so little, to himself or to them. He didn't even mind the stiff cold wind that came in the door at him as he watched the three men walk away across the courtyard to the church. Cold was good. Cold would keep him awake—at least until he made it upstairs to his bedroom to lie down.

For the first time in hours, Father Robert Healy thought he could sleep.

2

By the time Mary McAllister got Chickie George back to St. Stephen's, she was exhausted, and she still had at least an hour of studying ahead of her if she hoped to pass her weekly quiz in Systematic Theology. She was also sliding into one of those irritated moods that had been plaguing her for almost a month. It was four o'clock in the afternoon and already dark, although not so dark as it would have been before New Year's. When she got out of the van and came around to help Chickie down, she could feel the sting of freezing rain against her cheeks. They were gearing up for an ice storm, the worst kind of weather possible. Too many of the homeless people she looked after were too mentally ill, or too damaged from alcohol, to have sense to come in from the cold.

Chickie had an Ace bandage around his ribs. Four of them were broken, and neither he nor she had been happy to hear the doctor say there wasn't much that could be done about it but to feed him painkillers and wait.

"I've always tried very hard to stay away from drugs of all kinds, even the legal variety," Chickie had said, in that high-camp squeal he affected around people he didn't know. Later, when they were alone together, he dropped most of the act, and said, "It's a very sensible policy, Mary. You know what happens to so many of us over at St. Steve's. I've got to stay off."

In the end, Mary had convinced him to take at least a half dose of the painkillers they had given him—Demerol and Percodan; they weren't fooling around—and now she could see it was a good thing she had. The van was not the smoothest ride in the world. They had been bumping over potholes for miles. Chickie's face was a mask of pain, which meant, of course, that it was a mask of pretense. Mary held out her arms to him and felt his weight against her shoulders.

"I wish you wouldn't do that," she said suddenly. "With the doctor, I mean. I don't understand why you do. It doesn't help you any. And it's not natural."

"Do what?" Chickie said innocently.

"Do that flaming-queen act," Mary said, moving back a little. When she was sure he could stand on his own, she left him, and went around his back to slide the van door shut behind him. "You know by now the effect it has on people. They stop taking you seriously. And it's not as if it's natural. You're not really like that at all."

"Not really like what, Mary? Not really gay?"

"Not really affected."

"Some people are like that," Chickie said. "Some people really can't help it. They're like that all the time. Why should people hate them for it?"

"I didn't say people should hate them for it. I said it didn't make any sense for you to behave that way when it wasn't natural for you. Don't you want people to like you for yourself?"

"Yes," Chickie said. "That's exactly what I want. Do you understand that?"

"I think so."

"I'm gay, Mary. I don't see why people shouldn't know it. I don't see why I shouldn't act gay."

"Aaron is gay. People know it. It has nothing to do with fluttering your hands and sashaying when you walk."

"Aaron can pass."

"Aaron doesn't pass, even if he can," Mary said firmly, "and you don't have to either. Just be yourself. That's all I'm asking you. Especially with health insurance as bad as yours is. You're very lucky that that doctor saw the riot on television and really hated Roy Phipps. It saved you a couple of thousand dollars."

"It doesn't look like there was a riot here last night, does it?" Chickie asked. "The street is absolutely clean. I can't even see lights down there at the hellhole. Do you suppose they've moved out?"

"We've none of us got that kind of luck."

"No," Chickie agreed. "We don't. Do you mind if I lean on your arm a bit? I'm still not feeling good about standing up."

Mary let him lean. It seemed to her that she had been letting him lean for a long time now, and that it was one of the few things that she still enjoyed, in this odd tangle of discontent that she had become locked in. The rain made the sidewalk tricky, but they went slowly, around to the side of the church and into the door of the annex—where, Mary suddenly remembered, Scott Boardman had died. Or had started dying. Convulsions and vomiting. She thought of Sister Harriet Garrity and frowned a little, because even though the connections between the deaths were now very clear, there was still something that seemed off about it all. At the door, she left Chickie standing on his own and opened up. The walls of the annex were lined with pictures, just like the walls of the basement over at St. Anselm's, but here the pictures were simple drawings of the Anglican flag and the symbols of Easter, rather than the productions of Sunday school children trying to express what they felt about the star of Bethlehem.

"Dan?" Chickie called out.

"He's not here," Aaron called back. A door opened down the hall and Aaron came out, dressed in good slacks and a good sports jacket and a black sweatshirt. "You're later than we thought you would be. He had to go out. How are you?"

"Prostrate, my dear, just prostrate. You have no idea—"

"He has four broken ribs," Mary said straightforwardly. "And a big Ace bandage around his middle. And he finds it difficult to walk. He's supposed to take painkillers."

"Oh, he must love that," Aaron said.

"I'd love a chair," Chickie said.

Aaron waved them in the direction of the office he'd come out of, and they followed him there. Mary looked around with a certain amount of curiosity. She had been over here before, but she'd never paid much attention to the place. Offices, after all, were offices. Now it seemed odd to her that the walls were so bare and so clean. In the offices at St. Anselm's, there was stuff everywhere. There were even books in stacks on the floor.

"So," Aaron said, "I thought that as long as I had the afternoon free, I'd try to tidy up Scott's files, and it's impossible. None of it makes any sense. You don't happen to remember somebody named John Strodever, do you?"

"Of course I do," Chickie said.

Mary helped Chickie ease down in the only chair other than the one next to the computer, that Aaron was using. It was not a good chair. It swiveled.

"You ought to remember him, too," Mary said. "He was the man who started the lawsuit. You know. Against the archdiocese. Because of the priests who, uh—"

"We get the picture," Chickie said quickly. "Mary's right. He was the first one. Later, there were a whole slew of men coming forward, but Strodever's the one who started it."

"Is he gay?" Aaron asked.

"I haven't the faintest idea," Chickie said. "Why would I know that? How could you possibly expect me to know that?"

"Look at this." Aaron tapped the computer screen, and Mary saw Chickie give him a withering look. Of course, Chickie had just sat down. His ribs were broken. He didn't want to get up again.

Mary went around the side of the desk herself instead, and looked at Aaron's computer screen. She seemed to be looking at the photograph of a bill of some kind, rather than an ordinary computer document.

"What is that?" she asked.

"It's a memo," Aaron said. "It's been scanned into the computer. Look. September 9. You see that?"

"Yes," Mary said.

"Now watch this." Aaron tapped at the keyboard. Mary saw

the screen blink and throw up what seemed to be the same scanned memo. "What's this?" Aaron asked.

"It's the same memo," Mary said.

"You think so? Watch this. Let's go back to number one." He went back to number one. "Now," he said. "Read the heading. After 'subject.' "

" 'Payment schedule in the settlement of the case of John Strodever, et al. vs. the Archdiocese of Philadelphia.' " Mary read.

"Okay," Aaron said. "Read the next line."

" 'Plaintiffs,' " Mary read. " 'John Thomas Strodever, Michael Charles Wheelan, Stuart Carl Dodd, Stephen Thomas Roderick.' "

"Okay," Aaron said. "Now for number two."

" 'John Thomas Strodever,' " Mary read obediently. " 'Michael Charles Wheelan, Mark Henry O'Mara'—wait."

"Yes, exactly," Aaron said triumphantly. "Wait."

"There's an extra name," Mary said. "Is it just the one?"

"Just the one," Aaron said. "Why do you think that is?"

"It's probably nothing," Chickie said. "One of the documents was a draft, that's all, and they left somebody out or put somebody in that they shouldn't have, so they rewrote it."

"If that's all it was, why would Scott have scanned them into the computer? And where did he get them? How could he get them?" Aaron shook his head. "It isn't like Scott was part of the lawsuit. And I don't know any of these names. I don't think it's plausible that he was trying to look after somebody he didn't know."

Chickie shifted uncomfortably in his chair. "It's no problem how he got them, for God's sake. Scott was a book and publications designer. He worked for all sorts of people. He did year-end reports for companies, and for law firms, too, when they put out those big glossy booklet things they like to to advertise how wonderful they are. Where is the memo from? It's a law firm, isn't it?"

"Brady, Marquis and Holden," Mary said.

"A big law firm," Chickie said with satisfaction.

"Well, all right," Aaron said. "Let's say he was designing something at this law firm and he ran across these documents, that still doesn't explain why he scanned them. And it must have taken a bit of work, too, because he must have either snuck them out of the law firm and then snuck them back in, or else he scanned them onto a disk there and then brought them here and loaded them—"

"Why would he have had to sneak them back in?" Mary asked. "Why not just take them and throw them out?"

"Why not just take them and keep them, then?" Aaron said. "Why bother to scan them at all? The only point to that is that he couldn't keep the originals of the documents."

"You're both turning this into James Bond, and there's no reason to," Chickie said. "So Scott was nosy. A lot of people are nosy. I'm nosy."

"Scott was murdered," Aaron pointed out.

Chickie shifted in his chair again. Mary bent down and looked at the document on the screen. It was a perfectly ordinary document. It was dated. It was on letterhead memo paper. She shook her head.

"Maybe," she said, "we ought to tell the police about this. Or that Mr. Demarkian. I mean, if Scott was murdered because of this—why would he be murdered because of this? Chickie's right. It could be just two drafts and one draft was wrong so the other one was written. It just doesn't make any sense."

Aaron clicked at the keyboard again, and the printer began to whir. "I'm going to make copies of both of them, just in case. Lots of copies. And I'm going to leave them all over the place. Then I'm going to have a good long talk with Dan. We probably should go to the police, but I want to know what we're going to say before we do it."

Mary backed away and went to where Chickie was sitting. He was looking pained and very tired. She thought it might have been a mistake to bring him out here, even though he had wanted very much to come.

"Maybe you should go someplace and lie down," she told him. "You look exhausted. And you're not well, even if you think you are."

"No, no," Chickie said. "I'll sleep in a pew. I want to be at that service. In case we get picketed."

"We won't get picketed," Aaron said confidently. "We've got an army of police coming down to cordon us off. And he wouldn't try anything so soon after last night anyway. He's a smart asshole. He knows when not to push his luck."

"I'd like to push his luck," Chickie said. "I used to think

he was gay and in the closet, but I've changed my mind. Nobody that foul could ever be gay."

"I think I'd better get back to school before I don't have any time to study at all," Mary said. "Are you sure you're going to be all right? Do you want me to come back and get you and take you home?"

"In the van with the homeless people?" Chickie said.

"Behave," Mary told him. Then she kissed him on the top of the head, waved good-bye to Aaron, and left.

Out in the parking lot, she saw that she had left the van's passenger side door open. She did the sensible thing of checking through the backseats to make sure she hadn't picked up a mugger or a rapist, then she climbed in behind the wheel and started up. She wondered if Chickie really did mind being in the van with the homeless people, and then thought that most people would. They smelled, and they could be frightening. She pulled the van out onto the street and headed back across town to St. Joe's.

There was a blue crystal rosary hanging from the back of her rearview mirror. It had a Miraculous Medal at the place where the long strand and the short strand were held together, and the Medal glinted every time she passed under another streetlamp. By the time she was four blocks away from St. Stephen's and St. Anselm's, there had begun to seem something eerie about that, as if she was receiving messages in a form of Morse code.

If she was, she thought, they were coming through in a language she didn't understand, and maybe didn't want to.

Then she turned her mind firmly in the direction of Aaron and Scott Boardman's scanned documents, and thought that she would get in touch with Gregor Demarkian about them as soon as she had a minute to spare.

3

At the chancery, Dan Burdock had come and gone, and the tea and coffee things had already been cleared up, when the call from Rome came in. The Cardinal Archbishop had been expecting it for hours—he had, after all, made a call to Rome himself, earlier in the day—but the fact that he hadn't gotten it hadn't stopped him from doing what he had just done. He tried to think of what *could* have stopped him, and decided that the only thing would have been a call from His Holiness himself. Barring, of course, a direct communication from the Almighty. The Cardinal Archbishop did not have direct communications from the Almighty. He had had them, once, very early in his years as a priest, but the lines from heaven had been silent for decades. Some men who experienced that silence became mired in aridity and lost their faith. The Cardinal Archbishop knew that this was just adulthood. When you were young, you heard God talk because you needed it, the way children needed candy, and the Cardinal Archbishop was convinced that children actually *needed* candy. Once you were grown you were expected to take responsibility for yourself and to worry about your teeth. He was, he thought, almost infinitely tired. It surprised him to remember how exhilarated he had been when he had been told he would be sent here as Archbishop, and made a Cardinal.

There was a knock on the door. The Cardinal Archbishop called out, and the door opened to let Father Doheny in.

"It's Rome," Father Doheny said. "It's Ratzinger himself. Not even a secretary."

"Well," the Cardinal Archbishop said, "at least they're still answering my phone calls. How does His Eminence sound?"

"He sounds the way he always sounds. Like God left something out of his voice. Are you sure you want to do this? You're not obliged to, you know. Bishops act on their own all the time. They always have. And take the consequences later."

"Maybe I didn't want to take the consequences later. No, never mind, Father. I'm only very tired. And yes, I'm sure I want to do this. I suppose I want to give them a chance to forbid me. Just to see if they would do it."

"They won't do it. They can't do it. You know that."

"Yes, I do know that. All right, Father, why don't you transfer the call in here, and I'll talk with His Eminence the Director of the Congregation for the Doctrine of the Faith. I think it had more of a ring to it when we were calling it the Holy and Roman Inqusition."

"People kept getting it confused with the Spanish Inquisition. They thought we burned heretics at the stake in caverns in the Vatican. Or something."

The Cardinal Archbishop thought it was more likely to be "something," but he took Father Doheny's point. People always seemed to know half of history, and to get it confused with the other half. Father Doheny left the room and closed the door behind him. The Cardinal Archbishop got up and went around to his desk. It was odd the way things worked out. He had been a defender of the faith all his life. He believed in a Catholic Church united to Rome, and speaking in one voice with Rome. He was an almost infamous purveyor of all things religiously conservative: the ban on birth control; the definition of marriage as the union of one man and one woman; the idea that abortion was always and everywhere murder. He could be counted on to approve the Tridentine Mass in any parish that wanted one. He could be found at the head of any pro-life rally put together by a Catholic organization in the city of Philadelphia. And yet, here he was—and no matter how hard and long he thought about it, he really couldn't see how he could be anywhere else.

The phone on his desk beeped mildly. You couldn't say it rang. The Cardinal Archbishop stared at it for a moment, and while he did it beeped again. When he tried to imagine Ratzinger, what he saw was a tall, thin, ascetic-looking man with an emotional temperature far too low. He was aware that that was exactly how most people imagined him. The phone beeped a third time, and the Cardinal Archbishop leaned forward to pick it up.

Cardinal Ratzinger spoke English, but the Cardinal Archbishop didn't want to conduct this conversation in English. For one thing, he didn't want to be overheard. For another, he didn't want to be misunderstood.

"*Guten abend, mein Herr,*" he said, and then he heard Ratzinger's voice, cool and deep, begin to stream out in its native German.

At the last moment, he began to wonder if he should have told Ratzinger's secretary that his mind was made up beyond the possibility of changing, but then he decided that it would have been beside the point.

SIX

1

Gregor Demarkian had never wanted to be a private detective. Even being a consultant had, at the beginning, seemed like more of a commitment than he would be able to handle. These days, he didn't know what to call himself. He still wasn't set up the way a business should be, even though what he did was certainly a kind of business. Bennis had tried to show him how to use Quicken to keep books and prepare bills to be sent when his work was finished. He had listened politely to everything she had had to say and then gone back to playing Free Cell as soon as she was out of the room. Even Tibor was better at this sort of thing than he was. Bennis had shown him how to keep books for the church, and he had followed directions and kept them. Gregor hated to admit it, but he would rather not be paid at all than go through the complicated procedure of sending bills and keeping records for tax purposes. He reminded himself, often, that he had more than enough money for his needs and no desires that could be called particularly expensive. He would have liked to have bought a coffee machine, but the fact that he hadn't had nothing to do with what one cost. It was more a matter of not being able to understand the choices, and being afraid that if he bought the wrong one, he'd be condemned to drinking cappuccino forever.

Today it was the day before Valentine's Day, and he had a list of things to do. At the top of it was buying a card and a big, gaudy box of chocolates for Bennis. Bennis liked boxes with ribbons and bows on them, as ridiculously ostentatious as possible. Bennis was out. If he got going fairly soon, he ought to be able to do some shopping without her knowing about it and without Garry Mansfield and Lou Emiliani jumping down his throat, hot on the heels of a new theory. Bennis was always nudging him to get a cell phone, but Gregor knew better. A cell phone meant he would never be left in peace.

Out on Cavanaugh Street, Donna Moradanyan had outdone herself. Her own house—the new town house she and Russ had renovated last summer—looked like it had been turned to silk. Red and white silk ribbons covered every inch of the facade, dotted here and there with metallic glittered hearts. In fact, metallic glittered hearts seemed to be what she was most committed to, this particular holiday season. There were a dozen or more on the front of Holy Trinity Church, and even more than that around Lida Arkmanian's front door. Gregor's own house had been decorated weeks ago. Donna always did this one first, because it was where she had started to do them in the first place, all those years ago, when they had all just met.

Bennis was not only out, she was at a local writers' conference, teaching a seminar on How to Make Fantasy Reality. Her notes were taped all over her refrigerator, which seemed to exist for no other reason than to hold notes. Lord only knew there was never any food in it, and when there was it tended to have grown green mold and taken on a life of its own. They should do something about the apartments, like knock them together and put a staircase between them, but everything he could think of to do seemed to have implications that would lead to repercussions on Cavanaugh Street. Of course everybody knew that they were sleeping together, and most people were relieved, since they'd gone on for years in a kind of relationship limbo where neither of them knew what was happening between them. Still, unmarried people didn't move into apartments together in neighborhoods like this, unless they wanted to spend most of their time explaining themselves to the Very Old Ladies.

He was procrastinating. He hated going out to shop. He also hated being in Bennis's apartment rather than his own, because he couldn't get to any of his things, and she filled her life with bits and pieces that made no sense to him at all. She had sachet in her underwear drawers. She had silk flowers all over the windowsill in the living room. If he went down to his own apartment, the phone might ring, and it might be

Garry or Lou, and then he would be stuck. He picked up his
coat where he had left it on Bennis's couch and went out
instead and down the stairs.

He couldn't visit old George Tekemanian, because old
George was having lunch in the city with his nephew Martin.
Martin was always taking old George to restaurants where they
set things on fire, and old George was always ready to order
something that would be set on fire. Gregor went out on the
street and looked up and down. Hannah Krekorian and Sheila
Kashinian were standing together a few blocks up in front of
Hannah's house, looking at something in what seemed to be
a magazine.

Gregor went up a block and a half and turned in at Holy
Trinity Church. He went down the alley at the side and around
the back to Tibor's apartment. The front door was unlocked.
No matter how often or how loudly Gregor lectured people
on Cavanaugh Street about the importance of keeping their
doors locked, nobody listened to him.

"Tibor?" he called out.

"In the kitchen," Tibor called back.

Gregor went into the kitchen, where Tibor's computer was
set up at a small table set against one wall. There was also a
big table in the middle of the room, with enough chairs to
accommodate an old-fashioned family of eight. Tibor's computer screen was the largest Gregor had ever seen, and the
brightest. Bennis had bought it for him for Christmas.

"What are you doing?" Gregor asked.

"I am reading a newsgroup," Tibor said. "I have become a
subscriber to several newsgroups. Also to several e-mail discussion lists. The discussion lists are easier than the newsgroups, but the newsgroups have a more interesting mix of
people."

"A newsgroup is what?" Gregor asked. "The same thing as
a chat room?"

"No, no," Tibor said. "Krekor, you really have to learn the
Internet. Your ignorance is embarrassing. Chat rooms are not
worth the trouble. They're full of people making bad sex
jokes, and then it turns out that half of them are FBI agents
looking for sexual predators. Back in Armenia, Krekor, I
would not have believed that so many men could be pedophiles."

"Ah," Gregor said.

"Well, it makes no sense, Krekor. What does a man want with a child? By the time I was twenty-six, I couldn't look at a woman much younger than thirty."

"You're an unusual human being," Gregor said. "What do you talk about on this newsgroup?"

"It's called alt.atheism. We are supposed to talk about atheism. Most of the time, there will be someone from a Christian church who comes to try to convert, and the atheists will swear at him. We have flame wars. Do you know about flame wars?"

"No."

"They are fights, but silly fights. Everybody calls everybody else names. Everybody swears. Well, I do not, Krekor, but you understand what I mean."

"What do you do? Do you try to convert people?"

"No. I discuss the historicity of the Bible with one or two people who are actually very knowledgeable."

"It seems like the whole street is having conversations with atheists these days," Gregor said. "There's Bennis with that woman, and some group she talked to. It seems odd to me, that atheists would join groups."

"Why are you so interested in atheism, Krekor? You're not even interested in religion. You said to me the other day that nobody commits murder for religion, do you remember that? I thought it was silly."

"I meant that nobody commits these kinds of murders for religion," Gregor said. "You know what I mean by these kinds. Poisoning. Hiding. When people commit murders for religion, they get a machine gun and raid somebody else's church."

"Or the houses of doctors who do abortions, yes," Tibor said. "So what are you doing here? Hiding from the Philadelphia Police Department? You seem distracted."

"Pedophiles," Gregor said.

"You have found more pedophiles?"

"No. No, what you said about pedophiles reminded me. Do you know about that case, the scandal in the archdiocese? I don't mean have you heard about it, I mean do you know about it, for real, with the details."

"I know some, Krekor, yes. You would know some, too, if you ever paid attention to the news. I don't understand why

you buy the newspaper. You never seem to read anything in
it but the editorial page."

"It's the only thing I can be sure is completely accurate.
People usually know what their own opinions are. But seriously, that case. How many priests were involved? Were the
victims all boys, or were there girls—"

"Wait." Tibor tapped at his computer. A second later, something came up that seemed to be a list. He tapped again. "Here
it is, Krekor. They have a web site."

"Who has a web site?"

"The victims. I ran into it the first week I was on the Internet. I was looking for religion in Philadelphia, and I found
it. They were all boys, yes, Krekor, at least the ones who put
up this site. And there were a lot of them. Maybe sixty or
sixty-five."

"Sixty or sixty-five priests were molesting their altar boys
in the Archdiocese of Philadelphia in the 1960s?"

"No, no," Tibor said. "You don't understand. There were
not so many priests, maybe five. But one priest can go through
many boys—here it is. See, Krekor, the pictures of the priests
are here. Mug shots. One of them was already dead when the
suit started, though."

Gregor looked at the screen. "THE SHAME OF CATHO-
LIC PHILADELPHIA," the headline read, and underneath it
there were what did indeed look like mug shots: five men in
early to late middle age, wearing clerical collars. Gregor sat
back.

"One of them was dead," he said. "What about the rest of
them?"

"Three are retired, Krekor, and live in retirement homes for
priests. The last one was still in a parish when the scandal
broke, and he was removed and has been sent to a psychiatric
facility. This was a large matter for discussion in the religious
community when it happened, Krekor, because there are implications that may not be immediately clear. It is very difficult
to defend yourself against a charge that you committed a crime
thirty years ago. There are many possibilities for abuse."

"Do you think that happened here?" Gregor asked. "Do you
think the priests may have been innocent, or that some of them
were?"

"No," Tibor said. "In the case of Father Corrigan, the one

who is dead, the one who was the most outrageous offender, there are diaries and other material. He kept very good records. The others have all admitted to the crimes. In this case, there are no implications, only mess."

"What about the one who was still in a parish when the scandal broke?" Gregor asked. "What parish was he in?"

"That would be Father Murphy. He was at Our Lady of the Fields."

"Had he been there long? Had he been in other parishes?"

"Yes, Krekor, of course he had been in other parishes. That was the practice in those days, when a priest had charges of this sort leveled against him by the parishioners, the archdiocese moved him to another parish. But you have to understand that people did not look on those things then the way we do now. They didn't understand—"

"No, no," Gregor said. "I'm not trying to make out a case against the Catholic Church. I'm just trying to figure something out. Was Father Murphy ever at St. Anselm's?"

Tibor looked startled. "No, Krekor, he was never at St. Anselm's. But Father Corrigan was. I'd forgotten that that was where you were looking into the murders."

Gregor peered at the computer screen again. "Father Corrigan was the biggest offender," he said.

Tibor nodded. "Yes, Krekor, the biggest and also the most determined. The other men, there are a few incidents, and then that seems to be all. With Father Murphy, there were three boys. With Father Roselli, there were two. You see? But with Father Corrigan—he was out of control, we would say now. There were dozens."

"All of them at St. Anselm's?"

"Most of them, yes. He was there for twenty-five years." Tibor clicked at his keyboard again and brought up a page that seemed to be devoted to Father Corrigan alone. The mug shot was reproduced there, at three times the size it had been on the main page. Tibor scrolled down and pointed to a triple-column list of names. "There they are," he said. "The men who have come forward to claim that Father Corrigan molested them when they were children."

"Good grief," Gregor said.

"Yes, Krekor, I know. A shameful thing. An evil man."

"But how could he have done all that without anybody

realizing?" Gregor asked. "I mean, even in the sixties, after a while, wouldn't the archdiocese have begun to suspect that the man had something psychologically wrong—"

"But Krekor, Krekor. It is possible that they did not know there were so many. It is possible they didn't know there was even one. The boys would not have been likely to tell anyone. And if they did, they would not necessarily have been believed. And the parents, even if they did believe their children, wouldn't have wanted the incidents to become public. It was a time when children were blamed for causing these incidents, don't you see?"

"I worked for twenty years with serial killers," Gregor said, "and I know something about patterning in behavior."

"Yes, Krekor, but the archbishop of the time was not a policeman, or even a psychiatrist. He did all the wrong things, yes, but he did them with the best of intentions. The man who came after him, now, that was panic. He wasn't thinking at all. He was only trying to escape."

"This was the man who tried to effect the cover-up? The last archbishop before this one?"

"That's right, Krekor. But it's all been taken care of now, you know. There has been a settlement." Tibor clicked at his keyboard again. A window came up that said "WE WON!!!!" "The men were triumphant, but that is to be expected. Some of them had been trying for years to be taken seriously. One of their mothers, too, who had done the unusual thing at the time and told the archdiocese about Father Murphy, she felt vindicated. She has her own web page. Would you like to see it?"

"No," Gregor said, and then, "thank you," so as not to be rude.

Tibor looked at him oddly, then clicked the keyboard again. The mug shot disappeared. In its place was a small rectangular billboard that said "Read My Newsgroups!"

"You are all right, Krekor? Does this have something to do with your murder that you are investigating?"

"I don't know."

"Oh. Well, there is much information if you want it. There are many articles in the local papers and there is an organization, the Freedom from Religion Foundation. Well, you can imagine. But if there is something you want to know, and you do not feel you can ask the Cardinal about it—" Tibor shrugged.

"I'm going to go buy Bennis a Valentine's Day heart," Gregor said. "Thank you for all the information. It probably means nothing, but you know how that is. I'm going to see Anne Marie this afternoon, did I tell you that? Henry Lord set it up. She wants to talk to me."

"It would be of more moment if she wanted to talk to Bennis," Tibor said. "Or to Christopher, who is coming from California. They will not witness the execution, but they want to be together when it happens. I think it was very wrong of Howard Kashinian to suggest they make popcorn."

"I think Howard Kashinian is going to be a murder victim one of these days if he keeps it up," Gregor said. "Okay, Tibor. I'll talk to you later. I have to get something that glows in the dark. Literally."

"Try Martindale's," Tibor said solemnly. "They have them the size of blackboards that play music. It is even very bad music."

2

Gregor went to Martindale's first, because it was on the way to the station, and then, coming out with the box under his arm, wondered why he wanted to be saddled with the thing halfway across the state. He was going up to the state penitentiary in Henry Lord's car. He could leave the box in the backseat if he wanted to, instead of carrying it with him through the prison. It still seemed odd to him to be carrying a box of chocolates for one sister while going to visit the other on death row. At any rate, the boxes in Martindale's were as big as Tibor had said they were, and covered over with so many ribbons and so much glitter they might as well have been wired for neon. They played music, too: "Yes, Sir, That's My Baby" and "Making Whoopie" being the two favorites. Gregor chose "Yes, Sir, That's My Baby." All euphemisms for sex embarrassed him, as if there was nothing wrong with committing the act, but something wrong about pretending not to.

He was coming out of Martindale's when he saw the copy

of the *Inquirer* in a vending machine, with Dan Burdock's picture on the cover, dressed in ceremonial robes and doing something at an altar. Usually, Gregor got the paper either going to or coming from breakfast, but this morning he had been distracted, and he hadn't even seen it. Now he put his money in the slot and got a paper out to give it a better look. Once he had it unfolded he could see that there was another picture, of the outside of St. Stephen's Church, where Roy Phipps and his parishioners were picketing. Roy Phipps looked, Gregor thought, entirely unscathed. No police truncheon had come down on his head during the riot, and he had found clothes in his closet that were cleanly and carefully pressed. Gregor scanned the story. It said nothing much he didn't already know. Dan Burdock and the parishioners of St. Stephen's were giving a private prayer service for the victims of the riot. A public, more elaborate service was scheduled for later in the week. Roy Phipps and his people were protesting the "normalizing" of "perversion," and intended to be back when the formal service was in session, "to bring a little sanity to these times in this place." Sanity seemed to include more parishioners dressed in bedsheets and crowned with angel's halos, but that wasn't the kind of thing Gregor thought he could safely go into.

He looked the story over one more time. He folded the paper up and put it under his arm. He went back into Martindale's foyer and headed for the pay phones. Here was a reason to have a cell phone. You could call anyone anytime from the middle of the sidewalk and not have to waste time at a telephone booth.

Except that there were no telephone booths anymore.

Gregor called Henry Lord, and asked, "You've got to go right by St. Stephen's, don't you, to get out of the city from where you are? Could you pick me up there?"

Henry had been willing to pick up Gregor on Cavanaugh Street, which was considerably farther out of the way. He would be more than happy to pick up Gregor at St. Stephen's, even if it meant pulling into the parking lot and searching through the church to find him. Gregor said thank you and took off, turning first left and then right, conscious all the time that neighborhoods changed quickly and—worse, and more annoying—so did the infrastructure. Whoever it was who had decided, sometime in the 1950s, that it made sense to put concrete highway overpasses over ordinary city streets must have been on drugs.

He got to St. Stephen's without incident, although he found himself counting homeless people along the way. There always seemed to be more of them instead of fewer, even in good economies. There was something he had never been called on to deal with. He had never been that kind of policeman, and he was glad he hadn't been. Alcohol and mental illness were beyond his understanding. Drug abuse seemed to him so monumentally stupid he couldn't imagine what it was people were thinking of when they took their first joint or their first shot of heroin. It was like hanging out a twenty-story window screaming: *kill me! kill me!*

When he got to St. Stephen's, the street was quiet. The doors to both St. Stephen's and St. Anselm's were propped open, but Gregor had the impression that they always were. There was no sign of Roy Phipps or any of his angels, although if Gregor tilted his head the right way he could see the tall white cross on Phipps's town house's front door.

Gregor went into the church and looked around. It was empty. He went to the back and out the back door to the courtyard and saw lights on in the annex. He went across the courtyard to the annex and let himself inside. It was warm and light in here. Most of the office doors were open.

"Can I help you?" somebody said.

Gregor turned to see Chickie George sitting behind a desk in the office to his left. He hadn't recognized the voice, because for some reason Chickie wasn't putting on the camp this morning. "I'm looking for Father Burdock," Gregor said. "Is he around somewhere?"

"Up the stairs, first office you get to," Chickie said. "I'd show you up, but I'm being held together by plaster of Paris."

"So I heard. I hope it isn't too painful."

"It wouldn't be painful at all if I could use it to sue that son of a bitch up the road. Dan's in. Just tell Mrs. Reed who you are."

"Do you know who I am?"

"Of course I do," Chickie said, and suddenly the camp was back. "You're the Armenian-American Hercule Poirot."

Gregor went down the hall—he had only himself to blame

for that one; he'd been asking for it—and found the stairs with no difficulty. He went up and around, thinking as he did that he was being routed back toward the church proper, and found a pleasant-looking middle-aged woman in a flowered dress, typing away at a computer on a desk.

"Is Father Burdock here?" he asked. "My name is—"

"Gregor Demarkian," the woman said.

"Gregor Demarkian," Dan Burdock said, sticking his head out the door of the inner office. "Hello. Is this the official interrogation? I've been waiting for you."

"It isn't an interrogation at all," Gregor told him. "I'm actually on my way to somewhere else. I have a friend picking me up in your parking lot in less than half an hour. It was just something that struck me, that's all, and since you were more or less on the way—"

"Sure. Come on in. Mrs. Reed can get you coffee, if you like."

"No, no. I don't have time for coffee. It really is a small thing."

Dan Burdock stepped back and shooed Gregor through the door into the inner office. Gregor found himself in a high-ceilinged, paneled room with a wide fireplace, like the libraries in private clubs for men that used to dot the better neighborhoods of the city. There was an enormous leather wing-backed chair just in front of Dan Burdock's desk. Gregor sat down in that and waited for the priest to settle himself.

"Well," Dan said. "What's the problem? I can't imagine we've done anything in the last few days that hasn't been thoroughly documented on the evening news."

"You probably haven't. No, it isn't anything you've done. It's—" Gregor tried to think of a way to make this sound sensible, and realized he couldn't. "It bothers me, in a way, that you and the Reverend Phipps are on the same block. It seems like too much of a coincidence. So I thought that perhaps it wasn't one."

"You're right," Dan said. "It isn't one."

"So the Reverend Phipps moved into his town house in order to harass St. Stephen's. Was that before or after you became pastor here?"

"I've been pastor here for twenty-five years," Dan Burdock said. "Roy has only been up the block for the last ten. And he didn't come to harass St. Stephen's. He came to harass me."

"You personally?"

"Got it in one."

"But why?"

Dan Burdock sighed. "We were in college together," he said. "At Princeton. We were roommates one year. We were in the same entryway for two years. I'm the one he knows."

"The one what?"

"Gay man."

"Are you gay?" Gregor asked.

Dan Burdock sighed again. "Of course I'm gay," he said. "I'm not practicing, as the church likes to put it, but I'm gay. Everybody knows it. Nobody will talk about it. Except, of course, Roy. Sometimes I think it would be easier if I posted a sign on the church bulletin board out there by the sidewalk that said, 'The pastor of this church is a homosexual. Other homosexuals welcome to worship.' Except that everybody knows that, too. It drives me nuts."

Gregor nodded. "What about Roy Phipps? Is he also gay?"

"You mean, as a handy explanation for why he feels the need to persecute homosexuals? If you want my private opinion, and that's all it could be, the answer is no. I threaten the hell out of Roy, and I always have, but it's not because he's latent."

"What is it, then?"

Dan Burdock stood up. "Do you know anything about Roy? I mean, beyond the rhetoric and the newspaper stories about picket lines at gay funerals?"

"No."

"Well, I do. He came from a dirt-poor family in some backwater hollow in West Virginia, at a time when kids like that didn't get to places like Princeton. He fought his way through high school. He fought his way to a scholarship. He spent four years of college working three jobs and studying his head off and managed to graduate salutatorian of our class. He's a very unusual man, Roy is. He could have been anything. I've always thought of what he did become as a form of reaction formation. He finally couldn't stand it anymore. He wanted to bring us all down. Those of us who didn't have to fight, if you know what I mean."

"But why pick on homosexuals?"

"I don't think he decided to pick on homosexuals. I think he decided to pick on me. And since I happen to be gay—well, there it is."

"He's going to a lot of trouble, just to pick on you."

"I agree. But I do think that is what this is. I always have. Is that really all you came here to find out? Why Roy took up residence on this block?"

"More or less, yes. And I'm interested in the coincidences. The two churches, for instance, with their layouts so similar, the courtyards, the annexes, the parking lots."

"Except that St. Anselm's has the school. But that's not a coincidence either," Dan Burdock said, "and you must have known that. Sometimes I wonder what it would have been like to live in a world where everybody wanted to be an Episcopalian."

"I think I lived through that era," Gregor said. "But then, I'm a lot younger than you are. I'd better go downstairs and make sure my friend isn't freezing in his car in the parking lot. I told him to come in if he didn't see me, but I don't really know what he'll do. Thank you for your time."

"You're more than welcome. Is there going to be an official interrogation one of these days? With the cops present, and all that sort of thing?"

"I don't know."

"I've been getting ready for it for days," Dan Burdock said. "No, longer than that. I've been getting ready for it since I first knew Scott hadn't died a natural death. Does that make any sense to you?"

"Yes. Some."

"Let me come down with you and see you out."

Gregor nodded slightly, and Dan Burdock led the way to his own office door. Outside the office windows, the day was already grey and dark, and it wasn't yet noon. It was lucky they hadn't had snow.

Gregor realized, at the last minute, that he'd left the Valentine's Day box on the floor next to the chair he had been sitting in, and went back to get it.

SEVEN

1

There were funeral arrangements to be made for Sister Harriet Garrity. It wouldn't be a quick funeral, or even necessarily a local one, but Sister Scholastica felt as if life would make a bit more sense if she could get the details straightened out, and so that was what she was trying to do. The first requirement had been to notify Harriet's order, which was called the Daughters of the Immaculate Conception—a name, Scholastica thought, that had probably made Harriet's teeth grate. It was strange to think of the things they had all taken for granted in 1962: the First Fridays and First Saturdays devotions; the brown scapulars and Miraculous Medals; the intentions made in the hopes of gaining indulgences for the suffering souls in Purgatory. Scholastica still remembered the kinds of indulgences there were—partial and plenary. A plenary indulgence got the soul out of Purgatory immediately. A partial indulgence got some of the years of suffering taken off that soul's sentence, and the years were long. There were partial indulgences that took off hundreds of years, and yet, since they were only partial, there must still be years left. Once, when she was eleven, Scholastica had found herself kneeling in the middle of the cathedral in Rochester, thinking that there would never be an end to it. No matter what the nuns said, Purgatory was forever, and if you got stuck there you would suffer only a little less than if you got stuck in hell, and you would never get out. For a moment, the room had seemed to dissolve, and she had thought herself surrounded by souls in agony, crying out to God for the cool relief of water. Then she had snapped back into the present, and there had been Judy Sullivan, sitting in the pew right in front of her, wearing a blue angora sweater over her parochial-school uniform skirt. The colors clashed, but Scholastica had wanted that sweater even so.

The nun from Sister Harriet's order had been more gracious than Scholastica had expected her to be. Maybe, being used to Harriet, Scholastica had expected an argument, just as a matter of principle.

"We'll send somebody up, of course," Sister Hilary Etchen had said. "Although I must admit I don't know who it will be. We only have four of us now in the motherhouse, and two of us are over seventy. You don't have that problem, do you, at Divine Grace?"

"We're short on vocations," Scholastica had said. "Everybody is."

"Yes, everybody is. But last year you had eight. And the average age of your Sisters is under fifty. Sometimes I think we should have kept the habit, just for its drawing power. Do you take girls right out of high school?"

"Sometimes. A lot of the time now we prefer to take them out of college."

"And they come?"

"Well," Scholastica had said, "some of them do, although not as many as used to when they all came as soon as they left parochial school. But it's mostly from the Catholic colleges, anyway, and from the conservative ones at that. We don't get a lot of candidates from the public universities."

"No," Sister Hilary had said, "I don't suppose you do. It makes me wonder, sometimes, if I had my head screwed on right, when I voted in favor of the changes we made in this order. I used to think that people would want to be part of us more if we were authentic, if we didn't traffic in ceremony and formality. But it seems the opposite is the case."

"I think adolescent girls like to play dress-up," Scholastica had said.

"We'll find somebody to come up. Sister Joanne Fuselli is serving in a parish in Wilmington, maybe she can get away. And we'll inform the relatives, of course. Harriet had quite a few relatives. It's hard to believe, isn't it? Sisters get murdered sometimes, on the street, in muggings, but something like this. . . . Do you have a place to put the body if, you know, if it takes us some time to get this organized?"

"The body is at the medical examiner's. There has to be an autopsy. It won't even be released for a couple of days."

"Oh. That's fine, then. I can manage something in a couple of days. Thank you so much for calling. We managed to get the news to her brother before it hit the newscasts. That was worth everything."

"Yes," Sister Scholastica had said. Then she had put the phone down and stared out her window, and fifteen minutes later she was *still* staring out her window. Reality had lost its edges, once again.

She got out from behind her desk and went into the hall. The office women were all at work, which meant that it was either before or after the noon rosary. She made it a point to attend the rosary every day, if only to set a good example for the other Sisters. The laywomen were always so grateful when their rosary was joined by the Sisters. Sister Scholastica went down the hall and stopped in Sister Thomasetta's doorway.

"So," she said. "Where are we? Or aren't you getting much done today, either?"

"I'd be getting more done if the police didn't call every twenty minutes to ask silly questions. Where did Sister Harriet sleep. What did Sister Harriet have for breakfast. As if I were supposed to know. You remember what Harriet was like. She wouldn't eat with us. She wouldn't stay with us. Sometimes I think she would have been happier if we'd disappeared from the face of the earth."

"It was a difference in political agendas," Scholastica said, coming inside. "Except I never think of myself as having a political agenda. Have the police really been calling every twenty minutes?"

"That Detective Mansfield, yes. I've been imagining him sitting in his office somewhere, obsessing about Sister Harriet and her murder. But the thing is, there are better people to ask about the things he wants to know than me. Why should he ask me, just because I'm the one who happens to be answering the phone this morning?"

"You can send him down to me, if you'd like to."

"What I'd like is for Sister Peter Rose to get the day off so that she can talk to him. I'm sorry, Sister. I don't mean to sound so irritated. I suppose I've had a bad day, with one thing and another, all day."

"We all have." Scholastica paced around the room. Sister Thomasetta was a woman of the old school in more ways than one. She had a framed picture of Our Lady of Fatima on her desk, and another of her niece and nephew, dressed to the death for Christmas. "So," Scholastica said. "What else has been happening around here? Did Mary get the things she needed for the soup kitchen?"

"They sent somebody else. Mary went to take that young man from across the street around to do some things. You know the one. He's always sort of swishing around. He got a couple of ribs broken in the riot."

"Chickie George."

"That's it. Anyway, then she had to study. I have no idea how that girl does it. She's been Dean's List at St. Joe's for the past three years, did you know that? Peter Rose told me. And the soup kitchen and the Sodality and praying the Office every day. And that boyfriend of hers treats her like cornflakes. Someday she's going to wise up and walk out on him, and then he'll be sorry."

"I guess. Is that it? Have we really managed to go through a day where nothing happened?"

"Pretty much," Thomasetta said. "Oh, I managed to go through those records you sent me. Only once, mind you, I've been doing payroll. But I looked through them. You're right. They're a mess."

"I thought so. Father Healy is a nice man, but he's hopeless when it comes to things like this. And you know if the archdiocese catches the discrepancy, we'll all be in trouble whether it was our responsibility or not. The Cardinal Archbishop isn't the world's easiest person. Do you think you can fix it?"

"Give me a day or two, yes. It's just sloppiness. It isn't even unusual sloppiness. Maybe you ought to go over to the house and have something to eat."

"Maybe I should," Scholastica said. "Don't you wonder how they did it? Whoever killed Sister Harriet. How they got her to eat the arsenic. You'd think she would have known that the person hated her."

"Harriet? Harriet had the emotional intelligence of a sea slug."

Scholastica wanted to laugh, but she caught herself at the last minute. Then she left Sister Thomasetta's office and went down the hall again, but in the other direction. When she got to the end, she opened the fire door and stepped into the cold. She looked up at the big brick building that was St. Anselm's School—and that had been, for almost a hundred years now— and decided that she just couldn't face playing principal at the moment. She was being very unfair to Sister Peter Rose, she knew, but she couldn't help herself. Maybe she *wasn't* cut out to be a nun, at least not a nun of the kind that Reverend Mother General was. By now, Reverend Mother General would have solved the crime and provided Gregor Demarkian with incontrovertible and fully admissible evidence of the same.

Scholastica went in the side door of the church, looked around at the people praying in the pews, and then went around the back to the stairs that led to the basement. She checked the boxes that had been set out for the food drive, and the other boxes, left against the wall in piles on the floor, that held the rosaries and the scapulars for the First Holy Communion classes. Then she reminded herself that somebody else had already seen to all this, and that none of it was her job at all. She was just looking for a way to waste time that would not make her feel guilty. She felt guilty every time she thought of the way she had behaved at the sight of Sister Harriet's body.

She came back up to the first floor and went out the front door of the church. She looked across at St. Stephen's and wondered what they were doing in there. There was more activity than there usually was in the middle of the day in the middle of the week. She looked up the street in the direction of Roy Phipps's place, but that was calm enough, too, this morning. Maybe they were tired of picketing. It always surprised her that nobody had ever done any damage to Roy Phipps or his church. You would think, given the nonsense he pulled, that violence would be inevitable.

Scholastica started to turn back to the church, but as she did she saw a woman coming up the street, and because the woman was familiar, she stopped. A second later, she realized who it was: that Edith Lawton person, the professional atheist, who lived with her husband in one of the single-family town houses on the block. Scholastica didn't want to know what one of those town houses cost, or how you could afford one on the money you made by being a professional atheist—but then, Edith Lawton was supposed to be married. At the moment, she looked oddly mismatched, as if she were the living embodiment of one of those Picasso paintings from the 1920s. The parts of her didn't go together. She was dressed like a teenager, in jeans and a down jacket, and she was almost thin enough to pull it off, but her face was the face of a fifty-year-old woman. In the harsh light of the intermittent sun, it looked even older.

"Mrs. Lawton," Sister Scholastica said.

"Hello, Sister."

"What are you doing this morning? You look ready to go skiing."

Edith Lawton stopped, and hesitated, and looked at the church. "I was going to go to Mass. That's all right, isn't it, even if I'm not Catholic."

"It's more than all right. We encourage it."

"Even if I've never been a Catholic?"

"Even if you've never been a Catholic. I thought you didn't believe in God."

"I don't. God is just a fairy tale, like Santa Claus. People only believe in him because they're afraid of dying. Do you mean I can't go to Mass if I don't believe in God?"

"No," Scholastica said wryly. "We *especially* encourage you to go to Mass if you don't believe in God."

"Religion is a terrible thing," Edith Lawton said piously. "Look at all the harm it causes. Look at what happened to those poor boys and right here in this very church. Don't you think it's a shame, that those boys were hurt and then the faithful gave their donations just so that they could be used to pay the lawyers? The Church has a lot to apologize for." Then she turned her back and hurried down the walk into the church.

Scholastica watched her go with some amusement. Then she folded her hands under her scapular—to get them warm; in the old days they walked with their hands like this all the time, to keep them out of sight—and crossed the street to St. Stephen's.

There was going to be a big prayer service over there for the victims of the riot, and she had volunteered the Sisters to help out with the details.

She wondered if Edith Lawton would have a vision at the Consecration and want to become a nun. She could just see the program on EWTN, with Edith in a postulant's habit, telling the story of her conversion.

The road was empty of traffic, so she crossed the street. If she went on like this much longer, she was going to give herself a serious case of the giggles, at a time when she had no right to laugh at all.

2

Bennis Hannaford had never been one of those people who could tell herself that God arranged all things for the best. If she lost her bank card, she didn't think it was because God was protecting her from a trip to the theater, since a trip would have ended in an accident. If she couldn't sleep one night, she didn't think God was trying to make her so exhausted that she wouldn't have the energy to worry when something came along to worry about. Part of that was the simple fact that Bennis had a hard time believing in God, but more of it had to do with the fact that she was a pessimist. Bennis Hannaford did not think things worked out for the best. In fact, if she believed in any occult power at all, it was the one that was working overtime to make sure things worked out for the worst. That was why, when she found the capital-punishment essay up on Edith Lawton's website, she didn't gloat about its being there. The only reason it was going to be up on the web was that Edith had found it impossible to publish. Web publication was just as bad, as far as Bennis was concerned. Millions of people would be able to read the thing, and, what was worse, it was tucked in among all of Edith's other obsessions, like the priest pedophilia scandal and the endless blather about the Catholic Church and abortion. Bennis couldn't understand why so many secular writers presented the Catholic Church's stand on abortion as if they'd just uncovered a well-hidden scandal under a very large rock. It was like people who were shocked—just shocked—to realize that cigarettes caused lung cancer. The only people who didn't know those things by now had to be brain-dead.

She was, she thought, having a nicotine fit, except that these days she didn't actually feel like smoking, only like killing someone. Edith Lawton would have been a good choice, but she wasn't available on Cavanaugh Street in the early afternoon, and probably never would be. Bennis tried to imagine what Father Tibor would make of Edith Lawton. He'd read some of her work—that's what happened when you pointed Father Tibor to a website—but all he'd been willing to say of her was that she "lacked seriousness."

I am avoiding the issue, Bennis told herself, and then she let herself out the front door of the small apartment building. On just the other side of the street, Donna Moradanyan was standing near the top of a tall ladder, putting red and white crepe paper across the front of the facade of Lida Arkmanian's house. The crepe-paper strands were curled on each other, so that they made a kind of barber-pole effect, except sideways. Lida was standing at the bottom of the ladder, in her three-quarter-length chinchilla coat, fussing.

"She is going to fall off," Lida was saying, as Bennis came up. "She is going to break her neck. That is what is going to happen here."

"I'm going to put the light cord through the window," Donna Moradanyan called down. "Then you can plug it in when you get back inside. Or this evening. When it gets dark. You know what I mean."

"Please be careful," Lida Arkmanian said.

"She cannot be careful," Hannah Krekorian said. "If she's careful, she won't get anything done. She has to be brave."

"I don't understand why she doesn't just hire somebody to put that stuff up," Sheila Kashinian said. "I mean, for God's sake, Russ is a lawyer. He must make a mint."

"Don't say 'for God's sake,' " Lida Arkmanian said. "You know what Father Tibor said last Sunday in church. We all take the Lord's name in vain far too much around here."

"I don't see why anybody should bother me about taking the Lord's name in vain," Sheila Kashinian said. "I'm not the one who swears every time I lose the lottery. And what *about* the lottery? Isn't that supposed to be against Christian principles?"

"Only if you're a Protestant," Hannah Krekorian said.

Bennis went around the other side of the ladder. "You okay?" she called up.

"I'm fine," Donna said. "I shouldn't have used crepe paper for this. It gets ruined in the weather. But then I have to worry about the lights, and crepe paper works with the lights. What's with you? Aren't you working again today?"

"I was looking for Gregor," Bennis said. "He doesn't seem to be around anywhere."

"He left the neighborhood a couple of hours ago. I assumed he was off to talk to the police about the murders. Can you look around down there and see if there's a red satin heart with a tab on the end of it? I'm missing one."

Bennis went to the pile of materials lying in a heap at the bottom of the ladder and started to look through them. Most of what was there was paper, bits and pieces that looked as if they had been wrongly cut and then discarded, but not exactly thrown away. The heart was very small. Bennis nearly missed it. She picked it up and stood back.

"Do you want me to climb up there and give it to you?"

"No. I'll be right down. You ought to do something with yourself. You're driving yourself and everybody else crazy."

"Well, I was going to do something with Gregor, but then he disappeared. You're not going to be able to reach over to the other side of the building from where you're standing."

"I know."

Donna let the crepe paper fall from the last place it had been taped. It hung down the front of the building like a ponytail. Then she came down the ladder and rubbed her hands against her slacks.

"Thanks," she said, taking the heart. "I'm going to move the ladder. You should move yourself. When is your brother coming in?"

"It depends on which brother you're talking about. Christopher will be here at the end of the week."

"Are the other two coming? I thought they weren't coming."

"Teddy's already here. He's in a hotel somewhere holding press conferences. Or he would be, if this whole thing hadn't been overshadowed by the problems at St. Anselm's. What do you think Hannah would say? Maybe that the murders happened so that they would chase Anne Marie off the front pages and save my privacy."

"What about Bobby?"

"God only knows," Bennis said.

Donna took the heart and went back to the ladder. Then

she performed what seemed to Bennis to be an unnecessarily complicated series of tugs and bumps to get the ladder to move down the front of the building and rest somewhere near the middle.

"Do something," she said. "Why don't you write a column about being harassed by what's-her-name. I'll bet you anything you can get it published somewhere good. *The Atlantic Monthly. Harper's.* That ought to make you feel better."

"Don't you ever wonder where people like that get their money?" Bennis asked. "I mean, I was born with money, and I still had to work before I started to get seriously published. And I know she's married, but still—"

"Maybe her husband makes a mint."

"It's like other people know where to find money and I don't," Bennis said. "It's like some secret nobody ever let me in on. Not that I need money now, of course, but when I was first starting out and nobody would take my stuff, I couldn't have lived in a town house in a major city and bought my bags at Coach. And her hair clips, too. Did I tell you she buys her hair clips at Coach?"

"She's got a husband."

"She's got a husband who does something with computers. He can't be making that much money. Oh, I don't know. She probably has it from her family, or her husband's got it from his. Except I know everybody with family money in Philadelphia and on the Main Line, and I've never heard of them."

Donna unearthed something that looked like Christmas lights, except the bulbs were all either white or red. She wound the strand around her arm and started up the ladder again.

"Go do something," she said again. "Go buy food for when Christopher gets here, unless he's staying at Lida's, then go buy him something else. Go buy Gregor a Valentine's Day card. You're making us all nuts. You're worse like this than you were when you first quit smoking."

"When I first quit smoking, I threw an end table through my living-room window."

"I know. Trust me, it was less annoying. Go down to the Ohanians and volunteer for the Armenia Relief Committee. Just *do* something."

"Right," Bennis said, but all she did was to step back a little and watch Donna on the ladder, stringing lights through crepe paper. The things that went through her head at times like this—that she wished somebody would rent the top-floor apartment in the building she shared with Gregor and old George Tekemanian; that she wished she had remembered to buy chocolate at the little store she liked near Independence Hall—were sane enough, but didn't have to do with anything. Donna would probably find them . . . annoying. She watched as Donna taped the strand of lights to the brick and then taped crepe paper over it, to hide the wires. Then she nodded a little to Lida and Hannah and Sheila and went down the block toward the Ararat and the church and Ohanian's Middle Eastern Foods. Lida's coat was the most spectacular, but all three of them had fur. Bennis couldn't imagine herself wearing something like that in public.

At Ohanian's she stopped and bought a copy of the *Inquirer*. She paged through the first section and checked the editorials and op-eds, but it was all right. There was nothing about Anne Marie today. She folded the paper up and put it in the nearest wastebasket. She wouldn't read any more of it today, or any other day. She couldn't make herself concentrate on the news. She thought about going to the Ararat and decided there was no point. She wasn't hungry, and the last thing she needed was more coffee. She thought about going to see Tibor and decided that she couldn't sit still for a tour of his fifteen latest websites, even if some of them would be funny and others would be scary as hell. Some people visited websites for research. Some people visited them because they were looking for a cause that would let them vent their rage. Tibor visited them out of curiosity—not about hate, but about human nature.

In the end, she went back to the wastebasket and retrieved the paper. Then she checked her bag and made sure she had both money and credit cards. Then she walked all the way to the corner past Ohanian's and looked up the cross street for a cab. There were cabs. There were always tons of cabs near Cavanaugh Street, because cabbies loved to pick up people who lived there. Generations of being told not to be stingy about tips had had its effect.

Bennis got in and asked to be taken to Gump's. She had no idea why she wanted to go there, since she never bought any jewelry but earrings, and she almost never bought those.

She settled in the cab's backseat and went back to reading the paper, looking now through the stories that bored her silly, the announcements of weddings and funerals, the two-paragraph squibs about Little League games and zoning-commission meetings on the Main Line. She looked over the television listings and realized that she had never heard of half the shows being listed. She looked over the book and movie reviews and realized that, although she had heard of most of what was mentioned, she wanted no part of any of it. She was about to fold the paper up and tuck it away in her bag, when she saw the picture of a man she thought she recognized. She stared at him for a moment and came up blank. She was sure she had met him, but not where, or why, or with whom, if it had been with anybody. She leaned over and read the caption under his picture. "Ian Holden," it said, "senior partner at Brady, Marquis and Holden." She looked for the story and found another two-paragraph squib, announcing some charitable committee he had been named to chair. She rubbed the side of her face compulsively.

Brady, Marquis and Holden was the law firm that handled the work for the Archdiocese of Philadelphia. Gregor had mentioned that. She didn't remember his mentioning Ian Holden, or any other lawyer in particular. Besides, she was convinced that she'd actually *met* him, shaken his hand, seen him in the flesh. Something like that. She had no idea why.

Outside the cab, the traffic was getting worse and worse. It was the middle of the day, and too many people wanted to be in the same place at once. Had Holden been an assistant district attorney, back when Anne Marie was tried? He looked too old for that, and he seemed too senior. She rubbed her eyes again.

She met people every day, in all kinds of situations. She met them at workshops and signings. She met them at cocktail parties given by the organizations she supported. She met them on the street, when they recognized her from *Vanity Fair* or *Good Morning America*. It was probably nothing, really. She was making too much of it, the way she made too much of everything lately, because it was either that or deal with reality.

She folded the paper firmly into quarters and put it in the

pocket on the back of the front seat. Then she stretched out her legs and closed her eyes.

If she was going to act like a ninny, she might as well get some rest while she was doing it.

3

Out at St. Joseph's University, in the middle of a class called Roots of the Western Philosophical Tradition, Mary Mac-Allister had a sudden revelation. Actually, she had two, but she was only aware of the first one, the answer to her moods of the past several months, the light at the end of her particular tunnel. The class was being taught by a priest who tended to lecture in the same way he had once given homilies at Mass. He modulated his voice until it sounded as if it were coming from a synthesizer. He gestured with his arms, moving them in big arcs from the shoulders, so that some of the students in the first row had to flinch away to avoid being hit. Worst of all, he explained too much, and too often. Mary already knew St. Thomas's proofs for the existence of God, and why they didn't really prove anything. She could do the Argument from Design in her head, and recite the sophisticated spins that had been put on it by modern religious philosophers like Plantinga and Swinburne. She was doing a minor in theology, and sometimes—like now—she didn't know why, because what she really wanted to do with her life was what she was already doing with it. Bag ladies and winos didn't care about the Argument from Design, or the Argument from Morality, or even the Argument from Miracles. Most of them were too far gone to understand anything but brutality and kindness, and most of them weren't really human anymore, most of the time. "Respond not to the man but to Christ in the man," Mary's favorite grade-school nun had told her, over and over again, as the very core of religion. It had taken her a while to figure it out, but finally she had. Mr. Morelli and Mrs. Carstairs and Mr. Hemmelwaite and Miss Janns were old and sick and crazy, but she was called to see beyond that. She was called to see inside each of them, where they really were still human, because Christ lived in them, Christ was part of them, as Christ was part of all people everywhere even if they had banished

Him from their hearts. It didn't matter that Mr. Morelli wouldn't be the way he was if he had only been able to stop drinking. It didn't matter that Miss Janns had never had a chance at anything, because she was born with the schizophrenia she had never been able to shake. Nothing mattered except that they were human, and they deserved to be treated as human, and if nobody else would do that, then she would have to.

You need two different documents, a voice in her head said, when you've got two different files.

She came to, startled, and realized that she had zoned out completely, she had no idea how long. Father was talking about the philosophy of the Scholastics and the importance of the Aristotelian synthesis to the medieval construction of reality. Some of the students around her were taking notes. Others were only doodling, the way you could often in this class, because Father repeated everything four or five times. Mary wondered what his parishioners had thought about it, all those years ago, when he had been assigned to a parish and expected to preach. She suspected that he hadn't lasted at that parish very long, much the way she expected Father Healy wouldn't last long at St. Anselm's.

You need two different documents when you've got two different files, the voice in her head said again, and then she looked up, past Father's shoulder, and saw the crucifix on the wall above the chalkboard. It was an odd moment. Like most other Catholics she knew, Mary had devotions she felt comfortable with and devotions she couldn't make meaningful at all. For her, Christ Crucified had always been an uncomfortable image. Even Christ Triumphant, in the Resurrection, had made her feel oddly out of place. Christ on the cross had sometimes made her cringe. She liked mangers, and Virgins, and the star floating over the cold desert night in Bethlehem far more than she would ever be able to like the Stations of the Cross.

"Aristotle," Father was saying, "could never have been accepted as a source of Christian philosophy if St. Thomas hadn't found a way to disguise his religious skepticism, but once that skepticism had been disguised—"

Mary blinked, and the Crucifix on the wall seemed to waver. She felt a wave of dizziness roll over her, as if she were about to faint, except that she didn't feel faint. She felt as if she were floating. The floor had dropped out from under her feet. The air had become tactile and electric. The light no longer seemed to be the light from the fluorescent lamps above her head, but another kind of light entirely, coming from nowhere, going to nowhere, purely white.

A second later it was over, except for the slight feeling of nausea that presented itself as a rush of acid to her throat. Mary swallowed as hard as she was able. Then she closed her notebook and put her pen in her pocket, deliberately and carefully. She was afraid that if she moved too quickly, she would find that she had forgotten how to walk.

"Miss McAllister?"

"Sorry, Father," Mary said. "Don't feel well."

This was not exactly true. She didn't feel unwell as much as she felt claustrophobic. She had to be out of this room, and after that she had to be out of this building, in the air, in the cold, anywhere where she couldn't be confined. She put her notebook into her backpack and stood up. Father had come down the row to her, a half-panicked frown on his face. She could hear him breathing.

"You don't look well," he said. "Are you sure you'll be all right? Would you like to have somebody come with you?"

"I just want air," Mary said, and then blushed a little, because that was rude, and she was never rude to priests. She got one of the straps on her backpack over one of her shoulders and headed out of the room, into the long corridor that went the entire length of this wing of the building. It was a beautiful building, picture-perfect college Gothic, made of marble and almost brand-new. It must have cost the earth, and it occurred to her that it was strange she'd never thought of it. At the end of the corridor there was a fire door. She went through it and out into the quad.

Out there, there was a statue of St. Francis, in habit, holding out his hands to the birds. St. Francis was one of the saints Sister Harriet Garrity had actually been able to like, although, of course, she had disapproved of his relationship with St. Clare. She liked St. Teresa of Avila, but disapproved of her relationship with John of the Cross. She positively hated The Little Flower, who had seemed to her to be the worst sort of male-identified woman. Mary rubbed her eyes and walked past the statue, farther into the quad. There were statues everywhere. She had, she thought, liked Edith Lawton more than she had liked Sister Harriet Garrity. Edith might be annoying, but at least she didn't pretend to be a Catholic.

When she got to the statue of St. Clare with the stone bench wrapped around it, she sat down. She had, she thought, known this was coming. Somewhere at the back of her mind, it had always been with her, waiting for her to stop long enough to notice it was there. The problem was, now that she had noticed it, she wasn't too sure what to do with it, or even how to go about deciding what to do about it. Her head ached a little. Her hands were cold. St. Clare's veil was as long as a waterfall.

All right, Mary thought. This is it. I'm going to be a nun.

EIGHT

1

Execution in Pennsylvania was by lethal injection. Gregor Demarkian had known that all the time, but for some reason he had been blanking it out, especially when Bennis had been the one asking him. He didn't know why that should be so. Of all the possible forms of capital punishment, lethal injection was certainly the best—although the idea of calling one method of killing someone "the best possible" made his head ache. He could imagine other situations, and other people, with other answers: Homolka and Dreen, up in Canada, who only thought a killing was good if the victim screamed. Still, there really were worse methods. The gas chamber, which was a matter of being fully conscious while being asphyxiated in a booth with windows all around it, so that you could be seen by the largest possible audience. The electric chair, which was not only obviously painful—you *would* scream if your mouth wasn't muzzled shut—but which kept malfunctioning, doing only half the job, causing buckets of blood to gush out of the mouths and eyes of its victims, causing burns. With lethal injection, they put you to sleep first. The element of righteous retribution was removed. The apocalyptic undertones were banished, once and for all, to the minds of the lunatic fringe who came to stand at the gates on execution evenings, cheerleading for death.

And that, Gregor thought, as Henry Lord pulled the car through three sets of electrified gates into the "official visitors" parking lot, is what I don't like about lethal injection. It may be the most humane method we have, but it normalizes the whole process. It makes capital punishment appear as no more serious a policy decision than farm price supports.

The electrified gates were guarded by uniformed officers with rifles—with machine guns, Gregor noticed. Being used to federal prisons rather than state ones, he was a little surprised. Federal prisons were often minimum security. Stockbrokers who had traded on a little inside information and bankers who had scammed a few federal loans weren't going to do much that was physical except notch their daily running time from thirty minutes to an hour. State prisons got the kind of prisoner whose idea of an interesting afternoon was to kill all five of the people in the convenience store they were robbing, and then to try to kill the cops who came to arrest him. Of course, federal prisons also got interstate kidnappers and Timothy McVeigh, but Gregor had no idea what they did about those people. McVeigh, if he remembered rightly, was on a federal death row. That one was probably not minimum security.

"What's the reverie about?" Henry Lord asked, pulling into the parking space one of the guards was indicating with a waving machine gun.

"Timothy McVeigh," Gregor said. "I hope that idiot has his safety on."

"I hope he's not an idiot. I never have liked this place. I used to have clients here, when I was younger, but I never have liked it."

"I don't think you're supposed to like it," Gregor pointed out.

"I know that. That's not what I mean. I've been to other prisons, though, and it doesn't give me the feeling this one does. I really hate being in this place. Maybe it's because of death row."

Henry got the car settled in the space and turned off the engine. The guards suddenly surrounded the car, staying just far enough back to give the impression that they didn't really think they'd have to shoot anybody, but close enough in so that they could if they decided they wanted to.

"Maybe it's because they treat visitors here as if they were potential escapees," Gregor said drily. He opened his car door and stepped out, unfolding a little from the car, because it was a compact and he was so tall.

Henry got out, too, unfolding less, because he was shorter.

A thin, small man in a neat brown suit came through the guards, holding out his hand.

"Judge Lord," the small man said, shaking vigorously. "Mr. Demarkian. I'm very pleased to meet you. I've read mountains of print on you. You lead a very interesting life."

"This is the warden, Ed Nagelman," Henry Lord said. "You've got to introduce yourself, Ed. Gregor was with the Bureau. He doesn't know the first thing about wardens."

"Actually," Gregor said, "I was thinking about wardens. About the one at the federal facility that has Timothy Mc-Veigh."

"We're very happy not to have him here," Ed Nagelman said. "We've got enough trouble with the SGN."

"What's the SGN?"

"The Seamless Garment Network," Gregor said. "That's very odd. Sister Harriet Garrity was a member of the Seamless Garment Network."

Ed Nagelman looked momentarily blank. "Oh," he said finally, "you mean that woman who died, the murder you're looking into. Well, I wouldn't be surprised. Most of the members of SGN seem to be nuns. You may have seen some of them out in front of the gate. They're already gearing up to protest this one."

Ed Nagelman nodded at the guards, and then led the way through them and across the parking lot to the path that led around the front of the large building.

"Everybody has to come through the front," he told Gregor, "even me. And anybody who comes in or goes out of the secure area has to have an armed escort."

"Even on visitor's day?" Gregor had this vision of dozens of wives and small children, waiting for men with machine guns to follow them everywhere.

"Visitors of that kind aren't admitted into the secure area. We have a visitor's room where people can sit at booths and talk to each other through bulletproof glass. But for somebody like you, who will be meeting with a prisoner face-to-face, within the prison's secure compound itself, we've got armed escorts."

Gregor cleared his throat. He did not repeat his line about hoping that the idiots had their safeties on. He just thought it.

They got to the front door, which oddly enough—at least

oddly to Gregor's mind—did not seem to have anything in the way of security on it. It just opened, like a door. Inside, in the lobby, there was plenty of security, including four more uniformed men armed with machine guns.

"It makes you wonder how anybody ever escapes from places like this," Gregor said.

"If it makes a difference to you, nobody has ever escaped from this one," Ed Nagelman said. "It's our job to make sure they don't. And it's in their best interests, although they think it isn't. I don't know of a single escape attempt from a maximum-security facility anywhere in the last ten years that has resulted in somebody successfully getting out and staying out alive. They die of cold. They die of exposure. They get shot dead on the main street of some godforsaken small town somewhere when a concerned citizen who watches too much television recognizes them and panics. Do you know how many people in the Commonwealth of Pennsylvania carry handguns?"

"I don't think I want to," Gregor said.

Ed Nagelman led them to an inner door. One of the armed men came forward to open it up for them. They stepped into a small space with another door on the far side of it. Then the door they had come through closed and snapped locked behind them. Only then did a uniformed man from the other side of the far door open that one, so that they could go on through into yet another room full of men.

"The whole place is set up like this," Ed Nagelman said. "They've got scientists who work out the possibilities and devise ways to protect us from them. I would expect that this system would be much the same in federal prisons."

"Not so many guns," Gregor said politely.

They went through another door, into another secure lock, and out the other side through yet another door. Gregor had the odd feeling that they were caught in a journey to the center of the earth, or—what was that movie, with Gregory Peck, or maybe with Cary Grant, where the man had amnesia and kept remembering himself going down to subbasements that didn't exist? Beyond this set of doors there was another room with another set of doors. Beyond that, there was yet another room and yet another set of doors. Gregor had not seen a single prisoner yet, as far as he knew. It was as if this place had been so thoroughly occupied by an invading army, all its inhabitants had left.

After this next set of doors, they found themselves in a long corridor with rooms on either side. They were still not actually in a cellblock, but they at least seemed to be in a functional part of the building.

"These are conference rooms," Ed Nagelman said. "They're here so that prisoners can talk to their lawyers—death-row prisoners, by the way, and only death-row prisoners. Contrary to the people who picket us at the gate, we do not indulge in summary executions here. Most prisoners stay on death row for over ten years, and, if anything, they have the best accommodations in the place. Their own individual cells, without roommates. Their own exercise yard, very uncrowded and very carefully policed. Their own communications facilities, including telephones and Internet access. I'd be a fool to think that prison rapes never happened here, but I can guarantee they don't happen to condemned prisoners. Here we go. A smallish room, but adequate for the purpose."

It was, Gregor saw, thoroughly adequate for the purpose, sort of a cross between a police station's interrogation room and a law firm's conference room. There was a carpet, but no paneling. The table was made of wood but the chairs were made of metal. At least they weren't bolted to the floor.

"I've sent somebody out to tell Miss Hannaford you're here," Ed Nagelman said. "As soon as she's ready, she'll be brought down."

"Miss Hannaford?" Henry Lord said.

Ed Nagelman shrugged. "She objects to the use of her first name. I don't feel like arguing with her. Some of the guards are not so polite. She has quite a manner, though, our Anne Marie."

"She always did," Gregor said.

"Yes, I gathered that," Ed Nagelman said. "It's odd how they are, you know. Of course, most of the prisoners I know are men. The only women I deal with are the ones on death row. But it's surprising how many of them have an exaggerated sense of their own importance—of their own virtue, I'd guess you'd call it. In all the time I've been here, I've only met one man who hasn't been convinced that he's innocent as the day is long, and that was Father Murphy."

"Father Murphy?" Gregor stopped in the middle of taking off his coat.

Ed Nagelman nodded. "Father Murphy. Brian Murphy. From Our Lady of the Fields. I was thinking about him when Henry told me you were going to come up here. Because the papers have been saying you're helping the police with a murder at St. Anselm's, and that was Father Corrigan's old stomping grounds. Not that Corrigan was ever here, of course. He was dead as a doornail before the lawsuits started."

Gregor dropped his coat on the nearest chair. "But Father Murphy was here?" he said.

"Oh, sure," Ed Nagelman said. "For three years. There are people who say he would never have ended up here if it hadn't been for Corrigan, but I don't believe that. It isn't 1964 anymore. Kids who get molested tell their parents, and their parents believe them, and there are laws that prevent anybody from keeping it all quiet. At the time the scandal broke, Murphy had a boy at Our Lady of the Fields, so they could prosecute him, and they did. Gave him ten years. He lasted three."

"Do you mean he was paroled?" Gregor asked.

"Paroled and shuttled off to a monastery somewhere in Wisconsin, from what I remember. The archdiocese promised he wouldn't be permitted anywhere near children, and they kept their promise. If you want my opinion, from what I've heard about cloistered monasteries, I'd prefer jail. But I've got to give this to him. He knew he was guilty. He accepted that he was guilty. He was ashamed that he was guilty. I've often wondered if it had anything to do with his being a priest, and if Corrigan would have been the same way. But I doubt it. Corrigan had that look in his eye, you know what I mean? The look that says, as far as he was concerned, the world, the universe and everything came right down to him."

"Well, Jesus," Henry Lord said. "What was it in the end. Thirty kids?"

"Exactly sixty-two corroborated," Ed Nagelman said. "We got that information as part of the package on Brian Murphy. And when I saw it, I hate to say it, but all I could think of was that we'd all gotten lucky. I mean, at least he didn't kill them. Most of the ones I see, the kids are dead. You know what I mean?"

"Yes," Gregor said.

There was the sound of a door opening and shutting in the hall. Ed Nagelman went to the door of the conference room and looked out.

"Here she comes," he said. "Good luck with your conversation. Where you think you're going to get with it is beyond me."

2

Here, as in all prisons, inmates were expected to wear the clothes the prison issued them, but Anne Marie Hannaford had found a way to make that uniform appear to suit her self-perception. Gregor Demarkian watched her curiously as she came in. She was, he thought, his first extracurricular murderer. If she had not decided to murder several members of her own family, he would not have met her sister Bennis, and he might never have developed this retirement consulting business, which he still insisted to himself was not a business at all. Looking back, he remembered thinking that an "ordinary" murderer ought to be different than the serial killers he was used to tracking. Now he knew that she was not different at all. Like the most intelligent of the serial killers—the ones, like Ted Bundy, who were not schizophrenic or bipolar or otherwise mentally impaired—she lived in a world of her own making, where nothing really existed but herself. It was the first requirement of murder, that ability to blank the rest of the human race out of existence at will, and that was why Gregor had always thought it was hogwash, the idea that anybody could be a murderer. Anybody could kill in the heat of passion, or if they were afraid for their lives and panic—that was true. Most people could not do what Anne Marie Hannaford had done, or what was being done now at St. Stephen's and St. Anselm's.

Anne Marie was a daughter of the Main Line. She had gone to Agnes Irwin and Bryn Mawr. She had come out at the Philadelphia Assemblies. If she had been prettier, she would have been the kind of person he would have expected to find on the cover of *Town and Country*. But she hadn't been prettier. It was Bennis whose picture had appeared on the cover of *Town and Country* the year she was a debutante, and in

Vogue, too, that same year, dressed in riding clothes and carrying a whip. Bennis still had both of those pictures, framed, in her own bedroom.

Anne Marie, on the other hand, could spend the next fifty years of her life in a maximum security prison and never be anything but what she was: a Main Line society lady; a volunteer for all things charitable; a devotee of the arts. Her body under the shapeless prison shift was thin and hard and wired strong. Her hair was carefully cut and curled back away from her face. Sometime not too far in the past, it had been dyed, and dyed well.

Henry Lord and Ed Nagelman left the room. So did the two armed men who had brought Anne Marie in. Gregor supposed they had searched her thoroughly before they had ever allowed her to leave her cell, but he wasn't actively worried about it. He could imagine Anne Marie Hannaford doing a lot of things, but pulling a gun on him and trying to bull through an escape were not two of them.

He had stood, instinctively, as she walked in. Now he sat down as she did, stretching his legs out under the table a little ways. She sat with her legs crossed carefully at the ankles, the way girls were once taught to do at dancing classes, in the days when crossing legs at the knees was a signal that a girl was "fast."

"Well," he said, when it became clear she didn't intend to say anything until he did. "I'm here. It's been a long time since we've seen each other."

"Since the trial," Anne Marie said.

"That's right. Since the trial. You asked me to come, Miss Hannaford. I came. It's Bennis who wants to come."

Anne Marie looked away. It was, Gregor thought, the first time she had blinked since she had come into the room. Then he realized that that couldn't be right. She must have blinked a dozen times. It only seemed as if her eyes were propped wide open, as if they were arc lights on an empty roadway.

She stood up and rubbed her arms, seeming annoyed. "I know Bennis wants to see me. I don't want to see Bennis. What would be the point of my seeing Bennis?"

"She's your sister."

"Myra was my sister. Emma was my sister. What difference

does it make? I did see her once, you know, at a distance. At the funeral."

"Funeral?"

"Our mother's funeral," Anne Marie said. "They let me attend. Sent me out there with enough of an armed guard to secure Panama City. I could have talked to her then, I suppose. I didn't want to."

"I think," Gregor said, "that she feels that, under the circumstances, it would be a way to say good-bye, or to make amends—"

"Or to feel sorry for me, because that's what she's always felt for me. Sorry. I was a good person to feel sorry for. When we were young, she felt sorry for me because she was popular and I was not. When we were older, she felt sorry for me because she was pretty and I was not. When we were older still, she felt sorry for me because I was stuck taking care of our mother and she was making herself famous. Except, of course, that I didn't feel stuck. I would have done that forever, if my father hadn't been a son of a bitch. Did you know I could use words like that? Son of a bitch."

"Everybody can use words like that," Gregor said.

Anne Marie nodded. "I suppose so, yes. But I'm glad it's over, if you want to know the truth. I know there won't be a stay of execution this time. Our bloody-minded governor wouldn't allow it. It means I don't have to go on pretending anymore. Pretending I'm sorry. Because I'm not sorry. Did you know that?"

"Yes."

"Maybe if you tell Bennis that, she won't want to come."

"She'll want to come."

Anne Marie sat down again. "Tell her to come for the execution. They issue invitations. It has to be witnessed. Teddy is coming for the execution, did you know that? It's just like Teddy, wanting to see somebody dead."

This, Gregor thought, was the stupidest situation he had ever been in in his life, and he had spent some time escorting vice presidents of the United States to official FBI functions. He had no idea why Anne Marie had wanted to see him, but she didn't have anything of interest to say, and so far she hadn't said anything he wanted to hear. He ought to get up and walk out on her. It would be better for Bennis if Bennis didn't get a chance to talk to her. It would be better for him if he could get past this feeling that he had no right to make these kinds of decisions for anybody but himself.

"Want to leave?" Anne Marie asked him.

"Very much," he told her.

"Why don't you?"

"Because your sister Bennis wants very much to talk to you before you die. And I am trying to make that happen for her."

"Are you in love with her?"

"Yes."

"How convenient. But then, Bennis always had half a dozen men in love with her. She was that kind of woman. Does she see only you or does she still sleep around?"

"Your brother Christopher," Gregor said carefully, "is coming up to be with Bennis during the day you are to be executed. He won't watch the execution, either. But he will come to keep Bennis company."

"I think you ought to be very sure what your arrangement is, because she does sleep around. She always did. And she always had such interesting people to sleep around with. Writers. Artists. Rock stars. Did you know about the rock star?"

"I know that I don't intend to engage in a conversation about Bennis's sex life with you."

"Well, that's typical, too, isn't it?" Anne Marie laughed. "When we were growing up, we were taught that bad girls do and good girls don't, but it was a lie, like all the rest of it was a lie. Some girls are good even when they do and some are bad even when they don't and you're born with that. It's all luck. Bennis got lucky, and I did not."

"Do you really think that your decision to kill three people was a matter of luck?"

"I think you ought to tell Bennis, for me, that she's not wanted here. Christopher isn't wanted here. Even Teddy and Bobby aren't wanted here, and I have a lot less to hold against them. Tell Bennis I don't want her here to gloat."

"Bennis doesn't want to gloat. You know she doesn't want to gloat."

Anne Marie stood up. "Tell her from me that I'm glad I did it. I'm glad about Myra. I'm glad about Emma. I'm glad about our father. I'm only sorry I couldn't finish the job. If

they had ever let me out of here, I would have tried. Now call
them back. If I go to the door, they'll panic."

"Are you sure this is it? Once I leave, I won't come back.
If you want to see her, tell me now."

"I don't want to see her. And if I change my mind, they'll
bend over backwards to make it happen. You know they will.
They don't want to get charged with brutality or cruelty or
any of those other things the protesters are always screaming
at them. Are there going to be protesters at my execution?"

"Protesters and cheerleaders, from what I gather. The protesters are from something called the Seamless Garment Network."

"Excellent. Nuns. When I was growing up on the Main
Line, nobody would admit to being Catholic. Being Catholic
was being Irish. It was being—low-rent. Are you going to get
me out of here?"

Gregor stood up and went to the door. It had a window in
it, and he knocked on that until the guard outside understood
what he wanted. Then he stepped back, and the guard came
in. Anne Marie stood up.

"It was pleasant to have spoken to you, Mr. Demarkian.
Give Bennis my message. Give her all of it. I don't want to
have to hear from her again."

Out in the hall, Ed Nagelman came up behind the two
guards who were coming to get Anne Marie. He stood back
politely, because the guards' work would always come first.
It was the most dangerous. Anne Marie, though, was not dangerous in that way, and she went out without a protest, her
head held up and back as if she were entering a ballroom.

Ed hurried into the conference room. "That was lucky. I
was afraid I'd have to interrupt your talk. There's a call for
you at the security desk."

"A call for me here? From whom?"

"A Mr. John Henry Newman Jackman, who identified himself as the deputy commissioner of police for the city of Philadelphia. I looked him up. There is such a person, and his
caller ID matched the phone number we've got for him. He
says it's serious. And urgent. He sounded"—Ed Nagelman
spread his hand—"highly agitated."

"All right," Gregor said. "I wonder what could be urgent."

"I did, too, but all he told me was to tell you that it had

happened again, and this time all bets were off, because it was Father Healy. I don't like to make guesses about things like this, but I assumed it had something to do with the murder you were looking into. Wasn't there a Father Healy involved in that murder you were looking into?"

Gregor didn't answer him. He was half running down the hall in the direction of the security desk, and he thought he was having a heart attack.

PART THREE

Organized religion is a crutch for weak-minded people.

—JESSE VENTURA, GOVERNOR OF
MINNESOTA

ONE

1

It was too long a drive. Gregor knew that by the time he got to St. Anselm's, the worst of the emergency would be over. The police would have the scene taped off. The witnesses would have been rounded up and shunted off to the sidelines somewhere to talk to uniformed officers whose only purpose would be to record whatever they said on steno pads. Of course, there was another possibility, and that was that Roy Phipps had taken to the streets again with his little band of followers—but nothing like that was coming over the radio on the sporadic news broadcasts they were able to pick up as they wound through the hills. It was funny how, living in Philadelphia, Gregor often forgot that Pennsylvania was a mountain state. They were real mountains, too, not as high or as intimidating as the Rockies, and not as new, but not "hills" the way any sane person thought of "hills." Most of them were rounded at the top and had vegetation all the way up, but for roads people had found it easier to go straight through the middle of them rather than over and around them, and Gregor and Henry seemed to keep getting caught in tunnels. They couldn't hear anything in tunnels. They couldn't even hear each other.

Eventually, the mountains and the tunnels were behind them, and the exits on the turnpike were closer together than every fifty-six miles. Gregor began to relax. The worst of his subconscious fears—that they would never be able to find their way back at all—finally appeared on the surface of his mind and made him feel embarrassed. He played with the radio dial until he got what sounded like talking heads and found that he had hit on a talk show instead of a news broadcast. The talk show was called *Feels Good*.

"Today," the talk show's hostess said brightly, "we're discussing role reversals. Can women reclaim their power by using prosthetic dildos to show the men in their lives what it really feels like to be a woman?"

"Jesus Christ," Henry said.

"What's a prosthetic dildo?" Gregor said.

Henry sighed. "It's a dildo. You know, a plastic version of a man's penis. It comes on a strap thing so that you can buckle it on and . . . and . . . oh, hell—"

"Right," Gregor said.

"That's the city," Henry said.

What he really meant was that that was the suburbs. They had to go through several towns on the Main Line before they reached Philadelphia itself. The traffic was getting thicker by the mile. The drivers were getting angrier. Gregor picked up a real news station.

"There is no word at this time who is dead at St. Anselm's Church, or what weapon was used in the killing," the announcer said. It was another woman. She was just as sprightly as the woman who had been talking about dildos. "We do have word that the police have cordoned off the entire block, including the cross streets, to prevent a recurrence of the riot that occurred there earlier in the week—"

Gregor turned the sound down. "That isn't very helpful."

"It tells us that Roy isn't burning down the barn."

"I suppose."

"That's the exit," Henry said.

Gregor looked up and saw that it was true. He'd lost a block of time, playing with the radio, thinking about nothing. Now he tried to pay attention as Henry shot off the turnpike and onto the complicated series of ramps and overpasses that would land them in city traffic. Gregor had actually learned to drive, once, when he was about thirty years old, because the Bureau had required it, but he had never gotten behind a wheel if he could avoid it, and most of the time he had been able to avoid it. The truth was, he was bad. Most people who had driven with him would just as soon do the driving themselves. Eventually, he had ended up behind a desk in the District of Columbia, and there had been no point at all in having a car.

It had been years since he let his last driver's license lapse. He was almost positive he couldn't pass a driving test if he were given one.

Henry had actually made it onto a city street. Gregor saw small grocery stores, and butcher shops, and the kind of store that sold newspapers and candy. Gregor had never understood how those stores made enough money to stay in business. Henry turned a corner and then another corner and then another. Neighborhoods got good and bad in succession, without any pattern that Gregor could see. Then there were police cars and pulsing red-and-blue lights, and Henry pulled over.

"Go," he said. "They won't let me in in any case."

"You're a judge."

"I'd have to create a fuss, and I don't want to. Go. Call me up later and let me know what happened."

Gregor got out of the car and looked around. He could, he thought, have gotten a police escort to bring him up here—if he'd called Jackman and asked for one, he would have gotten it—but it hadn't even occurred to him, and it didn't matter now. He was at the end of the block on the cross street. At the other end, St. Anselm's sat on the corner, its side to this street. There was a small knot of people pressing up against the barriers. Most of them seemed to be homeless people, winos and bag ladies, not so much curious as confused.

Gregor pushed through them to the uniformed officer at the gate. The uniformed officer was very young, and he looked scared to death.

"Gregor Demarkian," Gregor said. "Talk to Detective Mansfield or Detective Emiliani. They called for me."

"Nobody can pass the barrier," the uniformed officer said.

Gregor thought for a moment of what he could do—go down a few blocks and use a pay phone to get Jackman to get Mansfield to come out and get him—but all the alternatives meant getting this young man in trouble, and that wasn't what he was here for.

"Look," he said. "It won't kill you to get on that walkie-talkie and ask Detective Mansfield and Detective Emiliani if they're looking for a man named Gregor Demarkian. If the answer is no, you'll be in no different a position than you are now."

The young man in the uniform hesitated. Then he nodded

a little, said "just a minute," and turned his back to the crowd.
Gregor watched him punch in a code, talk into the receiver,
and then hesitate again. He turned around and looked Gregor
up and down. He went back to talking into the walkie-talkie.
Then he was done. He put the walkie-talkie into a little holster
arrangement at his belt and came back to the barrier.

"You do," he said.

"I do what?" Gregor asked.

"Look like a sort of out-of-shape Harrison Ford. You ought
to think about using some weights, Mr. Demarkian. Weight
training can change your life."

Gregor was of the opinion that his life had already been
changed as much and as often as he wanted it to be. He slipped
through the gap in the barrier that the uniformed officer made
for him. The crowd was nonexistent on the other side, and the
light was getting to be that way. Sometime, in all the running
around, while he hadn't been noticing, it had started to become
night. Why was it, he wondered, that everything that happened
on this block seemed to happen in the dark?

When he got up close to the side of St. Anselm's, there
was light again, coming across the parking lot from the courtyard. It was artificial light, but there was a lot of it, training
on a building on the far side of the space that Gregor was sure
he remembered as the rectory. He tried to get through the
wrought-iron gate and couldn't find a way. He walked all the
way to the entrance to the parking lot and went in there. There
was another uniformed officer stationed there, but this one
seemed to recognize him. He even nodded.

Gregor crossed the parking lot and walked onto the frozen
ground of the courtyard without worrying about finding the
pathways. The ruts in the ground stabbed against the slick
leather of his shoes and hurt his feet. The rectory door was
open, propped back by something he couldn't pick out in the
shadows. Policemen were walking in and out. None of them
seemed to be carrying anything. No ambulance was parked in
the parking lot.

Gregor got to the rectory door and introduced himself to
the officer stationed there. The officer nodded slightly and
called up the stairs for Mansfield.

"It's all over but the shouting," he said apologetically.

"They took the body out half an hour ago. Had to. We had hysterical nuns all over the place."

"We had *one* hysterical nun all over the place," Garry Mansfield said as he came down the stairs from the second floor. "Hello, Mr. Demarkian. You should come up and see the scene. Not that it means anything. It's just like the last one. No telling where he got the stuff or when he ate it, except, you know, that arsenic kicks in pretty soon so he'd have to have eaten it pretty soon. No vomit anywhere but in his bedroom. Lou Emiliani is so frustrated, he's threatening people with death."

"Do you know when he died?" Gregor asked.

Garry Mansfield was hurrying back up the rectory's stairs. Gregor was hurrying behind him, except that he didn't find it possible any longer to really hurry up stairs. Maybe the uniformed officer had had a point with that business about weight training.

"This one's fresher than the last one," Mansfield said. "Sister Peter Rose found him. She said she thought he must have fainted, and then when she touched him he was warm. You can talk to her."

"Do you think she's telling the truth? About the body being warm?"

"I think she thinks she is," Garry Mansfield said. "I guess it's not impossible. He wasn't long dead when we got here. But he was on the other side of the bed."

"On the other side of the bed from what?"

"From the vomit," Garry Mansfield said simply. "On the side of the bed that you can't see from the door, he'd done a lot of vomiting. There was an ocean of it. But he seems to have come around to the door side before he collapsed. Trying to get out, I'd guess."

"So would I. He didn't leave vomit anywhere else? Only on that side of the bed?"

"I think there might not have been much of anything left in his stomach to come up," Garry Mansfield said. "If you know what I mean. Sister Peter Rose said the room smelled funny, if that's any help to you."

"I think it's perfectly natural."

"Yeah, so do I," Garry Mansfield said. "You don't think this is something the nuns are doing, do you? I mean, I'm not a religious man myself, but I don't have anything against it. But you hear all these stories about convents, and the women go nuts in them, and that kind of thing."

"Ah," Gregor said. "Well. I think you'll find that that's mostly an urban legend."

"Yeah? Well, I think it's weird anyway. Shutting a bunch of women up together like that and telling them they can't, you know, have any. It would make me nuts."

Gregor was about to say that Sister Scholastica was one of the sanest women he knew, but they had reached the top of the stairs and Lou Emiliani. What Gregor assumed must have been Father Healy's bedroom was cordoned off from the rest of the empty building, and full of men in lab coats. He stood aside a little as one of the technicians brought a clear plastic bag full of something out the door.

"Shit," Lou Emiliani said. "I mean, excuse me, Mr. Demarkian, but—shit."

"I take your point exactly," Gregor said.

"You know what I want to know?" Lou Emiliani said. "What was this nun doing in the Father's bedroom to begin with? I mean, what was she doing there? Do they run back and forth to each other's rooms like a bunch of college students?"

"Did you ask her?" Gregor said.

"She's the one who's having hysterics all over everywhere," Garry Mansfield said.

Gregor went to the door of Father Healy's room and looked inside. From where he stood, he couldn't see where the vomit had been. The bed was made and unrumpled. The single chair was a straight-backed wooden one he couldn't imagine any visitor wanting to sit in. He went back to Mansfield and Emiliani.

"What about food?" he asked. "Was there any food in there?"

"Chocolate chip cookies," Mansfield said. "But I wouldn't pin your hopes on that. They were as stale as rocks."

"But you sent them to be analyzed," Gregor said.

"Absolutely." Garry Mansfield sighed.

Gregor went back to the door of the room and looked inside again. It was a plain room, with a crucifix on one wall and a religious painting on another. There was a wooden kneeler in front of the crucifix. It was the sort of thing Gregor knew people had, but didn't know why. He went back to Mansfield and Emiliani.

"Well," he said, "why don't we go talk to Sister Peter Rose."

2

The convent parlor was smaller than the rectory living room— smaller and plainer, even though it housed eight nuns when the rectory housed only two priests. All of the nuns seemed to be in attendance when Gregor knocked on the door. Sister Thomasetta let them in. Sister Angela Marie ran back and forth with tea and cookies. Sister Scholastica was sitting with Sister Peter Rose, making the kind of shushing noises a mother makes to a child who has had a bad fall, but not really done himself any damage. Well, Gregor thought, it's true enough that Sister Peter Rose hasn't done *herself* any damage—but then, he didn't believe she'd done damage to anybody else, either. Sane people had motives when they committed murder. Even half-sane people did. Unless he was terribly wrong about Sister Peter Rose, she was as sane as a rock.

Garry Mansfield and Lou Emiliani wiped their shoes carefully on the indoor mat. They'd already wiped them carefully on the outdoor one. Sister Scholastica looked up as Gregor and the two detectives came in and called out,

"Angela Marie? Do you think you could get these three gentlemen some coffee? They're probably going to need it."

Gregor nodded politely to the young nun hurrying out, and sat down on the couch across from the chairs where Sister Scholastica and Sister Peter Rose sat.

"Well," he said.

"I'm sorry," Sister Peter Rose said. Then she buried her face in the oversize handkerchief she was holding and started to cry again.

"I keep telling her not to worry about it," Sister Scholastica said, "considering the way I behaved yesterday. Then I get to thinking about the handkerchiefs."

"The what?" Gregor said.

"The handkerchiefs." Sister Scholastica reached out and

touched the one Sister Peter Rose was holding. "It's been a regulation in the order at least since I entered. We carry men's plain white linen handkerchiefs. I don't think I realized, before this week, just how large they were."

"Ah," Gregor said.

Sister Peter Rose put down the handkerchief and blinked.

"You know," Gregor said, "you're wrong. You'd make an excellent Mother Superior."

"Mother General," Scholastica corrected him.

Sister Peter Rose looked startled. "Oh, yes," she said. "What a wonderful idea. Not right away of course, because I wouldn't want Mother General to be ill, but in the long run—"

"Let's try to remember I haven't even been elected a provincial yet," Scholastica said. "Are you ready to talk to Mr. Demarkian, Sister?"

"Oh," Peter Rose said. "Yes. I'm sorry. I know I'm acting like a child."

"You're doing fine," Gregor told her. "You're not supposed to take finding a dead body in stride. Even people who are paid to do it don't take it in stride. The question, at the moment, is why you went up to Father Healy's room. That's what you did, isn't it? You went up to the second floor of the rectory and into his room."

"That's right," Sister Rose said. "I'd never been there before."

"So it wasn't something you usually did."

"Oh, no," Sister Peter Rose said. "I wouldn't think of it under ordinary circumstances. We've got very strict rules about that sort of thing. The whole archdiocese does. Well, most archdioceses would frown on a nun going to a priest's bedroom for almost any reason, except, you know, if he were dying and she was needed to nurse him, which would be an entirely different thing, of course, because—"

"Sister," Scholastica said.

"Oh," Sister Peter Rose said. "Sorry."

"That's fine," Gregor said. "Don't worry about it. So it wasn't your habit to go up to Father Healy's room, and ordinarily you would never have thought of it. That's as I'd thought. But you did go up to his room. So you must have had a reason."

"Oh, yes," Sister Peter Rose said. "It was because of the pounding."

"The pounding?" Gregor asked.

"I could hear it all the way down in the rectory living room," Sister Peter Rose said. "It was like he was trying to throw furniture. Things seemed to be smashing into the floor, except it was the ceiling over my head. So I went out into the hall and called up the stairs. And he didn't answer me. That's when I started to be worried."

"When he didn't answer you," Gregor repeated.

Sister Peter Rose rubbed her hands together. "I thought I'd catch him before he had a chance to go upstairs, you see. I mean, when I come in from outside I always spend a couple of minutes in the parlor or I go to the kitchen before I go upstairs. So I thought he would be on the first floor. But then I couldn't find him, and the pounding started, and he wouldn't answer me—"

"Wait," Gregor said. "When did you think you could catch him?"

"Oh." Sister Peter Rose took a deep breath. "Well, you see, I was at the school, and I'd had a conference with this parent, and that was over. And I looked out the window of my classroom and Father was standing in that little arched side doorway that goes into the Mary Chapel. You know the one I mean."

"Yes." It was the one Gregor had been going in and out of on a regular basis since he first started coming to St. Anselm's.

"Well, he was standing there, talking to someone—"

"Who?" Gregor asked.

Sister Peter Rose shook her head. "I don't know. I couldn't see. But it wasn't an angry talk, or anything. It didn't look confrontational. Father was just sort of bopping along and talking full tilt. I mean. You know what he was. He was such a *naif* really."

Gregor bit his lip. Standing at the doorway, Garry Mansfield and Lou Emiliani bit theirs, too. Gregor took a deep breath.

"So," he said, "Father Healy was standing at the side door talking to somebody. Do you have any idea what he was doing before then?"

"I do," Scholastica said. "I was there. He was in the church, leading a Chaplet of the Divine Mercy."

"A what?" Gregor asked.

"A Chaplet of the Divine Mercy," Sister Angela Marie said, putting a tray with coffee things down on the small round coffee table at Gregor's side. "It's a devotion, with a set of repetitive prayers, to the Divine Mercy. It's been televised endlessly on EWTN over the last few years—"

"Eternal World Television Network," Sister Scholastica said. "Mother Angelica and those people. It's very popular in this part of the country."

"Yes. So there were requests for us to do the Chaplet here, and Father liked devotions of that kind, so he led them. Once a week, every week, at this time."

"How long does it take to pray a Chaplet of the Divine Mercy?" Gregor asked.

Sister Peter Rose wiped her eyes. "About half an hour, if you get really fancy with it and chant. Father loved to chant."

"He did that," Sister Scholastica said. "He had a beautiful voice for plainchant."

Gregor thought about it. "Tell me something about this devotion. Does it require anything else besides praying and plainchant—"

"It's not praying and plainchant," Sister Angela Marie said, "you pray *in* plainchant."

"All right. You pray in plainchant. But does it require anything else, like Communion, or any other thing that might require Father Healy or anybody else to eat anything?"

"Oh," Sister Peter Rose said. "Oh, no, it's nothing like that. And the only thing you'd ever have to eat in a Catholic church would be the Body and Blood, anyway. But it was just prayers, like the rosary. You didn't receive Communion."

Gregor turned to Scholastica. "You said you were there. There was nothing to eat while the Chaplet was going on?"

"Of course not," Scholastica said.

"Were you watching him at all times? Could you say for certain that he didn't eat anything or drink anything while the devotion was going on?"

"Of course not," Scholastica said. "I wasn't looking at him at all. I was looking at my beads, or I had my eyes closed, which is what I was supposed to be doing. But I can almost guarantee that he didn't eat or drink anything during the Chaplet, anyway."

"Why?" Gregor asked.

"It's because of the format," Sister Thomasetta said, coming in from the foyer. "It's a proclamation and response format. One person said the first half of a sentence, then the congregation said the next half. Over and over like that. In sentence fragments."

"What Sister is trying to say," Scholastica said, "is that Father Healy wouldn't have had time to eat much of anything. To swallow something small like an aspirin, maybe, but other than that he would have been caught up short the next time he was supposed to speak, and we would probably have noticed the break."

"Probably but not definitely," Gregor said.

Scholastica fluttered her hands in the air. "It's hard to say definitely about anything. But I didn't notice any hesitations. The devotion is very hypnotic, in a way. Nothing broke the rhythm that I noticed during the whole half hour."

Gregor looked at Garry Mansfield and Lou Emiliani. Lou Emiliani shrugged. It was weak, but if they could trust it, they would know that Father Healy had to have been poisoned after the Chaplet devotion. Half an hour was far longer than it would take for arsenic to start to make him sick.

Gregor turned to Sister Scholastica again. "What happened after the Chaplet? Did he stand around talking? Was there a coffee hour?"

"No, nothing like that," Scholastica said. "We do that sort of thing sometimes, when we have devotions or meetings in the evenings, and after the early Mass on weekday mornings, so that people can have some coffee before they go to work—"

"Because they've been fasting," Sister Angela Marie said. "For Communion."

"Right," Scholastica said. "So we've got that. But with something in the middle of the day like this, no, we don't do any coffee or refreshments. It's mostly older people who come. I think they go off to a diner a couple of blocks away and have something on their own."

"Did Father Healy stand around in the church after the Chaplet and talk to the people who had come?" Gregor asked.

"He said hello and how are you to a couple of them," Scholastica said, "but he didn't get involved in conversations."

"And then he left."

"Yes."

"And you saw him leave," Gregor said.

"Yes," Scholastica said. "Well, to be exact, I saw him go out behind the Mary Chapel in the direction of that door. There's a little buffer space or something back there, the actual door is hard to see from the center of the church. But he went that way and he didn't come back and there's no place else to go."

"Did you go out that way, too?"

"No," Scholastica said. "I went out the front of the church. I had to go over to St. Stephen's and tell Chickie George that Mary McAllister wouldn't be able to pick him up until seven. She'd been held up at school."

Gregor thought it over again. "What about the other people who had been at the devotion. Did they leave by the Mary Chapel door?"

"Some of them might have," Scholastica said, "but most of them wouldn't have. Like I said, we get mostly older people. The Mary Chapel door comes out on a stoop—well, you've been on it. A concrete-block stoop. It ices over this time of year. We should take better care of it. But the way it is, most of our older people prefer to go out the front, where we've got salt down when it ices and the going is relatively flat."

"But you can't say that one of them *didn't* go out that door," Gregor said.

"No," Scholastica admitted. "But do you really think one of our older people poisoned Father Healy, and Bernadette and Harriet and poor Scott Boardman from across the street? I mean, I know they get cranky sometimes, but—"

"I'm just trying to determine if we can rule out that part of Father Healy's day," Gregor said. "So it was most likely one of your older parishioners he was talking to when Sister Peter Rose saw him."

"Well," Sister Peter Rose said, "yes, I suppose so. I just didn't think it was. If you know what I mean. I mean, none of the other people from the Chaplet were around, or coming out that door, or even in the parking lot. So I just assumed, you know, that it was somebody else."

Gregor let it go. "What happened then?" he asked. "He came back to the rectory?"

"That's right." Sister Peter Rose nodded. He came across the parking lot and then across the courtyard, and I called out to him, but he didn't hear me. So I ran around to the back door—I was at school, you see, I couldn't go right out the way I could have if I had been here—and just as I got outside, I saw him go into the rectory. So I ran up to the rectory and rang, but nobody answered. Well, I mean, I didn't wait for him to answer, really. I mean, there's no need. I rang to let him know somebody was coming in, then I came in."

"And Father Healy wasn't in the living room," Gregor said.

"In the living room or the dining room or the kitchen. I checked all those places. And then I knew, you know, that he'd gone upstairs. So I went to the bottom of the stairs and called up to him."

"And?"

"And nothing happened," Sister Peter Rose said. "He didn't answer back. So I called again. And then next thing I heard was the thumping."

"Thumping like somebody falling or thumping like somebody pounding?"

"I don't know," Sister Peter Rose said. "Thumping like somebody was taking something big and blunt like one of those weight bags boxers use to practice on and slamming it against the floor, over and over again. Like that. It didn't make any sense really. I couldn't understand why he wasn't answering me. And I thought, I don't know, that he was having a heart attack or maybe this was a home invasion and there were people in the house and then I don't know what I was thinking, but I ran up the stairs to find out."

"You could have been killed," Sister Thomasetta said. "Think what would have happened if it was a home invasion."

"Well, it wasn't," Peter Rose said. "And I got up to the top of the stairs and the door to his bedroom was closed, but I could hear the thumping in there, so I opened it. I know I shouldn't have opened it. When the Cardinal Archbishop finds out about this, I'm going to be sent right back to the motherhouse. But I did open it, and there he was, on the floor, all sort of contorted—I'm not sure how to describe it—all bent up and creased, sort of, his skin was creased and I just lost my composure. I just—I screamed and screamed and then I could see that he was dead and I didn't know what to do about it."

"There wasn't anything for you to do about it," Scholastica said. "What do you think you were supposed to do about it?"

Actually, Gregor could think of a number of things—call the police; call the ambulance; get help; not panic—but he didn't mention any of them, because most civilians could not do anything but what they did. Training could teach you to handle the surprise of somebody dying violently before your eyes. Without training, people mostly did what they could do.

Gregor got up and went to the parlor window to look out. A little way across the courtyard, tech men were going in and out of the rectory while a young dispirited-looking priest was standing by.

Gregor retreated from the window. It was dark out there, now. Other than the police and the parochial vicar, the courtyard was empty.

"I suppose," he said, "we'd better find out what the autopsy says about what the man ate."

TWO

1

Ian was with her when the sirens started, and he was with her an hour later, when the street was calm again and only the lights at the end of the block gave any indication that there was something wrong at St. Anselm's. Edith knew it was a mistake. Will almost never came home before the middle of the night anymore, but this might be the time, and to have Ian sitting here naked wouldn't do. She looked across Ian's lap at the night table. He had laid out his Rolex watch and his Coach accessories: leather card case, leather credit card case, leather wallet. Everything Ian owned that wasn't gold was mahogany leather. Edith got up and found a robe to wrap around herself. Then she sat back down on the bed and stretched out her legs.

"It can't go on forever," she said finally. "Will knows now. Nothing we do will make any difference to that."

"It will make a difference if he can prove it."

"He can say he walked in on us. He did walk in on us. Isn't that the same as proof in a divorce court?"

"Not if you deny it."

"I thought I wasn't allowed to deny it," Edith said. "Under oath, I mean. I thought you told me, when we started—"

"I know what I told you.'

Until now, the room had been dark. Ian never seemed to like the light on when they were together. Now he switched on the bedside lamp and sat looking up at her, the pale hair on his chest seeming to rise and fall in a stray draft. Edith's roll of Life Savers were lying on top of the dresser. She got it down and popped the one on top into her mouth, fingering it along the smooth small curve first, as if she wanted to memorize the shape with her fingers.

"Everything we've done," she said carefully. "From the very beginning. Everything we haven't done. It was so that Will wouldn't find out."

"But Will did find out, Edith. So that's over."

Edith went to the window and looked out. "There's been another one, down the street. Did you know that. Father Healy. Didn't you know Father Healy from your office?"

"Vaguely. Mostly, I only knew the Cardinal."

"You knew that girl. That Bernadette Kelly."

"Of course I did. She was a receptionist."

"She could have ruined you."

Ian got very still. Edith could feel it. "I wouldn't say that," he said finally. "She wasn't a very bright girl. Everybody knew that."

Edith turned the soft mints over and over in her hands and then put them back on the bureau. It was worse than still in this room. Everything had come to a dead stop. The lights in the church's courtyard down the block were spilling into the street. Every time somebody walked past there, he looked as if he had been lit up. Edith went from the bureau to the window to the bed and back again.

"She could have ruined you," she said finally, "and you knew it, and I knew it. She could have stopped you. She told you so. I heard her."

"She never said anything of the kind. Edie, don't be a fool. You didn't hear anything like that. Even if you think you did, you can't corroborate it."

"I don't have to corroborate it. I heard it. And then a week later, less than a week later, she was dead. Out in that trailer park where she lived. They never would have known it wasn't diabetes if that silly husband of hers hadn't brought her into church. Nobody would ever have known. But he did."

By now, the room was beyond dead stop, beyond anything Edith could remember experiencing in her whole life. Ian could have been a block of marble. If he had smoked cigarettes, he would have brought one out to have something to do with his hands. With the light on, there were no shadows in the room. Edith thought that she must look like those women in movies, lit to be hags. The light was wrapped around her, making her look creased.

"You," Ian said, "are making mountains out of molehills. Because if you think I killed Bernadette Kelly, you're crazy. There are other ways of getting out of trouble if you have to. I'm not about to go around offing people with arsenic and risk a death sentence. And besides, you can explain Bernadette Kelly, but what about the rest of them? That gay boy. And the nun. And now—what? What's going on down the street?"

"I'm not sure."

"Maybe it's another one," Ian said pleasantly. "What did you think I did, Edie, drop in over at St. Anselm's and off somebody on my way here to pork you? One of the other nuns, maybe, or one of the altar boys. If they still have altar boys, after everything that's happened there."

"I'm not saying you killed anybody."

"Well, you're saying something, Edie. Maybe you ought to come right out and just say it. Because if you think you can blackmail me, you're very wrong."

"I thought you didn't want publicity. I thought you said it was dangerous."

"Dangerous isn't the same as lethal." Ian got out of bed and grabbed for his pants. He had no robe here—he had never kept any of his clothes in this house—but his underwear was lying right on the floor at the side of the bed. He wore boxer shorts with prints on them. It was one of the things Edith had found most fascinating about him when they had first met.

"I think you're underestimating the problem," Edith said. "You can't really think that nobody is going to find out. Not now. The new Cardinal isn't like the old one. He's going to do an audit one of these days, and he's going to find those extra names you put on the victims' list. And he's going to know it was you. Even Bernadette Kelly knew it was you."

Ian stopped with his trousers halfway up his legs. "I don't know what you're talking about," he said.

"Everybody else will," Edith told him.

Ian pulled his pants the rest of the way up and buttoned them. Then he reached for his shirt. "I think it's time we cooled this off a little," he said carefully. "You've gotten too wound up in it. You're under too much stress. We need a vacation from each other."

"Every time somebody came up who could expose you, they died," Edith said. "Did you notice that? Bernadette Kelly. And that gay boy, as you call him, who was the lover of one of the victims on that list. I'm not a detective genius, Ian. If I found out, everybody else will."

"I think you're insane," Ian said. "I think you've walked straight into one of your fantasies and can't find your way out. You've got no idea if that gay boy was the lover of one of the pedophilia victims, and even if he were, what would he know that could hurt me? And what about the other one, the nun? I've never even met the nun. And what about what's going on down there now?"

"There are four extra names," Edith said carefully. "On one of the lists of victims, there are four extra names. They change the calculations. You slipped it by the old Cardinal Archbishop because he was practically senile, and now you're stuck with it, and everybody who knows anything about it has died."

"If that's the case, Edie, I'd be more worried than you are to have me in the house. If I've already killed at least three people, I might not be fastidious about killing one more."

Edith looked at Ian standing at the side of the bed. He had started to put on his shirt, but it was still unbuttoned. It was a good shirt, cotton oxford, with a button-down collar. Sometimes it seemed to her that Ian dressed entirely out of a novel by F. Scott Fitzgerald, or maybe John O'Hara.

She walked out of the room and down the hall to the bathroom. She turned on the light and closed the door. She had jogging things hanging in the cupboard. She put those on, because she couldn't stand the idea of going back down the hall to her own bedroom. Everything in this house was cramped and old. Everything was—ordinary. Her jogging things were bright red. The pants had racing stripes down the outsides of the legs.

Dressed, she came back into the hall and listened. Ian was still in the bedroom. She could hear him swearing under his breath.

"I'm going down to the kitchen," she called to him.

He didn't answer, but she didn't expect him to. For days now, she had known what was going on, what was happening to them. She had been in enough love affairs in the course of her life to understand when one had suddenly become unglued.

The energy was gone. The passion just seemed hallucinatory. Except that she had never been in this particular love affair for energy, or for passion. The truth of it was, Ian disgusted her, physically. He was the kind of pale, half-soft man who made her feel as if he were oozing.

The truth, she thought, as she got the coffee things out of the cupboards in the kitchen, was that lately all sex had started to disgust her—an offshoot of the onset of menopause, maybe, except that she'd heard that menopause had exactly the opposite effect. Her hands were shaking, but she wasn't frightened. She could hear Ian moving around upstairs, but he didn't threaten her. She kept trying to get a handle on her emotions and couldn't. She wasn't sad. She wasn't upset. She wasn't scared. She wasn't anxious. Even that deep pit of envy that she carried everywhere at the center of her heart had disappeared, dissolved in the acid of a rage so righteous and so complete that it was burning it up.

That's it, Edith thought. I'm angry.

Then she put the kettle on to boil and turned around to face the door that led into the dining room. He was coming, very slowly, as if he needed to let her know that nothing she did and nothing she said could make him hurry. She could hear his shoes, first on carpet and then on hardwood. He had taken the time to get dressed. She could hear him breathing. That was not as calm.

When he came through the door, he had a gun—and Edith found, to her surprise, that she had half expected that. She knew nothing about guns. This one looked big, and black, and could be held in one hand. Names flitted through her head— Smith & Wesson; Colt—but they meant nothing to her. She had all the lights on in the kitchen, but she could have looked out the bank of windows over the sink and seen those other lights, over at St. Anselm's.

"If it's really true," Ian said, "that I killed at least three people, I don't think you should be trying to threaten me when you aren't even armed."

"I didn't threaten you."

"I think you did."

Edith giggled. "I saw what you did," she said, "and I know who you are."

"It isn't funny, Edie."

"I think it is."

"I can't have you going around the city of Philadelphia telling people I added four extra names to the victims' list on the pedophilia case."

"And pocketed the cash."

"They'll assume I pocketed the cash, Edie. They'll assume that."

"They'll be right."

Ian did something to the gun—cocked it, Edith thought it was called. She wasn't sure. It was odd how she could be so little afraid of this thing. If it were loaded, it would be more than capable of killing her. She was sure it was loaded. She really didn't care.

"I thought you'd get away with it, when this started," she said. "I thought you were smart enough for that. But I was wrong. There's no way you can get away with it. And now I don't really want you to. So that's that."

"I could shoot you right here."

"You won't."

"You're the one who thinks I've killed three people."

Edith turned her head to the side and looked through the windows at the lights coming from St. Anselm's. Four, she thought. That's what that is over there. That would be four. She crossed her arms over her chest and looked back at Ian. She had gotten to him, finally. He was not only posturing, now. He was furious, almost as furious as she was, furious enough so that his hands were shaking, and the gun was jiggling up and down.

"I don't understand why you thought you could get away with it," she said. "Coming in here, and taking what you wanted for free."

"I don't know what you're talking about."

"It doesn't matter what I'm talking about," she said.

Ian raised the gun higher in the air, and steadied his hands. Edith turned her back on him.

2

Roy Phipps knew, as soon as he saw the lights coming from the courtyard at St. Anselm's, that there had been another one.

He knew it the way some people know that rain is coming by the pains in their joints. Of course, he sent Fred down the street anyway—he had to send Fred, if only to save Fred's pride—but when he had the few details that could be learned by eavesdropping at the edges of the crowd, he knew nothing more than what he had already divined. It was funny, the way it worked out. If he had been a different sort of man, with a different sort of background, he might have become a psychic. He thought he would have been a good one. It was all one, really, ESP, speaking in tongues, transubstantiation, being slain in the spirit. It was all magic, only some of it, like the gifts of the Holy Spirit, was white, and some of it, like the Catholic Mass, was black as pitch. Except that Roy didn't much like calling the Evil Things "black." No matter what else he was, he had never been an instinctively racist man. He would have welcomed black members into his church, if any had been interested in joining, but none ever were. The real divisions in the world were not between black and white, but between good and evil. He had always known which side was evil—but no, that wasn't true. For a few short years, at Princeton and later in graduate school, he *hadn't* known, and what he remembered of that time was an agony of confusion so great he had sometimes woken in the night in a panic, thinking that his head was about to split open. But it was funny the way *that* worked, too. He had seen it as soon as he had gone to the seminary, which was why he hadn't stayed, and why he hadn't allowed himself to be ordained in any of the small denominations that would have had him. Nothing that you allowed to become part of you ever really left you. He ministered to Fred, but he did it in a J. Press suit. He preached to men with dirt ground into the creases on their hands, but his own hands were as soft and clean and well kept as any New York banker's.

Now it was nearly nine o'clock, and the street was something like quiet. Roy had been standing at the windows of his office for nearly an hour, doing nothing. Sometime ago, a noise that sounded like a shot had come from the general direction of the house belonging to the atheist Edith Lawton, but it had probably been some kind of illusion. Roy had sent Fred up to check, and Fred had seen nothing worth reporting. Somebody was moving around in the kitchen, but he couldn't tell who. Nobody was panicking. Nobody was screaming. Maybe it was a premonition. The atheist Edith Lawton was also the whore Edith Lawton. Her fancy man had come to visit hours before. His car was still parked in the street. Maybe the atheist Will Lawton would come home and find them together and shoot them both. For some reason, the thought of that made Roy feel extremely pleased, as if some part of his life had been vindicated.

Around him, the town-house church was quiet. Fred was leading a Bible study in the living room, but other than that there wasn't anything going on for the rest of the evening. Roy sometimes stopped in to the Bible study meetings to straighten out whatever mess they'd gotten themselves into. They read the King James, because they believed that was the only true version, but then they stumbled on the language. Sometimes Roy would read to them from the original Hebrew or Greek, and they would sit solemnly, listening and nodding, as if they understood him. If nothing else proved that it was all magic, that did.

Roy went out into the hall and listened. The living-room door was closed, and all he could hear was the low murmur of hesitation. They were "struggling" with a passage, meaning most probably that they were refusing to accept the plain truth of it. It took a long time to convince people that when God said "hate," He meant hate, and when He said "kill," He meant kill. America had been corrupted with the False Christ of compassion and love, as if heaven were supposed to be a vast kindergarten whose denizens could commit no more serious a wrong than running with scissors or drawing on the walls. Calvin had had it right. The vast majority of men were born destined to burn forever in the pit of hell.

Roy went out the front door and down the steps to the street. It was cold, and he wasn't wearing a coat, but he didn't particularly mind. He walked up the block until he got to the Lawton house and stopped. Fred was right, for once. There was no sign of anything wrong here. The front of the house was dark. The back of the house was lit up—there were lights on in the kitchen and the sunroom—but there was nothing to see, and no sounds of panic. He walked past and up to the end of the block, where St. Anselm's was, but there was still a police barrier there. It was set up in such a way that people could enter the church, if they wanted to, and some people were doing just that. They looked like the homeless people Father Healy had insisted on allowing to sleep on the pews. Roy himself had no patience with homeless people. If they were mentally ill, they belonged in mental institutions. If they were drunks or drug addicts, they belonged in the gutter. If they were anybody else—but Roy knew all too much about the ones who were anybody else. He had grown up with the ones who were anybody else.

He crossed the street to St. Stephen's and stood for a moment at its front gate, resting his hand for a moment on the wrought-iron railing. Two men came out together and looked him over as they passed, but if they recognized him, they didn't say anything. Roy went up the walk and into the church, which reminded him eerily of the Princeton University chapel—but then, that made sense, because that was "affiliated" with the Episcopal Church, too. He went through the foyer and into the church and saw that, unlike St. Anselm's, there were no homeless people here—but then, he thought, there wouldn't be. It was one of the first things he had ever known about religion, and he had known it all the way back in West Virginia, when he was barely old enough to talk. Churches came and went, but the Episcopal Church was now and always would be the Church of the people who had the most money.

He was just thinking that he ought to go home—he had no idea what he was doing here—when he felt someone at his back and knew, with that same sense that had told him about the murder at St. Anselm's, who it was. At that moment, he was looking at the gold latticework that framed a picture that had been left on the marble altar, and for a moment he went on looking at it, although he couldn't make out what the picture was about. Then he straightened his back a little and turned, to see Dan Burdock standing behind him.

"I never understood where Episcopalians got the money for all that gold," he said pleasantly. "Even in West Virginia, where I grew up, the Episcopalian church was full of gold. And it wasn't as if anybody there had anything like money."

"Do you want to tell me what you're doing here?" Dan Burdock asked. "Are you trying to start another riot?"

"I'm standing in the middle of a church, admiring its altar.

I don't see how that could start a riot. Among normal people."

"From what I remember, it wasn't my thoroughly normal people who started the riot the last time."

Roy swung his head back in the direction of the altar. "No," he said. "That's true enough, and on camera, so I won't bother to deny it. On the other hand, the blame for the escalation is entirely on you."

"What are you doing here?" Dan Burdock asked again. "What could you possibly hope to accomplish? I've got one person dead myself and across the street—"

"The priest died. Yes, I know. We hear everything down the block, you know. We're not exactly in Siberia. Tell me, was it the same thing? Was it arsenic?"

"They'll have to wait for the autopsy."

"They must have a guess," Roy said. "I sent Fred down to find out, but you've met Fred. He isn't exactly a superspy."

"Yes," Dan said. "They think it's arsenic. I haven't actually been over there. I don't exactly have the nerve for that. Or the bad taste—"

"Oh, let's not get started on my bad taste."

"Why not? Why not, Roy? You've chosen to make a vocation out of it, why not talk about it?"

"Why don't you just come out and say it? Why don't you just tell everybody that you're gay? Everybody knows it anyway. Your bishop must know it, by now. It's the cowardice I can't stand. It was the cowardice I couldn't stand at Princeton."

"I thought it was the prep school you couldn't stand at Princeton."

The pews in this church were made of carved and polished wood, with swirling ridges on the ends of them. Roy sat down on the arm of the one just behind him. He had entered the little Episcopalian church in Millard's Corner only once or twice, and been suitably impressed, but it had been nothing like this—or, for that matter, like the college chapels at Princeton and Yale and all the other places he had been since. He knew something about the Gothic aesthetic, about the idea that the house of God ought to reflect the glory of God, but he could never get used to it. In his mind, Christianity would always be a religion of the disenfranchised—of what, in his childhood, would have been called the deserving poor.

"I won't go away," he said finally. "Oh, I'll go away now, in a bit. I've got work to do, and it's getting late. But I'm not going to disappear from down the block, and I'm not going to fall off the face of the earth. I'll be here as long as you're here. I'll move to wherever you decide to go next. As long as you stay in the ministry, I'll be here."

"Would you disappear if I left the priesthood?"

"But you won't leave the priesthood," Roy said. "You know that, and I know that. And your bishop won't throw you out. Oh, you'd be a little safer if you were in Newark with Spong, but not a great deal safer. You're safe enough. So you won't leave, and I won't leave, and I won't be quiet about what I see going on here. With the men. With you. Even if you're more discreet about it than most."

"Roy, you could have taped every second of my sex life for the last twenty years, and it would be suitable viewing on *Sesame Street*."

"Really? How very intelligent of you. But then, you were always very intelligent. Not as intelligent as some other people, but very intelligent." Roy got up off the pew's arm. "I came to look around, because I hadn't been in here before. I don't know why not. I should have come in and watched you on Sunday one week, but I never did. Have you ever come to watch me?"

"You know I haven't."

"But you must have seen me, once or twice, at least in clips. I think they've broadcast me giving sermons a million times by now. They don't broadcast the whole sermon, and they're always trying to find the three seconds out of two hours when I look like I might be sweating, but they do broadcast me."

"I don't know what you're getting at," Dan said.

Roy stood up and brushed lint off his jacket. It was probably true. Dan probably didn't understand what he was getting at. On the other hand, as much as he would like to be understood, he had what he had come here to get, and there was no reason for him not to leave. He brushed lint off the arm of his jacket and wondered what it meant, that Dan was wearing a clerical collar and he was not. Really, it was worse than that. Dan was wearing one of those agonizingly tacky black polyester shirts meant to take a clerical collar, the kind you bought out of a catalogue of clergy supplies, and Roy was wearing his best Brooks Brothers camel hair. Roy thought suddenly of D. James Kennedy, with his Coral Ridge Ministries, always dressed in academic robes to preach. Maybe it was just a kind of social anxiety. When you were not to the manner born, you had to rely on costumes.

"What's the matter now?" Dan asked.

Roy stuck his hands in his pockets. "Nothing is the matter. I wanted to see your church. I've seen your church."

"Everybody is welcome in this church," Dan said.

"Something tells me that I wouldn't be, if the men going back and forth around here realized who I was."

"They realize who you are."

Since this was possibly true, Roy let it go. He stretched a little and pivoted, taking in the choir loft, the altar, the tall stained-glass windows that lined both of the long sidewalls. It was a beautiful church. He wouldn't have expected anything else.

"Well," he said, "I think that we've carried this as far as it can go. I'll talk to you later."

"Of course."

"Of course."

Roy backed away, then turned around and went as slowly as he could out the doors to the foyer and out the doors there to the walk that led to the street. Men were still coming in and out, and he thought that Dan might be right. They might know who he was, and just be too polite, too circumspect, too God-damned private school to do anything about it. He wondered if they looked at him after he had walked past, but he knew that the one thing he couldn't do was to turn around to check. He went all the way onto the sidewalk and turned toward home without a backwards glance. He looked at St. Anselm's and saw that girl who worked with the homeless coming out the front doors and half-running to the corner. If he had had any sex drive at all, he would have wanted something like that girl to take to bed.

What he wanted instead was more coffee, and as he started down the street he began to hurry, just a little, so that he would be closer to getting it.

3

If Mary McAllister had been at the church right after Father Healy's body was discovered, or even heard about the death anytime in the next two hours, she would have been able to talk to Gregor Demarkian directly. Instead, she had had an evening class and then a quick run to the library. Lately, it seemed as if she never had the materials she needed to do what she needed to do. Then she had been in a hurry, because she was late for the soup kitchen and also for the boxes she was supposed to pick up at St. Anselm's. If she had listened to an ordinary radio station on the drive over, she would have heard all about it. Instead, she'd tuned in to the station that played chant and medieval motets. She had no idea where they broadcast from, but wherever it was seemed to have no news bureau at all. It wasn't until she had pulled into the parking lot at St. Anselm's and seen all the strange lights in the courtyard that she'd realized something was wrong. It wasn't until she'd found Sister Scholastica, looking as if she'd been drenched and wrung out in her habit, that she'd known *what* was wrong. Then, for a while, she'd simply behaved like a fool. It wasn't that she had been inordinately fond of Father Healy. As priests went, he hadn't been too bad, but he hadn't inspired her in the way that the Pope did, or made her feel as if she were in the presence of holiness, the way Father Dougan at the soup kitchen did. He was just a nice, ordinary, harmless man who meant well and tried to do good. Maybe that was why his death came as such a shock. She could almost understand somebody killing Sister Harriet Garrity. She had had urges to do that herself. Then, without realizing it, she had been bracketing away the deaths of Bernadette Kelly and Scott Boardman by telling herself they were probably the work of somebody deranged, like a psychopath. But this seemed like such an . . . ordinary . . . murder, so sort of matter-of-fact, as if whoever had done it had killed in the same spirit in which he got himself breakfast or decided to change the channel on his television set.

Gregor Demarkian and the two police detectives were already gone by the time Mary got to St. Anselm's. Mary didn't really want to talk to the police detectives, because it would seem too much like something official. A deposition. A witness report. Gregor Demarkian seemed safer. Mary had seen enough of him on the news and in the papers to feel as if she almost knew him. His best friend was a priest, that was one thing. The woman he went out with was the one who wrote the fantasy novels about good and evil that one of Mary's English professors at St. Joe's had said had "a very Catholic intellectual foundation," whatever that was supposed to mean. None of it meant anything, except that she would be more comfortable talking to Demarkian than to the police, and she knew where to find Demarkian. She called the soup kitchen and told them she would be late with the boxes. Then she put the boxes in the back of the van as fast as she could and crossed the street to St. Stephen's. Just as she was coming out St. Anselm's front door she saw that man—Roy Phipps; for a second she hadn't been able to remember his name—coming out of St. Stephen's. He looked at her briefly but didn't register what he saw, and she looked away. It was Mary McAllister's personal opinion that Roy Phipps was an agent of the devil himself, determined to make all Christians look like evil fanatics and make sure nobody who wasn't one would ever want to be one, but this didn't seem to be the best place or the best time to have it out with him.

She went into St. Stephen's front door and looked around. Nobody was there that she knew. She went around to the back and into the annex. Most of the office doors were open, but the offices were empty. She went around to the back of the church again and looked into the small reading room behind the sacristy, and there he was, sitting with his legs propped up on an ottoman, reading David Leavitt's *The Lost Language of Cranes*.

"There you are," she said. "I was afraid you'd left without me."

"I can't leave without you." Chickie put his book down in his lap. "You're the only one who can get me in and out of a car. I'm in no shape to take a taxi by myself."

"Where's Aaron?"

"Marc's play opened tonight. It ought to be just about over by now. There's going to be a party to wait for the notices.

We're invited, if you want to go." Chickie's head shot up. "I don't think I meant that the way it sounded."

"I know the way you meant it," Mary said. "Oh, rats. We really need Aaron."

"Why?"

"Because we have to talk to Mr. Demarkian, that's why. And Aaron is the one who figured it out. He'll be able to explain it better than we will."

Chickie fingered the back of his book. "Don't you think you're jumping to conclusions here? Gregor Demarkian is a professional. The police are professionals. If they really need us, they'll come and find us."

Mary marched over to Chickie's chair and put her hands on its arms. She was leaning all the way over him, with her face only inches from his, and she was breathing hard.

"Look," she said. "I know it's an act. The swish thing you do. And I know you've got good reason to do it, even if you haven't told me what it is, but I believe you, and mostly I'm okay with it, but I'm not now. Okay, Chickie? I can't handle it now. Do you know Father Healy is dead?"

"Yes," Chickie said. "Everybody in Philadelphia knows Father Healy is dead."

Mary retreated to a standing position. "I didn't know he was dead. I was in class and in the library, and then I was listening to that station that makes you so crazy. But you must see it, don't you? What Aaron found out, about the extra name, that Scott knew about. I'm not crazy, you know, I'm really not. It must have something to do with all this."

"But even if it does, Mary, what are we supposed to do about it? Even Aaron isn't sure he knows what it means, and I don't understand it any better than I understand Swahili. In fact, considering some of the situations I've gotten myself into over the years, I probably understand Swahili better."

"Don't get started on that sort of thing, either. I get nightmares that you're going to pick up AIDS."

"I do try to be somewhat more careful than that. My point, however, stands. We don't have anything to say to Gregor Demarkian. Or to the police. We don't know what we're talking about."

"Did Aaron make copies of those sheets?"

"Dozens of them. They're all over the place. According to

Aaron, you can't be killed for what you know if everybody else knows it, too."

"Good," Mary said. "What we'll do is get some of the copies and take them out to that place Demarkian lives. Cavanaugh Street. I can find it on a map. And then we'll just tell him the truth. About Aaron finding the stuff on Scott's computer. And like that."

"And then what?"

"I don't know what. That's what Mr. Demarkian is supposed to know."

"Has it occurred to you that Aaron might not be overjoyed to be turned in to the police? I don't know what his life is like at the moment, but he may have issues—"

"Like what?"

"Like an apartment full of marijuana."

"Oh." Mary always forgot that people like Aaron and Chickie lived lives very different from hers. They seemed—Chickie, especially, seemed—so close to her on the emotional level, she was never prepared to hear that they did things that horrified her even to think about. The sex, she didn't think about. It was easier that way.

"I know," she said. "Aaron has a cell phone, right?"

"Right."

"And you must have the number, or Father Burdock must—"

"Dan isn't here. We had a visit from Reverend Hell Incarnate down the road."

"I know. I saw him leave. Why does that mean that Father Burdock isn't here?"

"I haven't the faintest idea. He was upset. He came through here and said he'd be out for a while. Why do you want Dan?"

"I don't know," Mary said. "Somebody in authority, maybe. Somebody official. It doesn't matter. You call Aaron and tell him what we're going to do, and he can meet us at Cavanaugh Street or he can not and wait to talk to Mr. Demarkian tomorrow and if his apartment really is full of marijuana, he can flush it down the toilet or give it to the neighbors. I'll call Mr. Demarkian and tell him we're coming."

"Is he listed?"

"On the front page of the Philadelphia *Inquirer*, two days ago. There's a contact number for anybody wanting to reach him with information. Come on. If we hurry, I'll be able to get this all done in time for me to pick up the homeless people to bring them to the soup kitchen tomorrow morning. Which reminds me. Sometime on this trip, we have to drop off the boxes I've got in the back of the van. Go on, go call Aaron, and I'll call Demarkian."

"I think you're insane," Chickie said.

"I'm not insane." Mary swept the hair away from her face and wound it into a knot around her hand. She used the other hand to search around in her pockets for an elastic band, found one, and tied her hair back. She was breathless and exhilarated at once, as if she had taken some kind of drug. "Hurry up," she said. "I'll go down to Aaron's office and see if I can find those copies. I'll be back in a minute. You call Aaron."

"May I tell him that I think you're insane?"

"Tell him anything you want. Just make sure he knows what's going on. And hurry."

Mary chugged out of the little room and back across to the annex, moving as fast as she ever did when one of the homeless people was losing control. She got to Aaron's office without coming close to getting out of breath. The copies were stacked up on his desk in a little pile, collated. She took three sets and folded them into a square that would fit into her jeans. Then she took the phone and punched in for a line. She didn't really have the number they'd printed in the *Inquirer* for Gregor Demarkian. It wouldn't have occurred to her to keep it. She was just sure that if there was a number in the newspaper, there would be one listed in the directory. She got Aaron's phone book from off the bookshelf and looked up Demarkian. The number was there.

It was only later, standing next to Aaron's desk while the phone rang over and over again in her ear, that it occurred to her that she had told Chickie nothing about thinking that she wanted to go into the convent. She hadn't changed her mind. If anything, her conviction had grown stronger by the hour, so that now she was sure that her next step would have to be to talk to Sister Scholastica to find out how the wheels could be put in motion. It made her a little uncomfortable, to know that she hadn't said anything about it. She was closer to Chickie than she had ever been to any of the best girlfriends she had had growing up, or to any of the ones she had met at college. She told him everything. She even told him when she had cramps.

All of a sudden, the phone on the other end of the line was picked up. After so long a ring, Mary expected to hear an answering machine. She heard, instead, the low throaty voice of a woman with the kind of Main Line accent that reminded her a little of Katharine Hepburn.

"Bennis Hannaford," the voice said.

Mary McAllister forgot all about Chickie, and about wanting to be a nun, and even about herself, and launched into a complicated explanation of what it was she was calling about.

THREE

1

It wasn't that Gregor Demarkian thought the information brought to him by Mary McAllister and Chickie George was unimportant. It was only that he had anticipated it. From the moment that he had first heard that there had been a "huge" damages case against the archdiocese, he had expected somebody, somewhere, to have been using it to cheat. Bennis would probably call this cynical—although, Lord only knew, she was cynical enough herself—but Gregor didn't believe it was possible for an opportunity like this to crop up without somebody taking advantage of it in some way. Not only was there a damages case, but the man who had been at the head of the fountain of money was an incompetent fool. Whatever else could be said about the old Cardinal Archbishop, that much was without question, at least when it came to matters of the law. The new Cardinal Archbishop was much better, but he was also in the middle of a whirlwind. Somehow, somewhere, some way, somebody would have figured it all out, but Gregor didn't think there had been a fairy's breath of a chance that that would be anytime soon. That was why he sat calmly at the desk in the corner of Garry Mansfield's office reading witness reports, while Garry and Lou Emiliani jumped around making phone calls, taking faxes, and jumping around with all the abandon of disgruntled employees who'd gotten dead drunk at the office Christmas party.

"I don't understand what's wrong with you," Garry Mansfield said, when Gregor had been particularly unresponsive to some piece of news. "This could be it. This is the first sensible lead we've had since this whole mess started."

It was edging on to noon, and Gregor had been at the station since eight that morning. He'd been up and restless until well after three, too, so that he was now tired enough to have very little patience for amateurs. He especially had no patience for Garry and Lou, who should not be behaving like amateurs. Both of them had to have been at this long enough to know that they shouldn't jump to conclusions. Both of them had been with the department through its own agonizing series of scandals, which ought to have taught them caution for a whole different set of reasons. Instead of being cautious, they were partying, and Gregor's head ached.

"You really are being too uptight about this," Lou said after a while. "This is real, what you uncovered here. There really is a scam going on in the offices of Brady, Marquis and Holden."

"I know," Gregor said.

"Well?" Garry said. "What more do you want? Look at what we've got here. The archdiocese has been paying restitution to sixty-two men, but the firm has been distributing restitution to seventy one. See that? We're going to have to do a lot more work, of course, but this is spectacular. It really is. It amounts to tens of thousands of dollars already."

"If it has gone on the full payment term, it amounts to over two million," Lou Emiliani said. "Garry's right. We can't ignore this. It all fits together."

"I'm not asking you to ignore it," Gregor said. "I brought it to you. Don't you remember?"

"We remember." Garry said.

"Well, then."

"I just want to know what you're so down about," Lou Emiliani said. "It's not unclear who pulled the scam. It was this guy Ian Holden. Partner in the firm's name and everything. Don't tell me you think we're going to get all the paper, and it's going to turn out not to be him."

"No," Gregor said.

"We've got traces out on the checks that were sent to the extra nine men." Garry ticked the points off on his fingers. "We've got requests in for information about his bank accounts. If we can get this moving without his realizing we're onto him—"

"Have you been able to find him yet?" Gregor asked.

"No," Garry admitted. "He seems to have disappeare[...]

"You've sent people to his apartment?" Gregor aske[...] but it wasn't really a question.

"We sent uniforms, yeah," Lou admitted. "He didn't answe[...] the door. Under other circumstances they might have found it open, if you know what I mean, but seeing as he's a lawyer—"

"Never mind." Gregor waved it away. "I take it he hasn't been at work."

"No," Garry Mansfield said.

"So," Gregor said, "that most likely means he knows the news is out. Don't you think? Somehow or the other, he's got word, or he knows something that makes him think that the news will be out and he's anticipating. And he's gone."

"Maybe it was panic," Garry Mansfield said. "He was around yesterday afternoon, right after lunch. People saw him. People talked to him. Maybe he went down to St. Anselm's and killed Father Healy—"

"Why?" Gregor asked.

"Because Father Healy knew," Lou Emiliani said. "That's what all this is about. Who knew. Keeping people quiet. Bernadette Kelly because she worked in the office—"

"—as a receptionist," Gregor said.

"She did extra work for the partners on the side," Garry Mansfield said. "We knew that before. And she was smart about numbers when she wasn't smart about anything else. I mean, can't you see it? Holden takes a look at her and figures she's too dumb to catch on to what he's doing, gets her to help with the paperwork, and—wham. Doesn't that ring true to you? Doesn't it? And don't tell me it won't pan out."

"I won't," Gregor said. "I think that part will pan out. That's not my point. There are too many loose ends here. Why arsenic, for one thing. Why would he use arsenic?"

"Maybe he had some handy," Lou said.

"Is there any evidence of that? I can't imagine that a major law firm like Brady, Marquis and Holden would buy rat poison at the local pharmacy if they had a problem. They'd hire a firm of professional exterminators. Don't you think so?"

"Maybe," Lou said, half-sullenly. "But maybe it wasn't from the firm. Maybe he had it at home."

"No," Gregor said. "Listen. If he had rat poison at home, or arsenic in any other form, then he bought it openly without

murder anybody. In that case, if he used it to
...ebody, he would leave himself open to being iden-
...ving bought it. Never mind the fact that there would
... of the stuff around the house. Why would he do
...nething like that?"

"Panic," Garry Mansfield said.

Gregor sighed. "Be reasonable. Four times? That's how
many people are dead. Four. Do you really think he panicked
four times in a row?"

"Maybe he used the stuff that was in the church," Lou said.
"We don't know where Bernadette Kelly was killed, not yet.
He could have given her something at the church and then
moved her body—"

Gregor sat up a little straighter in his chair. "Wait," he said.

"Look at the great detective," Lou said. "I thought of something. I thought of something he didn't."

"He couldn't have moved the body," Gregor said.

"There goes that," Garry said.

Gregor rubbed his forehead and stood up. This was what
he hated most about not sleeping well. Other people could
operate at full power on no rest, but he was always left logy
and disoriented and slow.

"He couldn't have moved the body," he said again, "but he
wouldn't have had to. Nobody would have had to. Nobody
has to move a body before it's a body yet. I want to go talk
to the Reverend Phipps."

"What?" Lou Emiliani looked startled.

It felt better to be up and moving. His coat was laid over
an old-fashioned metal filing cabinet in a corner of the room.
He couldn't believe either Lou or Garry ever used it, or anybody else either, with computers all over the department. Gregor put on his coat and felt around in the pockets for his
gloves. They weren't there. He must have left them at home
on the bed.

Garry and Lou were standing side by side, staring at him.

"It would be helpful if one of you came along," Gregor
said. "He's not a stupid man, the Reverend Phipps. He isn't
going to talk to me if I don't have a police officer with me.
He may not talk to me even then."

"We were talking," Garry said carefully, "about Ian Holden. And how he probably committed four murders."

"He didn't," Gregor said.

"Why not?" Lou asked.

"Because the timing is off, for one thing," Gregor said. "I should have realized all along that the timing mattered more than anything, but I was so tangled up in—you know, it's a dangerous thing. Nobody who deals with real crime ought ever to read Agatha Christie novels."

"What are you talking about?" Garry asked.

Gregor wound his scarf around his neck. "Agatha Christie novels. In an Agatha Christie novel, the poisoner would have tucked the arsenic into something innocuous, and then he could have been miles away when the death actually happened. The poison would have been, in, say, the chocolates on Sister Scholastica's desk—"

"We had those checked," Lou said quickly.

"I'm sure you did," Gregor said. "And I'm sure they were fine, too. As a murder method, that one always bothered me because you couldn't be sure of getting the person you wanted. Anybody could eat the chocolates. Death and destruction could rain down like confetti at a New Year's party, and then what? Trust me. Check out his schedule. Ian Holden couldn't have committed these murders, not all four of them, anyway, because he couldn't have been in the right place at the right time. I've been forgetting the timing. I've been thinking like Agatha Christie."

"Right," Garry Mansfield said.

"Come with me, one of you," Gregor said. "It's only a couple of blocks away. It won't take more than half an hour. There's something I've got to find out."

"Nobody would be angry at you if you could prove the Reverend Phipps did it," Lou Emiliani said. "The precinct would probably get together and throw you a party."

"Come," Gregor said.

Garry Mansfield got his coat off the back of his chair and started to put it on. Gregor stood, shifting from one foot to the other and feeling dense. There are only two reasons for individual murder, love and money. He knew that. He had always known that. And there was something else he had known, too. In real life, murderers did not construct elaborate plots for no other reason than to make themselves look clever. Not that anybody had constructed an elaborate plot here, of course. This was so simple, he had gone days missing the whole thing.

The *Philadelphia Inquirer* didn't know what it was talking about when it called him the "Armenian-American Hercule Poirot."

2

In the end, it was Garry Mansfield who came with him. Gregor had the feeling that neither of them wanted to go, and that their reluctance had more to do with their distaste for Roy Phipps than with any work that might be lying around the office, waiting to get done. Garry wanted to cut down the side streets and come up on Phipps's place from the side, but Gregor insisted on going the long way around, past St. Anselm's and St. Stephen's, so that he could see what the situation was. The situation was nonexistent. St. Stephen's was having its service for the men who had been hurt in the riot later this afternoon. There was a notice to that effect on the sign at the end of its front walk, made of colored cardboard and printed in metallic paint, as if to attract as much attention as possible. Whatever effect Roy Phipps had had on this neighborhood, he had not driven the men of St. Stephen's into hiding, or even into discretion. Gregor approved of that very much. He looked at St. Anselm's and noted that there was a short note on its sign, indicating that Masses would be said as usual even now that Father Healy was dead. Gregor who would say them, since the parochial vicar was away. Gregor thought it had all been easier in the day when every parish had had nothing more than a parish priest and the nuns who ran the parochial school.

He turned down the street on the same side as St. Anselm's and picked up speed. Halfway to where he was going, he reached Edith Lawton's house and stopped. The house looked shuttered up and dead, but he was sure that somebody was supposed to be inside. Hadn't Bennis told him that Edith Lawton worked at home? The front window shades were pulled down tight. There were no lights coming from inside, in spite of the fact that the day was gray and dark. Still, if there had ever been mail in the wrought-iron mailbox, it was gone.

"This is what's-her-name's house," Garry said politely. "You know. The pain in the ass. The bitch."

"Edith Lawton."

"That one."

"Why isn't she home?"

"She probably went out shopping. Do you want to talk to Roy Phipps, or do you want to talk to Edith Lawton?"

"I want to talk to Roy Phipps," Gregor said, even though he really wanted to talk to both. He turned away from Edith Lawton's house and went on down the street. He wasn't in a hurry, at the moment. It seemed to him that now that everything was reasonably clear, he had all the time in the world. He only wished that he could walk into Roy Phipps's town house and catch the man smoking crack cocaine in the foyer, or something else equally egregious, so that he could do his part to make St. Stephen's evening service a success. It was the unfortunate truth that people like Roy Phipps almost never did things like that. They were too . . . focused.

They stopped in front of Roy Phipps's town house, and Gregor looked in the closer of the two front windows. The shades were open, and the room behind them was empty and conventional: a couch, a couple of chairs, a coffee table. Gregor climbed the stoop and rang the bell. There was a cross screwed into the brick next to the door on one side, and another, smaller one screwed into the doorframe above the button for the bell. They were crosses, not crucifixes, which made Gregor unaccountably grumpy. The Armenian Church used crosses rather than crucifixes. Gregor didn't like the idea that there was any similarity at all.

Nobody had come to the door. Gregor rang the bell again and stood back a little to look through the windows. That room was still empty. It still looked too clean. Then Gregor heard footsteps coming up to the door, and the sound of panting, somebody out of breath.

The door opened on an overweight man in a suit a size too small for him. He looked as if he were strangling in his shirt collar.

"Yes?" he said.

"I'm Gregor Demarkian," Gregor said. "This is—"

Garry Mansfield had his badge out, but the man in the tight suit was barely looking at it. "Yes, yes," he was saying. "We were expecting you. Reverend Phipps asked me to make sure you came right in, as soon as you got here—"

"Excuse me?" Gregor said.

"We want to cooperate with the police," the man said, gesturing them to come inside. "We want to cooperate fully with all the necessary, uh, things that the, uh, that the police want of us, and—"

"Fred." The voice sounded oddly preppy, as if some exclusive boys' school accent had been laid on over the West Virginia twang. Roy Phipps was standing at the back of the long front foyer, dressed in a suit that most definitely fit him perfectly, looking slightly pained. "I think Mr. Demarkian and his friend have taken your point," he said.

"Detective Mansfield," Garry said.

Roy Phipps nodded politely and stepped aside. Gregor went up to him and saw that there was a narrow hall leading to the side, and near the end of it an open door. That would be the door to the room with the other window that faced front. Gregor went in and saw that he was right. He had a full, high-ceilinged view of the street, nearly down to the end where the churches were. He could see St. Stephen's more easily than he could see St. Anselm's, although it was a stretch for both.

Garry Mansfield came in, and Roy Phipps came in after him. Gregor sat down in one of the visitor's chairs that faced the desk.

"So," Roy Phipps said, "are you going to arrest me now, or are you going to wait to make a splash in the papers for a few days and do it then."

"I'm not aware that we're going to arrest you at all," Gregor said. "I couldn't arrest you if I wanted to. I'm not a police officer."

Roy Phipps sat down behind his desk. "Very neat. Are you going to arrest one of my parishioners?"

"Not that I know of," Gregor said.

"This gets more interesting all the time. I thought it was the official position of the Philadelphia Police Department that I am personally responsible for any untoward thing that happens to any homosexual within the city precincts."

"Do you mean to say you think that Father Healy was a homosexual?"

"No," Roy Phipps said, smiling faintly. "Father Healy was

a Satanist and a devil worshiper in the pay of the Whore of Babylon, but as far as I know, he was as heterosexual as he was damned. I was thinking of the man who died at St. Stephen's. Scott Boardman."

"Were you responsible for the death of Scott Boardman?"

"If I was, I wouldn't tell you. But you know that. So that can't be what this is about. Was it me you wanted to talk to, or one of the men of the church?"

"It was you," Gregor said. "If you don't mind. I'd like to know why you decided to found your church here, rather than, say—"

"In a neighborhood closer to where my parishioners live?"

"You can't draw much of a crowd from the surrounding blocks," Gregor pointed out. "You're mismatched for the area. You have to admit it."

"Christians are always mismatched for the world they live in," Roy Phipps said. "At least, real Christians are. There aren't a lot of us left anymore. Most of the people who call themselves Christians in the United States are anything but. They're children of their times. They don't like to hear the truth when it's pointed out to them."

"And the truth is?"

"That sinners go to hell and God hates sinners. I'm not in the wrong neighborhood, Mr. Demarkian. I'm in the right one. The only chance these people have is to hear the truth preached to them and to repent. If God will let them repent. God doesn't give the gift of repentance to everybody."

"Were you here, on the street, yesterday afternoon?"

"Yes."

"In this office?"

"Most of the time, yes."

"When you're here in this office, do you keep watch on St. Stephen's and St. Anselm's?"

Roy Phipps shrugged. "I do what I can. I can't really see the churches clearly from here. If you're expecting me to have seen some particular person come in or out, the chances are nearly nil. I do see people when they walk by here, but they almost never do."

"Do you know who Mary McAllister is?"

"No."

"She works with homeless people. She brings a van from a soup kitchen—"

"Wait," Roy said. "I do know who she is, by sight. I wasn't sure of the name."

"Did you see her anytime on the afternoon of the day Father Healy died?"

"No."

"What about Sister Scholastica and Sister Peter Rose?"

"I assume they're nuns," Roy said. "But that isn't very helpful, is it? There are a fair number of nuns down at St. Anselm's. I couldn't tell one from the other at a distance, and I don't think I know any of them by name."

"Did you see any nuns on the street the afternoon of the day Father Healy died?"

"Of course I did. They're everywhere, aren't they? But I don't think that means anything, either. What difference would it make?"

"What about Father Healy?" Gregor said. "Did you see him?"

"No." Roy stirred in his chair. "Why don't I save you some trouble, Mr. Demarkian. The only person I saw down this end of the street all day yesterday was the whore atheist, Edith Lawton. I saw her come down the street and go into her own house. Dozens of people could have gone into and out of the churches without my ever seeing them. I don't have a good enough view."

"And that was it? Edith Lawton."

"That was it. At least, that was it on the day Father Healy died. Since then, of course, the street has been hopping. There are half a dozen people skulking around this morning. I assume they're all reporters."

"Fine," Gregor said. "What about you, on the afternoon of the day Father Healy died. You said you were mostly in this room. Where else were you?"

"In the bathroom," Roy said.

"That was it?"

"I didn't go out even once all afternoon. I had work to do, and that evening I had a Bible study. In case you didn't notice, I didn't even manage to put together a picket line after the murder, although I should have. Sometimes, I can't do everything at once."

"Were you here alone?"

"I am never alone," Roy said solemnly. And then he smiled. "I live in a fishbowl, Mr. Demarkian. There's always somebody here, Fred or one of the other men. They man phones day and night, for one thing. And I'm not exactly easy to lose in a crowd, am I? By now, my face must have been on every news broadcast in Philadelphia. I wasn't wandering around the street by myself that afternoon. I couldn't have been and gotten away with it."

"Shit," Garry Mansfield said.

Gregor only sat back in his chair and tried to think.

FOUR

1

The Cardinal Archbishop had never had any patience for the sort of cleric who thought of himself literally as a Prince of the Church: the kind of man who wore robes everywhere, or traveled with an entourage, in order to make himself as conspicuous as possible. He had the same feeling of distaste for those of his parishioners who insisted on wearing expensive Christian jewelry. Christ died on a cross of wood. It made no sense to wear a cross of eighteen-karat gold with a diamond in the middle of it, the way so many of them had been after Christmas, because Tiffany and Company had had the piece in its Christmas gift catalogue. People called him an ascetic, but it wasn't really true. An ascetic denies himself things he wants, out of a sense of duty and a will to self-discipline. The Cardinal Archbishop simply had no taste for certain kinds of luxury. If he had a failing as a pastor, he thought this was it. Most people craved luxury, and they were positively addicted to self-indulgence. He seemed to have been born without the genes for either.

Of course, at the moment, he was decking himself out with as much splendor as a Renaissance Pope, and with a good deal less money in his treasury to back himself up. Even the present-day Pope wouldn't go out on the streets of a major city looking the way the Cardinal Archbishop was looking now. Every once in a while, the Cardinal Archbishop could feel Father Doheny staring at his back, confused and concerned, as if he thought the Cardinal Archbishop might have had a psychotic break while he wasn't looking, and now they were all going to be stuck with the consequences. Even so,

Father Doheny did his job. He handed pieces of heavily embroidered cloth across the table when the Cardinal Archbishop reached out for them. He straightened things at the back where the Cardinal Archbishop couldn't see them. He kept a straight face, as bland as the face of a bad statue in the sort of church which bought its art from the same sculptors that manufactured its funeral monuments.

The Cardinal Archbishop looked into the mirror and straightened the bright red skullcap on his head. He had a traditional red Cardinal's hat, but nobody ever wore those anymore, not even in Rome, and he hadn't been able to bring himself to order it brought down from the wall of the cathedral where it hung. Even so, a scarlet cap and a scarlet cape were obvious enough, and under them he had all these . . . things.

"So," he said finally. "Do you think I've finally lost my mind?"

"I was wondering what you were doing, Your Eminence, yes. This isn't, uh, standard street attire in this day and age."

"Some of it isn't street attire at all." The Cardinal Archbishop brushed what might have been lint and might have been a thread from the wide cummerbund that spanned his waist. "I feel like I'm about to go trick-or-treating on Halloween. Do you think it was actually the case that there was a time when people were impressed with this sort of thing?"

"I think people are still impressed with this sort of thing. Some people, at any rate."

"Yes, so do I. And that's part of the reason why I'm wearing all this. The other part is the press. Have we managed the press? Do they know I'm coming?"

"Absolutely, Your Eminence."

"Good. We're going to get a lot of phone calls when all this is over, but I wanted to tell you now that I'm not taking any from the Conference. Not a single one. I already know what they're going to say, and I don't particularly care."

"If you've cleared this with the Holy Father, I don't see that you have anything to worry about with the U.S. Conference of Catholic Bishops."

"I keep telling you. I haven't cleared this with anybody. I've only kept them informed. Except that I haven't kept the Conference informed. I think it was easier when we really were Princes of the Church. I'd like to be an autocrat for a day. It would be considerably more relaxing than being what I actually am. Have you kept tabs on that damned fool with the money?"

"Uh, not exactly," Father Doheny said. "Which damned fool with the money were you referring to?"

"The one who was in here the other day. The one we wanted to put at the head of the committee. Never mind. It doesn't matter. Either he's going to quit outright, or he's going to lecture me and I'm going to tell him off, and then he's going to quit. It can't be helped. I doubt if the bankruptcy can be helped, either. I'll think about it tomorrow. Are we ready to go?"

"Of course. I'm ready if you are, Your Eminence."

"Do we have press at the door?"

Father Doheny gave him a very odd look and went to the window to check. "Yes," he said finally. "It seems we do. We do have press at the door."

"Good. There ought to be even more when we get across town. I'm ready to go if you are, Father. It's about time we got this show on the road."

The Cardinal Archbishop never used phrases like "get this show on the road." His English was as formal and correct as a set of model sentences in a grammar book. He didn't care. He swept out of his office and into the hall with Father Doheny trailing behind. He let Sister call the elevator for him, then swept inside the elevator cab when it came. In these clothes, the only movement possible for him was sweeping. The cape could have been designed for Zorro on a night with more assignations in it than sword fights.

"Make sure the car is ready when we get down," he told Sister, as the elevator doors closed. She scurried back to her desk, and he looked at the crucifix that had been put up in the cab next to the security mirror.

"There are people who think we should abandon the crucifix for a plain cross," he said to Father Doheny. "They want Christ risen and triumphant, not dying in agony. But you know, Father, I think they're wrong. We preach Christ and Him crucified. That's what St. Paul said. He knew what he was talking about."

"Yes, Your Eminence," Father Doheny said, sounding thoroughly confused.

They had reached the first floor. The elevator doors were opening again. The Cardinal Archbishop stepped out and walked across the broad foyer to the front doors of the chancery, moving so quickly that Father Doheny had to half run to keep up. Outside, the wind was bitter and full of ice. The Cardinal Archbishop felt it as needles against the skin of his face. He got into the car and let the driver close the door on him as half a dozen reporters pushed in to ask him questions. He wasn't answering questions, at the moment. He would answer questions when he got to Baldwin Place.

"Are they following us?" he asked Father Doheny when the car pulled out into traffic.

"They seem to be."

"With any luck, there will be more of them when we get to St. Anselm's and St. Stephen's. That was a pretty poor showing. You'd think the Cardinal Archbishop of Philadelphia could command more press attention than that just by going to a baseball game."

"Your Eminence, would you mind very much if I asked you what we're doing?"

"We're going to see Father Burdock."

"Well, yes, I know that, but—"

"Something else occurred to me. Now that Father Healy is dead, he's no longer a suspect."

"Your Eminence?"

"Never mind. We'll have to come back for Father's funeral, too, of course, when the time comes. But that will be later. Is that Baldwin Place up there?"

"Yes, Your Eminence."

"Is that a television van?"

"Your Eminence, if you could just tell me—"

The car pulled up to the curb in front of St. Stephen's. To pull up in front of St. Anselm's would have required going against the traffic. There was indeed a television van—in fact, there were two of them—but what the Cardinal saw the most of were nuns. Sister Scholastica had done what he had asked of her. She had her nuns out on the street in force, in full habits and capes, so that there looked like there were a lot more of them than there actually were. Maybe there really were a lot more of them. The Cardinal Archbishop would not have put it past Sister Scholastica to bring in recruits from other schools in other parts of the city, or even from other traditional orders. All that mattered was that the nuns looked like nuns. They had to be easily recognizable to non-Catholics who had only a quick glimpse of them on television. The driver came around the side of the car and let the Cardinal Archbishop out. He stepped into the street and looked around.

"Your Eminence?" Father Doheny asked anxiously, hurrying around from the street side. "What's going on here? This looks like the start of another riot."

"It is. It's my personal riot. Mine and Father Burdock's."

"Your Eminence—"

"Don't worry," the Cardinal Archbishop said. "The police are already here."

It was true, too. The police were already there. The Cardinal Archbishop could see them, lined up on either sidewalk but standing well back so that they didn't become too obvious either to the television cameras or the crowd. There was a crowd, too, just building up, coming from both the St. Anselm's side and the St. Stephen's side of the street. The Cardinal Archbishop looked down the street, but everything at the other end seemed to be quiet and dark.

"I only hope Father Burdock and his people did their part," he said. "We're going to look pretty silly if we've gone to all this trouble and they're not at home."

"Your Eminence—" Father Doheny said again.

The Cardinal Archbishop walked away without listening to the rest of what Father Doheny had to say, mostly because he had already said it himself to himself several times over the past few days since the riot. He walked across the street to St. Anselm's and mounted the steps. He should have brought a censer to waft incense at the crowd. He could hardly believe he'd been so stupid as to forget it. He got to the top step in front of St. Anselm's front doors and held his hands out at shoulder height.

"*In nomine Patris, et Filii, et Spiritus Sanctus.* Amen," he said, in the loudest voice he had, which was very loud. He had a good deep bass when he wanted to use it.

In front of him, the crowd calmed down. The nuns fell into ranks and repeated the Latin to him. People began spilling out of St. Stephen's Church. Some of them sat down on the frozen sidewalk to listen.

"*Pater Noster*," the Cardinal Archbishop started, and after that it was a piece of cake. He was old enough to have been taught all these prayers in Latin as a child. He had been trained as a priest in the days when speaking Latin was expected of everyone who took Holy Orders. The words rolled out of his throat the way thunder rolled out of a valley before a storm.

Over on the other side of the street, the doors to St. Stephen's opened one more time and Dan Burdock came out, looking far less impressive in green-and-gold vestments than he might have—but then, the Cardinal thought, even High Church Episcopalian wasn't as high church as Rome was on an off day.

Since the Pater Noster was over, the Cardinal Archbishop started in on the Ave Maria.

2

For a long time after the Cardinal Archbishop arrived on Baldwin Place, Dan Burdock had stayed inside his own church, his hands resting on the green-embroidered cassock he had made up his mind to wear, hesitating. He had not been surprised, and he had thought he should not be afraid. This was what his meeting with the Cardinal Archbishop had been about, and as he watched men stream out of St. Stephen's front doors into the street, he thought that he ought to be glad of it. God only knew, the men were glad of it. Aaron was nearly euphoric. Dan had been careful about security, as the Cardinal Archbishop had been careful. He had called the men he needed and told them it was urgent, but he had not told them why. Given the events of the last few days—maybe even of the last few months—they had all assumed the emergency had something to do with Roy Phipps, and they had not been wrong. What Dan had not done was call his own bishop. His bishop was a gentle, wise, intelligent man who believed more of the Christmas story than Bishop Spong, but he was essentially cautious. He would worry, as Dan had worried, about what would happen if something went wrong. Then, looking out on the street at the crowd swelling slowly and relentlessly, Dan realized that, of course, something was going to go wrong. The Cardinal Archbishop had always expected that something would go wrong. He was not afraid of what the wrongness would bring, or what it would mean, or how he would look tomorrow morning on the front page of the *Inquirer*. That was when Dan had finished up dressing in his silly ritual clothes. They weren't even the right ritual clothes. Episcopalians didn't have pompous costumes for everyday life. He'd had to put on Mass vestments, although he was sure there was some rule telling him he couldn't. Even so, he could see the Cardinal Archbishop's point. The brighter their clothes, the more easily they would be seen on television.

Dan finished dressing and went out to the front steps of the church. Aaron was there, hopping from one foot to another, hard-pressed not to double over, he was laughing so hard.

"Why didn't you tell us?" he demanded. "We would have loved this. We would have helped you."

You would have told the immediate universe, Dan thought. Instead of saying it, he pressed forward toward the middle of the street, where the Cardinal Archbishop had now gone to stand and wait for him. A man ran forward and thrust something into his hands and ran away again. Dan looked up to see that he was holding the gold cross mounted on a pole that they used for procession at the start of the Sunday service. He hadn't realized it was as heavy as it was. He wasn't the one who usually carried it. He held it over his head and thought that it must be visible for blocks. Somebody parked in a car at the diner this moment would be able to see only two things, the mass of people in the middle of the street and the cross. Then he thought that he should have worn something under all this embroidered linen, like a sweater. It really was February. The air was cold enough to make his bones ache.

He got to the middle of the street where the Cardinal Archbishop was, and stopped. He was, he thought, outclassed in every way. The Cardinal Archbishop was taller, and thinner, and more splendidly dressed. It didn't help that he was also the sort of person who drew people's attention, something Dan had never been. Roy Phipps was, though. He had been that way all the way back in college. Dan thought about that for a second and put it aside.

"People," he said, leaning close to the Cardinal Archbishop's ear, "are going to think that Canterbury and Rome have reunited, under the direction of Rome."

"Want to change your mind?" the Cardinal Archbishop said.

"No."

"Want to go ahead of me?"

"I'll look like your altar boy."

"Want to be first when we get to the spot?'

"Want to toss a coin to decide which of us will give his superiors the worst heart attack?"

"Mine are having their heart attack as we speak. We should have arranged for a band. Excuse me."

Dan stepped back a little and let the Cardinal Archbishop go forward. The street was now so full of people, he could barely move, but they were all quiet, and all well behaved. Nobody was shouting. Nobody was throwing anything at all. He recognized a dozen or more of the men he had called over the last several hours, and those men all seemed to have brought friends with them. He recognized the men of his congregation. Chickie George was holding hands with that Mary McAllister who ran the homeless center—but then, if Chickie were straight, he'd be married to that girl by now.

The Cardinal Archbishop raised his hands high over his head and started the Angelus, blessedly in English, because it had been thirty years since Dan had had a course in Latin and the most he remembered now was a series of swear words he'd been taught by a particularly unsavory classics teacher at his prep school. Now that he thought of it, Dan was sure that that particular classics teacher had been gay.

"The Angel of the Lord declared unto Mary," the Cardinal Archbishop said.

"And she conceived of the Holy Spirit," the crowd answered—all the crowd did, because even High Church Episcopalians knew the Angelus.

Then the crowd moved, slowly but deliberately, with the Cardinal Archbishop at its head, and in no time at all Dan found himself pushed to the front of it. Out in front, there was suddenly air to breathe, and space. The crowd was concentrated at the end of the block near the churches. There was nobody at the other end of the block or a block and a half away from that, where Roy was. Dan said the words of the Hail Mary—how he remembered them, he couldn't say—and moved forward slowly, the way he processed in on Sunday mornings when the organ was working very slowly and the church was hushed. Along the street, lights went on in town houses and front doors opened. People came out to see what was happening. That hadn't happened when the real riot had been going on. When the real riot had been going on, the neighborhood had locked down tight, hoping to stay out of it.

Once, years ago, when Dan was still in the seminary, he had thought there might be a way out of it. He couldn't be the only gay man who had entered the ministry, or who had pledged himself to celibacy, either. In those days you never heard about Roman Catholic priests falling from the path of righteousness into the muck of sex—but then, in those days, they might have fallen less often. It had been easier to stay clean in an era when sex had been vigorously repressed in all parts of the culture, when there had barely been a hint of it on television or in the movies. It startled him sometimes to realize how shocked people had been by books like *Ulysses*, or, even funnier, things like *Valley of the Dolls*, where there was no real sex on the page at all. Now sex was everywhere. It was on the billboards he passed when he came back to St. Stephen's from a trip across town. It was on television, butt naked half the time, men and women both. It was, especially, in the books he read. There now seemed to be something like an Obligatory Sex Scene, so that no novel was really a novel without five pages of intimate description.

No, Dan thought, as he inched his way down the street and the crowd inched behind him, the Cardinal Archbishop intoning the Angelus with every step—no, he could not have been the first gay man to enter the ministry and decide to solve his problems with celibacy, and he could not be the first one to realize that celibacy was not the point. Sex was not the point. Even having somebody to wake up next to in bed was not the point. He wasn't particularly horny. His loneliness came and went. *Identity* was the point, and the need not to feel that he had been born in some way defective.

Of course, according to Christianity, everybody was born defective. That was the point of original sin. Maybe, Dan thought, that settled the question of whether he was an orthodox Christian or not, in the negative. He did not believe in original sin. He did not believe that anybody should believe in original sin. It made him feel a little odd to realize that the

Cardinal Archbishop mostly likely not only believed in original sin, but celebrated it.

They were all the way down the street and at Roy Phipps's door. Dan had no idea how they'd gotten there so quickly. It had felt to him as if they were barely moving at all. He looked at the windows that flanked the door and saw that the lights in the rooms beyond them were all on. Roy was a lot of things, but he was not a coward. He would not retreat. It struck Dan suddenly that there was something wrong in this, something wrong in the way they had defined religion from the beginning, something whacked-out at the core, because he shouldn't be here now. None of them should be. Roy Phipps should not be what he was in this place and at this time, because it was a betrayal of everything else he was and had been, from the very beginning.

Dan took a deep breath and mounted the steps to Roy's front door. The crowd behind him was quiet. The Cardinal Archbishop was not intoning prayers. Dan rang the doorbell and stepped back. Then everybody began to pray the Our Father, as if it had been arranged in advance.

Years ago, at Princeton, Roy Phipps was a phenomenon. He was the sort of boy the system had been designed to celebrate, the diamond in the rough, the genius in the muck pile. He was supposed to go on to graduate school and then a career in academia or law, with an avocation in cultural alienation. Dan himself was supposed to go on to a career in academia or law, and then, and then—what?

The door opened wide, and Roy stepped out, dressed in sports jacket and tie, looking like a businessman checking to see if his newspaper had come in the morning. He looked Dan over from head to foot, then turned his attention to the Cardinal Archbishop. Dan could see the rhythmic twitching of a muscle in the side of his face, the only one that Roy had never been able to control when he was angry.

"The Catholic Church is the Whore of Babylon," Roy's voice boomed out—and it did boom. The man had a deep and carrying bass that Dan never quite got over the sound of. "The God of wrath will bring down the apostates and the adulterers and the sodomizers and on the last day He will cast you all into the pit of fire, into the pit of hell, to suffer an eternity of agony in the company of Satan and his fallen angels—"

The Cardinal Archbishop, it turned out, had an even deeper bass voice, and it carried even farther. He began to intone something in Latin, and for a few moments, Dan couldn't figure out what it was. The crowd had become very still. Dan didn't know if they understood what the Cardinal was saying or not. The Catholics might. His own men almost certainly would not, except for the one or two of them who had been to seminary or studied classics.

Then the flow of the words began to seem familiar, and one or two of the words themselves began to seem familiar, too. The wind had picked up and was coming down the street at a furious pace. Dan felt it in his ears and on his neck and wished he were off the steps and down in the crowd where the press of people would shield him from the cold. Some of the crowd had picked up the rhythm, too, and a few people were saying what seemed to be responses.

And then, somehow, Dan knew. It had been thirty years since he had heard any version of this rite, but he knew—and as soon as he did, the responses began to come quite naturally to him, too, although he had no idea how. He had never performed this rite in his life, or known anybody who had. He didn't even think Episcopalians believed in it. What he remembered, he remembered from a theology class so far in his past it might as well never have existed, and he thought he must have learned the old version, the before–Vatican II version, although it didn't seem to matter.

The Cardinal Archbishop mounted the steps in front of Roy Phipps and raised his hands above Roy's head. Dan stepped back and down. Did Roy know what this was? Of course he knew. Anybody who was looking into Roy's face at this moment knew he knew.

The Cardinal Archbishop was performing a rite of exorcism.

3

In the back of the crowd, so far back that she found it difficult to hear exactly what the Cardinal Archbishop was saying, Mary McAllister was holding on to Chickie George's arm. Chickie was so excited, he looked feverish, feverish and triumphant, as if he were liable to explode at any moment. It didn't help that he was not well, or that he was solving his problems—Mary was sure—by taking double the prescribed amount of his pain medications. It didn't help that it was so cold out here and he was wearing nothing but a cashmere sweater over a thin cotton shirt over good wool pants. Why was it impossible to get Chickie to take care of himself? Why was it impossible to get him to wear a coat?

"Listen," she said, tugging desperately at his arm. "Listen, there's something I've been meaning to tell you—"

"Who would have believed it?" Chickie demanded—and it wasn't in that high-queen voice of his, either. Mary bit her lip. "The Cardinal Archbishop of Philadelphia. The old son of a bitch. On our side."

"Oh, no," Mary said. "I mean, I don't think—"

"I don't either," Chickie said shortly. "I know the old fart will be back on television tomorrow talking about how gay sex is objectively evil or whatever it is he says. That's not what I mean. Listen to him. Listen to him. Old Roy is going to bust a gut."

"Please *listen*," Mary said, trying to brush hair out of her face faster than the wind was brushing it in. Roy Phipps had tried to go back into his house, but the door was blocked behind him. Two of the men from St. Stephen's had come up and got in his way. Chickie never used phrases like "bust a gut."

"Listen," she said again. "There's something I have to tell you. I should have told you before. I'm—I mean, you know, at the end of the school year—I'm going to go into the convent. Into the Sisters of Divine Grace convent. In New York. I mean, I talked to Sister Scholastica, and she said—"

"I know," Chickie said.

"What?" Mary said.

"I know," Chickie said again. "I've known for a year. Haven't you known?"

"No."

"Well, it was obvious to everybody who cares about you. Which just goes to show that that idiot boyfriend of yours didn't give a damn about anything but getting in your pants, which I sincerely hope you haven't allowed him to do, because he isn't worth it and—"

"Chickie."

"Sorry."

"Do you mind?"

"No," Chickie said. "I don't mind. If you invite me, I'll come up for that ceremony they have where they put the veil on your head. You know. I won't even, ah, be too obvious about, ah, things."

"Be as obvious as you like. Just be yourself."

"Right," Chickie said.

Mary looked up at the town house again. The Cardinal Archbishop was still intoning in Latin. The words seemed to go on and on, and the crowd seemed to know how to answer— but Mary didn't. She didn't have the faintest idea what was going on, or why Chickie was so ecstatic. She wrapped her arms around her body and shivered.

"What's he doing up there?" she asked. "Is there something in particular that's supposed to happen?"

Chickie looked at her with wide eyes, momentarily shocked.

And then he burst out laughing.

FIVE

1

Gregor Demarkian was in the offices of Brady, Marquis and Holden when news of the exorcism came, sitting in a large and expensively outfitted conference room with both Garry Mansfield and Lou Emiliani, a junior partner, and Delmark Marquis himself. The news was brought by a secretary who was running when she came, but Gregor was only momentarily surprised about that. Surely there were radios in these offices, and even small television sets, that belonged to the support staff and that were kept running, surreptitiously, throughout the day. Even more likely, everybody, senior as well as junior, management as well as staff, had computers that were plugged into the Internet for e-mail purposes. One way or the other, the news was out. Delmark Marquis demanded that the conference room's own television be taken out of the carved mahogany cupboard where it was hidden when it wasn't needed and turned on to the station that promised the most extensive coverage. How he knew which station this would be was anybody's guess. Gregor sat back and watched the set and the room together. He was neither surprised nor particularly upset. He had gotten past his simple personal distaste for the Cardinal Archbishop. Now he thought that the man was—complicated—to say the least, and where he wasn't complicated he might be unusual. But watching him on the screen, making the sign of the cross over Roy Phipps's balding head, Gregor still didn't much like him.

Delmark Marquis was a small, round, neat man in the kind of suit that would have looked better on somebody who was tall and thin. It was so expensive, though, that it didn't look

ugly even on him. He raced back and forth in front of the
television set, clapping his hands together in front of his face
like a kindergarten teacher calling her class to order.

"This is extraordinary," he kept saying. "Extraordinary.
What does this man think he's doing? What can he possibly
imagine is the advantage of this sort of behavior? I know it's
the fashion these days to deplore the inadequacies of the old
archbishop, but at least that man had a sense of decorum. A
sense of dignity. He would never have gone in for—something
like this."

Lou Emiliani had gone out as soon as he had heard about
what was happening on Baldwin Place. Now he came back in,
looking relieved. "I called the precinct," he said. "There's no
problem. No fights. No vandalism. They're all just out there
praying.'

"Which means, of course, we won't be able to say anything
about it." Delmark Marquis made a face. "You can't complain
about a Cardinal Archbishop wanting to pray, now can you?
Not even if it's right out loud and right in public. That man
has been nothing but a problem since he came to the city of
Philadelphia. Nothing. What the Vatican was thinking is beyond my comprehension."

"Maybe," Gregor said politely, "we could go back to these
records for a moment. I'd like to get some sense of what happened here, and how much money was involved—"

"I thought I told you." Delmark Marquis stiffened. "We
can't possibly know the answers to those questions until we've
done a thorough investigation. And it's going to take weeks.
You can't expect us to simply jump in and make speculations
about a client's affairs without—"

"The client has given his permission," Gregor said.

Delmark Marquis made another face. "Ah, yes. Right off
the cuff. Just like that. The man has gone off his head. He
thinks it's Christmas morning, and this is Jerusalem. I detest
dealing with religious people. I really do. They have no sense.
They're always abandoning prudence for purity, and all purity
ever gets them is trouble."

"There they go," Garry Mansfield said. "They're marching
back down the street. Look, there's Roy Phipps. He looks like
he ate a lemon."

"Quite," Delmark Marquis said.

Gregor looked down at the papers on the table in front of him. They were only his notes, not official documents, but they contained as much information as he needed for his purposes, if he could only get Marquis to answer questions instead of having fits. It was going to take weeks to get hold of the official documents, even with the Cardinal Archbishop authorizing their release, but Gregor thought he could manage to get enough of what he needed for his purposes, if only he could keep Delmark Marquis on topic.

"Mr. Marquis," he said. "Try to concentrate. We have four people dead, that we know of—"

"That you *know* of? What in the name of God do you think you're dealing with? This is beginning to sound like a slasher movie."

"We have four people dead that we know of," Gregor repeated. "The one solid motive we have in any of this is the payments being made by the archdiocese to this office, so that this office may disburse those payments to the litigants in the civil suit in which several priests of this archdiocese were accused of sexually molesting several young boys in the 1960s—"

"I know what the case was about, Mr. Demarkian." Delmark Marquis sniffed. "I've been at this firm for thirty years. I was one of the founding partners."

"I just wanted to make sure we were clear."

"Of course we're clear. We've been clear since you got here. I am trying to be cooperative, Mr. Demarkian, but as far as I'm concerned you're barking up the wrong tree. Ian Holden may be a thief—I suppose it's hard not to think of him as anything else, under the circumstances—but if the same person killed all four of those people, then Ian Holden isn't a murderer, and that takes care of that."

"That's assuming you're right," Garry Mansfield put in quickly. "You don't know that he was in court the entire day Harriet Garrity died. He could have said he was but—"

"Tut, tut, tut," Delmark Marquis said. "It has nothing to do with what he said. It was the Bellwether Corporation bankruptcy. He's the head of the legal team in the Bellwether Corporation bankruptcy. For God's sake, man, there were clips of him marching around looking like he had egg on his face on the network news. Although why he took on Bellwether to begin with, when anybody with any brains in his head at all could see that they had to be a pyramid scheme, I don't—"

"Please," Gregor said. "I believe you. Ian Holden was in court when Harriet Garrity was killed—"

"Not that it matters," Lou Emiliani put in. "This is poison we're dealing with. He could have planted the poison at an earlier time and then have been safely in court when the death occurred—"

Gregor sighed. "Could we, please? Let's see how this worked. The archdiocese paid a court-ordered amount of money every month, into a fund administered by you—"

"Administered by the firm," Delmark Marquis corrected. "Yes, that's right. The actual amount of money was determined by the courts in a lump sum. Then we divide it up."

"Of whom there were sixty-two real plaintiffs," Gregor said.

"Yes," Delmark Marquis said.

"But Ian Holden divided the money into seventy one payments. Is that right?"

"Yes," Delmark Marquis said again. "At least, that is what appears to have happened from the documents you've brought me and the information we've managed to retrieve. We're not really going to know what happened until we can get into Ian's computer, and I don't think that will happen until we find Ian. I hate these new computer systems. They make everything impossible. They're nothing but trouble."

"Let's go through how it could have happened," Gregor said. "The archdiocese sent Ian Holden a check in the amount necessary to pay the monthly lump sum restitution installment. Then Ian Holden paid the real plaintiffs. Then—what? He just took the rest of the money out of the account on his own?"

"One way or another," Delmark Marquis said. "I suppose that when we really get into it we'll find that he had shell accounts in the names of the imaginary plaintiffs, and then other shell accounts from there. You have to go through a certain amount of silliness to hide financial tracks, but it can be done. Of course, the real experts would never be caught at all. This is something more in the way of an amateur effort."

"Fine," Gregor said. "So that's how he got the money. What did he do with it?"

"What do you mean, what did he do with it?" Delmark Marquis looked blank.

"Did he spend it?" Gregor asked. "Did he drive expensive cars, keep up an expensive apartment, buy all his clothes custom-made from Brooks Brothers? What?"

"Oh. Well, most of the partners buy custom suits. Ian's remuneration would have covered that."

"What about the rest of it?"

"I don't think he spent more than any of us did, in any obvious way," Delmark Marquis said. "We're not undercompensated here, Mr. Demarkian. He lived on his income, as we all do, but I don't remember there being anything unusually lavish about the way he lived."

"What about gambling?" Gregor asked. "What about drugs?"

"Don't be ridiculous." Delmark Marquis was appalled. "The man was a lawyer, for God's sake."

"Lawyers have been known to gamble," Gregor pointed out. "And lawyers have been known to work themselves up to right royal cocaine habits."

"Well, Ian didn't have a cocaine habit here," Delmark Marquis said. "If he had, we would have noticed. He was an efficient and conscientious attorney. He came in on time. He worked weekends. He showed no signs of . . . mental disintegration."

"What about the gambling?"

"I wouldn't know," Delmark Marquis said. "But I can hardly see where he would have had the time. We work very long hours here, Mr. Demarkian. We don't have time to play the horses or attend illegal poker games."

Gregor wanted to say that there were many more ways to gamble than those, ways that did not require someone to take time off work, at least in the early stages. He didn't because there was no point to making the comment. He already knew what had happened here, or he thought he did. He wanted only to confirm some things that needed confirmation.

"If he wasn't spending the money," he said carefully, "what do you suppose was happening to it?"

Delmark Marquis sighed. "He's got it stashed somewhere, I'd expect. At least I hope he has. If he's got it stashed, we can get it back. If we can't get it back, we'll be liable for it.

We're a partnership. There's a mess, for you. God, if I get my hands on that man, I'll kill him myself. You won't have to wait for the Commonwealth of Pennsylvania to ask for the death penalty."

"I thought you said you didn't think he was guilty of murder," Garry Mansfield said.

"I don't," Delmark Marquis said.

Gregor looked over at the television set, which was still on, only turned down low. It had gone back to soap operas.

"If you had to guess where Ian Holden had hidden this money," Gregor said, "where would you guess? He isn't married. You told us that. So there isn't a wife. Is there a girlfriend?"

"Of course there is. Several girlfriends. The man was awash in girlfriends."

"No girlfriend in particular?"

Delmark Marquis shrugged. "Ian liked them young. As young as he could legally get them. Eighteen, nineteen. They had more on their chests than in their heads, and he never saw any of them for longer than a few weeks. But he always had a mother on the side, if you know what I mean."

"No," Garry Mansfield said, "I don't know what you mean."

"He means that Mr. Holden always had an affair running with a relatively older woman who provided him with more stability and more extensive nonsexual services," Gregor said blandly. "And this woman, this time, was named Edith Lawton."

Delmark Marquis blinked. "Good God. How did you know that?"

"Do you mean Edith Lawton helped kill them?" Garry Mansfield said.

"I told him he was a fool to have anything to do with her," Delmark Marquis said. "It's not that I'm prejudiced about atheists, mind you. Half the lawyers on the planet are atheists. But that woman is abrasive. She's worse than abrasive. And she doesn't know how to behave in company. He brought her to the Christmas party a couple of months ago. I thought the wives were going to die of embarrassment."

"Damn," Lou Emiliani said.

Gregor stood up. "I want to go out to Bernadette Kelly's

trailer," he said. "I want to talk to Marty Kelly's mother. Can we do that?"

Of course they could do that. They would work overtime as long as they had to. That was what they were paid to do. Gregor only wanted to get out of Delmark Marquis's conference room and back into real life.

He had no way to tell, at this moment, whether there was going to be another murder or not.

2

The trailer park where Marty and Bernadette Kelly had lived was well out of the city, in some township whose name Gregor never was able to catch, but it didn't matter. Garry and Lou made the arrangements with the local police, who were more than happy to have them all out questioning witnesses on their own. The real problem the surrounding townships had with the city of Philadelphia was the city's tendency to want them to perform services without compensation: question suspects and witnesses; search for discarded weapons; verify dates and times. There might be an economic boom, but many of the townships hadn't seen the best of it. There was too much in Pennsylvania that was still mired in rust-belt technology and rust-belt thinking. There were too many people who could not seem to move into the new century. Hell, Gregor thought, watching the landscape deteriorate around him into scrub brush and discarded vehicles, there were too many people who couldn't seem to move out of the century before last. It was shocking, in a way, how much of a difference it made, which way you went when you left the city, and how far you traveled. On the Main Line and in Bucks County, there was money to spare—so much of it, sometimes, that it got wasted on ostentation and silliness. Out here there were seats torn out of the backs of cars, their fake leather upholstery ripped to tatters, their metal frames rusted at the edges. There were also shopping strips, which was a form of urban development Gregor had never understood. God only knew, he wasn't green, or anything close to it. He wasn't opposed to stores or restaurants or even malls. He just didn't understand how shopping strips made any money, when they were so hard to get in and out of from the traffic that passed them by. He watched Burger King melt into Taco Bell and Taco Bell melt into Arby's, and thought that Father Tibor could eat here for a week and be perfectly happy. It wasn't true that people only liked fast food because they didn't know anything better. Some people seemed to like fast food *because* they knew something better.

Garry turned in at a tube metal frame gate with an arched sign over the top of it that said: BLUE HAVEN SHORES. There was no water around that Gregor could see, and no access to water, either. Pennsylvania was not an oceanfront state. They drove far down the center drive that started at the gate and parked in between two trailers that looked like trailers, rather than like the prefab houses that were so common in trailer parks these days. Double wides, Gregor thought. That was what they called them. None of these trailers were double wides. Instead, they were narrow and seemed flimsy, as if their walls were too thin for this weather. Maybe they were. The state had regulations for trailers, Gregor was sure, but he was also sure it was one of those things. The people who lived here could not afford to be squeaky wheels. If the regulations were inadequate, they wouldn't be the ones to report them.

Garry stopped the car and got out. Lou got out of the front passenger seat. Gregor, who had been sitting in the back, hesitated only a moment. Then he climbed out of the car and looked around. The drive the car was standing on was dirt. Nothing in this trailer park was paved, even in the places where lack of paving left ruts so deep and so hard-edged, they were dangerous to tires. There were a lot of cars, and just as many motorcycles, but everything there was ancient. Gregor saw makes and models that he was sure had been discontinued years ago. Most of the vehicles looked as if they would not be able to move no matter how hard anyone tried to make them. Nobody was out and around. One or two of the trailers had lights showing from inside them, and one or two of the others showed flickering in the windows that meant a television set was playing somewhere inside. Otherwise, the place seemed deserted.

"You can see the trailer where Bernadette lived with Marty," Garry said, "but it won't do you any good. It was clean as a whistle when we found it, and it's been gone over thoroughly since then. There was a report on it in those papers we sent you when you started to work with us. Did you see it?"

"I saw it," Gregor said. "I don't want to see Bernadette's trailer. I don't think it's necessary. Are we all agreed that she must have died here?"

"We're agreed, but it won't do us any good," Lou said. "We can't prove it."

"I know. Sometimes that's just the way it is. But look at this place. She could have died on the ground anywhere around here, and nobody would have noticed. Even if somebody had seen her, I doubt if they would have noticed. How many times do you think the people around here have seen somebody collapse on the ground while being thoroughly sick to their stomach?"

"Drunks," Garry Mansfield said solemnly.

Gregor pointed a toe in the direction of the nearest trailer. It was up on cinder blocks, and peeking out from under it were dozens of beer cans and wine bottles. The wine was of the sort that came with screw caps and had names like Strawberry Nectar.

"Mrs. Kelly is down the line here," Garry said, chugging off between the trailers. "We call her Mrs. Kelly because we don't want to get accused of prejudice. I'd bet you anything you want she's never been married."

"I hope you're right that we didn't need to call before coming," Gregor said.

"She'll be here," Lou Emiliani said. "And if she's not, there's only two other places she could be—the pawnshop or the liquor store. You can walk to both of them from here. She lost her license years ago, and she never has enough money for a car, which is good news for the innocent motorists of the Commonwealth of Pennsylvania. She had fourteen convictions for DWI between 1964 and 1973. That was when she lost her license—1973. She was still hooking then. It must have been a hardship."

"Cars are how the hookers operate on this stretch of road," Garry Mansfield said. "They drive out to the less particular parts of the strip and just sort of sit on their hoods. Maybe we shouldn't have been so worried about being prejudiced, though. I mean, she's white, this woman. It's not prejudiced to think some white woman is trash, is it?"

"Jesus Christ," Lou Emiliani said.

They had reached the door of a trailer that actually looked to be in somewhat better shape than the ones around it. Gregor started out to be surprised, and then he remembered that one of the notes he had been given had said that Marty and Bernadette had looked after Mrs. Kelly's trailer, out of Bernadette's apparently boundless sense of duty. That was the most important thing to remember about Bernadette. She took the idea of duty very seriously, and she expected her husband to take it seriously, too.

Garry Mansfield knocked on the trailer's narrow door and stood back. The three of them listened while somebody inside banged and rattled against what must have been furniture. Garry knocked again.

"Fucking hell," somebody said, and then the door was opened and an old woman was standing in front of them, wearing a dress that seemed to be longer on one side than it was on the other and a cardigan sweater whose buttons were done up unevenly. Other than that, she was wearing nothing at all. Her legs and her feet were bare. Her head was not only bare, but nearly bald. What hair she had left was half-grey and half-ginger, as if she had dipped pieces of it in dye and let the rest of it go.

"Shit," she said, looking at the three of them. "Cops. More cops. What do I want with cops?'

"There's just a couple of things we wanted to check out with you," Garry Mansfield said politely. "If you wouldn't mind. This is Mr. Gregor Demarkian—"

"I know who it is. I got a TV set just like anybody else. I don't got cable, but I got a TV set. And I don't got any extra in the liquor cabinet, either. I'm not entertaining guests. So you can just pack up and get on out and leave me alone."

"Maybe if we could come in for a minute, Mrs. Kelly," Garry said. "There are just one or two things we need to ask. We won't take up much of your time."

Mrs. Kelly looked from one to the other of them, then stepped back from the door. She didn't go very far. There wasn't very much room. Gregor went in first, and as soon as he did he was overwhelmed with the smell. Walking between the trailers outside, he had been afraid that their walls were too thin to keep the cold out. The walls of Mrs. Kelly's trailer not only kept the cold out, but the heat in. It was as hot as a greenhouse, and the atmosphere was thick and moist and acrid, the smell of stale vomit, left where it was to rot. Gregor blinked. Lou Emiliani flinched.

"I don't have time to pick up around here the way I'd like," Mrs. Kelly said. "And I don't give a shit anyway. You knew that, didn't you. I never thought I'd say it, but I miss Bernie the Saint. Did you know Bernie was a saint? Fucking sanctimonious asshole, but a saint."

"Yes," Gregor said. Garry and Lou had left the trailer's door open, and he didn't blame them. To breathe the smell of this place with no air coming in from the outside would be lethal. He looked around and saw that the kitchen was right behind him. The sink was full of dishes that seemed to have been left where they were for days. They all had food encrusted on them. To his left there was a living room, but he couldn't imagine himself going in there to sit down.

"It's about the day your daughter-in-law Bernadette died," Gregor said.

Mrs. Kelly shook her head. "Nobody knows what day she died. The police said that. It's a mystery."

"Let's talk about the day your son died, then," Gregor said.

"That was six o'clock in the morning," Mrs. Kelly said. "I wasn't even awake. I don't get up early in the morning. There's no point to it."

"What about the twenty-four hours right before that," Gregor said. "Do you remember anything about them?"

"I might."

"Well, good." Gregor rubbed his face. Thank heaven for small favors. "What I want to know is, was Bernadette here during that time? That day before Marty died."

"She might have been," Mrs. Kelly said. "But she might have been dead, too. How am I supposed to know?"

"She quit work, didn't she," Gregor persisted. "She wasn't going to work anymore because of the diabetes—"

"That's right." Mrs. Kelly looked triumphant. "Fucking sanctimonious saint. Didn't do her any good, did it, all that praying? The diabetes would have killed her quick enough even if nobody else did. I'm not surprised somebody did. I wanted to, a million times. There's people can't keep their noses out of other people's business."

"Yes, fine." Gregor nodded encouragingly. Lou Emiliani had gone into the tiny living room and was standing over the couch, watching in fascination as a couple of roaches moved around on a square couch pillow that seemed to be encrusted with mud. Gregor turned away, to make it possible for him to concentrate.

"Now," he said. "She wasn't going to work anymore, and she hadn't been, for a while. So if she was alive, then she must have been at home."

"Or at the doctor's," Mrs. Kelly said. "She went to the doctor's a lot, and not to the cheap charity clinic at the hospital, either. She had health insurance. From her job. Isn't that a fucking hoot?"

"Yes," Gregor said. "But the police talked to her doctors, and she'd had no appointments for two weeks before Marty brought her body to St. Anselm's. Did she do the shopping?"

"Not after she got sick. Marty did that."

"Fine. Do you remember anything at all about the last time you saw Bernadette? What she was doing? How she seemed, if she was sick, if she was tired—"

"She was sick. Of course she was fucking sick. What the fuck did you expect? She was talking to that priest from the church she went to. He came out to visit her."

"Father Healy?"

"I don't know. A priest. In a collar. They were standing right out there in the road talking to each other, and I watched them, too. You know what priests are like. They stick it in any port they can find, they're so desperate for it. I thought they'd go into Bernie's trailer and then I'd give it a minute and go over and catch them at it, the fucking sanctimonious saint, but they stayed outside."

"Do you know how long they talked?"

"Nope."

"And you're sure it was Father Healy you saw."

There was a bottle of beer on the edge of the kitchen sink. Mrs. Kelly got hold of it and drank whatever was in it, which didn't seem to be much. Then she made a face and dropped the bottle in the sink. It cracked.

"I don't know who it was I saw," she said, with exaggerated patience, "because I can't tell one fucking sanctimonious saint from another. Got that? It was a priest, with a black priest suit on and one of those collars. Tall. Christ, what difference does it make? They were always coming out here, the people from that church of hers. They were some kind of fucking support group. Christian community. You should have heard that fucking sanctimonious saint talk about Christian community."

"Do we mean Father Healy now, or Bernadette?"

"Bernadette. I don't talk to priests. They meddle too much. I don't talk to nuns too much, either. There were nuns over there all the time."

"But not the last time you saw her."

Mrs. Kelly got another beer bottle out of the six-pack box on the floor and opened it with a can opener. Gregor found himself wondering why she bought bottles instead of cans. "The last time I saw her," she said with deliberate slowness, "the priest was gone and she was going into her own damned trailer, which was always as clean as a hospital. Maybe nobody killed her at all. Maybe she killed herself from all the cleaning stuff she had in that place. It's poison, most of it. It's worse than cyanide."

"Maybe," Gregor said.

"She wasn't sick the last time I saw her," Mrs. Kelly said. "She was walking just fine, like there was never anything wrong with her. I always thought she put it all on, with the diabetes and all that. I always thought she was going to stage a miraculous cure one day and say she saw the Virgin Mary. You know what I'm talking about?"

"Maybe," Gregor said, but he only said it because he was afraid that if he said no she would try to explain. He looked at Garry and Lou and nodded. The trailer door was still open, and cold air was still pouring in. Lou had gathered up the cockroaches and killed them.

"Right," Garry said, suddenly perky. "Well, Mrs. Kelly, thank you for your time. With any luck, we won't have to bother you again."

They were out of there so fast, Gregor found himself facing Mrs. Kelly on his own in no time at all.

It was not a comfortable moment.

SIX

1

When the "exorcism" was over, Sister Scholastica went back to St. Anselm's convent and sat in the single small chair in her own room, with the chair pulled up to the window so that she could look out. It was not what she should have been doing. At the very least, she should have been at her own desk in her own office, so that anyone who needed her could consult her about—things. She didn't have much she could have told them. She didn't know why she and the Sisters had participated in that charade, set up by the Cardinal Archbishop. At base, she supposed, it was mostly anger, because she was so sick and tired of Roy Phipps and his posturing and the way it all intruded on her life. Still, there were a thousand things she ought to be doing, about the school, about the parish, about the Sisters she had been sent to take care of. Mary McAllister's request papers were sitting on her green felt desk blotter, waiting for her to put them into shape and send them to upstate New York. Reverend Mother General would be waiting for them. Sister Scholastica couldn't make herself do anything but look out the window and wonder what Roy Phipps was doing now. She had expected him to have some kind of reaction that would be both public and dramatic. Instead, the street was so quiet, it might as well have been deserted.

In this order, Sisters did not have clocks in their rooms, unless they were serving as bell ringer, which Sister Scholastica never did. They did have watches, but Scholastica hadn't turned on the light when she came in, and in the deepening dusk she found it impossible to look at hers. Outside, the streetlights had begun to glow, faintly, against the failing light.

She always thought of February as the deepest part of winter. She forgot that it was really a time when the light had begun to return to the early evenings. She wished she could see beyond the courtyard to the street itself. If Roy Phipps wasn't doing something to mark the exorcism, maybe the people of St. Anselm's were, or the men of St. Stephen's. She wished she knew, for certain, how she felt about the entire question of homosexuality. It wasn't enough to know what the Church said and to believe that the Church was bound to be right—that the Church was right, really, when it came to questions of faith and morals. Right and wrong were not the issue here. She wanted to know what she *felt*, and every time she tried to get to the bottom of that, she stumbled over a pit of confusion. She didn't know how she felt. She didn't know what she thought. She only knew that she wished she could stop obsessing about it, and both St. Stephen's and Roy Phipps stood in the way of that.

When the courtyard outside was dark enough so that she could no longer see the grass, Sister Scholastica got up and put on her cloak. Somebody else might have called it a cape, which it was, technically. It was black and had a rounded collar like a raincoat's, with slits at the sides near the slash pocket openings for her hands to come through. She buttoned the top four buttons and let it go at that. The cloak had buttons going all the way down, but she had never seen anybody use all of them. She left her room and went down the convent stairs, listening for the sounds of Sisters in the parlor or the kitchen. She heard nothing, which possibly made sense. It was likely to be much earlier than she thought it was. They were probably all over at the chapel for Office, or maybe even in the cafeteria.

When she got to the convent's front door she went out, and then across the courtyard and around the side of the church to the street. St. Anselm's was lit up for the evening, its front doors propped open so that the homeless men and women Father Healy had been so meticulous about admitting would be admitted still. There was no way to know if the new priest, brought in from God only knew where, would maintain the practice. When they released the body from the medical examiner's office, it would lie in its plain pine casket in front of this altar. Father Healy's family would come in from wherever they lived in suburban Philadelphia. She thought about going in and looking at the altar—why?—and then she passed by down the street on the St. Anselm's side. St. Stephen's was lit up, too, but, as usual, it looked far more deserted than St. Anselm's ever did. Far more deserted and far less chaotic. There was something concrete she could hold on to. In a church whose parishioners were mostly gay men, life was far less chaotic.

She thought she was going all the way down the two-block stretch to Roy Phipps's church, although she had no idea why, but when she was halfway there, she found herself stopping in front of Edith Lawton's house. It was dark, except for a light way in the back on the first floor that Scholastica assumed must be the kitchen, or a room just off the kitchen. All the town houses in this neighborhood were alike. She looked at the door and the steps in front of it, but they were no different than the doors and steps in front of any of the other houses on the street. She looked at the narrow driveway to her left and saw that it was empty of cars. Either everybody was out, or whoever was in didn't drive. Then she wondered what it was she was looking for. Everybody in the neighborhood knew that Edith Lawton made a profession of being an atheist. Were there symbols that atheists hung on their doors, the way Christians hung crosses? Scholastica shook her head slightly and backed away from the door. The cloak was heavy but not as effective against the cold as she wished it could be.

She intended to turn around and go back up the street to St. Anselm's, or, if she were still feeling restless, down a little farther to look at Roy Phipps's place once and for all. Instead, she went down the short drive and around to the side of Edith Lawton's house. From there, she could see even more light. It looked as if whatever was lit was some kind of sunroom. She went farther to the back and pushed against the door of the high wooden fence. It slid open without protest. If it were meant to be some kind of security, it was woefully underused. She stepped through the fence and into the backyard and looked around. The ground was mostly taken up with paving bricks. At the far end of it, there was a brick barbecue that looked blackened and worn in the light that spilled out of the back windows. The overhead security light was not on. Past

the wooden fence at the back, the nearest neighbor's house
was absolutely dark.

I should turn around and go home, Scholastica thought.
What am I doing here?

She went farther around to the back again. The windows
were indeed to some kind of sunroom. It jutted off the kitchen
like a wooden rendition of a sugar cube, and there was enough
light coming from inside it to have served adequately as il-
lumination for major surgery. There was light in the kitchen
beyond, too, but with both the overhead and the desk lamp lit
to full in the sunroom that hadn't been immediately apparent.
Scholastica pulled her arms inside her cloak and held them
against her body, hesitating. She most certainly ought to go
home. She just didn't want to.

She went to the door of the sunroom and tried it, telling
herself that if it didn't open she would take it as a sign from
God that she ought to turn around and go straight back to her
convent. It opened easily and without complaint. She stepped
into the sunroom and looked around. The computer was on
and set to a word processing program and a file entitled "The
Evils of Public Piety." Behind the computer, there were piles
of papers that looked like manuscripts and another pile that
seemed to be copies of a single magazine. That pile had a
huge black glass cat sitting on top of it as a paperweight, so
that all Scholastica could read of the title was *Free Think*.

She turned away from the computer and went into the
kitchen. There was nobody there, either, and for the first time
since she had begun this nonsense she began to feel ashamed
of herself. What was she doing, breaking into somebody's
house, and especially this somebody, who would surely make
a fuss about it if she were ever to discover it? Scholastica
could see the headlines now, from the pages of everything
from the *Philadelphia Inquirer* to the specialty atheist magazines. *The Housebreaking Nun. Sister Home Invader.*

The hall next to the kitchen was dark. Scholastica turned
on the light at the switch just outside the kitchen door and
looked down into the dining room and the living room. Then
she went down to the dining room and turned the light on
there, too. On the dining-room table there was a copy of the
Vanity Fair that had the interview with Bennis Hannaford in

it. She went through the dining room and into the living room and stopped.

For some time now, she had known she was not alone in the house, but she hadn't been able to put her finger on why. Now she understood. She could hear breathing, heavy, labored breathing, as if somebody with emphysema had fallen asleep. She felt around on the walls closest to her for a light switch, but found nothing. She reached out to see if her hand would hit a lamp on the floor or on a table, but found nothing of that, either. Finally, she just moved forward, toward the breathing, thinking that if she could just find out who was here and where they were, she could get them to tell her where the lights were.

"Hello?" she said.

All that answered her was yet more breathing. She moved forward inch by inch and then her shins hit a low table. She bent down and put her hands on the table's surface and leaned across it. The breathing was closer now, but just as labored.

"Hello," she said again.

Her eyes had adjusted to the lack of light just enough for her to know that somebody was lying on the couch. She put her hands out to touch whoever it was, to shake them awake—
—and then the lights went on.

They went on right over her head, so that she was blinded for a moment, and stumbled. She would have fallen if she hadn't felt so desperately that she mustn't do any such thing. A moment later, the form on the couch began to come clear. It was a man, apparently fast asleep, bound hand and foot and mouth in masking tape. Scholastica had the sudden, inexplicable urge to laugh out loud. What else could you do in this situation but laugh out loud? She even knew who the man was. She'd seen him a dozen times. It was Ian Holden, the lawyer for the archdiocese, but he was wearing a shirt and no trousers and he had on green argyle socks.

"Turn around," somebody said.

Scholastica turned, and saw that Edith Lawton was standing over her, holding a gun pointed more or less in her general direction. The more or less was important. Edith Lawton was shaking, and every time she inhaled the gun wobbled in her hands. Scholastica wasn't afraid at all. She almost felt as if she were playing a part in a soap opera. The scene felt unreal,

and was unreal, and nothing Edith Lawton did from here on
out could change that.

"Go and sit down in the chair," Edith Lawton said.

"I don't think so," Scholastica said.

"Go and sit down in the chair or I'll shoot you," Edith
Lawton said. "I should have shot him, you know. I could do
it right now."

"I don't think so," Scholastica said again.

Then she took three large steps across the room to where
Edith Lawton was and took the gun out of the woman's hand.

"You can't shoot a gun when the barrel's open," she said
gently, chucking the two bullets still left in the chambers into
her hand. "What's the matter with him? Does he have a concussion?"

"He's a thief. I hit him on the head."

"He's probably got a concussion. He looks all right, though.
We ought to call him a doctor. Do you have emergency numbers next to your phone?"

"There's another one," Edith Lawton said. "In my bedroom.
He's awake, though. I'll bet he doesn't have a concussion."

Sister Scholastica blinked. "Another one? Another man?
You've got another man tied up in this house?"

"He's my husband. Will. He came in and I—" Edith Lawton looked around, confused. "It isn't fair. Did I tell you that?
It isn't fair. But I couldn't do anything about it. And I wanted
them both to stop yelling at me. So I hit them on the head.
What do you think of that?"

Sister Scholastica thought Edith Lawton had had a psychotic break, but she didn't say it. She put the gun in the
pocket of her habit and nodded toward the stairs.

"Let's go," she said. "Let's get the other one, and call the
ambulance, and sit down and talk. I think you're going to be
in a lot of trouble."

2

Bennis Hannaford had wanted her brother Christopher to come
to Philadelphia by plane. After all, what sane person came to
Philadelphia from California any other way? Christopher had
had another way, one that involved going to New York first

and seeing some people and coming on by Amtrak from Penn Station, and now Bennis was standing next to a long bench in the train station, wondering where all the homeless people came from. She wasn't unaware that some people were homeless. She'd written an op-ed about it for the *New York Times*, and several times a year she forked over a significant amount of cash for one of Father Tibor's relief funds. What bothered her was how the homeless seemed to congregate in some places rather than others. There were none living on Cavanaugh Street, or on any of the blocks near it, but here there seemed to be dozens, and the police were making it clear that they were barely welcome. Or worse. Bennis wrapped her arms around her body and paced back and forth in front of the ticket booths, listening to the sound of her clogs on the hard floor under her feet. Once, after one of her novels had been chosen for Oprah's Book Club, she had been recognized in this station, and approached, too. It was the only time in her life she had ever been asked for an autograph on something besides one of her own books. She didn't expect to be approached today. She had a feeling that she didn't look anything like herself today. Her hair, thick and wild and as black as a little help from L'Oreal could make it, felt flat against her head. Her body felt four inches shorter than it normally was, and she wasn't tall by anybody's measure. "Bennis Hannaford," somebody had once said, "is the sort of person who glows in the dark." Bennis was fairly sure she didn't glow in the dark at the moment. She barely had wattage in reflected light.

There was a newspaper vending machine against a wall near the benches. The paper was full of the death of Father Robert Healy. It even had a picture of St. Anselm's Roman Catholic Church on the front page, in badly tinted color. It bothered Bennis a little to realize that she thought of this as good luck. Four murders on Baldwin Place meant that Anne Marie's story had almost ceased to exist as far as the media were concerned. This was not turning into a circus, the way the execution of Karla Faye Tucker had. On the other hand, maybe it couldn't have. Anne Marie was no Karla Faye Tucker, except maybe in bloody viciousness. Anne Marie was not a creature of the camera, and nobody in her half-long life had ever called her attractive. Anne Marie, the ugly one. Anne

Marie, the stupid one. Anne Marie, the one without prospects.

I'm losing my mind, Bennis thought, and then people began streaming out into the waiting room from the tall archways that led to the trains. There were a lot of them—why were so many people coming to Philadelphia on this particular day?—and it wasn't until they were almost all gone that she saw Christopher, still as tall and lean as a caricature, carrying a large leather grip in one hand and wearing his sports jacket open. That was all he had, a sports jacket, made of camel's hair, with a sweater under it. The sweater was probably cashmere, but Bennis didn't see how that was supposed to help. He was going to freeze to death.

"Hey," she said, when she came up next to him.

He dropped his grip on the floor and gave her a hug. This was something he had picked up in California: hugs.

"Hey to you," he said.

"Why didn't you bring a coat?" she asked him. "It's minus nine out there."

"We don't have minus nine in Santa Barbara. Don't worry about it. If I get too uncomfortable, I'll buy something to wear. How's Lida?"

"At home. Cooking you something."

"Excellent."

"Are you going to stay over there this trip?"

Christopher picked up his grip. "I think it's the only sensible thing, don't you? I mean, not only do I want to, but from what I gather your life is not exactly solitary any longer. Not that it was ever really solitary. You know what I mean."

"I know what you mean. Are you going to go up there for the execution?"

"No," Christopher said. "That I definitely am not going to do. But Teddy is."

"You talked to him."

"He says your phone is unlisted. I didn't give him the number. I figured you didn't want me to. I talked to Bobby, too, by the way. He's out of jail."

"And living on the Main Line," Bennis said, turning so that they could start the long walk to the front doors and to find a cab. She could have brought her car, but she hadn't. She'd been feeling far too distracted to drive. "Trust funds are forever," she said. "You've got to wonder what Bobby was thinking. If he thinks. And no. I don't want to talk to Teddy."

"I didn't either, but I got stuck. He called the station. Look, what about you? Are you all right? We've had some news out west about this thing your boyfriend is involved in—"

"Oh, for God's sake," Bennis said. "Don't call Gregor my boyfriend."

"Whatever. The thing is, I figure by now it doesn't upset you when he gets caught up in this stuff, so I wasn't worried about that. But I was worried about the other thing. About Anne Marie. Did you ever get to see her?"

"No." Bennis bit her lip. "Gregor saw her. He went up there yesterday."

"Without you?"

"She didn't ask for me," Bennis said. "He got in touch with her lawyer to, you know, see if he could get her to talk to me, but in the end she only wanted to talk to him."

"Did he tell you what she said?"

"No. But I have a feeling that it was really nasty. If it wasn't nasty, he probably would have told me. If you see what I mean."

They were out on the street. Bennis had no idea how they had gotten there. In the however-long-it-was since she had been waiting at the station, it had gotten dark again. Why was it that this February it was almost always dark? Daytime was supposed to happen sometimes. She was sure it was. At the very least, there were supposed to be a couple of hours of sunlight in the morning. Maybe she slept through it. Maybe that was the explanation. She was getting a migraine.

Christopher was getting a cab. It was as true in Philadelphia as it was anywhere else. A good-looking white man in expensive clothes could get cabs to appear out of thin air. One of them pulled up at the curb next to them, and Christopher leaned forward to open the door for her.

"Cavanaugh Street," he told the driver. "It's—"

"I know where it is," the driver said.

Bennis climbed in and slid as far over toward the opposite door as she could. The cab's seats were torn and grimy. The window between the backseat and the front had had so much dirt ground into it for so long, it would never again be able to be clean. Christopher got in and closed the door beside him.

His legs were so long they didn't really fit in the back of the cab.

"Anyway," Bennis said.

Christopher held out his hand and let Bennis put hers into it. It made her feel as if she were nine years old again, and her father was downstairs, screaming, threatening, promising death and destruction, if she didn't immediately change everything about herself and apologize while she wasn't doing it.

"Do you think it's inherited?" she asked. "Schizophrenia is inherited. Maybe this is, too. Psychopathy. Sociopathy. Whatever."

"I don't know."

"We certainly have a lot of them in this family, though, don't you think? Not just Anne Marie. Bobby. And Teddy. Sometimes it seems to me that most of the normal ones are dead."

"I think that if you haven't been drinking, you ought to start. You can't do this to yourself, Bennis. It isn't your fault. It isn't even your responsibility."

"I helped them catch her," Bennis said. "That's my fault."

"And what was the alternative? To leave her running around loose? She'd already killed three people, and the next on the list was you, and you must know that. Demarkian must have told you that. I mean, hell, you were there."

Bennis looked out her window. Stores were going by, their windows lit but empty-looking all the same. She was wearing a heavy wool jacket, but she was cold.

"Gregor says that poisoners are particular kinds of people," she said. "They're—they're psychologically different. People who murder with guns and knives tend to be angry. Either they're angry right at the moment and they go off like bombs, or they're really furious and have been for a long time and it gets obsessional. Gregor says that to kill with a gun or a knife in anger, you're looking to avenge yourself or somebody else. Even if that's not really real, it's what you think you're doing. Am I making any sense?"

"Some, yes. I just don't know what this is getting to."

"Well," Bennis said, "he said people who used poison were different. They weren't angry like that. They felt," Bennis drummed her fingers against her knee. "It was like the gun and the knife murderers were angry in the explosive sense.

Something in particular happened and they got mad. But poisoners were—resentful, rather than angry. That's the word. They believed that life should have been better for them, and it wasn't, so they believed they had the right to make it better by any means necessary. I'm getting this hopelessly messed up."

"I don't think so," Christopher said. "It sounds like Anne Marie, don't you think? I don't mean that our father was fair when he set his sons up with trust funds and didn't do the same for his daughters, but you and Emma and Myra never thought you had to kill to make up for it."

"He also said that nobody ever really committed murder for religion," Bennis said. "No, I know what you're going to say. I said it, too. But he meant this kind of murder. Anne Marie's kind of murder. And the ones he's investigating now. So I've been thinking about it, you know. I've been thinking about his case, because I guess it stops me from thinking about Anne Marie. And something occurred to me."

"What?"

"Well, that there's only one person I can think of, of all the people he's told me about, that would fit the description. And it seems stupid to think so, because, you know, I don't know most of those people. I've never met them. But in this case there only seems to be one, but nothing he's said has given me any indication that he suspects that person. And I was wondering, you know, if some people have some kind of cosmic purpose, if they're fated—"

"Bennis?"

"Oh, hear me out, for once."

"You're an agnostic and a skeptic. You don't believe in fate," Christopher said.

"I believe that I don't want her to die," Bennis said. "Anne Marie, I mean. I don't want them to execute her. I don't want them to execute anybody, but I especially don't want them to execute her, because she's my sister, and I don't care if she's a psychopath. Does that make any sense?"

"It makes about as much sense as anything else you've ever said. And we're at Cavanaugh Street. Let's get out of the cab."

"Right," Bennis said.

Cavanaugh Street looked ready for Valentine's Day. Donna's house was decorated to death. Even Holy Trinity Armenian Christian Church had its front door wrapped in ribbons and bows. The cab had stopped on the curb outside her own apartment. Across the street, Lida's house was lit up in every window.

Bennis got out onto the sidewalk and let Christopher pay for the cab. When he was out, too, she crossed the street to Lida's side and waited for him to come after her.

"I don't want her to die," she said, and then she buried her head in his chest the way she had once wished she was able to do with their father. It was, she thought, crazy the way that had turned out. Engine House, where they had all grown up, and their mother, and their father, and each day crazier than the last. Now she thought that she was going to freeze here on Cavanaugh Street. She would turn absolutely solid, and when she did they could put her body up on display in a public park.

"I don't want her to die," she said again.

Christopher put his hand on her head and stroked her hair.

3

It was the anticlimax that bothered Dan Burdock, the feeling that he had been wound up and raised up and pumped full of excitement, only to have it end at . . . nothing. For more than a day now, he had been primed and ready, so tense with knowing what was about to happen that he had sometimes found it hard to breathe. For a single short hour out on the street, he had nearly been flying. The cold had meant nothing to him. His feet hadn't seemed to touch the ground. He wondered now what it was that he had expected. Maybe he had thought that the exorcism would be real, that Roy really had the devil harbored in his soul and this rite would bring it out, into the open, complete with horns and tail and pitchfork. That said something he didn't much like about how he really felt about the Roman Catholic Church—and, for that matter, how he felt about Roy. Aaron would say that he had a secret attraction, but Dan knew it wasn't true. Aaron thought everybody had a secret attraction to everybody else, or at least that all homosexuals did, and that all men were probably homosexuals. Dan knew something about the fascination with disgust. Looking at Roy was like looking at a body on an autopsy table, or those pictures of the body parts in Jeffrey Dahmer's freezer that had shown up in one of the tabloids the week after Dahmer's trial. Sometimes you had to look at those things and make yourself feel them, just to make yourself believe that they were real.

Now he looked out over the choir balcony onto the body of the church, just as he had on the night before Scott Boardman's funeral, and found himself thinking the same kinds of thoughts. Granite and marble were difficult to maintain, and expensive, but they were worth it. They made this place a house of God in the only way that had ever made sense to him. The high ceilings, the soaring arches, the delicate carved latticework, the stained glass—Roy was wrong, and so were all those low-church Protestants, who thought you could only approach God through poverty of mind and body. Poverty of mind and body was epidemic in this world. If you were going to approach God, you had to approach him through majesty.

Dan looked down at his hands and saw that he was holding one of his tubes of soft mints and rolling it back and forth between his fingers. He put it in his pants pocket without taking one, then went out the door and down the stone steps to the hall beside the church. When he got to the first floor, he stopped and opened the arched door into the church proper. There were a lot of people in there now, because the march and the exorcism had worked them up, and they didn't want to leave. Dan saw Chickie George and Mary McAllister, sitting in a pew in the back and looking over something they had laid down on the seat between them. There had been rumors all day that Mary was going to enter the Order of the Sisters of Divine Grace at the end of the college term. Maybe she had brochures or something to show Chickie. Did convents put out brochures? Dan had no idea. He looked around the church a little longer and found Aaron and Marc, sitting with two men who were unfamiliar to him. Maybe that would be the best man and the man of honor, if that's what they were going to call it, when the wedding finally happened. Dan knew that the wedding would finally happen, even if the bishop had apoplexy and the papers screamed for weeks. That was what he was doing here. That was why he had *been sent* here, and no matter how hard he had tried to be prudent over the years, he had always known it. Now he only wanted to make sure that the church would survive no matter what he did—the church was a small "c," not the one with the large "C"; St. Stephen's, not the Anglican Communion.

He drew his head out of the doorway and closed the door as quickly as he could against the air lock. He went down the hall and then out the door there to the foyer. The foyer was full of people, too, but they were either people he didn't know well or didn't know at all. He went out the front doors onto the street and found that far less was happening there. The homeless people were coming into St. Anselm's. Mary McAllister would have work to do in a little while. Dan saw an old woman with her brown paper shopping bags on a wheeled rack that she pulled behind her, like one of those luggage carts people had in airports. He wondered how she'd managed to get together the money to get it.

He was just coming out of St. Stephen's front gate and onto the public sidewalk itself when the police cars began arriving farther down the street, and the ambulance came around the corner and stopped there, too. He hesitated for a moment, thinking that the traffic must be for Roy or one of Roy's people, before he realized that the vehicles were much too close. It wasn't Roy's church they were stopping at, but one of the ordinary town houses on the street. They weren't making all that much fuss, either. None of them had sirens blaring, and except for the fact that one of the police cars was pulsing its red-and-blue top lights, they might have been ordinary cars arriving for an ordinary party. Then an ordinary car did arrive, and Dan recognized Gregor Demarkian being helped out of it. He walked down the block until he was directly across the street from the action. The police had left the town house's front door open, but looking inside it, Dan couldn't see anything but a coat tree and a small framed picture whose content he was too far away to make out.

People went in and out, in and out. Dan looked up the street and saw that the door to Roy's church was open and that Roy himself had come out, alone, to check out the situation. Dan didn't think he'd ever seen Roy alone anywhere near the town house. The "church" seemed to have something going on every minute of every day and night. Dan walked up the sidewalk until he was standing directly across the street from Roy, and waved.

"The view is better from over here," he said, loudly enough so that he knew he had been heard.

Roy looked at him for a moment, and then at the police cars and the ambulance. Then he crossed the road in the middle of the block. If this were an ironic movie, something Swedish or Italian, a car would have come out of nowhere and run him down.

"Do you know what's going on?" Roy asked, when he was safely on the sidewalk.

"I don't even know whose house it is," Dan said. "There doesn't seem to be much in the way of an emergency, though. No sirens. No hurry. Gregor Demarkian is here."

"Is he? That's Edith Lawton's house. Edith Lawton the atheist."

"You mean like John Paul, the Pope? I didn't know atheist was a job description."

"In her case it is. She writes for atheist magazines."

"Roy—"

"Give me some credit, for God's sake. I mean atheist magazines, magazines about atheism. She writes for them. She also sleeps with her lawyer."

"What?"

"You ought to get out more, Dan. You don't know anything about anything."

It was true. He really didn't know anything about anything. He looked at the town house again and saw that a man was being taken out on a stretcher and put into the back of the ambulance, but no sirens went on, and for some reason he couldn't pinpoint, he didn't think the man was seriously hurt.

"I wonder if that's the husband or the lawyer," Roy said. "Did I mention that? She sleeps with her lawyer, but she's also got a husband."

"Are they separated?"

"Not that I've noticed. But maybe I'm a little out-of-date. These days, the family comes in all kinds of new and interesting forms. Maybe the three of them felt they were all married to each other."

"Maybe."

"It would be convenient to think that they were coming to

arrest Edith Lawton for the murders, wouldn't it? It would be convenient if they'd arrest somebody for those murders. This whole thing is getting entirely too complicated. What did you expect me to do during that farce you engineered this afternoon? Fall on my knees and embrace the Church of Rome?"

"I didn't engineer it. It was the Cardinal Archbishop's idea. If it hadn't been, he wouldn't have come."

"True enough."

"I expected you to lose your temper," Dan said.

Roy laughed. "I never lose my temper. I haven't lost my temper in thirty years. I'm a block of ice. Take a look. They're bringing her out."

Dan looked. A woman was coming out the front door with her arms in handcuffs. She was a prettyish but obviously middle-aged woman, and she had tears streaming down her face. Maybe she was sobbing. There was just enough noise so that Dan couldn't tell. Dan saw Gregor Demarkian come out the front door, talk to the woman for a moment, and then start down the street in the direction of the churches again. Dan watched him go for a little while and then turned his attention back to the woman.

"I know who she is," he said. "I've seen her around. I thought she was a Catholic. She's always going in and out of St. Anselm's."

"She was there on the afternoon the nun died. She was there on the afternoon the priest died, too."

"Interesting."

"My deacon thinks it's all of a piece. Devil worship is devil worship. Atheists worship the devil, and so do Roman Catholics."

"Atheists don't worship the devil," Dan said.

"And Roman Catholics do?"

Over at the town house, another woman had come out. It took Dan a moment to place her, because she was wearing a habit and habits tended to make all the women who wore them look alike, but in a moment he saw that she was Sister Scholastica, who had come after Christmas to take over the running of the school. She went to the police car where Edith Lawton was now sitting and leaned through the door to talk to her. A police officer put a hand on her arm, and she shook him off. He didn't insist.

"So," Dan said, "this is it. The murders are solved. Don't you think so? They seem to be arresting her."

"They brought a man out of her house on a stretcher."

"They didn't bring him out in a body bag. He wasn't dead. What does he have to do with the murders?"

"I would think he had something more to do with her arrest."

Dan swung back, but the nun was standing away from the police car now, and the police car's door was closed. As he watched, the car started up and pulled away from the curb. It went up the street in the direction of the churches and turned right at the corner when it got to them. The ambulance pulled away from the curb, too, and as it picked up speed on the street it started its siren. Dan flinched.

"Damn," he said.

"I've got to get back," Roy said. "Stay glued to your television set. Maybe you'll hear the news that the case has been solved."

"Maybe I'll just go over there and ask Demarkian to his face," Dan said, even though he no longer had any idea where Gregor Demarkian was. He'd gone up the street, and Dan hadn't seen him come back down. Dan put his hands in his pockets and felt the roll of soft mints sitting there. He took it out and handed it across to Roy.

"Would you like one?" he asked politely.

Roy reached for a mint out of the top of the tube without taking the tube out of Dan's hand and said, "What do you see in these things? They might as well be made of plastic."

"They're also very easy to fill with arsenic," Gregor Demarkian said. "I don't think I'd eat one if I were you. The experience is not likely to be pleasant."

SEVEN

1

Gregor would have gone home, if he could have. The next several hours were inevitably ones of excruciating boredom, at least for the police and for the people like him, who had seen men arrested and booked too many times to find the process interesting. Maybe Dan Burdock found the process interesting, but it was difficult to tell. From the first, when Gregor's hand had come down on his wrist to prevent him from giving Roy Phipps one of his doctored soft mints, he had been carefully and meticulously blank. It was as if he had read far too many of those books where the master criminal manages to escape punishment for the almost-perfect crime by simply keeping his mouth shut. What Dan Burdock expected to do about the fact that he had been caught holding the doctored soft mint in his hand, Gregor didn't know. Maybe he didn't realize that that, in itself, was a punishable crime—or rather that trying to hand it to Roy Phipps was. Gregor was sure, though, that the cases brought against him would be more solid than that. There might be no way to charge and convict him for the death of Harriet Garrity, but there would be no problem at all in the death of Scott Boardman, and they only needed one. He really ought to go home, Gregor told himself. He had nothing to do here, and if Garry and Lou wanted the particulars, they could always get them over the phone at a decent hour of the morning. In all the fuss and nonsense, the day was already sliding into night again. There was something about this case that seemed to cause the hour always to be close to dark. If he could go home, he could lie on his couch and plug away at the laptop Bennis let him use when he wanted to get on the Internet without sitting at a desk. Gregor really hated the Internet, but he wanted to hit the newsgroups and see who Tibor was arguing with now.

Unfortunately, Garry and Lou had no intention of allowing him to go home. They had arrested Dan Burdock on his say-so, and they expected him to stick around long enough to let them know they hadn't done the wrong thing.

"All we need is to make a wrong arrest on a priest," Lou Emiliani said. "Even an Episcopalian priest. And a gay-rights priest. We'd get crucified."

Gregor had been able to see his point. He had taken up residence in a small conference room on the precinct's first floor, doing crossword puzzles, until he couldn't stand it anymore. Then he had found a phone and tried to call Bennis, who wasn't home.

"Her brother is here and they have gone out to a restaurant for dinner," Tibor said, when Gregor finally got hold of him. Gregor could hear the clicking in the background that said Tibor was on the computer again. Sometimes he wondered if Tibor thought God was on-line. "They have not gone to the Ararat," Tibor said, "because Bennis wanted to be private. I do not know how she expects to be private, Krekor. Everybody here knows everything. Even Howard Kashinian knows everything, and he is so stupid he has to be told by his wife."

Gregor had hung up and gone back to the conference room to wait. At one point he had wandered down the hall to see Dan Burdock booked, but there had been nothing to see, really. A man with a stone face being fingerprinted—surely somebody would come to see him, hire a lawyer for him, give him a shoulder to cry on? Gregor had always had the impression that the parishioners of St. Stephen's were very tightly knit. Maybe they didn't know.

He had gone through both the *Philadelphia Inquirer* and *USA Today,* as well as three cups of coffee, when Lou and Garry finally came in to see him. They looked even more exhausted than they had right after the arrest, but they also looked a little calmer, and that made Gregor feel a little better.

"Not as bad as you expected?" he asked them, as they came in.

"If you're talking about the media, it's worse," Garry said.

'There's a circus out there. The only good thing is that they can't get back here."

"We're going to be on the news at eleven," Lou said. "I don't think the portrait is going to be flattering."

"But," Gregor said.

"But the lab got back with a preliminary," Garry said. 'There's arsenic in three of the mints Burdock tried to give to Roy Phipps. Which is really good to hear, because I didn't know how we were going to justify this if there wasn't. I mean, do you actually have any idea what went on here, or were you just guessing?"

"Mostly, I was being an idiot," Gregor said. "I was thinking like Agatha Christie. I kept looking for things like chocolates left in a box, or pastries left on a table, and not finding them. Which makes sense, if you think about it, because that would be a ridiculous way to commit a murder. You could never know if the person you wanted dead would be the person who ate the tainted food. You could never be sure that nine other people wouldn't eat it instead. I used to read those books when Tibor gave them to me and wonder what the woman was thinking. Agatha Christie, I mean. The one scenario was so unrealistic."

"Right," Lou Emiliani said. "Good. Okay. So—"

"So," Gregor said, "I finally asked myself the only sensible question. Who would have been able to give arsenic to each of the victims and know that the victims would actually *be* the victims? And over and over again, I came back to Dan Burdock and those damned mints. He always had those damned mints. He offered one to me, once."

"Do you figure it was poisoned?" Garry asked.

"No." Gregor shifted in his chair. He hated the chairs they used in precinct conference rooms. They were always made of metal and hard as rock. "None of the other, more usual questions did me any good," he said. "Access to the poison was out as a filter, because Father Healy had bought the stuff and strewed it all over the basement at St. Anselm's. Anybody could have gotten hold of it. Motive was out, too, because although it was perfectly clear what kind of motive there could be, half a dozen people had the same one—"

"What motive?" Lou demanded. "Why do you figure Dan Burdock killed four people?"

"Money, of course," Gregor said. "It's always money. Did you really think it was going to be religion?"

"I was sort of hoping it was going to be Roy Phipps," Lou said.

Gregor shook his head. "A murder may occur in Roy Phipps's vicinity, or even at his instigation, but it won't be this kind of murder. It will be somebody bashing somebody else on the head in one of those riots he orchestrates so well. And the Reverend Phipps won't be the one doing the bashing. No, listen, it was always money, all that money from the settlement of the pedophilia suit, which was wandering around the landscape with very weak controls, even nonexistent controls, on where it went. That's what I kept hearing when I first came here, that the old Archbishop, the one before this one, was hopeless when it came to practical matters of this kind. He committed the archdiocese to make payments so high that they threatened to bankrupt the institution. He signed off on papers and deals he didn't even read. Nothing about that deal was ever set up properly, and that meant it was ripe for being ripped off. As Tommy Moradanyan Donahue would say."

"Who's Tommy Moradanyan Donahue?" Garry asked.

"He's five," Gregor said.

Lou cleared his throat. "So the settlement funds were ripe for being ripped off, and they were ripped off. But I don't see how you can say they were ripped off by Dan Burdock. I mean, he didn't have access to the funds. Now Ian Holden—"

"Had tons of access and did a lot of ripping off," Gregor said. "Yes, I know. You can take that up with him. But he didn't kill anybody."

"Why not?" Garry demanded. "Bernadette Kelly was a receptionist in his own office. She could have found out all kinds of things—"

"She could have, and she might have, but that has nothing to do with this," Gregor said. "Dan Burdock wasn't ripping off the archdiocese. He was ripping off Scott Boardman."

"What?" Lou shook his head.

"He was ripping off Scott Boardman," Gregor repeated. "And, I think, if you look through the church's books, you'll find he's been ripping off a few of the others. It's only a guess, but it makes sense. Tibor would get an enormous kick out of this. We'd have known all along, somebody would have sus-

pected from the first, except that we've none of us managed
to free ourselves from stereotypes."

"You're sounding like the department's diversity hand-
book," Garry said.

"Somebody ought to," Lou told him.

Gregor got up and stretched. He more than hated those
chairs. They were going to kill them. "St. Stephen's had a ton
of money. Everything about it was beautiful. It was well kept
up, even in ways that are demonstrably expensive. It costs
money to clean stained glass and marble so that they look the
way they look there. And yet, you know, the Episcopalian
Church is steadily losing membership. That much is regularly
reported in the press. And St. Stephen's doesn't have that large
a membership—less than two hundred and fifty, I think, is
what Dan Burdock told me."

"Well, yeah," Garry said. "But—"

"But what?" Gregor shook his head vigorously. "But gay
men have no dependents, so they have more money to give to
their churches than straight men do? But gay men care more
about appearances than straight men do? But gay men want
exquisitely beautiful things around them and are more willing
to pay for them than straight men are? That's what I mean by
stereotypes. If St. Stephen's had been an ordinary church without a reputation for being a 'gay' one, we'd have seen the
anomalies immediately. We'd have wondered where all the
money was coming from. Instead, we looked at all the expensive, elaborate accoutrements and dismissed them as being just
what we'd expect of a 'gay' church."

"I don't see how he could have gotten enough money out
of Scott Boardman's settlement to do all the things he was
doing," Lou said.

"He didn't. His parishioners really do contribute more than
the parishioners of St. Anselm's, because it really does matter
that they don't have families to support. They're just not Bill
Gates. If you check his books, I think you'll find that he's
been stealing from all six of the men at St. Stephen's who are
part of the pedophilia settlement, and probably from a few of
the others. Remember how he's got that place set up over
there. What did he call it? A mutual-aid society. They run a
ton of programs—a health-insurance pool, a check-cashing

service, a short-term loan service. There's money going in and out all the time."

"And Scott Boardman found out what he was doing—" Lou started.

But Gregor shook his head. "No. My guess is that what Scott Boardman found out was that the amount of money he was receiving in his account every month was smaller than the amount he should have been receiving by about a couple of thousand dollars. He found it out from Bernadette Kelly."

"How?" Garry asked.

"Bernadette Kelly worked at Brady, Marquis and Holden. She was also—sympathetic, I think the word is. She and Scott Boardman talked about his troubles, and his big trouble toward the end of his life was financial. And so I think Scott told her how much he was getting, and she didn't think that was right, so she checked herself. And at that point, Dan Burdock had two choices—either let his scheme blow up in his face or take care of Scott Boardman and Bernadette Kelly both. If he'd killed only Scott, he'd have had Bernadette suspicious and dangerous right across the street."

"Okay," Garry said. "So he gave them mints laced with arsenic—"

"That he'd gotten by picking it up off the floor in the basement at St. Anselm's, which he could do because there was nothing strange about his being in St. Anselm's. Even though he and Father Healy didn't really get along, they cooperated on a practical level on a number of projects."

"What about Sister Harriet?" Garry asked.

"Oh," Gregor said. "It wasn't Sister Harriet per se. It could have been anybody. He could have quit after Scott and Bernadette if Marty hadn't gone off his head and pulled that stunt in St. Anselm's. Then all of a sudden, everything was out in the open and very highly visible, and people started asking questions. Especially Harriet Garrity. Think of all those organizations she belonged to. The Seamless Garment Network. The Alliance for Reproductive Rights. The—"

"Gay and Lesbian Support Advisory," Lou said. Then he blushed. "It didn't even occur to me."

"Well, we're not going to be able to nail him for Sister Harriet," Gregor said. "I know what happened. She nosed around long enough to figure out something about the way

Scott Boardman died. But we'll never prove it. We will be able to prove the Boardman murder against him. That ought to be enough."

"What about Father Healy?"

Gregor thought about it. "It depends," he said. "I'd bet my life that Father Healy died because he saw Dan Burdock take some arsenic from St. Anselm's basement—or saw Burdock take something and later figured out it was arsenic. That time frame fits. Burdock would have had to get more poison to kill Sister Harriet with. He wasn't expecting to need any. He wouldn't have kept it."

"I hate things like this," Lou said. "I hate knowing more than I can use. It ends up feeling so damned . . . incomplete."

"I still want to know how you knew it was Dan Burdock and not that sleazeball lawyer we're not even going to be able to arrest until next week," Garry said. "I mean, look at this. Dan Burdock was stealing small change, even if everything you suspect is true. Ian Holden stole at least a couple of million dollars—"

"Exactly," Gregor said. "Why murder four people? If you're going to murder anybody at all, murder the first two because they've put you in a bind and then just take off. The man had money. He had resources. He didn't need to stick around here. Dan Burdock did. He didn't have anyplace else to go."

"Maybe he'll confess," Lou said. "That would make everything a lot simpler than it is now. Why is it they never confess when you need them to?"

Gregor sat down in his chair again and stretched his legs. The reason they never confessed when you needed them to was that you only needed them to when you didn't have enough to be sure you could convict them. And then they thought they might be able to get off.

2

Half an hour later, having given Garry and Lou enough to go on with, Gregor Demarkian finally got his coat and got ready to leave for Cavanaugh Street. He checked his pockets to make sure that he had all the things Bennis was always accusing him of losing—the scarf she had bought him for Christmas one year; the leather gloves with the cashmere lining she had bought him for his birthday in another—and then headed out toward the front doors and the street. He would, he thought, have to walk several blocks to get a cab. There would be none cruising through the dismal neighborhood around the precinct house at this hour of the night. He went down the steps and stood just under the round precinct light. There was another one, on the other side, and he found himself wondering why police stations everywhere had settled on this kind of architecture.

He was just turning left to walk toward Baldwin Place and St. Stephen's and St. Anselm's when he saw a figure in the shadows, waiting, too, and because he knew who it was, he slowed his steps to allow this man to catch up with him. A moment later, the light from the precinct lamps glowed down over Roy Phipps's face, and Roy smiled a little.

"So," he said. "The Armenian-American Hercule Poirot has solved another crime."

"At the moment, the Armenian-American Hercule Poirot is going to go to Baldwin Place and find a cab. Why did you wait for me? You got what you wanted."

"I was wondering if you knew what was happening to the atheist Edith Lawton. Not murder, unfortunately, but she managed to cause enough damage. Hit her lover over the head and gave him a concussion. Hit her husband over the head and gave him a concussion, too. It's just wonderful. Silly cow. She's fifty years old. What made her think some rich man was going to take care of her at her age?"

"It happens."

"It happens to women much better-looking and much more intelligent than Edith Lawton. She's a damned fool and always has been. Atheism as enlightenment. Don't you just love it? These stupid people. They think that all they have to do is declare that God doesn't exist and it will add fifteen points to their IQ scores."

"Is that what you came to talk to me about, atheism?"

"I told you what I came to talk to you about."

They had reached the corner. Gregor turned left again, and felt rather than saw Roy Phipps turn with him. He didn't usually notice the fact that Phipps was a handsome man, but it

was true. He was handsome and photogenic, and he had the
kind of high-voltage energy that played well on a television
screen. Everybody was always so intent on vilifying Roy's
positions, nobody ever took note of how much charisma he
had or what he was really doing with it.

They were now only half a block from the corner where
St. Anselm's and St. Stephen's faced each other. On their right
was the wrought-iron fence that defined St. Anselm's small
compound. Lights were burning in the convent, but not in the
rectory.

"You know," Gregor said, "if I were you, I'd be more careful than I have been. You're not the only one who can go
poking around in other people's private lives."

"Aren't I?"

"Father Tibor had a field day with your deacon. From what
I understand, it wasn't difficult."

"No," Roy admitted. "It never is difficult with Fred."

"It's too bad there's nothing about my life that hasn't already been in the *Inquirer*. And *People* magazine. There is,
however, quite a bit about your life that has so far appeared
nowhere in public."

"I don't think so," Roy said pleasantly. "I don't think
there's anything to find at all. I don't smoke. I don't drink. I
don't womanize. I'm clean as a whistle. I'm a crusader, Mr.
Demarkian. I'm the hammer of God. This country has turned
itself into a haven for perversion, and I'm here to make sure
it knows that it's going to hell. I mean that literally, do you
understand that? Going to hell, the place."

"Then why bother to go after Dan Burdock?"

"Are you joking?"

"Of course I'm not joking," Gregor said. "If Dan Burdock
is gay, it's an entirely intellectual position. The man has never
had a love affair in his life, as far as anyone can tell. And we
did check. So I don't think you're going after Dan Burdock
because he's gay."

"It doesn't matter if he's gay himself. He—facilitates—the
homosexual agenda."

"All right. He facilitates the homosexual agenda. But that's
not what you're doing here. As I told you, Mr. Phipps—"

"Reverend Phipps."

"I don't think so. As I told you, your life may not be public, but it is traceable, and we traced it. Your ordination is bogus, although I doubt that that would matter to your parishioners, who don't really understand what ordination is. But what's more interesting to me is the fact that you never had anything to say about the homosexual agenda until exactly seven years ago, *after* you had moved onto Baldwin Place. In fact, it looks very much like your commitment to the anti–gay rights cause was dictated *by* your move to Baldwin Place. Before you came here, you did a lot of railing about pornography, and a lot of railing about evolution, but you never had a single word to say about gays."

"I don't see where that matters," Roy said. "I don't see what you think you're going to be able to do with that."

"I don't intend to do anything with it," Gregor said. "I do intend to make sure that the Philadelphia police have your record—your whole record, including the information that shows that you have been stalking Dan Burdock for over twenty years. That's not criminal, as long as he never swore out a complaint, but it is indicative. If I were you, I'd move out of Baldwin Place and take your parishioners with you."

"Don't be ridiculous. I wouldn't want to give up the real estate."

"That's up to you. But Mr. Phipps, if one of your thick-headed Bible thumpers does some real damage somewhere to a gay man, it would be possible, knowing what I know now, to charge you as an accessory. You've always been able to avoid that up until now. I'm here to tell you you aren't going to be able to avoid it again. You wanted to ruin Dan Burdock's life. He ruined it for himself. This vendetta is over. Get out of here."

"No," Roy said. "You're not as good as you think you are. And I'm not finished."

Gregor looked up and saw the lights at the front of St. Stephen's. Just a few feet from where he and Roy were standing, the homeless people were going in and out of St. Anselm's, the way they did every night. He wondered if it had been on television yet, if the parishioners at St. Stephen's knew that their pastor had been arrested. He hardly thought it mattered.

"I'm better than I think I am," he told Roy Phipps, "and what's more, I've got a very long memory. Move out of Baldwin Place. If you don't, I'm going to come after you. And if I do, I'm going to shut you down."

"You're not as good as you think you are," Roy Phipps said again, but for just one moment there was a crease of fear across his face, and a crease of doubt.

There was also a cab coming down the street, and Gregor hailed it. Surely it was as cold tonight as it had ever been this month, but he didn't feel it. He felt as warm as if he were in his own living room, in spite of the fact that his coat was open and he seemed to be wearing his scarf on his sleeve.

The cab pulled up and he opened the door to get inside it. At the last moment, he turned back to Roy Phipps on the sidewalk and smiled.

"Move out of Baldwin Place, Mr. Phipps. I'm not bluffing."

Then he got into the cab and told the driver how to get to Cavanaugh Street. The sky about his head was clear. Even in the glare of the streetlamps, he could see stars. He hoped Bennis was home from her dinner and ready to talk—but then, maybe she wouldn't be, under the circumstances.

All Gregor Demarkian had ever wanted in his life was a world he could make right when it went wrong. Lately, he had been learning to settle for the fact that he could sometimes make a small part of it right for a finite period of time.

The cab pulled away from the curb, and he sat back and closed his eyes, thinking of Cavanaugh Street.

EPILOGUE

... OF AN INWARD AND SPIRITUAL GRACE.

1

On the day Anne Marie Hannaford was executed for the murder of her father, Gregor Demarkian spent the afternoon in Father Tibor Kasparian's apartment, looking through the stacks of paperbacks on the kitchen table for something he might actually be able to read. Aristotle's *Nichomachean Ethics* wasn't going to do it, especially since it was in the original Greek. On the other hand, Jackie Collins's *Lucky* wasn't going to do it either. He was a little surprised that Tibor had so few of what had come to be called "serial killer novels," the kind of thing where dismembered bodies turn up every fifteen pages and the object is to see if the detective can catch the murderer before his haul reaches three figures. In a way, it was rather comforting. There were times when Gregor looked at what was on offer at the movie theaters and thought that Americans had become drunk on blood. What other explanation could there be for the popularity of films that seemed to be about nothing but people getting stabbed, often with ice picks? Then again, the movies that weren't about people getting stabbed with ice picks weren't very interesting, either. He had taken Bennis to see *Titanic*, and he couldn't remember being so bored in his life.

I'm trying to avoid the television, Gregor told himself. That's what I'm trying to do. The television was in the living room, and he hadn't been there once since he first came in. For a while, he had had hopes that the murders at St. Stephen's and St. Anselm's would knock the execution out of the headlines, but it had been more than a week since Dan Burdock had been arrested. The newspapers were looking for copy again, and, of course, Anne Marie Hannaford was copy. "The Society Slaughterer," one of them had called her, but it hadn't stuck. It was too clumsy. These days, they stayed with the conventional angle. No matter what she had done, Anne Marie Hannaford was a woman. The Commonwealth of Pennsylvania almost never executed women. Did they really want to start now?

Gregor would have been with Bennis if he could have been, but Bennis had gone off with Christopher right after breakfast. Gregor didn't know where to. He was sure they hadn't gone to witness the execution. Father Tibor was sitting at his computer, clicking through a website called Books 'n' Bytes, and stopping periodically to type furiously, Gregor didn't know why. He didn't understand how Father Tibor could have gotten so addicted to the computer so quickly. He was even in the process of getting his own Web page.

"So," Gregor said, pulling up a chair and sitting down just behind Tibor's left shoulder, "what is it you're doing, exactly?"

"I am at www.booksnbytes.com."

"You said that."

"It is a website devoted to mystery novels, Krekor. It is very useful. Vicki, who has put it up, has taste very much like mine. She has descriptions, so I am sure not to buy the things I do not like. Also she has links to Amazon.com."

"I know about Amazon.com."

"We must be grateful for even small signs of progress, Krekor."

Tibor bent over and began to type furiously. Gregor leaned forward and tried to see what he was typing.

"So what's this?" he said. "You're writing to this Vicki who owns the web-site?"

"No, Krekor. When I write Vicki, I use e-mail. Except this Christmas I sent her one of Lida and Hannah's honey cakes that they made for me especially to send, and then I used snail mail. This is a newsgroup."

"Ah," Gregor said. "So what are you having a conversation about?"

"The Monophysite heresy," Tibor said. He had turned around again and was typing furiously.

Gregor nodded. "So, this is a newsgroup whose theme is religion."

"No, Krekor. This is rec.arts.mystery. It is a newsgroup whose theme is detective novels."

"You're having an argument about the Monophysite heresy on a newsgroup dedicated to the discussion of detective novels?"

Tibor stopped typing and turned around. "Find something to do with yourself," he said. "You are making me crazy. I know you are worried for Bennis, and this is a good thing, but you are not helping her by coming here and being dense about the Internet."

"Old fart. Dense. You've been talking to Tommy Moradanyan."

"Tommy Donahue. You must remember to call him Tommy Donahue. The adoption went through. We had a party. You were there. This woman is so annoying. She thinks she knows everything. She will not admit she is wrong. It is incredible, what you learn about people on the Internet, Krekor. This woman, when she was shown to be wrong and could not deny it, disappeared for a month instead of apologizing. I could write a book about defensiveness, except that I could not write a book. Why are you still sitting there?"

"I still want to know why you're having an argument about the Monophysite heresy on a newsgroup dedicated to the discussion of detective novels."

"It is because this silly woman calls herself a pagan and doesn't know what a pagan is. Go down to Ohanian's and buy me some Pringles, Krekor. At least that way you will be useful."

"What worries me," Gregor said, "is that she's going to blame me for it. I mean, in a sense, I am to blame for it. If I hadn't come along, Anne Marie might never have been caught."

Tibor stopped typing again and turned all the way around. "If you hadn't come along, she would have been dead, and Anne Marie would have been caught anyway. The woman was not behaving sanely. It is unfortunate that Pennsylvania uses the death penalty. I do not support the death penalty. But Krekor, there is no question that Anne Marie is a murderer or that she would have gone on murdering if she had been given the opportunity."

"I know, Tibor. I didn't say I was being sensible."

"You would not feel this way in another case," Tibor said. "You will not feel this way about Father Burdock, if he is executed. This is true even though you do not approve of the death penalty any more than I do."

"I said I wasn't being sensible. I know I'm not making any sense. But this thing with Bennis and me is so new, and so fragile—"

"Nonsense. It's been going on from the very day you met her. You were only not aware of it. She was aware of it, though."

"When we met, she was living with someone in Boston. And right after she left him, she started going out with one of the Rolling Stones."

"So this is supposed to mean something? It does not mean something. She moved here into that apartment right over your head. She did not last very long with the rock star. I do not think he was a member of the Rolling Stones, though, Krekor. I think the Rolling Stones are perhaps too out-of-date."

"Right," Gregor said.

"There is another thing," Tibor said. "Bennis is not blaming you, because she is blaming herself. None of you are acting like sensible people at the moment, which is perhaps inevitable. Go to Ohanian's and get me some Pringles, before they all come back and start worrying about my diet. I have to post a message on the difference between latae sententiae and ferendae sententiae excommunications, because this fool woman thinks that Christian churches excommunicate people right and left and keep it secret. Why is it that people find it so difficult to check their facts before they give their lectures?"

"Are you still on that newsgroup about detective novels?"

"Go to Ohanian's, Krekor. It will be good for the both of us. I need to e-mail Vicki at Books 'n' Bytes about this new writer Karen Sturges. She has written a novel about musical people."

"Right," Gregor said.

He meant to say something else, but Tibor was bent over his keyboard, typing away industriously again. Gregor wondered what Vicki was going to say about Karen Sturges—and

hen he felt like an even bigger fool than he had all morning.
;ane people did not take Internet relationships as if they were
eal.

Or, at least, he didn't think they did.

2

Ialf an hour later, Gregor came out of Ohanian's Middle East-
rn Food Store with two large brown paper grocery bags. One
·f them had not only Pringles, but Marshmallow Fluff, Skippy
·uperchunk peanut butter, Cheez Whiz, Goldfish crackers, six
lim Jims, two cans of Durkee Fried Onions, and six packages
·f Twinkies.

"He comes down here for one thing and then he goes home
nd remembers something he forgot and then he comes back
ere again and it goes on all day," Mary Ohanian said. "It's
razy. Take it all, and that way he'll be able to pig out in
·eace. How that man manages to eat like this without gaining
ton of weight, I'll never know."

"Fifteen years of starving in Soviet gulags," Gregor said
·landly. "It changed his metabolism."

"Well, maybe I'll try that next. Nothing else has ever
·orked on me."

"Well," Gregor said. "You're a little late. There is no more
·oviet Union, so—"

"Bennis told me that the next time I saw you I should make
·ou buy a whole stack of *loukoumia* so she'd have something
> snack on when she couldn't sleep. Give me a minute and
'll package it up. She'd better watch herself, though. I mean,
know it's usual for people who quit smoking to eat a lot,
·ut she's—"

"Mary."

"I've got the *loukoumia*. Also a little of the marble *halvah*.
he likes that, too."

Now Gregor was standing on Cavanaugh Street, wondering
·here he ought to go first. The food in the bag meant for his
·wn apartment didn't need to be refrigerated. On the other
·and, Tibor had probably forgotten all about asking for Prin-
·les and called for takeout to the one Kentucky Fried Chicken
·lace that deigned to deliver.

He went down the street as slowly as he could withou
feeling silly, and as he passed the Ararat he looked into th
big plate-glass windows, to see if anybody he knew was there
Nobody was. It was the wrong time of day. People were a
work, or at home cooking, or off to some other part of th
city to get library books or birthday presents or something els
they couldn't find right on the street. Lately, Gregor had bee
realizing more and more that work was necessary to him
Without it, he felt too much at loose ends. He didn't vacatio
well.

He was just thinking that it would have been easier on hi
nerves if Pennsylvania had stuck to the practice of holdin
executions only at midnight, when a cab pulled up in front o
his own building a block and a half away and he saw Chris
topher and Bennis get out. Christopher seemed to be layere
into near immobility—he was now, Gregor thought, wearin
three sweaters under his sports jacket, and it was a new sport
jacket, made of wool. Gregor wondered where he had gotte
it—but Bennis barely seemed to be wearing clothes at all. A
turtleneck. A single sweater. A pair of jeans. Maybe she wa
being kept warm by her own anxieties.

Christopher leaned over and paid the cab. Bennis looke
up the street and saw Gregor standing there, holding grocer
bags. She called over her shoulder to Christopher and heade
up the street.

"What have you got?" she asked, when she finally reache
him.

Gregor looked into the bag with the *loukoumia* in it. "Som
things for Tibor. And some *loukoumia* for you. Mary said yo
wanted it."

"I did want it," Bennis said.

Christopher came up, too. "God, it's cold in this state. Hov
do you people stand it?"

"Most of us wear more clothes than Bennis does," Grego
said.

Bennis was rummaging around in the other grocery bag
"Cheez Whiz," she said. "Pringles. For God's sake. He can'
eat this stuff."

"He usually does. You want to tell me how you are, or a
I supposed to guess?"

Bennis dropped the Cheez Whiz back in the bag. "It's over," she said finally. "It was over an hour ago."

"Pronounced dead at 11:46 A.M.," Christopher said. "I thought Pennsylvania always executed people at midnight. I'm feeling a little disoriented."

"They used to," Gregor said.

Bennis wrapped her arms around her body. "I know I said I wasn't going to watch, but we went into this bar and they had the television on and I couldn't help myself. I couldn't drink, either. Do you know what, Gregor? Drinks taste really awful when you're not smoking. Even wine tastes really awful."

"She's okay with champagne," Christopher said, "but, under the circumstances—"

"It was a zoo," Bennis said. "There were those people from the Seamless Garment Network, carrying signs. And there were other people carrying signs, which were—I mean. Well. They were in favor of the death penalty. Let's put it that way. And then Teddy came on, pompous as hell—"

"He's turned it into an art form," Christopher said. "I usually think Bennis is exaggerating when it comes to Teddy, but in this case—"

"Anyway. Here we are. I wanted to walk around some after it was over, so we went to see the Liberty Bell. I don't know why. I never want to see the Liberty Bell. But we went."

"And you're back." Gregor shifted the bags from one arm to the other. His movement brought Bennis's attention back to them, and she leaned over to see what was under the Cheez Whiz.

"Pringles," she said. "Goldfish. Skippy—well, Skippy's all right."

"That means she eats it," Christopher said blandly.

"It's like the man is trying to poison himself deliberately. Is that Twinkies?"

"Don't blame me for the Twinkies," Gregor said. "I just shopped for him. I'm not responsible for feeding him. Why don't you come back to the apartment?"

"Why don't I meet you two for dinner later?" Christopher said. "I've got somewhere I need to go."

Gregor watched as Christopher hiked determinedly down the street, then turned to Bennis again.

"Where's he going?"

"To a Gambler's Anonymous meeting. This thing made me want to go back to smoking, it made him want to go back to gambling, so he found a meeting. They've got them practically around the clock or something these days. He says it's because of the lottery. I feel sick to my stomach. Is that crazy? Even when I'm not thinking about it, I'm sick to my stomach."

"It's not crazy. She was your sister, no matter what she'd done."

"Right."

"You want to go back to the apartment? I've got *loukoumia* and *halvah* and there are grape leaves in the refrigerator that Lida brought. And there's liquor. Maybe if you get worked up enough, it won't matter how bad it tastes."

"What's Tibor doing?"

"He's on the Internet, having an argument about the Monophysite heresy."

"Oh. He's on rec.arts.mystery. Gregor, do you know what I want to do?"

"No."

"I want to go back to the apartment, but I don't want to eat. And I don't want to drink. I want to—well, look, let's go and I'll show you. It's like, I feel like, somebody died and it could have been me, or something weird like that, and so—"

"So—what?"

"Let's just drop this stuff off at Tibor's so he doesn't come looking for it. And then we can bolt the doors as well as lock them, and that will take care of that."

"That will take care of what?" Gregor asked.

Bennis took one of the bags of groceries out of his arms and cast a long-suffering look at the stratosphere.

"I'm not going to go blurting it all out in the middle of Cavanaugh Street," she said. "Come on home and lock up with me, and I'll tell you all about it."

Then she went marching off down the street in the direction of Holy Trinity Armenian Christian Church, and Tibor's apartment, and the building they had shared now for almost six years.

She was just turning in to the alley that led around the side of the church to Tibor's place when Gregor finally realized what she'd meant.

"Clueless," she called out to him, stopping in the alleyway to let him catch up.

It was true, too.

In some ways, he was embarrassingly clueless.

The story of a woman on the morning of a war . . .
—RED HOT CHILI PEPPERS, "EASILY"

In the very early hours of that morning, it rained. The water came down in a steady hissing stream, so that, lying in the too-large bed under too many blankets, Liz Toliver was sure she must be hearing snakes. Later, she would wonder what she had been thinking of. It made no sense to buy a king-size bed for just one person. It was like sleeping in the middle of the ocean, too open and free, too abandoned and lost. The water brushed against her fingertips. She jerked away from it. The snakes slid silently through the folds in the sheets. All of a sudden, she felt suffocated.

Slit his throat. Slit his throat. Slit his throat. The words bounced back and forth across the walls, the wooden walls, much too close to her. The snakes were coiled against her skin. Everything was dark. *Slit his throat. Slit his throat. Slit his throat.* Somebody was singing it. The blood was everywhere on the ground. It seemed to be soaking up the dirt. *Slit his throat*, she thought she heard again, but this time the voice was high-pitched and eager, the voice of a woman who can't wait a moment longer to consummate an act of sex.

Slit his throat, something sang again—but then she knew what she was hearing. It was the phone. She sat up in the grey half-dark.

"Liz?" Jimmy's voice came through the answering machine. "Liz? Are you there? I thought you were having a nightmare."

Liz reached over to the night table and picked up. "I was having a nightmare. How do you always know when I'm having a nightmare?"

"I don't know. I just do. Are you all right?"

Liz leaned over a little farther and turned on the lamp. She saw the book on the night table—the Hollman High School *Wildcat*, 1969—and looked away from it. The walls of her bedroom were plaster. There were pictures in frames hung in a line across one wall, the original paintings from the covers of all her books.

"Liz?"

"I'm fine. I was thinking of the paintings. Does it make

any sense for me to keep the paintings? It seems so—conceited somehow."

"Jesus Christ."

This was the point where, ten years ago, Liz would have lit a cigarette. Instead, she sat up further and stretched. This week's copy of the *National Enquirer* was lying across the seat of the stuffed chair she kept next to the fireplace. She could see her own face on the cover of it. Her face and the picture of a snake.

"Liz?"

"I'm fine. I'm just not all the way awake yet. I think it's a really bad idea to try to do color on newsprint."

"What?"

"The *Enquirer*."

"What are you *talking* about?"

"Never mind. Like I said, I'm not all the way awake yet. And I've got a headache. And I've got to go into the city to teach this morning. What time is it?"

"Six fifteen."

"Maybe we're having a snowstorm."

"If you're coming into the city, we could have lunch. At the apartment."

"Good idea. Never mind the fact that there are probably twenty tabloid reporters outside the front door of the building right this minute."

"Not that many. And they know we screw."

"What a delicate way of putting it."

"We'd be married if you'd have me. Listen, Liz, let me ask one more time. Let me send the lawyers down to take care of your mother, okay? There's no point in your doing this."

"She's my mother."

"She also hates you. She always has. And the rest of that town isn't much better, and you know it. And you're worried about the tabloids? Watch what they do when you get down there."

"Watch what they do if I *don't* go down there. 'Elizabeth Toliver Abandons Sick Mother.' I can see it all now."

"Liz? *Listen* to me. Those stories aren't an accident. Somebody's doing that on purpose. Somebody's feeding the *Enquirer* all kinds of—"

"I don't want to have this conversation again."

"Jesus Christ," Jimmy said.

Liz threw off the covers and swung her legs off the bed. "I'll meet you at the apartment at one," she said. "I'm fine. Let me go check on the boys. I know you don't get along with Maris. You don't have to see her if you don't want to. I'm all right."

"I think of you as a saint," Jimmy said. "Sort of the Mother Teresa of public intellectuals. No matter what the provocation, your faith in human nature will never waver—"

"I'm not Mother Teresa, and I'm not a public intellectual. Get off the phone. I'll talk to you this afternoon."

"Somebody *is* planting those stories, Liz."

Liz hung up. Outside, the sky was getting a little lighter. It looked like the grey muslin curtain that hung across the wooden cells in Carmelite monasteries in France. Once, when she and Jimmy were first seeing each other, before she got used to the fact that anything he did showed up on *Entertainment Tonight* as soon as anybody got wind he'd done it, she'd taken him to visit a friend of hers who'd left Vassar their junior year to become a nun. The resulting headlines had been ridiculous—"Jimmy Card Converting to Catholicism!"—but the day had been a good one. That had been the first time she'd realized, deep down, that he was in love with her. Before that, she had tried not to think about what he might be feeling. That had been the first time, too, when she had known that he could hear her thinking, even when they were not in the same room. The monastery where her friend lived was in a little town on the Normandy coast. When the visit was over, Jimmy rented a hotel room overlooking the water, and they fell into bed together, wordlessly, as if they'd thought of nothing else in all their time together. They started at four o'clock in the afternoon and lasted past midnight. They left the window open so that they could hear the sea pounding against the rocks as a storm moved in across the channel. They came to at one, hungry and out of luck. Everything in town was closed. The wind was so strong, it broke the glass in the window they'd left open and sucked a discarded bedspread into the street.

Once, when she was just seventeen, she had beaten her hands bloody against the locked door of an outhouse latrine, beaten and beaten them until her pain and her fear had become so loud in her ears that all she could hear was her own wailing.

Above her head, the wind had become a shrieking howl—or maybe it hadn't. Maybe that was just her own head, too, maybe it was all inside her, just herself, trapped where she was in the dark with the snakes covering the floor under the latrine seat and moving, moving steadily, in and among and between each other, trying to climb up to where she was. Out there, though, there was something: that woman's voice singing—*slit his throat slit his throat slit his throat*—and then laughing as the blood poured out on the ground, and over the water of the river, and into the mouths of snakes, into the mouths of snakes, because the snakes were everywhere then, on the floor, on the seat, on her arms, crawling up into her clothes, crawling inside of her, until she felt full of snakes writhing and jamming and making her bleed.

She was standing next to the chair with the *Enquirer* on it. She had no idea how long she'd been there. Her mouth was very dry.

"I ought to go check on the boys," she said to the air. Then she looked down at the *Enquirer* and made a face.

"Shocking Secret Never Before Revealed!" the headline said. "Did Elizabeth Toliver GET AWAY WITH MURDER?"

In the picture under the headline, her hair looked the color of spilled ink.